# Only the Wind
# Remembers

# Only the Wind Remembers

## Marlo Schalesky

MOODY PUBLISHERS
CHICAGO

© 2003 by
MARLO SCHALESKY

Library of Congress Cataloging-in-Publication Data

Schalesky, Marlo M., 1967–
    Only the wind remembers / by Marlo Schalesky.
        p. cm.
    ISBN 0-8024-3324-3
        1. Ishi, d. 1916—Fiction.  2. Indians of North America—Museums—
Fiction.  3. Women museum curators—Fiction.  4. Yana Indians—Fiction.
5. California—Fiction.  I. Title.

PS3569.C4728O55 2003
813'.6—dc21

                                                                    2003009488

1 3 5 7 9 10 8 6 4 2

*Printed in the United States of America*

*For Mom*

# ACKNOWLEDGMENTS

*Only the Wind Remembers* started with a simple prayer—"Well, God, what do You want me to write next?" I expected an idea to fall from the sky and into my heart. But, as is often the case, God chose to use a friend to answer my prayer. That friend was John Olson. John sacrificed precious hours of sleep at the Mount Hermon Christian Writers Conference to help me bring Ishi's story to life. So I offer humble thanks to John for his brilliant brainstorming abilities, kindness, and especially his generosity of spirit.

I also want to thank Tricia Goyer and Maxine Cambra, friends extraordinaire, who read over the manuscript word by word and made invaluable suggestions. Thanks, too, to Cindy Martinusen, who took time from her own tight deadline to give my book a read and point out ways to improve it.

God also granted me a special blessing by allowing me to work with editor Karen Ball whose expertise, insights, kindness, and friendship made the editing process a joy. Thanks, Karen!

Thanks also to the great folks at Moody who have been wonderful to work with.

And finally, thanks to my incredibly fantastic husband, Bryan, who not only read through my first rough draft but also took care of Bethany (often with Grandma's help— thank you, Mother!) so I could have some much needed quiet time to think about Allison and the Great Eagle. Without his support, *Only the Wind Remembers* would have never become the story God intended it to be.

*Whisper to my heart of truth*
*And kill the doubt in me.*
*Whisper of a dawning hope*
*That all my fear will flee.*
*Whisper in my waiting ear*
*Of love I cannot buy.*
*Whisper of wooden cross*
*Where Jesus chose to die.*

# PROLOGUE

Wanasi stood on the edge of the world and wondered if he had the strength to step off. Behind him lay everything he'd ever known: the waters of the *Daha*, Grizzly Bear's Hiding Place, the great mountain *Waganupa*, and the graves of his people. Before him lay everything he feared—the world of the *saldu*, the white man.

In a distant field, cattle lowed. Wanasi shivered beneath the shelter of an oak. This was the place where the cattle died. He smelled it on the wind, heard it rustle through the leaves above him—death, like the buzzing of flies around his head. A small smile touched his lips, then faded. He had come to the death place, appropriate somehow for this thing he was about to do.

He raised his eyes and looked at the dusty field before him. Beyond it, a light glimmered against the dawn and beckoned him forward. "Saldu." He listened to the whispered word as the breeze swept it away.

From the hills behind him, a coyote howled, echoing the loneliness that drove him from his home.

"No, I will not be afraid. I will not turn back." He clenched his fist. "I am the last Yahi. But I will not die alone."

A hawk screeched overhead. Wanasi looked up and squinted into the rising sun. For one moment, his eyes followed the hawk's flight. Higher, higher, away from the dry, cracked earth, away from the fleeing night—away from the pain in his heart.

The vision blurred. Something was not right in his head. He could feel it. Soon he would follow the great Daha River south to the land of the dead. He would follow the path of his people. But he would not weep for them. Tears would sully their memory. Already he had burnt his hair short for his mother, the last to die. If she could see him now, he knew what she would do. He could see her shaking her head, could hear her low, rich voice muttering, *"Dawana ishi."*

Perhaps she was right. Perhaps he was a crazy man. But the gnawing in his belly, the gauntness of his frame, and the knowledge he had nothing left to lose had driven him here, to the very edge of a new world. And now . . .

There was nothing left to do but to go forward, to meet the future and do what he must.

Wanasi took a deep breath and stepped from the shelter of the woods. Nothing happened. No tingling beneath his feet, no chills over his bare skin. Nothing cried out that he now walked on saldu land.

Somewhere in the distance a dog barked. A second joined in until the air shook with the sound. But Wanasi didn't stop. He took another step, and another, each taking him farther from the place he had long called home.

Fat branches tooled into planks and tied in long rows

12

stretched across the white man's land like scars. Wanasi climbed through one row and stumbled forward, toward the sound of barking, toward the pinpoint of light that seemed to waver before his vision.

The wind stirred the dust at his feet and sent shivers over his naked frame. He thought about his breechcloth, which had washed away in the river two days ago. He had not gone after it. He would take nothing with him into his new life. He would enter the new world as he'd entered the old. With nothing . . . except his memories.

Wanasi staggered across an expanse of dirt to a second row of tied branches. His gaze fixed on the shimmer of light glowing between the planks. On the far side, a horse whinnied. Hooves stomped on hard-packed earth. Wanasi stumbled and then righted himself. It was almost over now. Shadows swirled through his mind. He must concentrate. He must finish what he started.

Wanasi crawled through another wooden row, his gaze still focused on the light. Flies swarmed through air heavy with the smell of manure, grass, and something sweet, like honey. He blinked and glanced down the long row of planks to see the eyes of horses staring at him. Eyes that watched him now, as if wondering what a man like him was doing among them. He heard the swish of a tail, and then the barking started again—louder this time and coming nearer.

Wanasi's gaze darted to a pile of dried grass on his left, to wooden planks on his right, to bare straw-scattered earth before him. There was nowhere to hide. Nowhere to run.

So here he would meet his destiny.

In the field beyond, a horse reared and screamed. Wanasi turned. And then they came, a blur of shapes from the darkness, like devils out of a pit. He fell to his knees. Bits of straw dug into his skin. He saw flashes of fur and teeth. He covered his head with his arms, and then they were upon him. Hot breath on his neck. Wet noses against his skin. Barking as loud as the shots that had killed his people.

But he was not afraid. He had no energy left for fear.

Through the haze of noise and weariness came a shout, a sound louder than the dogs' growling. It was the voice of a man, yelling words strange to Wanasi's ears.

He looked up through the mass of bared teeth and rope collars. His eyes fixed on the outline of a stick clenched in a huge hand, on a face dark beneath the brim of a hat.

*Saldu* . . .

The stick crashed down on his head and drove him backward. His shoulders hit the ground. But Wanasi felt no pain.

A face materialized before him, coming together like pieces from an old dream. A long nose, eyes squinted into thin slits, and a mouth saying something, something Wanasi still could not understand. He focused on the strange words. A response stumbled from his lips, unused to speech after so much time alone.

*"Saldu, aiku tsub. Nize ah Yahi. Aiku tsub. Aiku tsub."* But the man did not seem to understand. *"Nize ah Yahi."* His voice faded. "I am Yahi."

The stick raised again, high over Wanasi's head. And he knew that words were no good now. It was too late for peace. Too late for hope. But at least he would not die in the wilderness, alone.

Wanasi put his hands together, lowered his head, and waited for the killing blow.

# ONE

EARLY SEPTEMBER 1911, SAN FRANCISCO, CALIFORNIA

The stone angels wept tears of mist. Allison Morgan stared up at them, as if by looking long enough she could bring into focus the face that haunted her dreams. But, as always, it eluded her. Instead, all she saw was the angels, their eyes fixed on the sky, their features immobile.

"Where are you, Mama? Why can't I remember?" Silence surrounded her, swallowed her whispered questions.

She hugged her arms around herself and sighed. September had brought her back to the orphanage, just as it did every autumn. September—the month her mother left her, a skinny five-year-old, beside a trash bin. At least that's what the nuns told her. But that was twenty years ago. Too long to still carry the scars. Yet every September she found herself back here, staring at the faces, trying to turn back the years.

"Don't weep for me." She lifted her chin high. "I'm not trash anymore." She glanced down at her trim-fitting dress, tailored in the latest style, her spotless white gloves, the tiny lace parasol over her arm. Then she looked up into the cold, sightless eyes that would never warm, never see.

Five years ago she'd left this place for good, left the bleak walls, the iron doors, the condemning eyes . . . Allison lowered her head until her gaze fixed on the tips of her goatskin shoes. *Why can't I just walk away? Why can't I leave it behind forever?*

A breeze ruffled the hem of her skirt. She brushed her fingers over the brim of her hat, then raised her head one last time to glare at the angels. For a moment, they looked like Mrs. Whitson, the woman who came to the orphanage to teach the girls how to be ladies. Mrs. Whitson was Allison's picture of the perfect woman then, and in some ways, she still was. It was Mrs. Whitson who got her the job at the new museum of anthropology in San Francisco. It was Mrs. Whitson who introduced her to Thomas Morgan, the youngest anthropologist at the university. And it was Mrs. Whitson who, six months later, stood for her, as a mother should have, at her wedding.

Allison pressed her gloved fingers to her cheeks. "No." She made the word bold, loud, a solid declaration to her concrete judges that they no longer held power over her. "I'm not the ragamuffin child left next to a trash bin. I'm not the young girl with scuffed shoes and tattered hair, who Mrs. Whitson found scrubbing the floors all those years ago. I'm a *lady* now. I'm Mrs. Thomas Morgan, assistant curator at the only Indian museum west of the Mississippi." *And that makes me somebody. At least it will after today.*

In just a few short hours, Thomas would see all she'd done at the museum with the new Indian displays. He'd see her hard work, the elegant placement of artifacts, the perfect calligraphy of the signs identifying each tribe, the meticulous research penned onto tiny cards and slipped into each display for the public to read and learn. He would see, as would Mrs. Whitson, that she was the best assistant curator in the West.

The shrill beep of a horn sounded behind her. The parasol slid from her arm as she turned and found herself staring into the headlights of a new horseless carriage. She looked down the red painted sides, over the black leather roof, and squinted at the sheen from the front window.

A head poked out from the driver's side. Hair the color of coffee fell over deep blue eyes. "There you are, love. I've been looking everywhere."

Allison gasped. "Thomas! You didn't buy that thing, did you?"

Thomas grinned. "I did indeed. Isn't she a beauty?" He patted the shiny steering wheel.

"But, but . . ." She retrieved her parasol from the ground.

"Care for a ride, m'lady?" He leaned out the window and rubbed his hand over the car's door.

"It's a Model T."

"Of course it is. Brand-new from the factory."

Allison smoothed the pleats of her dress. The automobile was certainly impressive, but . . . She sighed. Maybe it would be okay. She walked over to the car and smiled. "Nice automobile, Mr. Morgan."

Thomas laughed. "Yes, it is, Mrs. Morgan."

Allison glanced at the shiny black seats and noticed Thomas's father sitting in the back. "Good day to you, Pop." She nodded and, as always, tried not to stare at the black mole that marred one side of the man's face. "How are the roses at the church?" Pop had been groundskeeper at Saint

Timothy's for ten years. Even though she and Thomas offered him a room in their house, Pop preferred his one-room cottage at the church. And Allison was glad he did.

Pop ran his hand through the edge of his peppery gray hair, then pulled at his collar. "Got aphids." The response was as sparse as the man himself. "Sprayin' ain't helping, either."

"Sorry to hear that."

"No need for sorrow, girl. I'm gonna get those little green buggers, even if I have to catch 'em and squish them with my own hands."

Allison hid her smile.

Pop's thick black eyebrows pulled together over eyes the same color as Thomas's. "So you approve, do you?"

"Of what? The automobile? Or the aphids?"

The old man grunted. "No, not them. This." He took a piece of folded newspaper from the seat beside him and tossed it toward her. Thomas caught it midair.

"There'll be time enough for that later." Thomas leaned farther out the driver's side and whispered, "Don't let him scare you, love. He's just testing you."

"I heard that, boy." Pop's voice rumbled like gravel down a hillside.

Thomas's tone returned to normal volume. "Don't let anyone tell you your hearing's going bad, Pop. Far as I can tell, it's as good as the day you caught me filching apples from Mrs. Lee's porch."

To Allison's surprise, Pop chuckled. "Better get going, boy, or you'll miss that ferry."

"Ferry?" The word caught in Allison's chest.

Thomas looked away. "Um, well, how 'bout you just get in and I'll explain." Allison saw the Adam's apple bob in his neck. She frowned.

"That is, unless you're not done with your business here?" Thomas gestured toward the orphanage. "What are you doing here, anyway? I thought you were just taking a short walk."

Now it was Allison's turn to look away. "It, um, it was such a nice day."

"Isn't this the orphanage where you lived when you were a girl? I wouldn't think you'd want to come back here."

"I only stopped to admire the statues. But I'm finished now."

"Oh. Well, all right. Get in then." The smile returned to Thomas's face. "Your chariot awaits. Isn't that what they always say?"

Allison touched her hat again and adjusted the reticule on her arm. The small drawstring bag bumped against her side. "Chariot, indeed."

Thomas ignored her murmured comment and stepped from the car to help her into the passenger's side. Then he walked back around the Model T and positioned himself behind the steering wheel. With a loud roar, the automobile lunged forward and began to rumble down the narrow street.

Allison jumped and Thomas chuckled. "First ride in a horseless carriage, love?"

She slapped his arm. "You know it is." She sat back and watched the buildings pass. Soon the orphanage disappeared from sight, replaced by shoemakers' shops, a cannery, a bank, and myriad tall buildings throwing shadows over the cobblestone before them. After a few minutes of silence, Allison turned to Thomas. "So are you going to tell me about the ferry?"

He winced. "I'd hoped you'd forgotten about that."

"Oh, Thomas!" Dread dripped down Allison's back. "You were supposed to see my displays at the museum today. You know how hard I've worked."

"I know I promised, but . . ."

*Not again!* Coldness congealed in Allison's gut. "But what?" That same coldness seeped into her tone, but she didn't care.

Thomas frowned. "It's not as if the exhibits will disappear overnight."

Allison clenched the fabric of her skirt until her joints ached. That awful sinking feeling started in her chest, the feeling that told her she couldn't count on Thomas. She couldn't count on anybody. She was alone.

"Well?"

Allison stared out the window, fighting to keep her voice calm. "It's always something." She blinked, attempting to focus on the shops, the buildings, the cobblestone street. But all she saw was the dim reflection of her chin, trembling in the glass.

The seat creaked as Thomas shifted beside her. "Don't say that."

"It's true."

"But this time it's a *big* something. You'll see." His tone begged her to understand.

Allison faced him. His eyes were wide, beseeching, but somehow they didn't reach her, didn't comfort her. At least not today.

"Not too big, eh?" Pop's voice came from the backseat. "Not much more than a hundred pounds, I'd say."

Thomas glanced over his shoulder. "That's enough, Pop."

"You gonna show her that paper? Or are you just going to keep yapping?"

"I'm going to show her the paper." Thomas grated the

words through clenched teeth, then handed Allison the newspaper.

She looked at the black print and frowned. Newspapers were so messy. She loosened her grip on her skirt and used her fingertips to picked up the paper by the edges. She turned to a section marked with blue ink. "Oroville Register, August 29." She paused.

"Took us a couple days to get it." Thomas motioned for her to continue. "Go ahead; you'll understand once you read it." His eyes added, *I hope.*

Allison swallowed the hurt lodged like a jagged pebble above her sternum and read. "An aboriginal Indian, clad in a rough canvas shirt that reached to his knees, was taken into custody last evening by Sheriff Webber and Constable Toland at the Ward slaughterhouse on the Quincy road. He had evidently been driven by hunger to the slaughterhouse, as he was almost in a starving condition. News of the presence of the Indian was telephoned to the sheriff's office by the employees at the slaughterhouse. They informed Sheriff Webber that they had 'something out there,' and they did not know what it was."

She lowered the paper just as the car hit a bump. Her heart beat faster. Thomas was right. She did understand. She understood all too well. "You're going to get him, aren't you?"

"Yes, I am."

"But why do *you* have to be the one who goes?"

"I don't have to. I want to. That—" he reached over and tapped a paragraph with one finger, then swerved to miss a carriage parked on the side of the road—"is exactly what Dr. Kroeber's been looking for. A wild, untainted Indian. This is a *miracle*, Allison."

She cocked an eyebrow at him.

"Keep reading. You'll see."

A hundred questions, a thousand objections raced through Allison's mind. But she silenced them, for the moment at least, and continued to read. "Not a single word of English does he know, nor a single syllable of the language of the Digger Indians, the tribe that lived around here." A chill spread through Allison's stomach. "Apparently the Indian has never come in contact with civilization. It is believed that the aborigine who was captured last evening is the last surviving member of his tribe." She dropped the paper and looked at Thomas. Words pushed past the sudden tightening in her throat. "He's all alone."

Thomas shook his head. "Not for long, love. Not if we can help it." He reached over and squeezed her hand. "Now you see, don't you? You know why I must go?"

"The last of his kind—"

"All this fuss for one old Indian." The querulous voice from behind them cut off anything further Allison might have said. "Don't see why the world's gotta stop its spinning just because some Indian walked out of the woods."

A few moments ago, Allison would have agreed. But something about this Indian's aloneness made the importance of Thomas approving her work at the museum less compelling. After all, the displays would be there tomorrow and the next day. Thomas had said so. Allison turned to see Pop's arms crossed over his chest and his brows bunched together like a fat caterpillar.

Beside her, Thomas scowled. His voice rose over the rumble of the engine. "Not just *any* Indian, Pop. They're saying he's the last Stone Age man in North America. Just think, what an absolute miracle, if it's true!" His features softened. "What a find he'll be for anthropology."

22

"Anthropology. Pah!" Pop uncrossed his arms and waved his hand in the air. "Who ever heard of such a thing? Theology, now *that's* something worth studying. Just like I've always said."

Thomas's jaw hardened, and Allison cleared her throat and shifted in her seat before the same old argument between the two could gain momentum. "Well, if it's true, at least it will put the museum on the map. Mrs. Whitson will be glad for that." She looked down at her small reticule. "But I don't have my things, Thomas. How can we be leaving on the ferry now?"

"Well . . ."

She stared at him, horror traveling from her stomach to her toes. "You didn't pack my bag for me, did you?"

"No." The word dragged like a long puff from a cigar. Then silence settled.

The car slowed to a near stop at Market Street as understanding dawned. Allison looked down at her lap. She twisted her fingers together. "I'm not going, am I?"

Thomas glanced toward her. "Not this time, love. You understand."

Allison turned away. *Oh, I understand. I understand perfectly. Something important is happening, and I'm being left behind. As usual.* She pressed her gloved hand against the cool glass of the window. *Don't think about it. It doesn't matter.*

The car slowed. An old gray horse plodded by, pulling a dray. The open cart bumped along the road, then turned a corner. A young boy stopped on the sidewalk and made shrill music on his pennywhistle. A man rode across the street on a bicycle. The world continued, just as it always had. But what would it all look like to a man who had lived his life hidden in the hills?

Before Allison could consider the thought further, Pop leaned over the front seat, squinted his eyes, and peered into her face. "Don't tell me you're all gooey-eyed over this wild man too? What's wrong with you people?"

Allison didn't answer.

Pop threw his hand in the air again. "You'd think this Indian was supposed to be your savior or something." He sat back in his chair. His voice lowered to a half-audible grumble. "Some heathen Indian. Don't know the first thing about what's really important. Worldly pursuits when the Kingdom's a'waiting. Young folk don't make no sense at all. Crazy. The lot of 'em."

Thomas reached over and gripped her hand again. "This is my chance. *Our* chance."

Pop jerked forward and squeezed Allison's shoulder. She glanced back and found herself impaled by a look as sharp as broken glass. Pop raised his finger until it was pointing directly at her nose.

Her eyes crossed.

"This Indian ain't going to save you." Pop's voice rasped against Allison's nerves. "But you just might save him. So are you going to tell this savage about Jesus or not?"

Something inside her froze. The same something that drove her to try to recall her mother's face, only she didn't remember why. She could never remember. Allison reached into her reticule and pulled out a clean pair of gloves.

Suddenly, nothing mattered except escaping the stifling atmosphere of the Model T, fleeing the beady, questioning eyes of Mr. Silas Morgan, and forgetting that somewhere out there a wild man waited, all alone.

# TWO

It was the first time in Wanasi's life that he couldn't smell the wind. He couldn't smell the flowers, or the trees, or the river as it rushed over rocks and branches toward the land of the dead. All he could smell were the saldu. More than he could count. More than the rocks in the Daha. More than the trees that swayed on the river's banks. Or, at least, so they seemed.

He rubbed the bump on his head where the stick had hit him. The bump felt smaller today but still tender. He glanced through the bars that formed one side of the enclosure they'd put him in. Were they only a dream, those endless eyes that stared at him from the other side? Perhaps he imagined the sea of mouths whispering words he didn't understand, or the fingers pointing, or the feet hidden in cloth and leather. They didn't seem real, these men with strange hair beneath their noses, or the woman clothed like a meadow flower with a blue feather in her headdress. He stared at a boy with hair cut short and a slender stick in his hand. Perhaps they were only spirits, watching from another world, waiting . . . but for what?

Or perhaps *he* was the spirit, looking out through bars of death into a world where he would never belong, the world of those who had killed his people. But that was long ago.

Wanasi reached out and touched the bars separating him from the saldu. The saldu nearest him jumped back, pressing into the feather-headed woman behind him. Wanasi ignored them. Instead, he focused on the bars. They were smooth to the touch and cold, like the fingers of an old man long dead. He shivered.

There were no dogs in this place, no sticks that fell on his head with increasing force. This was a better place, then. The saldu had not killed him, had not hurt him except for that one blow. These men saved him from the dogs and brought him here, to this odd cavern with bars and a floor made not of dirt, nor stone but wood—sheets of it. A floor unlike anything he had ever seen. Just like everything else. Except for the sunlight. He must remember the sunlight.

Wanasi turned his back to the saldu and glanced at the high, barred opening above him. Light splashed freely through the gap, though something clear and solid blocked the breeze. With measured steps, he moved into the stream of light. He closed his eyes and felt the warmth on his cheeks, his neck, his chest. He longed for the wind to kiss his forehead, to run its fingers through the stubble of his hair and remind him that he was not alone. But there was no wind, only the sun. And he *was* alone, despite the horde of saldu that stood gawking behind him.

"The wind is gone." Quiet words slipped from his lips, then vanished like morning mist. "But I will go on. I am not a spirit yet. I will stay. I will tell the story."

The babble of voices behind him grew louder. Wanasi pressed his hands to his ears and sat back on the wooden platform. His gaze focused on the patch of light on the strange gray floor. *It is not a dream. It is real.* He rubbed his hand along the cool white pine of the sleeping platform on which he sat. That, at least, was familiar. *Siwini.* He whispered the name of the wood and smiled. He would remember the sunlight; he would remember the siwini. He would remember who he was.

The last Yahi.

Once there were five of them living in Grizzly Bear's Hiding Place. Five survivors from a once strong people. But the others had taken the journey south to the land of the dead. All gone. All but one. Now it was time for him to travel south. How long had it been since he'd heard words in his own language? Three summers? Four? But he must not think of that now. He must forget the pain that drove him from the spirits of his people.

A loud rapping sounded from the bars behind him. He turned to see a man with a square white headdress, the same man who brought him from the cattle's dying place to this small cavern where no wind blew. The man again lifted a black stick and tapped it on the bars. Then he spoke more words Wanasi did not understand. Saldu words for a saldu world.

Wanasi shook his head.

The man pulled a small something from his pants and inserted it into a hole in the bars. Wanasi heard a click, and the barred door opened. A creak, unlike the sound of the wind in the trees, unlike any sound in the natural world, echoed in Wanasi's ears. And then his senses caught a new smell, a smell so good that it made up for the wind, for the floor, for the countless eyes that still stared from the other side of the bars. Wanasi smelled food.

The man in the headdress held out a bowl, and Wanasi took it. His hands trembled. The bowl held some kind of beans. He glanced at the man.

The man pointed to the bowl and then touched his fingers to his lips.

Wanasi smiled. "Thank you." But the man did not understand.

Wanasi dipped his fingers into the bowl and raised the beans to his mouth. They tasted like honey mixed with fire.

Minutes later, a second man slipped through the barred door into Wanasi's enclosure. Wanasi glanced up. He watched a bead of sweat trickle down the man's temple as he spoke. Wanasi focused on the strange words.

"Doe-nuh." The second saldu gestured toward Wanasi.

The hair twitched under the first man's nose, and Wanasi suspected the hair hid a smile. The man with the white headdress took something from the other man and nodded.

Then, he handed Wanasi an object that looked like bread with a hole in the middle. Wanasi put down the remainder of the beans and studied the bread. He weighed it in his hand, twirled it on a finger, put it up to his eye and looked through the hole. He tried the smallest bite. His eyebrows rose. It was good! Sweet. And it had no fire. Wanasi pushed the beans aside and took another large bite of the sweet bread.

The man beside him laughed.

Wanasi smiled back.

The man pointed at the bread. "Doe-nuh."

Wanasi repeated the word. He looked at the *doe-nuh*, then at the man beside him.

Suddenly the saldu world did not seem so terrible after all.

❧

Rare fury, like flame from a fire long banked, erupted in Thomas's chest and burned through his gut. He glared up at the two-story brick building before him. His eyes narrowed as he pulled his gaze from the word *jail* carved on the sign above the door. The bricks were faded to a dull orange, and the boards that formed the front steps were curved and worn. But none of that mattered. He didn't care that the paint was peeling or the window cracked or the brick crumbling. What made Thomas's stomach burn was that they'd dared to cage the Indian in a jail cell. And not just any cell but one reserved for the insane. They'd had the gall to set him up like a vaudeville sideshow! And now, Thomas was forced to do something about it.

He strode up the two rickety steps and pounded his fist on the door. It swung open, and he found himself staring into the black eyes of the sheriff.

"Dr. Morgan, I assume?" The sheriff's drawl flowed out like mud from a clogged pipe.

Thomas gave a curt nod. "You're holding the Indian here, Sheriff Webber?"

His tone caused the sheriff to scowl. "Couldn't find no better place for him."

"I had not heard he was a mad Indian, only an *uncivilized* one."

"Don't know what he is." Sheriff Webber removed his hat and scratched his head. "Seems, well—" he slapped his hat against his thigh and pierced Thomas with his gaze—

"seems kind of shy and lonely, if you ask me. Half starved, he was. Don't know if he thinks he's gone to the hereafter or what. Just stares at us. Won't tell us his name. Won't tell us anything."

Thomas smoothed his moustache. "It was rude to ask the Indian his name. The Indians from these parts never tell their personal names. It's considered undignified. A member of their tribe must tell it for them."

"Aw, it don't matter. I don't know as he understood us anyhow."

Thomas sighed. "So you brought him here and made him a prisoner."

"Like I said, thought this was the best place for him till you arrived."

"In a cell? Were there no rooms at the inn?"

At the sarcasm in Thomas's voice, the sheriff crossed his arms over his barrel chest and straightened his shoulders. "Now see here, Dr. Morgan. You don't understand. Not every day we got a wild man walking out of the woods. Caused a real stir. Couldn't just check him in to the local hotel." Twin creases formed between Sheriff Webber's eyebrows. "Here, maybe this'll make it clearer." He opened the door wider and swept one arm toward the stairs beyond.

Thomas's eyes widened. Men, women, boys—over two dozen people were crammed on the narrow stairs, pushing into the room above them. "Oh, no. The Indian's not—"

"Oh yeah, he's up there." Sheriff Webber's mouth twisted into a grimace. "They've been coming and going all day. I 'spect there's been nigh onto a thousand folks come to get their gawk. It's like a regular traveling circus in here."

Thomas pushed up his sleeves. "Not anymore." He stepped past the sheriff and stormed toward the steps beyond. The smell of tobacco and stale perfume assaulted his senses as he pressed through the crowd on the stairs. He reached the top, then paused, at a loss.

Now what?

The room buzzed like a hive of hornets over raw meat. No one glanced his way. A voice rose over the noise. "I bet it ain't got nuthin' under that shirt." The words jabbed through Thomas and spurred him to action.

"*Out!*" His shout rang through the room. "Everybody out. Now!"

No one moved.

He grabbed the collar of a boy with a fishing pole and steered him toward the stairs. "Heard the trout are good this year. Why don't you go find out?"

"But, sir—"

The boy's whine scraped against Thomas's nerves. "That's a *man* in there, boy. A real human being. This is not some carnival sideshow." He raised his voice. "And that goes for *all* of you. Give this poor man some peace."

"Now see here, Dr. Morgan."

At the sheriff's voice from close behind him, Thomas turned.

Sheriff Webber pushed his way up the last two steps and crammed his hat back on his head. "This here Injun's in my care till we get word from the Bureau of Indian Affairs."

"Word has arrived, Sheriff. I'll be taking him back to San Francisco with me. He'll be living at the museum." Thomas pulled a paper from his breast pocket and thrust it toward the sheriff.

Sheriff Webber glanced over the paper and cleared his throat. "Well, it's a relief, anyhow, to have him off our hands. He's all yours." He refolded the paper and handed it back to Thomas. His voice boomed over the drone of the crowd. "You heard the professor. Everyone *out* now. There'll be plenty of time to stare later. Go on."

Thomas moved aside as people began to file past him, their footsteps as reluctant as his students' coming to class on exam day. In time, the room cleared. Then he saw him— a thin, forlorn figure sitting in a ray of sunlight. He was more like a wisp of light than a solid being.

Thomas stepped forward.

The Indian turned.

For a moment, blue eyes caught in brown. Two worlds stood face-to-face, measuring, questioning, wondering. And then the moment passed.

The Indian smiled. Thomas smiled back. The Indian motioned for Thomas to enter his cell.

From behind them, the sheriff laughed. "Well, now I've seen it all." He picked up a small stool from alongside the wall, then stepped forward and unlocked the cell door. "You'd think the old Indian was a king inviting you to his castle."

Thomas took the stool and entered the cell. The Indian watched, unmoving, as Thomas placed the stool across from the Indian, sat, and pulled a group of papers from his breast pocket. He glanced down at the list of words in every known native language of California. Then he looked again at the Indian. "Who are you?"

The Indian did not answer.

"Well, let's find out." Thomas began to read.

The words again. Meaningless words spoken to him as if he was supposed to understand them. Wanasi stared at the man in front of him—a young man with no gray in his mud-colored hair and no deceit in his sky-colored eyes. A man of earth and sky. Wanasi pondered the combination as he listened to the hum of words. Was this a man who dreamed of flying like the winged eagle? Or was he one who dared not let his feet leave the earth? Maybe he was both.

*Who are you, strange saldu? Will I ever find out?*

Wanasi's gaze swept over the man's firm chin, over the odd hair beneath his nose, and up to the broad, unwrinkled forehead. Then again, he focused on the eyes, clear like a summer day.

All the while the man's voice droned on and on, like the persistent hum of a fly. With every word, the terrible aloneness seeped ever deeper into Wanasi's soul. He could feel it, colder than the ice pools on the big mountain, harsher than the wind that howled through the crags of Grizzly Bear's Hiding Place, fierce enough to freeze the hope that had begun to grow like a tiny flower within him.

In time, the sun dipped lower in the sky. The shadow of the bars lengthened across the floorboards. The man with the funny headdress came in and out, in and out, and finally made fire come from the end of a thin stick. Wanasi watched in amazement as the man touched the fire to the inside of a clear bowl. The fire stayed and lit the room.

And then Wanasi heard it. Like a sound out of a nearly forgotten dream. *Siwini.* A single drop of meaning in an ocean of babbling. He sat up straighter. His gaze riveted on the young man in front of him as he repeated the word. "Siwini." White pine.

The man leaned forward. "Siwini."

"Siwini." Wanasi breathed again. He ran his hand along the pine wood of the sleeping platform. "Siwini."

The man laughed. "Yahi."

Wanasi grinned and nodded. "Nize ah Yahi." And this time, he was understood.

Wanasi tipped forward and touched his fingers to the man's cheek. And at that moment, he knew who this man was. He was more than saldu.

He was a friend.

# THREE

Two months. Or, more precisely, eight weeks, two days, and sixteen hours. Then the museum would open to the public for the very first time. A tingle danced up Allison's arms as she walked along the displays she had worked so hard to perfect.

The cabinets holding each exhibit lined every wall and formed a long I in the middle of the room. Sun shone in from the open windows on her left, making bright patterns on the tile floor. From a far room, she heard the clank of a bucket as the janitor did his daily mopping. The rumble of a horseless carriage drifted through an open window, then faded into the gentle hum of distant city noise.

Allison's heels tapped on the tile as she passed the feathered tomahawks and clay pots in the Apache display. She glanced at the Cheyenne peace pipes, the deerskin moccasins of Ute children, and the Nez Perce headdresses in the large exhibit to her right. Nothing was out of place.

Farther on, she stopped to rearrange the woven baskets

in the Miwok cabinet. The large basket, she decided, should sit higher than the smaller ones nestled around it. She placed an ear of dry corn in the large basket and tipped it on its side.

*There, perfect.*

She rubbed her hand over the side of a smaller basket, feeling the dryness of the reeds, the smoothness of the tight weave. How odd to think that savage hands once used these very baskets to carry fish and grain. Years ago, old women wove them, never dreaming that one day their creations would sit as works of art in a museum and speak of their lives to strangers.

A chill raced through Allison. She mustn't think of those who'd worked by dwindling daylight to form the baskets. Must not think of people long dead, remembered only here, in the baskets, the moccasins, the spears, and tomahawks.

The janitor's tuneless whistle wafted through the room. Allison touched her fingers to the back of her neck. Tiny tendrils of hair stuck to the dampness there. She pulled a pin from her hair and removed her hat. The lace and muslin affair drooped in the heat. She tossed it onto a nearby cabinet, then rearranged the Yurok money purses with their *dentalium* shell money. Next, she focused on the toggle-heads for the salmon harpoon of the Deer Creek Indians. That tribe, at least, lived on, though they no longer hunted salmon. She moved the toggle-heads a bit to the left. The hemp rope joining them to the two sharp sticks was frayed, but unbroken. Many more salmon could be held with those toggle-heads. But none ever would be.

Allison continued on, tucking a feather in here, repositioning a knife there, until she came to a tiny display half hidden behind a large Chickasaw headdress in the far corner of the room. She pushed the headdress aside and considered the two baskets, blanket, and otter-skin quiver with four arrows made of yew. She frowned. There should be a tribe name written in beautiful black calligraphy above the hanging baskets. But these items came from an unknown group of Indians, whose tiny camp was discovered by surveyors a few years back. Only the artifacts had been found beside an old woman, who'd died in the woven blanket that now lay draped in the display. The blanket still held a hint of musty odor, as if it remembered the woman who had breathed her last in its folds. The rest of her band was never seen, though Indian hunters searched the mountains above Oroville for months afterward.

Oroville . . .

Allison paused. The lone Indian, who would come to live at the museum tomorrow, was found in Oroville. She looked down at the items in the display. Her fingers brushed the thick blanket, the woven basket, and clay bowl—then stopped on a delicately carved pine flute. Seven small holes were carved in its top, with additional holes on each end. Two thongs of beaded feathers lay near the blowhole, and a single carving of a bear ran along the side.

Allison glanced behind her, then picked up the flute. It was light, its surface worn smooth by many years of use. She raised the instrument to her lips and blew a single, soft note. It echoed across the museum and faded at the doorway that led to the room the wild Indian would soon occupy. What if . . . did she dare? Allison took two steps toward the far door, then turned back and replaced the flute in the display. She started to walk away but couldn't. She'd seen that room behind the door with its single cot, two bare shelves, and simple rag rug. Three days ago it had been an empty storeroom.

It was still no place to call home, but Dr. Kroeber thought it was fine for a wild Indian.

To Allison, it was as barren as a cement building, as unwelcoming as stone angels with blind eyes.

For a moment, she held as still as those statues and listened to the thumping of her heart. She would dare. She would.

Allison spun and grabbed the flute from its resting place. Before she could change her mind again, she hurried to the far door, pushed it open, and stepped inside to place the flute on one of the empty shelves.

A honeybee buzzed against the windowpane. Allison walked over, opened the window, and let the bee go free. Sounds from the outside trickled through the opening—the jingle of harnesses, the shouts of trolley-men up the street, the shrill whistle of a policeman, the clumping of horses' hooves, and the steady rumble of a horseless carriage. A breeze scampered through the room, bringing with it the salty aroma of the bay mixed with the pungent smell of horse manure from a stable two blocks away. Allison took a deep breath. Familiar smells to her, but not to a mountain Indian. What would the Indian think of this bustling place called San Francisco, so different from the caves and cliffs of his home?

Allison sat on the cot and smoothed the red-and-blue Indian blanket she'd brought up from storage earlier that day. A blanket and a flute. Poor weapons against the strangeness of a whole new world.

"Have you gone mad?"

Allison whirled at the snapping voice.

Mrs. Agnes Whitson stood behind her, in the doorway, her forehead creased.

Allison leapt up from the cot. Her gaze swept over Mrs. Whitson's expensive French hat, her impeccable steel-gray hair, her aged cheeks with just the proper amount of rouge, her immaculate Gibson girl dress with gigot sleeves, and finally her white leather shoes—one of which tapped out a rapid beat as Mrs. Whitson awaited Allison's answer.

Allison put her hand to her hair. Her hat! She'd forgotten it in the other room. Her heart thumped. "I'm, um, I was just checking to be sure the room was in order for the Indian's arrival." She adjusted her collar and tried to ignore her lack of headwear. Her gaze dropped to the floor, and she noticed a scuff on the tip of one pointed toe of her shoe. She swallowed. She should have polished her shoes that morning. She knew she should have. Why hadn't she?

"One must *never* enter a man's room. It isn't proper." Mrs. Whitson stiffened her spine. "Even if that man *is* only an Indian. Appearances, my dear."

"Yes, ma'am."

Mrs. Whitson clucked her tongue. "And to sit on his bed . . . Well! Need I say more?"

Heat surged into Allison's cheeks. "No. Of course not, Mrs. Whitson. Thoughtless of me, I know."

Mrs. Whitson's mouth tipped in what should have been a smile. "That's all right, dear. One cannot expect you to remember everything. You've done quite well, considering . . ." Mrs. Whitson did not need to finish her statement. Allison knew.

"Yes, well, now that we have that settled—" Mrs. Whitson touched two manicured fingers to her chest and cleared her throat—"I came today to speak with Dr. Kroeber. He tells me you have performed your duties adequately thus far."

*Adequately?* Allison's chin lifted. "Everything is ready except the arrowhead display. I'll finish that next week when the Choctaw arrowheads arrive from Oklahoma. Would you care to see what I've done with the other exhibits?" She clutched her hands together to keep them from trembling.

"Not today, dear. I'm in a hurry." Mrs. Whitson's gaze seemed warm, but it did nothing to relieve the tightness in Allison's chest.

Not today. Never today. Didn't anyone care how hard she'd worked?

"Perhaps tomorrow, then." Allison modulated her tone to polite indifference, then motioned toward the door and allowed Mrs. Whitson to precede her into the larger room.

Mrs. Whitson glanced toward the displays, then back at Allison. She stepped toward the first exhibit. "I have time for one, I think."

Allison hurried to retrieve her hat, then held her breath and waited for Mrs. Whitson's words.

Mrs. Whitson's shoes barely made a sound as she walked toward the Apache exhibit for, as Allison had learned, "a lady does not tromp about like a bull in a china shop." Mrs. Whitson held her handbag firmly but calmly as she examined the peace pipe and tomahawk, for "a lady does not feel the need to put her fingers on everything she sees." She lifted her glasses to her eyes, read the card above the hanging headdress, then turned and spoke to Allison in a tone befitting a lady—not too loud, as a fishwife might speak, nor too soft, as one who lacks confidence. "Your calligraphy is quite clear. The lessons did you well, I see."

"Yes. Thank you."

Mrs. Whitson nodded. "Well, I don't have time for more." She turned toward the outer door. "By the way, dear, those spears should be hung higher up." She motioned toward the long, pointed spears above the Cherokee exhibit. "And we do need some more colorful curtains in here. Those are rather dull." She glanced at the windows. "I will see to the curtains before tomorrow." Mrs. Whitson paused and studied Allison for a moment.

Neither spoke.

Mrs. Whitson adjusted her grip on her handbag. "Very well, then. I shall see you again when the Indian arrives. I will inspect the other displays at that time." She leaned over and gave Allison a dry peck on the cheek. "And do fix those spears, dear."

Allison turned toward the offending weapons. As she did, she heard the soft click of Mrs. Whitson's shoes on the tile.

"Allison."

She turned back to find Mrs. Whitson still behind her. The woman lifted her fingers and gently touched Allison's cheek. "Be careful, dear, won't you?"

Warmth spread through Allison. "Careful?"

"Of the wild man. You're so young. I would hate—" Mrs. Whitson broke off suddenly, sniffed, and turned away.

And for one moment, Allison believed someone really did care.

Wanasi stepped into the bright sunlight and felt the breeze tickle his cheek. For an instant he closed his eyes and breathed deeply of the scent of dust and oak. He touched the rough straw of his saldu headdress, then opened his eyes and looked at the cloth leg and chest coverings the saldu called *pan* and *shur.*

Wanasi looked like one of them now, the pale saldu ghosts. All except the foot coverings. Those he could not, would not wear. How would his feet feel the warmth of the ground beneath him? How would his toes grip the earth and rock to make sure steps into this new world? No, these things the saldu called *shooze* were not for him. He carried the leather things in his hand, walking out into a crowd that circled him like wide-eyed owls around a mouse. Their voices nipped at him as he passed men who chewed and spat; women who blinked through round, clear eye coverings; girls who stared and giggled; boys with bare feet like his and bare heads to match.

His new saldu friend reached over and patted him on the arm. The muscles in Wanasi's back relaxed. He had decided to call his friend *Majapa, headman,* for the others seemed to obey when the younger one spoke. It would not have been so with the Yahi, but the saldu were different. Very different. Would he ever understand them?

His gaze slid over their village. On his left, wooden structures hunched together like old women trying to stand in a winter gale. Horses were tied to posts in front of them. Above, thick planks held strange symbols painted in red and blue. To his right, toward the rising sun, two shiny bars lay an arm's length apart and ran together across the ground for as far as he could see. Flat pieces of wood sat crosswise between the bars as if to make sure they never touched nor drifted away from each other. And—Wanasi's eyebrows rose to his hairline—beyond them a boy sat atop a wooden contraption attached to two thin wheels. The boy rode the wheels like one would ride a horse.

Wanasi touched Majapa's arm and pointed at the boy. From a woven basket tied to the front of the contraption, a tiny dog barked.

Majapa laughed.

Wanasi grinned. "Dawana saldu." Crazy white man.

A sound, like the cry of a dying eagle, pierced the air. Wanasi jumped. He knew that sound. It belonged to the black demon of the saldu. He dared not turn, lest he see it there, like a fat snake filled with a dozen fat rats.

Wanasi shuddered and listened to the steady thrum of the beast's breath, growing louder every moment. He straightened his shoulders, then turned to face the monster. There, dark against the sun, the steaming demon hissed and slithered toward him along the two bars that ran on the ground.

His fingers gripped Majapa's arm. The demon raced toward them, but the saldu did not seem to notice. Was he the only one who could see the beast?

When he was a boy, his mother would make him lie down in the tall grass whenever they saw the black demon. They would hold their arms over their heads and squeeze their eyes tight shut until the demon was long past. It had never seen them, had never chased them with its hot breath. But now there was no tall grass to hide him, no rocks to shield him from the monster's fiery gaze.

Wanasi's breath came faster. He spotted a willow tree, dropped his grip on Majapa's arm, and ran toward the drooping branches. With each step, the demon drew closer. Its shrill shriek pierced him like a knife from the netherworld. "You will not take me!" He flung the cry over his shoulder. "I will not go to the land of the dead. Not now. Not yet!"

The willow loomed in front of him. He darted inside the cover of its branches and pressed his back against the far side of the trunk. *The demon will not find me here. I will be safe.*

Wind rattled the leaves around him. The chugging of the monster grew louder. Then another piercing scream spat from its throat, followed by a hiss more menacing than any rattler. Wanasi knew that black demon had stopped just outside the tree. He could hear its breathing. Could it hear his? He held his breath for one long moment, then another. Blood pounded in his ears. He pressed his palms into the willow's smooth bark and let out his breath in a quiet whoosh. Leaves rustled as branches parted behind him. He peeked around the trunk of the tree.

Majapa stood there, watching him. The hair beneath Majapa's nose twitched.

Wanasi peered through the branches to see the shiny side of the black demon standing just behind Majapa, but Majapa wasn't afraid. He beckoned Wanasi forward with one hand.

Wanasi shook his head. *"Hexai-sa!"*

But Majapa didn't go away as Wanasi insisted. He just frowned. "Ai-aiku tsub."

All is well? Clearly Majapa did not know what he was saying. Wanasi did not move.

"Aiku tsub," his friend repeated and extended his hand as if to say, "Trust me."

For three long breaths, Wanasi studied Majapa's clear eyes, then he stepped from behind the tree trunk. He was in the saldu world now. He must be brave. He must trust. As if weighted with skins filled with stone, his feet moved toward Majapa.

Majapa parted the branches of the willow and stepped outside their reach.

Wanasi followed, and there before him stood the saldu demon, puffing steam and snorting its fury into the wind. Would it leap upon him even now and devour him?

Majapa slowed his steps until he was standing at Wanasi's

side. He pointed to the shiny bars running side by side along the ground. Then he pointed to the demon. The bars, the demon. The demon, the bars.

Suddenly Wanasi understood. The saldu had caged the demon, had tamed it with the bars as a man might tame a horse and ride it.

Majapa motioned toward an opening in the demon's side. A saldu woman entered the hole and disappeared inside. A boy followed, and then two tall men. Majapa stepped up to the opening and pointed to Wanasi and then to the inside of the monster.

Wanasi stopped. Did the saldu expect him to step into the demon's belly?

Majapa looked into Wanasi's eyes. "Aiku tsub."

Wanasi stared down the long sleek body of the black demon. He glanced up at the smoke billowing from its head, and down at the shiny bars that held it. Then he lifted his chin and spoke directly to the monster. "Nize ah Yahi." His voice rang out. "I am Yahi. I am not afraid." He removed a single leather thong from his ear and tossed it on the ground. "I will ride the demon south, on the journey of the dead."

Without another word, Wanasi stepped into the belly of the white man's demon.

He did not look back.

⌒

Thomas watched the Indian conquer his fear and enter the train. He smiled. This man was nobler than most he'd ever met. His trust was a gift, one that Thomas prayed he'd never abuse.

45

To think he was standing here watching the last Yahi enter a train. It was amazing, incredible. Forty years ago the Yahi were thought wiped out by the Anderson attacks. This Indian would have been only a child then. Had he and a small band of survivors hidden in the hills for forty years? If Thomas had properly interpreted the Indian's gestures from the night before, the others were all gone now. Only this one was left, alone, with no one to give him a name.

Thomas watched the Indian make his way down the aisle and sit in a seat near a window. *The Indian*. He couldn't keep calling him that. It was too demeaning. Thomas would have to give him a name, at least for now. Perhaps he would call him *Ishi*, the Yana name for man. *Ishi*. It seemed right somehow. He stroked his mustache, then stepped up the last stair into the train.

As he did, the sheriff's voice sounded from the open doorway behind him. "You all set then, Dr. Morgan?"

He turned to the man. "Yes, thank you."

Sheriff Webber chuckled. "So you're thanking me now, are you, Professor?"

Thomas's cheeks warmed. "Come now, Sheriff, you can't blame me for objecting to a jail cell for a home?"

"Humph." The sheriff shook his head. "Don't see as how living in a museum will be much better."

The words struck Thomas like a slap. He raised his chin, much as the Indian had done moments before. "It will be better. We'll make it better."

The train gave a single sharp whistle. A puff of steam plumed from its engine.

"We'll see." The sheriff doffed his hat, then stepped down from the train. "If that wild man ain't run away or kicked the bucket by spring, I'll eat this here hat."

Thomas glanced at Ishi, sitting tall and still, like a tree unmoved by the wind. "Bon appétit, Sheriff Webber." A smile touched Thomas's lips. "Bon appétit."

# FOUR

It wasn't just the way the rain drove in spattering sheets across her skirt that troubled Allison. Nor was it the monotonous rumble of water on the fabric of the umbrella, or even the specks of mud that had formed a leopard pattern on her shoes and stockings. It was all of it, every last thing that had gone wrong on this worst of all days. Earlier that morning, she'd dressed in Thomas's favorite tangerine-colored dress, had her hair coiffed in the latest style, and made sure her gloves were sparkling white. She should have been the image of the ideal wife. She'd planned so carefully, but the ferry was late, she'd tripped over a stray mutt on the pier, and then the rains began.

Allison sighed. Now her dress was wet, her gloves soiled, her hair . . . well, there was no use thinking about her hair. She no longer looked like the ideal wife. But the *dutiful* wife—the one who braved the storm to meet her husband at the ferry—that was still possible. So Allison waited.

A strand of her hair caught in the wind and plastered

itself onto her cold cheek. Her gloved fingers tightened on the umbrella handle. Rain splashed into ever deepening puddles on the dock. But Allison did not move. Soon they would come. Thomas and the wild man. She would meet them, even if it meant ruining her new kidskin boots. They would all ride the cable car together to the museum. They would see her completed exhibits. And Thomas would be proud.

Allison squinted her eyes and gazed over the choppy water of the bay. There, like a speck of light on the waves, she could see something approaching. The ferry? She hoped so.

"Say, ma'am, why don't you wait inside, out of the rain?" Allison shook her head at the man speaking from behind her and raised her voice over the steady roar of raindrops. "No, thank you, sir. I'm fine here."

The man muttered something; then Allison heard the bang of a door. She pulled her coat tighter around her neck. The rain came down harder, making a million dancing divots in the water below.

Long minutes dragged by before Allison saw the shape of a ferry emerge from the grayness. Like an old bear, it lumbered up to the pier and bumped against the wood planking. Two men appeared and slid a short ramp between the boat and dock. One after another, passengers began to disembark. Allison watched wind-tossed women holding their hats against the wind; men, with their shoulders hunched and coattails flapping; a boy with his collar turned up and his cheeks the color of cranberries. Each hurried down the ramp and rushed past her. But still, Thomas did not come.

And then, as if the sky, too, held its breath, the wind quieted until all Allison heard was the rhythmic splash of raindrops on the taut fabric of her umbrella and the gentle bumping of the ferry against the dock.

Minutes passed. Finally, Thomas appeared. Allison gazed up at him and waved a greeting.

Thomas paused. He raised his hand. "Allison!" He strode toward her.

She watched him come, his hat a little askew, his shoulders beaded with raindrops. She longed to see his smile, but his lips formed a thin line as he came to a halt before her. "Whatever are you doing out here in the rain? You'll catch your death of cold." Her took her gloved hands in his own. "You're wet."

"Y-yes, but—"

Thomas glanced up to the umbrella, then down at her soaked hem. "You're certain to take ill in this weather, Allison. And you know we must be careful about Ishi."

"Ishi?"

"The Indian. He'll be quite vulnerable to our diseases." Thomas ran his hand through his wet hair. "I'd have thought you'd be a little more careful."

Allison turned her eyes away from Thomas. A chill swept from her ankles to her shoulders. Ice settled in her stomach. All at once, the rain seemed colder, the wind more piercing, the sky a dirtier gray. Why couldn't he just be glad to see her? Why couldn't he say how wonderful it was that she had made such an effort to meet him? She wiped a bit of dampness from her eyes and focused over his shoulder. "So where is this Ishi now?"

"I asked him to wait."

"He didn't." Allison pointed to the lonely figure at the top of the ferry ramp. His shoulders were covered with an old blanket, and his hat drooped so low that his face was hidden. "That's him, isn't it?"

Thomas glanced back. "Yes. That's him. Of course it's

him." Thomas put one hand on his hip, then threw his free arm around her shoulders. He drew a long breath, then blew it out slowly. "Well, what's done is done." He gave her a small smile. "I'm sure it will turn out all right. Come, meet our Indian." He offered her his arm and led her back toward the ferry.

Allison's eyes widened as she drew closer. She noticed that the wild man's hair was short and he held a pair of shoes in one hand. "He won't hurt me, will he?"

"Of course not. He's quite nice, really."

Words from the newspaper accounts of his capture flitted through her mind: *Savage, wild, brute, uncivilized, primitive* . . . But none of them seemed to fit this thin, shoeless creature, his pants spattered with mud. She remembered the look on Mrs. Whitson's face when she warned Allison to be careful, but that didn't seem to matter so much now.

The Indian tipped his head, and Allison noticed a leather thong in his ear that seemed at odds with the soggy straw hat. Thomas's grip tightened on her arm. She stepped up to the wild man and gazed into his face. Gaunt cheeks, square chin, and eyes brown and deep like the earth. Allison stared into those eyes, gold flecked and calm.

The Indian stared back.

What Allison saw wasn't a savage nor a wild man but just a man—a man whose utter aloneness touched something deep within her. At that moment, she knew that he was somehow seeing past her masks and into the secret places of her heart.

Only then was Allison afraid.

Wanasi looked at the strange creature, dressed like a poppy caught in the mud. She was a woman, a very young woman, young as his own daughter would have been if he'd ever had a wife and child. He'd noticed Majapa's arm resting over the woman's shoulders. From this he knew she was Majapa's woman. His wife. But if she was his wife, why did they speak like strangers? Why did she seem so alone? For a long moment, he looked into the woman's storm-colored eyes. He saw her loneliness, so like his own.

When he saw her fear, he stepped back.

The woman turned and walked down the planks with Majapa's hand on her arm. Wanasi watched the sway of the strange object she held over her head to keep off the rain. He watched the way the water slid off the covering and splashed to the ground at her feet. He watched as she and Majapa parted at the bottom of the ramp, looking back to see if he followed.

And as Wanasi watched, his heart began to pound. Could it be . . . ? Was this woman the person he sought?

The bell of the cable car jingled a discordant tune as Thomas helped Allison and Ishi to their seats. Strangers stared at Ishi, then looked away, as if embarrassed by their perusal. A woman scooted farther down the bench as Thomas settled between Ishi and his wife. Both sat beside him like twin statues, faces like stone, eyes forward, chins high.

The cable car's bell dinged one last time before the car began rumbling up the street toward Market. They passed a fishery, a warehouse, and a candlemaker's shop. Then the cable car turned and plunged into the heart of San Francisco. Tall buildings loomed on either side of them, some newly rebuilt from the earthquake that had wreaked havoc on the city just five years before.

Thomas leaned forward and tapped Ishi on the knee. Then he pointed to a tall structure on his left. Surely the Indian would be impressed with the sheer massiveness of the buildings.

Ishi looked, then smiled as if being polite. But he did not seem impressed.

Thomas pointed to an even taller structure. He stretched his hand up to indicate the remarkable height.

Ishi tipped forward and tilted back his head to look at the top of the building. Then he sat back and rubbed his hand along the cool metal pole beside his seat. He glanced at Thomas. *"Waganupa."* He stretched his hand, mimicking Thomas's motion for height. "Waganupa." He pointed north.

Then Thomas understood. Ishi was not comparing these buildings to his hut in the mountains but to the mountains themselves! Thomas laughed. No wonder Ishi wasn't impressed. Compared to God's mountains, the buildings of the white man must not seem like much at all.

Thomas sat back in his seat and chuckled. As he did, Allison turned toward him. "What did he say?"

Thomas crossed his ankle over his knee. "I think he just told me that Mount Lassen is a whole lot bigger than our puny buildings."

Allison smiled, then turned to Ishi. "Waganupa." She made the motion for "height." Then she pointed to the buildings and brought her fingers together to indicate small.

Ishi grinned.

Allison raised her hand to cover her mouth.

Thomas cocked his head. Allison had not changed her gloves once since she'd met the Indian. She didn't even seem to know they were soiled. That, at least, was something to be thankful for. But what caused her to relax enough to forget her obsession with her gloves? Had something happened on the ferry ramp? Something important? Ishi hadn't even looked at the women in the train and the ferry. He certainly hadn't engaged any in conversation. So what made Allison different? Why had she even come to the pier?

A hundred questions chewed at Thomas's mind. She could have met them at the museum where she could wait inside, out of the rain. Was she trying to make him feel guilty for going without her? Was she trying to push him into another quarrel, another confrontation? He'd seen enough of that in his years growing up. Too much, in fact.

Thomas wiped a droplet of rain from his sleeve. He supposed he should have been nicer when he first saw her there on the pier. He'd almost started to argue with her there. But no, he wouldn't let her push him into that. Even though, for heaven's sake, she should *know* better!

A smothered giggle interrupted his thoughts. He looked over to see Ishi making hand motions that looked like a bird in flight. On the other side of him, Allison was smiling. She looked so happy, free . . . so *normal*. Why couldn't she always be that way?

Thomas uncrossed his legs, and his gaze caught Allison's. She sobered.

Guilt slashed through him. He turned away and found Ishi's eyes locked on him. Ishi's eyebrows rose toward his hairline in the gesture Thomas had come to recognize as Ishi's sign for astonishment.

Thomas stood and walked to the far side of the cable

car. Was Ishi judging him for his relationship with his own wife? It was preposterous. Unthinkable.

Brakes squealed. Thomas looked back toward Ishi, but the Indian was gone. And Allison with him.

# FIVE

The Indian followed her. Allison could hear his footsteps, as soft as the pattering of old memories. She all but felt his curious looks like a hot brand on her back.

"Go away!" She spoke over her shoulder, but of course he didn't understand. How could he? Even she could barely comprehend the garble of words that pushed past the lump in her throat.

Why had Thomas looked at her like that? And why hadn't he helped her from the cable car? Instead, he'd just turned his back on her and kept it turned, even when the trolley came to a halt near the museum.

Allison's feet crunched on the gravel path leading to the front of the museum. She stared at the shimmering surface of rain-drenched rocks. Along either side of the path, delicate yellow daffodils lifted their teacup heads to catch drops of water. Beyond them, green lawns stretched toward a grove of sequoias. Midway across the lawn, a gray squirrel paused and sniffed the air. It looked toward her, then darted off in the direction of the trees. She watched it scamper away, and only then did she notice the rain had turned into a fine mist that settled in miniscule droplets on the grass.

She lowered her umbrella and shook the water from its fabric. Then she hooked it over her arm and fixed her eyes on the tall gray walls of the museum. Behind the museum, she could see the cluster of smaller buildings owned by the university and, across the road, the hospital. A shadow fell over the path, and Allison glanced up to see a seagull flying overhead. She focused again on the museum, refusing to look back at the Indian who still followed—or to see if that insensitive, rude, judgmental husband of hers—

"Ouch!" Allison stumbled to a halt. She glanced down at her shoe. Her ankle stung with dull pain, but she wouldn't limp. She wouldn't give Thomas the pleasure of seeing how he'd hurt her. It was all Thomas's fault, of course, every bad thing that had happened today.

Allison hit the end of her umbrella against the ground. He hadn't even cared enough to walk with her. A gentleman would have helped her from the cable car. She'd tried so hard to please him too. But it wasn't good enough. Nothing was ever good enough for Dr. Thomas Morgan.

The ringing of the cable car bell startled her. She paused.

"Allison, wait!"

Her shoulders stiffened at Thomas's shout. She continued toward the museum, picking up her pace despite the dull throb of her ankle. The crunch of long, loping strides sounded behind her.

In a moment, Thomas reached her. The Indian drew abreast on her other side but did not look at her. Thomas did. His blue eyes bored through her like a grinding stone on soft pine. He reached out and grabbed her arm. "What are you *doing*, Allison?"

She didn't answer.

"Slow down, would you?"

She didn't.

"Whatever is amiss?"

Her gaze flicked toward him, then returned to the tall gray walls. "Nothing. I'm going back to work."

Thomas relaxed his grip. "Are you okay? I thought you might have twisted your ankle."

"Don't bother pretending you care, Dr. Morgan!"

Thomas pulled back. "What are you talking about?" His voice cracked, and his fingers trembled against her skin.

Allison stopped short and wrenched her arm from his grip. "You . . . you . . ."

He stepped away, his brow furrowed, his face pale. For a moment, Allison thought he might be ill, but that was absurd. He wasn't ill; he was accusing. He wasn't afraid; he was reproving. And he was just trying to make her feel guilty.

Thomas's tone softened to a pained whisper. "How can you say that, Allison? Of course I care."

She dug her fists into her hips and glared at him. "Do you? Or are you just saying that to make up . . . to make up for—"

Thomas's eyes slid from hers. "I'm not going to argue with you."

*Of course not.* Thomas never argued. He never shouted. He just let her read the silent accusations in his eyes, hear the unspoken criticism he only sometimes tried to mask. And that was worse. Much, much worse.

"Please, Allison . . ."

Not this time. This time she'd make him say it. She'd make him tell her what he really thought. Allison jabbed her umbrella tip back toward where the cable car had been. "You didn't even have the decency to help me off the cable car. So I did it myself. Just like I do everything myself."

A blush stained Thomas's cheeks. For a moment, he didn't answer.

From beside them, the Indian leaned over and picked up a small stone. He examined it, shifting it from one palm to the other, then let it drop.

Thomas released a long breath. "Look, Allison—" he scrubbed his hand against his pant leg—"I didn't even realize the cable car had stopped. I'm sorry. I looked around and you were gone and I thought—"

"You *thought?* What did you think? That I'd taken your precious Indian?" She gestured toward the savage who was now rubbing his toe back and forth over the gravel. He still carried his shoes in his hand. Allison scowled. "Never mind. I don't care what you thought." She jerked her soiled gloves from her hands, took a clean pair of gloves from her bag, and slipped them on. "I was just trying to be a good wife."

"I know."

Allison stuffed her dirty gloves into her bag, then strode ahead, leaving Thomas behind. The Indian kept pace on her left.

*Breathe, Allison. A lady does not rush. A lady does not shout. A lady—*

"Allison Morgan, what*ever* are you doing?!"

Ice shattered Allison's nerves at the tone of Mrs. Whitson's voice. She looked up to see the older woman and Dr. Kroeber standing on the steps to the museum. *Caught!* Allison cringed. Mrs. Whitson was again clad in an immaculate gown. Dr. Kroeber, as usual, looked as if he'd dressed in a hurry.

Mrs. Whitson's quick stride brought her down to Allison in two breaths. Thomas nodded in the woman's direction, then hurried toward Dr. Kroeber.

Allison slowed, her anger fleeing like a deer before the hunter. Before she could think what to say, Mrs. Whitson stopped before her, one hand planted on a thin hip. "My dear, I thought I made myself quite plain about the Indian. Yet here you are with him."

Allison cleared her throat. "I'm with Thomas."

One of Mrs. Whitson's eyebrows arched toward her hairline. "That's not how it appeared to me."

"But—"

Mrs. Whitson waved away the word. "A lady does not make excuses."

For the briefest breath, Allison envisioned a brilliant defense. But it died a quick death in the face of Mrs. Whitson's next words.

"Must I remind you who this Indian is? A wild man. A savage. A *creature* that knows nothing at all of the niceties of civilization." Mrs. Whitson spaced each sentence with a dramatic pause. "Not at all the proper company for a lady. A person such as yourself must be particularly careful about appearances."

"Yes, I know." Allison followed Mrs. Whitson up the steps, the Indian at her heels.

When they reached the top, Mrs. Whitson turned. Critical eyes swept Allison's frame. "It's just as well Dr. Kroeber decided only we two would be present for the Indian's arrival." She sniffed. "You look frightful."

Allison turned away, and the Indian's gaze caught hers.

His mouth curved into a small smile; then he bent over to smell the pansies growing in a large ceramic pot near the door. He straightened and touched the fronds of a palm planted in an adjacent box. Then his gaze returned to hers.

Mrs. Whitson reached out and turned Allison's shoulders so that she could no longer see the Indian. "Obey me in this, Allison." Her voice dropped to a whisper. "Don't throw away everything I've obtained for you."

"Come, Ishi." Dr. Kroeber's pleasant tone silenced Mrs. Whitson's warning. He stepped to the front door and swung it wide. "Come see your new home." He motioned inside.

Allison caught snatches of Dr. Kroeber's conversation as she followed the others into the museum. Dr. Kroeber had one hand on the Indian's shoulder as he spoke to Thomas in rapid spurts. "Reporters driving me crazy . . . vaudeville . . . the circus . . . a sideshow, if you can believe it . . ." Dr. Kroeber approached the door leading to the Indian displays.

Allison caught her breath.

Dr. Kroeber gripped the doorknob. ". . . no idea of his value . . . offered me a hundred dollars."

The door opened.

" . . . last untainted Indian . . . as if we'd ever . . ." Dr. Kroeber stopped. The words died on his lips.

Allison smiled. Her work had taken his breath away.

Dr. Kroeber's arm dropped to his side. "Oh, *no*."

His words shot like darts into Allison's heart.

Shards of glittering glass; torn moccasins; broken arrows, tomahawks, clay bowls; a drum thrown on its side; bits of paper scattered over the whole like flakes of snow.

Thomas felt cold fingers touch his wrist as he struggled to comprehend the destruction. He turned. Allison swayed beside him, her face as white as the pieces of paper, her body stiff, with only her fingers quivering on his forearm. Her wide eyes did not blink as she surveyed the scene.

"Allison?"

She didn't turn. She only stared out over the rubble, and then she moved, like a ghost floating through a graveyard.

He heard Mrs. Whitson's voice behind him.

"What happened here?"

"I don't know." Dr. Kroeber stepped beside Thomas.

He swallowed. "Who was in the museum today?"

Then Dr. Kroeber and Mrs. Whitson spoke at once, their words mirroring the jumble that lay on the floor before them.

"I was."

"And I. But I didn't—"

"Did you?"

"—see a thing."

"How?"

"Why?"

Thomas raised his hands. "Neither of you know who could have done this?"

Dr. Kroeber shrugged his shoulders. "Someone must have sneaked in the back when I was in my office."

"I came directly to Alfred's office. I didn't see anyone else." Mrs. Whitson turned to Dr. Kroeber. "Shouldn't we have heard something?"

Dr. Kroeber shook his head. "Not if it was done earlier, before we came in. Or even last night."

Thomas sighed. "We'll check the locks. But other than that . . ." He let the sentence dwindle into silence. If only there were something he could do to make it better. But he couldn't. Not now, not ever. He'd learned that long ago. His gaze swept to his wife, who stood separate, removed. "Poor Allison." The words sounded hollow, helpless, even to him.

"Poor us." Dr. Kroeber leaned toward Mrs. Whitson. The two again began to speak.

Thomas watched Allison kneel by the fallen drum. She righted it, then bent to pick up a bow and arrow. The feathers on the arrow stuck out at odd angles. Allison smoothed them with one finger, her shoulders hunched. Then she stood and set the arrow in a broken display cabinet. He could see her arm tremble. Should he go to her? Should he try to comfort her? Or would she reject him again?

Before he could decide, he heard Ishi's quick intake of breath beside him.

*"Yahi!"*

Dr. Kroeber and Mrs. Whitson grew silent. They turned toward Ishi, but he wasn't looking at them. He didn't seem aware that any of them existed.

He weaved through the broken glass to an untouched display tucked in the far corner. Thomas followed, stopping behind Ishi and watching as the Indian ran his fingers over the otter-skin quiver and yew arrows. Silence hovered like the moment before a child's cry.

Then Ishi turned. A single tear shone on his cheek.

It was not at all what he'd expected, this white man's world. He had expected to die, and yet they cared for him. He'd expected their fear but received only curiosity. He'd gone to meet the enemy but found instead friends. But in his wildest dreams he'd never expected to find his own things set up like treasures, awaiting him. Of course, he wouldn't need those things in the saldu world. But he was glad they were here. Glad they would be in the room just outside his own. It seemed right somehow.

Wanasi looked around at the four white walls of the room they'd indicated would be his. They'd left him alone now. Alone in this strange place, with its wood floor, sleeping platform, and blanket woven with bright colors. He slid his footwear under the sleeping platform, then glanced toward the opening in the wall. Faint rays of sunshine shimmered through the raindrops that clung to the same clear material blocking the breeze. He walked over and placed his hand on the surface. It was smooth, cold, and hard. He could see through it, all the way across the grass to the tall trees beyond. He could see two gray squirrels running at the base of a tree and a blue jay pecking for a worm.

Wanasi turned away from the opening. Then he saw something that seemed like an image from a dream. The smooth wood, the two small hawk feathers tied with a leather thong, the seven precisely placed holes, and the familiar black bear running along its side. Wanasi had carved that bear when he was no more than ten summers old. He had carved it in memory of his brother.

Slowly, Wanasi made his way to the far side of the room. He picked up the precious flute and held it in his palm. Who could have set it there? And how could they have known? Three years ago it was taken from his camp, along with the other things they had needed to survive that winter, the things that now lay on red cloth in the room beyond. How had any of it come here?

Wanasi closed his eyes and focused on the feel of the

pine, warm against his skin. His hand moved to the rough cut of the finger holes, then to the bit of leather tied around the instrument. He held the hawk feathers gently between his thumb and forefinger. It was just as he remembered. Just as it was when he carved it so many summers ago, the summer when the *banya* were sick.

It rained that day, a hot, sticky rain that kept them huddled together inside the cave, telling stories of the old days and remembering. Wanasi hated days like that. Even now he recalled the way the small fire flickered and made shadows dance along the cave walls. He remembered his mother's voice, low and soft. He remembered the smell of cooking rabbit and the steady swooshing of his knife against the pine branch that would become his flute. But most of all, he remembered the story his mother told, a story that still chilled him despite the heat, a story that he had lived and wished he might forget.

But even after forty winters, Wanasi could not forget the day his people were massacred.

The saldu came like a swarm of bees, their sting carried in the sticks that shot fire. Wanasi could still see the blood, smell the death, and hear the screams and sounds that shook the ground like thunder carried in flame.

And the bodies.

They floated like so much driftwood down the blood-reddened waters of the river. He would have died that day but for the bodies. He remembered how his mother fell with him into the water, and together they floated with the dead. Icy waters swirled around Wanasi's head, drowning the sounds of fire and death. Lifeless bodies bumped into his arms, his legs, his side. He opened his eyes only once to meet the unseeing stares of his people, see the dark hair that

66

floated like giant spiders in the red river. And so he floated
—for an hour, for a day, for a lifetime—until the sun slipped
behind the siwini and his mother pulled him to the shore.
When he opened his eyes he saw the shadow of his mother's
face above him. They had fooled the sticks that shot fire.
They had fooled the saldu.

Wanasi stood on shaking legs and saw his uncle and two
others. They were all that was left. All that lived.

"We must go," his mother said. And so they walked, all
that night, the next day, and many days after that. They
walked far from the death place until they could no longer
smell blood on the wind.

They hid in their cave, told stories, cooked rabbits. But
nothing was ever the same. There were no more songs
around the fire, no more dancing in the moonlight. No
more laughter, no more dreams. Only hiding and hunting
and hoping to forget.

That was why Wanasi carved the flute. To forget the bad
and remember the good. And sometimes, it had worked.

He ran his hand over the smooth wood of the flute
again. Would it still work? Did the flute remember its music,
even here in the land of the saldu? Or was it dead too?

Wanasi raised the instrument, positioned his fingers,
and began to play. The notes came softly at first, then grew
until sweet music filled the room. He closed his eyes and
remembered his people. The song swirled around him, a living thing, then drifted out the door, flowing fingers reaching for someone who could hear the silent longings in his
heart.

# SIX

Allison refused to cry. It was indecent, weak. But the tears ran anyway. Not on the outside but down her throat and into the pit of her stomach. She thought she might throw up, but she quelled that feeling too. She must not break down now. She must go on. She must pull herself up by her shoe straps—or whatever the saying was that the men used.

The creak of door hinges sounded from a far room. Allison put her hands to her temple and rubbed, but the elephant dance in her head didn't stop. She closed her eyes tight, then opened them again. Nothing changed.

They had all left her, of course. They'd offered to help, but she refused. Somehow it made it worse to think of them picking through the remnants of her perfect displays. So Thomas and Dr. Kroeber retreated to their offices, Mrs. Whitson left with a simple "Such a shame, dear," and the Indian retired to his room. That left Allison alone with a thousand shards of broken glass, bolts of torn fabric, and priceless artifacts scattered from one end of the room to the other. Bits and pieces of her hope, her dreams, strewn about like garbage.

Somehow it didn't surprise her.

"Why can't anything turn out as it should?" Allison directed her demand toward the ceiling. *Is someone up there trying to ruin my life?* She silenced the thought. A good person didn't ask such questions. A good person did her Christian duty on Sundays and lived her life right for the rest of the week. But still, it hurt. And still, she wondered.

"Who you talkin' to?" A young boy appeared in the far doorway. Allison could see his shock of bright blond hair sticking out in every direction. The boy rubbed his hand over his nose. "You okay there, miss?"

"I'm fine. Everything's fine."

"Don't look fine. Looks like a right mess in here." He ambled over and squatted next to a hickory bow. He reached toward it.

"Don't touch that!"

The boy snatched back his fingers. "Why not?"

Allison crossed her arms. "It's an artifact, that's why."

"Looks like a bow to me." The boy grinned. Allison noticed that one tooth was only half grown in the front. "Nice bow too. Bet I could get a buck on the first try with that one. I'm a real good shot, you know."

Allison leaned back against a display cabinet and crossed her arms. "You ever shot with an Indian bow?"

The boy shook his head. "No, ma'am. But Dad says he's gonna teach me." He paused and twisted his mouth into a childish grimace. "Just as soon as the Indian teaches him, that is." He looked up at Allison. "Is the Indian here yet?"

"Yes, he is. But he's resting now. We're not to disturb him."

"Bet whoever made the mess disturbed him plenty."

Allison didn't answer.

"So who were you talking to, huh?"

"Nobody."

"I thought you was talking to . . ." His voice dropped to a whisper. "You know—Jesus."

A fist clenched in Allison's chest. "You . . . you'd better get going now. I've got a lot of work to do."

The boy stared up at her, then got to his feet. "Okay. Dad's probably looking for me anyway." He turned to leave but stopped and looked over his shoulder. "You'll tell the Indian I came to see him, won't you? Tell him I said hello. Tell him I'm sorry all his Indian stuff had to be behind glass like it was some kind of antique or something." The boy's grin was like a slice of watermelon over his face. Then he turned, trotted to the door, and was gone.

She hadn't even gotten his name. Hadn't found out how he knew about the Indian or the displays. Allison watched the door swing back and forth and finally settle in its place. "What a funny kid." She shook her head. "Half grown and wise as an old uncle." Not that she'd ever had an uncle.

Allison sat on the floor and pulled a basket into her lap. Was it Maidu or Deer Creek? She didn't know. She picked up a tomahawk. This, at least, she knew was Apache. She stood and put it near where the Apache exhibit had been, then turned again toward the mess on the floor. It would take weeks, months to sort through the rubble and put everything back in its proper place. Even then it would never be the same.

She knelt beside a large Shoshonean drum and tapped her fingers on the taut leather. *Thump, thump, thump,* like the beating of the blood in her temples. She stopped.

And then the music came, flitting into her friendless world like the song of some magical bird.

*The flute* . . .

He was playing the flute. Allison sucked in her breath and held it for one timeless moment. She closed her eyes and let the music wash through her. It was a sad song, its keening notes like tears dropping on her skin—tears that she would not shed for herself.

The tune changed, the notes deepened, but the song continued, like a call from a time long past. It reminded her of something . . . Yes, she remembered now—it was like the sound of the music box on her mother's bureau. But that music box broke. She could see it falling from the shelf. Shattering. Bits of wood over the floor. Its music had stopped then. Just as the Indian's music stopped now. She leaned forward and listened. But no more music came.

Instead, she heard another sound, a sound as lonely as a gull's call over the empty ocean. A man chanting. The Indian, his voice low but clear. Words, strange and eerie, floated in rhythmic waves. *Wowi. Hansi saldu, hansi saldu.* And one word, repeated again and again: *Yuna. Yuna. Yuna.*

Allison understood none of it, but the utter aloneness in his tone spoke more clearly than words. And that she understood all too well.

As quickly as it started, the chanting ended. The music came again. And the image of the broken music box flashed into her mind once more. Why had it dropped? And why did she remember it now?

She needed to know. She wasn't sure why, but deep within was the certainty that she *needed* to remember. She searched her memory, tapping her fingers again, softly, softly against the drum. *Boom, boom, boom,* like the sound of a fist on the door. *Boom, boom.* A fist . . . and the music.

A heavy fist.

Mr. Mayweather's fist, slamming against the door like thunder at noon. But it didn't start there. It started with Timmy. Yes, with Timmy Bear.

Allison leaned back against the wooden drawer of the Nez Perce exhibit and let the memory come.

The sky was gray, like an old sock worn too long into winter. Little Allison breathed in the damp air and looked over at Timmy, her stuffed bear. They were having a tea party for her birthday.

"Allison, get in here this instant!"

Allison turned toward the house. The shadowy figure of her mother stood on the porch. Allison jumped to her feet. "Coming, Mama."

She ran toward the house, and her foot hit a puddle. Mud sprayed up her legs and onto the fabric of her dress. She stared, horror filling her at the black splotches marring the material.

Then somehow she was in the house, the smell of cabbage soup pervading the room and the sound of the music box tinkling from the bureau. Behind a once yellow curtain, a bed lay rumpled and unmade. The drawers of the dresser sat open, and a full sack lay on the floor beside it.

Allison frowned. "Are we taking our clothes to the park too?"

Her mother did not respond. Her face was turned away, just as it always was in Allison's faded memories.

"We are going to see the grizzly bear, aren't we? Remember, you promised."

Silence descended between them like fog from the bay, then scattered at the sound of loud footsteps on the front porch.

"Shhh." Mama pressed a finger to her indistinct lips.

Together, they crouched beside the old stove.

"Why are we being quiet?"

Her mother's shadowy face looked down at her. "It's a game . . . for your birthday."

A thunderous pounding sounded from the door. A fist hitting wood. Once. Twice. Like the sound of the drum but louder. Much louder. Then a pause. And a voice like a knife chopping carrots. "I know you're in there. I saw the little girl. Open up!"

Dust shimmied from the rafters and fell over Allison's arms.

"I've given you plenty of chances to pay." Mayweather's voice, as strident and angry as Allison had ever heard it. "I ain't runnin' no charity house."

Allison wrapped her tiny arms around her knees and pretended to be as small as a water bug. This was a strange birthday game. She didn't like it at all. She didn't like Mr. Mayweather pounding on the door that way or the sound of his voice yelling things she didn't understand.

The door shuddered and groaned as a large weight hurled into it. The wooden bar bent, and a moment later, Mr. Mayweather crashed through the opening.

That's when the music box fell. Fell and shattered all over the floor. But Mr. Mayweather didn't care. "Get out!" His shout boomed through the room. His gaze darted to the bag of clothes that lay only half hidden behind the curtain. In two strides, he reached their bed, grabbed the bag, and threw it out the hole in the door. Then a long, fat finger pointed toward them. "You're next."

Allison could still see that finger, growing larger and larger until it filled her vision . . .

Fighting back a cry, Allison shook her head, and the memory faded. She was back in the present, back in the museum with her destroyed displays. She reached out and gripped a torn Sioux blanket, touched the colorful weave, and ran a finger over the tear down its center.

"This is my life—" her hand trembled—"a torn piece of fabric. But I'll mend it. Somehow, I'll make it right." She squeezed the blanket in her fist, the rough edges of the tear pressing into her palm.

From the other room, the music stopped.

If Thomas had been a drinking man, it would have been a good time for a tall one. But he didn't drink. He didn't smoke. He didn't curse.

Right now, though, he felt like doing all three.

He swiveled in his office chair and reached for a book on the shelves behind him. A hundred thoughts tumbled through his mind: Allison storming off through the rain, Ishi weeping over a basket and blanket, and a thousand shards of broken glass scattered over the floor. None of it made sense. None of it at all. Returning to the museum was supposed to be the easy part of the journey. But nothing had been easy since Allison met them on the pier. Who could have broken into the museum? And how could he stop it from happening again?

Thomas sat forward in his chair, flicked open the book, and propped it on his desk. He tried to read, but his mind was as jumbled as the Indian exhibit room. He glanced at the sketched drawing of a Yana Indian harpooning a salmon. Then he turned the page again and ran his finger over a photo of a woman weaving a blanket. He flipped back farther. A drawing caught his eye. Dozens of Indians floating down a river. Thomas closed the book.

The office door squeaked open. A head full of grizzled gray hair poked through the opening. "Here you are. Still wasting your life, I see."

Thomas grimaced. "Hello, Pop."

Pop strode into the office and shut the door behind him. "You hear me, boy?"

The smell of pipe smoke permeated the air. Thomas moved the *Native Tribes of California* book to the center of his desk.

*Not now, Pop,* he wanted to say but knew it wouldn't matter. When Pop was in this mood, nothing Thomas did would keep him from speaking his piece.

"Just throwing it away, I tell you." Pop flung his fist in the air as if Thomas's life were an invisible baseball in his hand. "Chasin' Indians." He clucked his tongue. "When you could have done so much more, been so much more."

*Like you did? Like you are?* Thomas bit his tongue to keep from saying the words aloud. He loved his Pop, but sometimes . . . He shuffled some papers on his desk and replaced his pen in the inkwell. "So I take it you want to see our Indian."

"*See* him? Pah! I don't need to see some heathen Indian."

"Then what are you doing here?" Thomas's chair groaned as he shifted position.

"Come to see you, boy. Heard the museum was broken into. Heard some exhibits were all smashed up."

Thomas leaned forward and placed his elbows on the

smooth oak of the desk. His hands tented over his mouth. "What do you know about that?"

Pop sat in a leather chair opposite Thomas. He ran his palm over the stubble on his chin. "So you suspect me, do you?" He stuck his pinkie in his mouth as if trying to loosen some food from between his teeth. "Didn't think you'd go so far as that, son."

Thomas sat back. "I'm sorry, Pop. Of course it wasn't you."

Pop's mouth quirked into a smile. He coughed. "Well, I might have done it if I'd had the chance." He dropped his hands and waggled a finger at Thomas. "But I didn't. Nope, wasn't me. I suspect one of those Indians themselves did it. Heard they're coming 'round here all the time poking about."

"We've had a Mill Creek Indian, a Blackfoot, and two Cherokees come to visit in the last two weeks, but I hardly think them likely suspects."

"And why not? Them Injuns are evil. Got no sense of right and wrong. Them and their devilish ways." He stabbed his finger in the air.

"Yes, you've told me."

Pop's voice rose to an indignant squawk. "Told you before, did I? But did you listen? Oh, no. Pop don't have no fancy degree. Pop's a dummy. No need to listen to old Pop."

Thomas dug his chin into his hand as his face warmed. Why did Pop have to start this now? He'd heard it all before, a hundred times. A million times. The same words shouted out, and his mother screaming, even louder, "I could have married better!" Then Pop hollering about religion and how he was making up for his mistakes. To which his mother always yelled that no matter how Pop preached, she wouldn't forget *her*.

Thomas could still see himself, trembling behind the door in his room, wondering about the mysterious *her* and knowing he was helpless to stop the fighting in the other room. He'd tried once. Just once. He'd prayed for God to help him; then he'd stepped into the fray. That was the only time he remembered his mother striking him.

An eerie chill shimmered down Thomas's back. If Pop wanted to bicker, he wouldn't oblige. He knew better. All those years had taught him one thing well: Praying was fine, but it was still best to stay behind the door.

Thomas placed both palms flat on his desk and drew a deep breath. "Listen, Pop, why don't you come see the Indian for yourself?"

Pop scowled. "I told you I didn't *want* to see him."

"Afraid, are you?" If Pop could only meet Ishi, he'd see he was no demon. He'd see he was just a man, a kind man, a gentle man, even if he was a heathen.

"Bah. Ain't scared of nothing, and you know it, boy." He jabbed a finger at Thomas. "Wasn't scared of that there rattler that nearly bit your leg off when you was seven. Wasn't scared of that wildcat that come sneaking on our property when you was ten. And I'm especially not scared of no fool Indian." His eyes narrowed to slits as they regarded Thomas. Then he grinned. "Was kind of scared of your grandma, though, afore she died."

Thomas chuckled, and the tension eased. "We all were."

"So I guess I'll see this Indian of yours. Suppose you haven't told him about Jesus yet, have you, boy?"

Thomas rose from his seat. "No, I haven't. I was leaving that for you." He walked around his desk.

Pop clapped him on the shoulder. "Sure you were. Two years I paid for your seminary training, and for what? Didn't teach you nothing."

"They taught me plenty, Pop."

"Plenty, did they?" Pop guided Thomas to the door.

"But not how to speak Yahi."

"Yahi. Humph. Ain't nothing but another heathen to me."

Thomas motioned for Pop to precede him out the door. This was going to be interesting.

# SEVEN

It was another Indian. But more than that, another Yahi! Wanasi stopped short and stared into the shiny circle on the wall. A man stared back at him. A man just like himself. Wanasi reached out trembling fingers. The man's fingers rose too. Their hands touched, but all Wanasi could feel was the cool, hard surface of the circle. He leaned closer. His breath misted the shiny material. He looked into eyes brown like his own. He looked at the high cheekbones, at the short black hair, and finally at the single feathered thong hanging from the man's left ear.

Then Wanasi understood. It was a reflection, like the one he often saw in the surface of water. Only this one was clearer. Much clearer. He flattened his palm on the shiny circle. A long moment passed; then Wanasi dropped his hand and turned from the image on the wall.

"Ishi?"

Wanasi heard the word for *man* spoken from the doorway. He glanced over his shoulder. Majapa entered with an old saldu behind him. Wanasi studied the man with hair like a badger, a black mark on his cheek, and eyes the same blue as Majapa's.

Majapa pointed. "Miss-tur More-gan."

The old man scowled and waved his hand in the hair. "No, no." He jabbed a finger into his chest. "Pop." He repeated the word twice more.

Wanasi frowned.

"Pop," the man said again.

*Could it be?* Wanasi walked across the room and stopped in front of the old man. Did the saldu name themselves? *How odd. How rude.* He leaned forward and looked into the man's sky-colored eyes.

The man didn't move. "Pop," he said and once again jabbed his finger into his chest.

Wanasi blinked. "P-ahhh-p."

The word seemed to please the man. He scratched his badgerlike hair until a chunk of it stood on end. He didn't bother to flatten it.

Wanasi heard Majapa sigh from the doorway. But before he could turn, the old man gripped Wanasi's shoulder and moved toward the sleeping platform. Then the man gestured for Wanasi to sit.

Wanasi sat.

Majapa leaned against the door and folded his arms. Something was troubling Majapa. Was it the jumble of baskets, blankets, and others tools in the other room? Or was it this strange saldu called *Pop* who now stood over Wanasi with something that looked like a square pouch in his hand. Wanasi could see that the pouch was made of black leather, but only one side was sewn shut. Something white peeked from between the leather flaps on the other three sides.

Wanasi placed his hands in his lap and waited.

Pop rubbed his fingers over the stiff, black pouch. Wanasi saw that the top held strange saldu markings, the same color as the flecks of gold that glittered in the Daha in spring.

Pop's hand touched the edge of the black leather, and then he opened the pouch. But it wasn't a pouch at all. It was some kind of strange thing with sheets inside. The sheets were thin, like snakeskin, and covered with black markings. Wanasi tipped forward. Many, many snakeskin sheets, all in a row. He reached out to touch them, to see if they were made of skin after all, or if they were yet another miracle of the saldu's making.

Before Wanasi's fingers could feel, Pop snatched the pouch thing away from him.

Wanasi withdrew his hand.

Pop pointed at the sheets and began to speak.

Wanasi didn't understand a word, but the old man didn't seem to mind. Wanasi waited as Pop stabbed his finger at the pouch thing and then up at the ceiling. Wanasi glanced at the ceiling. It was white, like the petals of a daisy. But he did not see anything there that looked like the marks on the sheet.

Pop rattled the snakeskin sheets again, then paced back and forth in front of the sleeping platform. He flung his arm in the air and shouted. Then he turned the pouch thing around and again pointed to the black marks.

Wanasi smiled.

Pop pushed the pouch thing under his nose.

Wanasi didn't dare to try to touch it again. Instead, he looked up into the old man's eyes and noticed the deep wrinkles on either side, the grooves in his forehead, and the redness of his cheeks below.

Majapa coughed.

Wanasi glanced at him. Their gazes caught and held. Majapa's eyes narrowed. Wanasi sat forward. Majapa was trying to tell him something, trying to communicate in a single glance. Wanasi watched for a moment longer, and then he knew. It was in the eyes. The same eyes that spoke from the old man before him. The man called *Pop* was Majapa's father. And if that were so, all this shouting and pouch pointing must be part of the saldu ritual to be accepted into their tribe. Yes, that was it. He need only sit quietly and let the old man complete the ritual.

Wanasi folded his hands in his lap and returned his gaze to Majapa's father. The old man pulled out a cloth and blew his nose. Then he stuffed the cloth back into his pants and sniffed.

Wanasi waited.

Pop turned toward Majapa and muttered something.

Majapa spoke to his father, few words, but each sharp as an arrow's tip. Then he threw up his hands, mumbled, and left the room.

Pop leaned over Wanasi. His cold-sky eyes searched Wanasi's face. Then as if bitten by a wasp, he straightened suddenly and thrust the pouch thing into Wanasi's hands.

Wanasi touched one finger to the white skin. No . . . not skin. It was like wood rubbed so fine and so thin that it was as smooth as water. He pointed to the pouch thing and then to himself.

Pop nodded.

Wanasi rose and placed the pouch thing with great care on the shelf next to his flute. His first gift from the saldu. He turned and smiled at the old man.

Pop grunted. And then something happened that Wanasi didn't expect.

Pop smiled back.

Mrs. Agnes Whitson was tired. Not the kind of tired that comes after a long day but the kind that seeps into one's soul over a lifetime. And lately, it seemed as if the weariness had only grown worse. Agnes removed her silk gloves and placed them on the small table in the entry.

Then she heard it. Whispering. Faint, indistinct, yet as unmistakable as the scurrying of a mouse in the wall. And coming from the direction of the kitchen. She touched her fingers to her hat. Above her, the gaslight chandelier shed no light into the grayness of the hall. She paused, listening.

The whispering continued.

Agnes strode down the hall and threw open the door to the kitchen. The whispering stopped, but no one was there. On the stove, a copper teakettle spat out steam. But that was not what she'd heard. Her eyes searched the kitchen, wandering over the large wooden table where the servants ate, over the hooks that held their aprons, over the half-chipped cube of ice that sat in a bucket near the outer door. The dishes had been washed and stacked, the floors mopped, and the dough for the evening's bread kneaded. It sat now, an oblong lump beneath a red-checked cloth on the table.

Agnes withdrew from the kitchen. The door thumped back into place. With quick steps, she returned to the entry. Her hands shook. She glanced at them, wrinkling her nose at the dark spattering of age spots. Blue veins coursed through paper-thin skin, like rivers in flood season. It hadn't always been so.

Once, her hands were as firm as ivory, as lovely as the carving of the white dove that sat near the ficus plant on the table. But that was long ago. Agnes smoothed her coiled hair and strained for the sound of voices, footsteps—anything that would tell her where the whisperers had gone. But silence pressed down on her like a smothering pillow until each breath felt like a burden.

She dropped her handbag next to her gloves and wished for the millionth time for the laughter of children, the scampering of tiny feet to banish the quietness. But such sounds weren't there. Never had been. Not a misplaced toy, or an infant's cry, or even another hand to touch the keyboard of the baby grand in the parlor.

She had not played since Teddy died. For a moment, the image of her young husband with a baby in his arms flashed through her mind. But that was just a dream, a fantasy that could never be more.

"He was a good man, a good husband." The words slipped from her lips, but she knew better than to believe them. Teddy had been anything but good. He'd taken her youth. He'd taken her hopes. And for what? A name? An old mansion? A reputation and a little wealth? It was not enough. It never had been. But it was all she had. A reputation—and if all went as planned, a museum that might someday bear her name.

Agnes's fists clenched until her knuckles turned white. If only there had been a child. If only she'd had a daughter of her own. Then maybe—

As though conjured by her thoughts, a child's voice drifted from the back of the house. "Thanks for the cobbler." A door slammed. The chandelier jingled. Then the silence came again.

Agnes loosened her fists and rubbed the divots her fingernails had made in her papery skin. Then she turned toward the parlor. There would be a fire laid in the grate, as always. Even in the hottest part of summer, she liked the merry crackle of the flames. Mary knew that.

But where was Mary now? She wasn't in the kitchen. She shouldn't be in her room. Was it Mary who'd been whispering behind the walls? Whispering with a phantom child who loved cobbler?

Agnes tapped her fingers on the table beside her. A servant ought always to be available when her mistress returned home. She pursed her lips. Mary wasn't an ordinary servant. She hadn't been for a long time.

A breeze blew in from an open window in the parlor. Agnes hurried to close it. As the window snapped shut, she caught a glimpse of her reflection in the glass. The woman who looked back at her was proper, as always. But when had her mouth turned as wrinkled as a raisin? When had her hair faded to the color of stone? She touched her cheek. Why did these thoughts plague her today? Was it because of the museum?

Of course it was. The museum was everything now.

Someone laughed, a high, bitter sound that crackled through the air. Agnes spun from the window. Mary. She was sure of it now. Steel coursed through her veins.

She marched over to the small table next to the fire and grabbed the brass bell lying there. She raised it, then paused. No, not yet. Mary would come soon enough. Then Agnes would see. Oh yes, she'd see if Mary had been whispering secrets to a cobbler-eating child.

Agnes perched on the edge of a stuffed Queen Anne chair beside the marble table. She stared into the dancing flames of the fire on the opposite side of the room. Above the mantle, a painting of Theodore Charles Whitson stared back. Teddy had been magnificent in those days—tall, dashing, with dreams that inspired even her hard-hearted father. It had seemed so easy to marry Teddy, except . . .

Agnes tore her gaze from the fire and from the man above it. Typically, she wouldn't retire to the parlor. She hated the feel of those eyes watching her. But today there was something about the way the sun slanted over the Persian rug and dipped through the muslin curtains . . . It was brighter in the parlor, happier. Here, she could confront Mary. Here, she might discover the truth behind the voices. If only she could ignore the face above the mantel.

Agnes rotated her ankles once, then tucked her feet under her chair. She longed to sit back, to allow her spine to melt into the cushions. But a lady did not sit that way. A lady always sat erect. Agnes laid her hand beside an ornate oil lamp on the table. As she did, her fingers brushed the open Bible that she kept there. What was it that she'd read just yesterday? Oh yes, "Take therefore no thought for the morrow." Jesus' words.

Yesterday, Agnes pondered the thought, but today it sounded like madness. *Don't worry about tomorrow? Too late.* Tomorrow had become today, and today she'd discovered the museum had an enemy. *She* had an enemy. And that meant she had to make some plans.

The museum could not fail. She wouldn't allow it. It was her legacy, the only one a barren woman could leave. Agnes closed the Bible. Her eyes watered. To see the displays ruined . . .

She rubbed her arms and reminded herself that the exhibits didn't matter so much now. They paled in significance beside the Indian. What did Thomas say his name was? Ishi. Yes, that was it. Ishi. *He* would make the museum shine. He would make it famous. Ishi mattered now.

She reached over and fingered the brass bell, then rang it. The sound pealed through the parlor and down the hall.

Mary appeared in the doorway.

Agnes looked over the woman's dark hair, only now getting a few strands of gray. She noticed Mary's firm hands and slim figure, still girl-like though the woman was nearing fifty. Agnes should have felt a pang of envy, but she was long past jealousy with Mary. Twenty years, ever since Teddy's death, Mary and she had been bound together as servant and mistress. It was the way it should be. The way it would be until one of them died. But sometimes Agnes wished it weren't so.

"You're wanting your tea now, mum?" Mary's voice held proper respect, but her eyes were as cold as a flagpole in winter.

"Yes, Mary. And—" her tone chilled to match Mary's eyes—"some cobbler, if you please."

"Cobbler?" The word came out in a squeak. "We don't have no cobbler, mum." She gripped the hem of her apron and twisted it into a tight ball.

"Really?"

Mary swayed from side to side, her fingers still squeezing the ruffle on her apron. "Crumpets. We got crumpets."

"No crumpets." Agnes rose from the chair.

Mary stumbled backward. "Just tea then, mum. Right away, then. Yes, mum." She bobbed once and darted out of the parlor.

Moments later Mary returned with a tray in her hands and a light throw blanket over her arm. Somehow she knew Agnes wanted it. She always knew. Mary removed the Bible and placed the tray on the table. She poured the steamy liquid and added two lumps of sugar. She stirred, lifted the cup and saucer, and handed it to Agnes.

Agnes sat, took the teacup, and raised it.

"Shall I open the window, mum? It's stuffy in here."

Agnes barely held back a grimace. Why did Mary insist on asking the same question every day? Especially when she had to know Agnes's reply would be what it always was. With a sigh, she spoke the same words she'd spoken for years: "No, Mary. Don't let in the wind."

Mary gazed at the window for a long moment, then turned away.

*One day Mary's going to open that window when I'm sitting here. One day she'll just walk over and do it. Then everything will change. But not today. Lord, don't let it be today.* Agnes set down her cup. "The museum was broken into."

"Was it?" Mary's eyes remained averted. "Sorry to hear that, mum."

"Many of the displays were destroyed." Agnes watched closely for Mary's reaction. If the woman knew something, it would show on her face. They'd been together too long for secrets.

Then again, Mary *had* fooled her once . . .

"Hmmm. Will that be all, mum?" She picked up the cup and saucer.

"*Allison's* exhibits." Agnes's voice was as sharp as a thorn.

The cup shook on the saucer. Mary looked into Agnes's eyes. For a flash, Agnes saw the depths of Mary's hatred. Then Mary lowered her gaze, and the mask of servant fell neatly back into place.

Agnes took the cup from the saucer in Mary's hand and lifted it halfway to her lips. She smiled. "Yes, that will be all, Mary."

"Good day, mum." The words sounded as if Mary had pushed them through a very small hole. She set the saucer on the table, picked up the tray, and turned toward the door. Her shoulders were held with such rigidity that it appeared as if she'd forgotten to remove the clothes hanger from her blouse.

"One more thing." Agnes rose from her chair.

Mary paused. She turned.

"I believe Teddy's picture needs a good dusting."

Mary's face turned as pale as the bone china teacup. She whirled and dashed from the room.

Agnes listened until the sound of Mary's footsteps faded into silence. Then she leaned back and chuckled. She had found her whisperer. Now she only needed to discover the vandal. She raised her teacup and toasted the portrait. "To you, Teddy. You've not defeated me yet." She lifted the cup higher. "And to the Indian called *Ishi*."

From the kitchen came the sound of breaking china.

Every day for over a week now Allison had listened to the chanting. It started just as the sun tipped over the tall sequoias. Low at first, then growing until the eerie sound pierced Allison's eardrums and twisted in her mind like a dagger. She had thought to escape, to leave the museum when the chanting started, but something in the stark lone-liness of the sound drew her. Words spoken in a language only Ishi knew. Words cried out to no one. So Allison stayed. And listened. And reminded herself that Mrs. Whitson did not approve of any contact between Allison and the Indian.

For thirty minutes he chanted his song, and then the silence came. That was when Allison returned to her work. There was so much left to do. She could labor for three months straight and still not have the exhibits perfected. She carried that knowledge like a stone in her gut. The museum would open in less than two months, and she would not be ready. All because someone had wrecked her dream. So Allison worked. And worked. And worked. From the early morning hours until far past her normal noon quitting time.

Sometimes the Indian poked his head through the doorway and looked at her. Just looked. He never spoke. Never smiled.

Nor did she.

And so it went, day after day. On a good day, the Indian played his flute, and Allison hummed along. On a bad day, he played his flute, and she remembered.

Today was a bad day.

The flute sang its bittersweet melody. Notes tumbled together like a stream in the springtime. Allison sorted through the museum's stacks of baskets, the largest collection of Indian baskets in the world. She wanted to choose just the right ones to display together, but she couldn't concentrate.

All she could think about was a five-year-old girl standing next to a trash bin. She could almost smell the rancid vegetables and rotting fish. Tears coursed down the child's cheeks. A gray alley cat hissed at her, then darted between two boxes. The girl ran. Ran as fast as her short legs could go, down the alley, out to the street.

"*Mama, Mamaaaaaa.*"

Allison heard the cry, like an echo across the canyon of time. But the carriage that held the girl's mother did not stop. It did not come back. Only the wind answered her. Only the wind, like the sound of a flute playing tunes that only the heart could hear.

Allison dropped the hemp basket and slumped over a cabinet. Three shiny arrowheads glinted at her through the newly replaced glass. She straightened and rubbed away the smudge her hand had made on the surface. Then she pressed her fingers into her forehead.

"Don't listen. Think about the exhibits." But the music played on. She put her fists to her ears. "Make it stop. Please God, make it stop!"

The music changed. It came now soft and lilting, like a butterfly whispering in a dandelion's ear. Strangely enough, it soothed her, called to her.

Allison straightened. She turned toward the Indian's door. Today, for just a moment, she would forget the displays. She would forget Mrs. Whitson's instructions. She would forget that she had to be a lady.

She snuck toward the Indian's room and slowly pushed open the door. He was sitting there, cross-legged on his bed. For a moment, he stopped his playing and lowered the flute. Their eyes met. Then the Indian raised the instrument again and the song continued. Allison stepped into the room and settled on the floor. She spread her skirt over her feet and rested her back against the wall. A breeze from the open window caressed her face. She tilted back her head and closed her eyes.

The music danced around her, masking the sound of carriages on the street, of the squirrel chattering beneath the windowsill, and the shade flapping gently against the wall. Allison drew a deep breath. She didn't care if she was sitting, unladylike, on the floor. She didn't even care if Mrs. Whitson found her here. Somehow, none of that seemed to matter. All that mattered was the melody.

Images formed in Allison's mind. Strange images that,

for a change, had nothing to do with her childhood or her mother. She saw a young boy dancing around a bonfire with his tribe. She saw him hunting deer. She watched him laugh, his chin lifted toward the sun, as he speared his first fish. A woman smiled and hugged him as he brought the catch back to the family hut. But then death came to the village. The boy escaped. He grew up in the mountains. There were so few others. And they died too. The boy was a man. The man was alone.

Allison opened her eyes. She studied the Indian on the bed. He was gazing out the window now, playing a happy tune. Was he remembering? Or dreaming of days to come? Allison rested her chin in her hands. He was dreaming, she decided. For how could anyone remember and yet be happy? She longed to ask him but couldn't. He didn't know her language. And she didn't know his. No one knew his.

No one in the whole, wide world.

Allison paused. Thought for a moment. *What if . . .*

She rose. What if she learned Yahi? She was good at languages. Would it make a difference? And would they even allow her to try? She thought of Mrs. Whitson's face the last time she caught Allison with the Indian.

But instead of the usual flash of shame, Allison simply dismissed the image. Mrs. Whitson or no Mrs. Whitson, somehow she would find a way.

# EIGHT

Four days later, Allison had still not found a way. She stood, her toe tapping, at the front window of her tiny box-shaped house, waiting to hear the quiet roar of Thomas's Model T. He should have been home hours ago. But day had turned to dusk, and she was still alone. Allison opened the window and listened to the shout of a grocery boy down the street. On the sidewalk across from her, an old woman pushed a cart that creaked and groaned as it crested the hill. A horse trotted by with a shiny black carriage behind it. Somewhere behind the row of houses, a cat yowled. The hair on Allison's arms stood on end.

The charcoaled scent of burning meat drifted through the room. She shoved the window closed and strode into the kitchen. Drippings sizzled against the hot metal of the oven. A thin line of smoke twisted from cracks around the oven's door. Allison bent over, opened the door, and eyed the shriveled lump of meat that had been her perfect pot roast. She grabbed a fork and jabbed the blackened mass. It would serve Thomas right to have to eat it like this. Except that he'd probably blame her. And it wasn't her fault.

Where *was* that man, anyway? And why did he have to be late tonight of all nights? Tonight when she had a million questions for him after he'd spoken again with the police? Oh, how she'd wanted to be at that meeting! But of course, women weren't allowed. Just as she, a woman, wasn't allowed to work with the Indian, as Mrs. Whitson, and then Dr. Kroeber, had so emphatically told her.

Even Thomas hadn't disagreed with them.

The room seemed too warm. She put a finger beneath her collar and tugged. The stitching stretched, and she let go. It wouldn't do to have a torn collar when Thomas finally got home.

Where was that dratted man?

The beep of a horn stirred her already heated emotions. She slammed the oven door and hurried back to the window. There, in front of the house, the Model T shone in the dying daylight. She patted her hair and took a long, calming breath as she watched Thomas's long legs stretch from the vehicle. Moments later he strode through the door and tossed his jacket onto the back of a wing chair. He pressed his hands into the small of his back and stretched. Then he removed his hat and plopped it onto the chair cushion.

"Hello, love. I apologize for my lateness." Thomas bent over and kissed her cheek. Then he straightened and sniffed the air. "What's that smell?"

Allison stepped away, snatched up the coat, and hung it on the rack behind the door. "Your dinner."

"Oh." He tried to smile, but the gesture failed.

Allison plunked his hat beside the coat. "Well, did you find anything out? Do they know who broke into the museum? Will the man be prosecuted? Will he have to pay damages?" Her eyes searched his.

"Whoa." Thomas held up his hands. "How about 'welcome home, dear; it's nice to see you'?"

She put her hands on her hips and stamped her foot. "I've been waiting half the day to find out what the police said!"

"Sorry, love." He stepped in front of the oval mirror and combed his fingers through his hair. "They still don't know any more than we do. And we don't know anything, at least not yet."

Allison's shoulders slumped. "But it's been weeks."

Thomas raised his eyebrows.

Allison pressed her fingers to her chest and cleared her throat. "Well, nearly weeks. When will you know?"

"Maybe never."

"What?"

Another horseless carriage rumbled up the street. Thomas glanced toward the window, then back at Allison. "No one seemed to see anything. So what can we do?"

"You can post a guard."

Thomas pulled off his tie and tossed it onto the sofa. Then he unfastened his cuff links and rolled up his sleeves. "You know we don't have the money for that."

"But we have the money to hire a linguist to work with the Indian." Her tone dripped with more heat than the blackened roast.

The sound of a baby's cry drifted from the house next door. Thomas frowned. "That's different. Besides, Dr. Sapir said he couldn't come."

"So what's going to happen to the Indian?"

"You know we can't have just anyone working with Ishi."

"I'm just anyone?"

Thomas plopped onto the sofa. "I don't want to argue with you. Ishi's the best thing that could have happened for the museum. Hundreds, *thousands* will come just to see him. Things are good. Let's be happy."

Allison sighed. "I know. It's just that . . ." She glanced at Thomas. He was brushing a bit of lint from his pant leg. Should she tell him about the Indian's music, his chanting? Probably. But she couldn't bring herself to say the words. The Indian's song seemed too ethereal, like a single strand of spiderweb that reached between the Indian and her. If she spoke of it, the strand would break. Allison turned toward the kitchen. "How about some pot roast? Well done."

Thomas leaned over and removed his shoes. "The roast can wait."

"I don't think so." Allison walked into the kitchen and opened the oven.

"I looked for you in the exhibit room this afternoon," Thomas called from the other room. "You weren't there."

She removed the pot roast along with two dry, wrinkled potatoes and placed them on the countertop. "I was in the back warehouse, looking for replacements for the things that were broken."

"Did you find some?"

"Not enough."

She heard the squeak of springs as Thomas rose from the sofa. "Come here, love."

She returned to the front room. Her hand touched the back of her hair.

Thomas pierced her with his gaze. She could see the confusion in his eyes, the questions, the silent longing for answers only she could give. But yet again words failed her.

Finally, Thomas sighed. "I can help you with the exhibits. We'll get them back together before the museum opens."

"No, I can do it myself." The words sounded weak, even to her. "Besides, you need to work with the Indian. Especially if Dr. Sapir isn't coming."

"I can do both."

"Can you?"

Thomas unfastened the top button of his shirt. "What does that mean?"

Allison let out a long breath. "Nothing, Thomas. It means nothing. I'm just tired tonight, that's all."

Thomas turned his back and walked to the window. He placed his hands on the sill and leaned toward the glass. For three full minutes, neither spoke. Just as Allison was about to return to the kitchen, Thomas's words reached out and pulled her back. "Why, Allison?"

"Why am I tired?"

He glanced back at her. "No. Why won't you let me help you?"

Suddenly she knew he wasn't talking about the displays anymore. "Thomas, please."

He turned away. "Will you be able to fix the exhibits in time?"

"I have to." Allison sat on the edge of the sofa, her back straight. She crossed her ankles and looked down at her hands in her lap. "They were so nice. They were perfect."

"I know."

"You *don't* know. You didn't see them."

"God saw them."

Allison's fists clenched in her lap. "He saw them being wrecked too." The accusation came out as a bleak whisper.

Thomas spun from the window. Three steps brought him to her. "You don't mean that."

Allison stood and smoothed her dress. "No?" She didn't meet his gaze.

Thomas's arms rose as if to embrace her, then fell back to his sides. "I won't let us fight about this. You believe in Jesus. That's all that matters. We don't have to know more."

She quelled the urge to slap him. "That's all that matters? Perhaps I should call you *Pop?*"

Thomas pulled back. "That's not fair." His voice wavered.

"It's all that matters to him too."

"He's got his reasons."

Allison sniffed, then rubbed her hands on her apron. "As do I."

"Let's not talk about this, Allison. Let's just eat that roast and talk about something else, something happy."

She stared at him for a long moment, noting the way his hair flopped down toward eyes that still pleaded with her; the way his shoulders slumped forward, just a little; the way his arms hung at his sides as if he'd forgotten how to use them. Then she turned her back. "Thomas, why did you marry me?"

It took him a full ten seconds to answer. "Because you loved anthropology, because . . . because we were so right for each other."

She turned back around. "But you don't even *know* me."

"I know your parents died and left you an orphan. I know that Mrs. Whitson took you under her wing. I know that you're a lady."

Allison laughed, a sad laugh without a trace of humor. "So that's what you know, is it?"

"And I know that I love you."

She had no response to that. Not a verbal one. But her heart cried out a desperate reply: *Show me, then! Show me.* But he wouldn't. He couldn't. And neither could she.

"Why did you marry me?" Thomas's quiet question seemed to echo in the growing darkness. He struck a match and lit the oil lamp on the end table. Shadows flared over the walls. "Was it just because Mrs. Whitson approved?"

Allison turned her face from him. "Of course not." Before he could say anything more, she escaped into the kitchen. Her hands trembled as she took two plates from the cupboard and placed them on the tablecloth.

"Then why?"

She jumped at his voice right behind her but still didn't face him. "Because. Because you talked with such passion, because you . . . because—"

"Not because you cared for me?"

"Of course I do."

Thomas squeezed her shoulders, then turned her with gentle hands into his arms. "Tell me the truth, Allison. For once, tell me. What's wrong between us?"

Allison swallowed. Hard. She did love him. She *did*. She wanted their marriage to be wonderful, amazing, perfect. But for that, he could never know the truth. He could never know what she really was.

And that meant she had to keep him at a distance when she was weak. When she was tempted to lean on him, to bare her heart and soul, to tell him everything . . .

The way she was now.

After a moment, Thomas dropped his arms and moved away. His back became a wall between them.

The late afternoon sun glinted through the window. Thomas put his hand to the glass and watched Allison in the garden outside. She'd been there for hours, digging, plant-ing, pulling weeds. Even from the kitchen window, he could see the dirt that smudged her face and dress. His clean, per-fect Allison. A smile brushed his lips. Somehow, she seemed more real out there with dirt on her nose and leather gloves two sizes too big.

He drummed his fingers on the glass. She didn't look up. They'd gone to church together that morning, as they always did, but it hadn't helped. Allison had changed her gloves three times during the service. Only now did she seem calm, only in the garden.

Thomas's gaze flicked over the wild roses that kissed the wooden trellis with their pink-and-white lips. Beneath them, a rock path wound through the opening and twisted through bunches of hydrangeas, azaleas, and a small plum tree. To the right of the garden, rows of vegetables lined up like soldiers in battle. The tomatoes and zucchini were still producing, even this late in the year. The tomatoes were small though. Even Allison couldn't get them to grow well in the fog of San Francisco. But the tiny sequoia that Allison planted in the corner loved the fog. Someday it would grow and overshadow the entire garden. Then, without sunlight, there would be no garden. No place for Allison to retreat. What would she do? Would she finally come to him? Somehow, he doubted it. His fingertips pressed into the glass. What had happened to them? Why was there always something between them, separating them?

At one time, he and Allison seemed to have so much in

common—a love for anthropology, a respectable faith, a passion for American Indian artifacts. But as soon as she'd started working on the exhibits, things changed between them. It was as if those cursed displays were all that mattered. And there was nothing left for him, or for their marriage. Perhaps that would be over soon. Maybe Allison would give up the idea of perfect exhibits and settle for good ones. Perhaps she would put the displays back in order and get on with her life—*their* life.

And perhaps pigs would sprout wings and soar through the skies of San Francisco.

Thomas gave a rueful laugh. If he knew Allison, she would be even more consumed now. And he didn't know if he could stand it.

He picked up a pitcher of water from the table and filled his glass. Light filtered through the pitcher, casting a rainbow of color over the countertop, reminding him of the first time he'd ever seen Allison. She'd been so beautiful standing there in her orange pleated dress and shiny white gloves, beneath a crystal gaslight chandelier. He'd taken her hand in his, and the sparkle in her eyes when Mrs. Whitson introduced them made his heart pound. The party to celebrate the dream that would become their Museum of Anthropology had barely begun. He'd held her gloved fingers a moment too long, and she'd blushed and slid them gently from his grip.

Allison had seemed so young then, so entranced by the things he had to say about his studies with the Indians. Was that only a year ago? His heart ached at the thought. He thought he'd found someone who understood him. Someone he could live with in peace, quietness. Too bad he hadn't taken the time to try to understand her. Or maybe he would never understand. Maybe that's just how marriage was.

Thomas lifted the glass and drained the water. Then he lowered the glass and stared at the white ceiling above him. "Lord, why does everything seem so wrong when it should be so right? Ishi is here. It's a miracle. It's everything I've ever hoped for. And what I thought Allison hoped for too."

From outside Thomas could hear the sound of a shovel impacting hard earth. He glanced toward the window but saw only leaves swaying in the breeze. "Please, God, make things right again. Don't let us become like my mother and Pop. I just want peace. Please . . ."

He stopped and waited for a sign, an assurance, anything. But the heavens seemed as silent as his wife when he tried to talk to her. Thomas sighed. He gripped his glass tighter and reached for the door leading to the garden. Perhaps he should try one more time.

A loud knock reverberated through the house. Again. And again. Someone pounded on the front door. Thomas turned as the pounding grew louder, followed by a voice raised over the dim noise from the street outside. "Dr. Morgan! Dr. Morgan, are you there?"

Thomas hurried to the front door and flung it open. "I'm here. What's happened?"

A young man stood on the porch, his hand still raised to knock again. Thomas got the impression of flushed cheeks beneath eyes rounded with panic. "Dr. Morgan, come quick!"

"What's wrong?"

The man grabbed his arm. "Ishi is missing."

The glass slipped from Thomas's hand.

# NINE

Thomas ran. Hard. His lungs heaved until his chest felt like an Apache war drum. Behind him, he could hear a voice calling his name. He ignored it. All that mattered was to find Ishi. Fast.

The street sloped in a sharp curve toward the bay. Thomas followed it. His calves burned. One block. Two. Five. The sound of horses' hooves blurred with the hum of streetcars. Thomas sprinted up a hill and down another, until finally the museum came into view. Shadows played over its gray exterior. He jogged up a final hill and then down the path toward the front door, his breath coming in great gasps. The morning glories had already hidden their faces for the night. Darkness crept up the path like a living thing. They would have to find Ishi soon, before the last bits of day were lost.

The harsh caw of a blue jay split the air. Thomas slowed.

Dr. Kroeber, his tie undone and his hair mop wild, stepped

through the door of the museum and paused on the steps. He put a hand to his eyes. "Is that you, Thomas?"

"Alfred, have you found him?"

Dr. Kroeber quickstepped down the stairs. "He's not anywhere in the museum. He was there this afternoon; then he was just, well, just gone. As if he evaporated into the fog."

Thomas paused at the foot of the stairs. He looked into the shadows of Dr. Kroeber's eyes. "Did you search the grounds?"

"Of course." Dr. Kroeber massaged his forehead, then glanced behind Thomas to the gravel path. "Is something wrong with your automobile?"

"My auto?"

"Your new Model T."

Only then did Thomas realize that he'd forgotten all about the Ford parked alongside his house. He'd also forgotten Allison. "Yes, um, of course, well—"

The sharp beep of the Ford's horn halted his words. He turned to see the Model T shudder to a stop on the road in front of the museum.

Allison jumped out, along with the young messenger. "Where is he?" Allison wore the same mud-splotched garden dress. Even the smudge on her nose remained.

Surprise pattered through Thomas's mind. Did the Indian mean that much to her? "Go home, Allison. You don't need to be out here in the dark. We'll find him." He turned toward Dr. Kroeber. "He couldn't have gone far. Not in this city. Surely someone will have noticed him."

Dr. Kroeber clapped a hand on Thomas's shoulder. "You head through those trees, toward the stables. I'll go the other way down the street."

Thomas nodded and attempted to hurry away. Before he took two steps, he heard Allison's voice behind him. "I'm coming with you!"

Thomas didn't turn back. "Go home. I'll meet you there with any news." He glanced over his shoulder and saw the stubborn tilt of her chin. Her gaze shot into him like twin tomahawks. He knew that look. Knew it all too well. Despite the urgency of his mission, he almost grinned. "All right, then. Come on."

Allison hurried toward him. "Thanks, Thomas. I won't get in the way."

"You can keep up?"

"I will. I promise."

"Let's go." They headed together across the grass toward the tall evergreens mixed with birch trees.

"I'll just leave the auto here, then," the young man called after them.

"Thanks." Thomas threw the shout over his shoulder, then broke into a jog.

True to her word, Allison matched his pace.

Soon, the trees closed around them. Shadows grew long and melted into one another, creating an endless stream of blackness. Still, Thomas saw no sign of Ishi. Fallen leaves crunched beneath his feet. He glanced at Allison. She stayed beside him, clutching at her dress with one hand. How could she run in those shoes, with her wet hem clinging around her ankles? But she did.

Thomas slowed. He called Ishi's name. Once. Twice. But only the crickets answered him. "Lord, find him for me." Then he called one more time.

No one called back.

Thomas ran farther until the trees thinned, allowing the

last rays of day to scamper through them. Something rustled off to his left. He stopped and called again. Again, nothing. He leaned over and put his hands on his thighs.

Allison paused beside him. "Where could he have gone?"

"I don't know. He's never left before."

"He's been so quiet lately."

Thomas gave her a sharp glance, but he couldn't make out her expression in the shadows. "What do you mean?"

"Nothing much. It's just that he usually, well, he usually kind of sings to himself. I hear him sometimes in his room. But not lately."

Then as if her words had beckoned it, Thomas heard a sound like the call of a nightingale. Sweet, lilting flute music drifted through the trees.

Allison grabbed Thomas's arm. "That's him!"

"Where?"

"The music."

"Are you certain?"

Thomas saw a flash of a grin in the darkness. How did she know?

"*Yes*. Hurry."

Thomas rushed forward and spotted a light through the trees. "The gaslight, at the stables."

"I see it."

The music drew them forward. The trees thinned farther, then cleared. The crickets quieted. Then Thomas saw them—two figures sitting on a bench outside the stables. Ishi and a boy. A horse whinnied in the paddock. The final ribbons of daylight sank and disappeared, leaving the two as black outlines against the flickering gaslight. Faint stars glittered overhead.

The music stopped as Thomas stepped forward. The Ishi silhouette stood and tucked what looked like a stick away in his shirt. Then he leaned toward the smaller silhouette. His arm raised.

And there, reflecting in the pale moonlight, Thomas saw the knife in Ishi's upraised hand.

Wanasi looked up to see Majapa racing across the grass toward him. He lifted his hand in greeting, but Majapa did not wave back. He didn't even smile. Wanasi stepped sideways. Was it the faint light that made Majapa's face seem so stern? Or was he afraid? Wanasi's eyes widened.

Was there danger? A cougar perhaps, waiting to pounce from the darkness of the trees? Or another saldu monster, this one untamed by silver rails? His hand gripped the knife tighter. In the field behind him, a horse stamped its foot and nickered softly. Wanasi frowned. The horses would know if there was something amiss, but they'd only grown more content as the darkness fell and wrapped them like a blanket from the sky.

The boy reached up and tapped Wanasi's arm.

Wanasi turned the knife in his hand and gave it to the boy. He had intended to only show him the blade, but if there was a demon in the trees . . .

"Majapa. Majapa come." Wanasi nodded toward Majapa and then rested his hand on the shoulder of his new friend.

Majapa's face became clear in the pale light. And with it, the figure of Majapa's woman running behind him.

Wanasi lowered himself to the bench.

"*No!*" The woman's cry shimmered in the air.

Only then did Wanasi realize he had done something wrong.

⁓

Thomas pulled to a stop before Ishi and the boy. He reached out his hand and encircled the boy's arm. "Are you all right?"

The boy pulled away.

"Did he hurt you?"

An owl hooted in the trees. A moment later, Allison came panting up beside him. The boy glanced from Allison, to Ishi, then back to Thomas. "You talking about the Indian, Dr. Morgan? 'Cause if you are, that's crazy talk, that is. Me and the Indian are friends."

"Friends?"

"Sure."

Thomas leaned over and looked the boy in the face. He noticed his blue, shadowed eyes and the light spattering of freckles over his nose. "You're Doc Pope's boy, aren't you?"

"Yes, sir." The boy sat up straighter.

"What are you doing out here with Ishi? And with that knife?"

The boy grinned. "Ishi! So that's his name. He wouldn't tell me, you know."

Ishi put a hand on the boy's shoulder. "Majapa?"

Thomas glanced up.

"Wee-lee. Fren." He spoke the words with slow precision.

"Told ya. Ishi and I are friends." The boy's grin was broad. "I'm Willy."

"What are you doing out here in the woods, Willy?" Allison squatted beside him and touched his knee.

Willy scratched his nose. "I thought I'd take Ishi for a walk. He was all alone in the museum. Even the janitor went home. Didn't seem right." He rubbed his hand over his head, further mussing his already rumpled hair. "I thought he'd feel more at home out here near the animals. Got kinda late, though. Dad's gonna be mad. Are you mad too, Dr. Morgan?"

"No, son. And Mrs. Morgan isn't either."

Thomas watched Allison brush the boy's hair behind his ear, an odd ache throbbing in his heart at the gentle action. Allison reached for the knife. "Where did you get this, Willy?"

The boy looked longingly at the blade. "Ain't it beautiful though? We brought it from the museum for the arrows." He scrunched his brow. "We was gonna put it back."

"Arrows?"

"Ishi was showing me how to carve 'em. Wanna see?" He held up a stick, smooth from where the knife had carved off the bark and branches. "Tomorrow we thought we'd put on the feathers and make the arrowhead. Isn't that right, Ishi?"

Ishi didn't answer.

"Ishi, here, is gonna teach me all that. Aren't you?" He smiled up at Ishi.

Ishi patted the boy's head. "*Haxa*. Aiku tsub."

Thomas saw Allison frown. "In the dark? You're carving arrows in the dark?"

Willy sighed. "Naw. We aren't carving anymore. Ishi was playing me some music. I think the horses liked it too."

"Hmmm." Thomas frowned.

Willy drew himself up to his full height. "It's like I said, Mrs. Morgan. He was pretty lonely up there in that ol' museum. He don't like being stared at and not even told hello or nothin'."

Thomas leaned forward. "What are you talking about?"

"That lady come poking her nose around but not even bothering to say hello, good day to ya, nothin'. I told her better, but she didn't listen."

Allison straightened. "What lady?"

"I dunno." Willy shrugged. "Don't remember her name."

"Mrs. Whitson?"

Thomas knelt down in front of the boy and put both hands on his shoulders.

Allison moved toward him. "Thomas, what are you doing?"

He shot her a glance, then looked into Willy's eyes. "Willy, have you seen someone sneaking around the museum who shouldn't be there? Anyone at all?"

Willy looked away and dug the toe of his shoe into the dirt. "I dunno who's supposed to be there and who's not. Dad says I'm not supposed to be there."

"Your father's right." Thomas stood back up. He turned toward Allison. "It was worth a try."

She nodded and rubbed her hands over her arms. "It's getting cold. Let's go back to the museum. Dr. Kroeber must be nearly frantic."

Thomas turned Willy toward the museum and gave him a gentle push. "Come on, boy. Time to go home."

"Sure." Willy smiled.

"And don't let us ever catch you taking the Indian out of the grounds again."

Allison's firm words earned her a frown. "You can't just keep him cooped up in there all the time." Willy's grumble was spoken half under his breath. "Who'd like that?"

As they all trudged back toward the museum, Thomas wondered if Willy was right. Was Ishi lonely? He hadn't seemed so. In fact, Ishi always seemed happy, willing to fit in and make a new life for himself.

Thomas watched Ishi glide through the trees, the dim moonlight reflecting off his white-man shirt. Yes, Ishi was fitting in . . .

Perhaps too much. Thomas thought back to the photo shoot a few days earlier. Ishi had insisted on wearing a regular shirt, tie, and pants. He scorned the breechcloth, which the photographer thought more authentic. Ishi had pointed to the clothes Dr. Kroeber, Thomas, and even the photographer wore. Then he'd done the familiar lifting of his chin, and the issue was settled. Ishi would have his photo taken in attire like that of everyone else, minus the shoes, of course. So the pictures that graced the Sunday paper had been of him in clothes like the saldu.

Thomas smiled. He wouldn't have guessed then that Ishi was lonely. But he supposed a man used to fresh air and lots of sunshine might feel shut off in a museum in San Francisco. Thomas watched a piece of moonlight slice through the trees and illuminate the fallen leaves on the path. In front of him, a branch snapped back into place. A flock of quail rose from the bushes, the sound of their wings filling the air. Ishi stopped short. He tensed and took the stance of a hunter. For a moment, the quail were silhouetted against the rising moon. Then they were gone. Ishi relaxed.

Thomas strode forward and put his hand on the Indian's shoulder. Yes, he supposed he'd have to get Ishi out into nature again. But how?

He looked up to see Allison lifting her muddy dress as she stepped over a small log. He remembered the dirt on her face, the splotches of earth on her hem—and a thought occurred to him. A wild thought, but it just might work.

*What if . . .*

Allison turned and smiled at him in the darkness. In that moment, he made up his mind.

# TEN

Sometimes, when the wind blew just right over the bay and the sky turned the color of hydrangeas, Allison could believe her life was everything she dreamed. But today was not one of those days. Today, her world seemed gray.

Allison dug her hand shovel into the ground and turned up fresh earth. Then she pushed a tulip bulb into the hole and covered it. In spring, a beautiful flower would come up. Yellow, she hoped. She loved yellow tulips. Pop gave her the bulbs, but he didn't tell her what color the flowers would be. *Tulips are much like life. You never know what will sprout up.*

She dug another hole and pressed in a second bulb. Then a third. The breeze grew stronger, sending curled brown leaves skittering across the ground. A worm wriggled in the newly upturned dirt, then plunged beneath its surface. Allison sat back on her heels and smiled. Maybe it didn't matter that the sky was gray or the wind cold. It didn't matter if her knees were stained or her hair out of place. This garden was her place, hers alone, like no other place in the world. Here, there were no long-faced nuns, no shadowy figure of a mother she couldn't remember, no stern eyes of Mrs. Agnes Whitson. There was just she and the earth and that little honeybee that kept buzzing around her head. On another day, she would have brushed it away, but today she let it be. It buzzed once more around her, then zoomed off to the wild roses on the trellis.

Allison felt the warm earth beneath her gloved hand. She lifted a clump and studied the way it looked against the thick leather that was so different from the white silk she was used to wearing. The worm slithered through her fingers and plopped onto the ground. Soon, it disappeared. Allison buried another bulb and patted the earth solid above it.

For a moment, the sun glinted through the clouds. Allison stopped, closed her eyes, and savored the warmth on her face. She smelled the heady aroma of roses and the spicy scent of the mint growing along the stone wall behind her. She opened her eyes, stood, and turned her back to the rose trellis. Then she put her palms on her hips and stretched. A hummingbird zipped toward her, then flitted off again. Somewhere in the branches of the crepe myrtle, a sparrow chirped. Allison drew a deep breath. Out here, life was everything it should be. Out here, she could almost believe there was a God who cared.

Almost.

The house's door latch clicked behind her. "Thomas, could you bring some water out for me, please?"

But no one answered.

Allison turned and her breath stopped. The Indian waited several yards behind her. He stood as stiff as the tiny sequoia beside him. Thomas was nowhere to be seen.

"Hi, Lissie." The Indian spoke ever so slowly, as if pulling the saldu words from out between his teeth like pieces of stringy meat.

Allison beckoned him forward, unable to restrain a smile. No one had called her *Lissie* since she was six years old, when Mrs. Whitson had firmly told the nuns to "call the child by her proper name." Since then she thought the nickname silly. But on the Indian's lips, it seemed more like an offering of friendship, of camaraderie. "Hello—" she paused for a single breath then spoke his name for the first time—"Ishi."

Ishi walked toward her, his bare feet making shallow indentures in the earth. He pointed to the bulbs and to the tiny mounds where she had planted eight of them. Then he knelt down and continued where she'd left off. His broad hands delved into the dirt. He brought up a fistful of dark earth and held it under his nose. His dark hair was growing out now, and his shoulders had lost that pitiful, thin look. Kneeling there, sniffing the earth and planting the last of her tulip bulbs, he looked as much a part of the garden as the rose trellis or the swaying myrtles. Suddenly, Allison was glad to have a friend in her private garden. No matter what Mrs. Whitson would say.

"Allison!" The door banged as Thomas hurried toward her. "He's here. Good. You don't mind, do you?"

"No, I don't mind."

"I told him to call you *Lissie*. He couldn't pronounce *Allison*."

She smiled. "I don't mind that either."

Thomas gave her a hug and kissed her hair. "I knew you'd understand. It's the best thing for him."

She leaned back in his arms. "Did Dr. Kroeber approve?"

"Well . . . um . . ."

"You didn't tell him?"

Thomas coughed. "I mentioned I was taking him to my garden at home. He seemed to think it was a good idea."

The image of Mrs. Whitson, nostrils flared and eyes narrowed, dashed through Allison's mind. "Did you mention it to anyone else?"

"No."

"Mrs. Whitson?"

"No. Why?"

Allison bit her lower lip. "Mrs. Whitson told me to stay away from the Indian. She said it wasn't proper."

Thomas made a fist. "Mrs. Whitson be—" Her fierce stare stopped him, and he dropped his hand. "No one needs to know, Allison. As far as Mrs. Whitson is concerned, I'm here too. We're not doing anything improper."

"Appearances." Allison whispered the word, but she didn't want to dwell on it. She wanted Thomas to be right. Maybe it *would* be okay.

"You worry too much about appearances."

Allison furrowed her brow. Appearances mattered. Mrs. Whitson said so. Constantly. But perhaps . . . if no one knew, no one could judge. It was just a little harmless gardening, after all.

Thomas stepped back and fixed his gaze on Ishi. "I know you respect that woman, but sometimes . . ."

Allison glared at Thomas. She read the implication in his unfinished words. How could he suggest Mrs. Whitson was anything but wonderful? "You know she's the only one who ever cared about me. She bought me clothes. She got me my position at the museum."

"I know. But still."

Allison put her hand on her hips. "To the nuns, I was just the same as every other little girl. But with Mrs. Whitson it was different. She taught me how to act in society."

Thomas clenched his fist. "That's the trouble. That's all Mrs. Whitson does."

"What is?"

He turned and pierced her with his eyes. "Act."

"Oh, Thomas."

"It's true."

Allison pursed her lips.

"And that's not the worst of it."

"No?"

Thomas went on as if he hadn't heard the sarcasm in her tone. "What's worse is that she wants to make you into a little Agnes."

Allison felt heat rise in her face. "Well, would that be so bad?"

"*Yes!*" His neck turned red, and he drew a breath. "Forget I said that. It's just that, well, I married you, Allison."

Her voice dropped. "Yes, you did." And it seemed that now he regretted it. No matter how she tried, there was always something she did wrong. Why couldn't she just figure out what to do, how to be, what to say so they'd all be happy?

Allison tugged on her gloves and walked back toward Ishi. Then she knelt down on the other side of the row, grabbed her hand shovel, and thrust it into the ground. The earth turned beneath the shovel's blade. She longed to look up at Thomas, to run back, throw her arms around him, and say, "Please, please show me how to be the wife you want." But she couldn't. A lady didn't do those things. And above all, Thomas's wife ought to be a lady. A real lady, not just someone who pretended, as he seemed to accuse her of doing. Allison shuddered. If he knew the truth . . .

She heard the door open and close as Thomas retreated into the house. A few moments later, the roar of the Model T's motor filled the air. The sound grew fainter and fainter, until it was swallowed up in the afternoon's silence.

Long minutes passed as she and Ishi dug holes and planted tulip bulbs. The sun drifted lower and spun the grayness in the sky into fluffy white clouds that settled around it like a winter collar.

Ishi began to hum, a gentle sound that seemed more like a lullaby than a wild Indian's song. In time, the humming broke into soft chanting, like at the museum, only this was more lyrical.

She inched closer. "Yahi?"

Ishi stopped his singing.

Allison touched her lips then pointed at Ishi. "Yahi. Teach me." She turned her finger until it was pointing at herself.

Ishi's eyebrows rose to his hairline. "Yahi?"

Allison nodded. "Yes, please."

His grin lit the garden like the sun breaking through storm clouds.

Weeks flew by, and Allison worked every day on the exhibits until not a feather, not a bone, not an arrowhead was out of place.

There were no more incidents at the museum. No break-ins, no strangers sneaking in through windows—nothing amiss in the displays she'd worked to perfect again.

And so Allison was content. The museum would open, the world would see her work, and life would be as she'd always hoped.

As she worked on the exhibits, Ishi chanted his songs while he cleaned the various rooms of the museum. He was quick to learn how to use the janitor's mop, broom, and duster, and quicker in his desire to be useful.

Sometimes, while he worked in a far-off room, if the day was going well, Allison would stop her work, close her eyes, and listen to the sound of words from a different world. Once in a while, she understood them. Often she did not. But as time passed, she comprehended more and more. For though her days were given to the museum, evenings belonged to Ishi.

Each day, as the sun dropped lower in the sky, Allison would stop work, walk home, and fix dinner. Then Thomas would come with Ishi. The three of them ate together, and later she and Ishi would wander into the garden to prune or plant, pick or trim. Then, for hours each night, he'd teach her the language that only he knew.

Allison hadn't told Thomas she was learning Yahi. Not yet, anyway. Would he be angry? Or glad? She didn't know. And she didn't want to find out until it was too late to stop her. True to his word, Thomas hadn't told anyone of her times alone with Ishi. Mrs. Whitson, of course, would gasp aloud if she knew. But the woman didn't know. Nor would she, as long as Allison had any say in the matter. And so the language lessons continued, becoming a secret that bound her to the Indian and gave her a glimpse into a world that no longer lived except when they were together.

The last leaves had turned golden as the autumn advanced and the time to open the museum drew near. On this

night, the maple that hung over her fence from the neighbor's backyard sported leaves of brilliant crimson and gold.

Allison and Ishi walked along the path of the garden. A
single maple leaf drifted to the ground before them. Allison
picked it up. She twirled it between her thumb and forefinger, then handed it to Ishi. Maples were rare out here in
California. Ishi, she assumed, had never seen one.

He studied the leaf for a moment, then lifted it to his
nose and let it fall again to the path. "Rose cut day?"

She shook her head at his broken English. No matter
how long they practiced, he never seemed to grow more
comfortable with the sounds of saldu words coming from
his lips. At times, she got the distinct sense that he actually
disliked the language. She sighed and spoke in Yahi. "Yes,
today we cut the roses." The language that had felt so odd
on her tongue so many weeks ago now flowed with increasing ease.

Ishi grinned.

The newborn in the adjacent house began to wail. Ishi
froze. "What is it? It is not a wildcat."

Allison laughed. "It is a . . ." She didn't know the word
for *baby*. "It is a very young person." She folded her arms
over her chest and pretended she was rocking an infant.

Ishi's eyes widened. "Ooooh, a *daana*." He mimicked
rocking a baby and she smiled.

*Daana. Baby.* Another new word.

Ishi nodded. "I remember. Yes. They sounded just like
that."

The baby's cry quieted to an occasional shriek and finally blended with the general rumble of noise from the city.
Allison pulled out two pairs of clippers from her apron
pocket and gave one set to Ishi. He turned and headed

toward the roses. Allison waited. She bent over and retrieved the maple leaf and placed it in her pocket. Then she joined Ishi.

Together, one on each side of the trellis, they began to snip the dying blossoms from the vine. Ishi held a dozen dry petals in his hand and crushed them against his skin. Then he tossed them in the air. The sweet scent of rose grew stronger.

Allison smiled. "Mama loved roses." She spoke the Yahi words with slow precision. "I remember that."

Ishi stopped cutting. "You have a mother?"

Allison shrugged her shoulders. "No longer."

"She has gone south."

"South?" Allison frowned, then realized what he meant. He thought she'd died. "No. Well, I do not know . . . I could pass her on the street and I would not know it."

His eyes widened. "You do not know your mother?"

Allison didn't answer.

Ishi clipped another rose. "Majapa told me you had no mother, no father. He said they have gone south."

"Yes, Thomas believes they are dead."

It was Ishi's turn to frown. "They are not?"

Allison looked away. "I don't know. I never knew my father, and my mother left me at the . . ." She stopped. There was no word for *orphanage* in Yahi.

A dry blossom fell apart in her hand and fluttered to the ground. "Mama loved roses. At least," she muttered in English, "I think she did."

Ishi set down his clippers on the rock wall behind him. He walked over to her and picked up the fallen petals. Then he tossed them into the breeze and smiled at her. "For your mama."

Allison smiled back. "What about your mama, Ishi? Tell me about her."

Ishi's face clouded. "I will not speak of her."

"Why not?"

"She has gone south."

For several moments, Ishi did not speak. Nor did Allison. Then Ishi retrieved his clippers and began to again snip the roses. "I have a story for you, Lissie. But not about my mother."

"Will you tell me anyway?"

"I will. It is a long story. We will not finish tonight. Or for many nights. I may grow old in the telling."

"I will listen tonight and for many nights."

He nodded. "I will tell you then. It is a story told by my grandfather and his grandfather before him. It will be your story now."

"My story?" A cool breeze pricked her skin.

Ishi tilted back his head until it seemed that he spoke to the sky above him. "I will tell it to no other. Not now. Not ever. You must keep it in your heart." He looked down. His face turned the color of the roses. "It is all I have, Lissie. Nothing else to give."

She wanted to deny it, to say he'd given her so much— his friendship, his language, his time. But something in his eyes stopped her. Her heart understood. What he offered was a gift she must simply accept. "Tell me, please."

Ishi ran a finger over the satiny surface of a rosebud. He bent over and breathed deeply of its sweet fragrance. Then he began, the Yahi words flowing around her with ease and beauty.

*It happened a time long ago, when the moon still shone orange and fat in the night sky. The stars were young then, and the rivers had only just learned to sing. The wind was old. But the eagle was older.*

He spoke without hurry, his words dropping clearly into the evening air so that Allison could understand each one. When he used a word she hadn't learned, she stopped him and he explained with hand gestures and more familiar terms. Then the story continued.

*By the great Daha River, a Yana girl lived all alone. One day, she sat grinding acorns against a big white stone. As the acorns turned to fine powder, she sang, Ai-ne-me ne-me-ne ai-ne-me hai-nem.*

*She called for someone to love her. Day and night, night and day she sang, until the moon grew old and the stars shone less brightly. Ai-ne-me ne-me-ne ai-ne-me hai-nem.*

*But no one came. She was alone. Only the wind whispered through the trees, speaking a language she did not know. And still Yuna sang and crushed acorns and waited.*

"Yuna? Her name was Yuna?" Allison remembered the word from Ishi's chanting.

"Yuna." Ishi nodded.

"She was named *acorn?*"

"Yes, her name was *acorn*. It was a good name."

Allison snipped another dead rose head and waited. After a few moments, Ishi continued.

*In time, acorn powder covered her dress. She tried to brush it away, but the flakes stuck on her hands, her face, her clothes.*

Ishi demonstrated by touching his fingers to his face and shirt. Then he rubbed his palms over his chest.

*She wiped her hands on the stone, but more bits of acorn shell clung to her skin. She wiped her hands on the ground. The powder was replaced with dirt. She rubbed them on her dress. Dirt covered her dress. She ran from the grinding stone and hid in the trees. If someone came, they would see she was dirty. They would not love her.*

Allison sighed. "That's terrible."

Ishi studied her for a long moment. "Yes." He looked back down at the roses and continued cutting.

Silence settled between them. Allison turned the clippers in her hand and tapped them against her thigh. "You said it was a long story. Does it stop there?"

"No. The story does not stop there. It is a very long story."

"Tell me more. Please."

"I will tell you more. A little more for now." He looked up into the sky again, drew a deep breath, then sat on the small rock wall near the roses. He put down his clippers and folded his hands.

*The sun cast long shadows through the trees. And still Yuna would not come out. The Great Eagle flew over her and called her name. He called and he called. But Yuna did not answer.*

*Soon the moon appeared. It looked for Yuna. But she hid from the moon.*

*In time, a coyote slunk into her camp and spotted her among the leaves. "Come out, Yuna," he called.*

*Yuna did not move.*

*"I see you, Yuna," Coyote called again. "You cannot hide from me."*

*Yuna climbed from her hiding place.*

*Coyote looked for a long time at her clothes. Finally he said, "You are very dirty, Yuna. I can see the dirt, even here by the moonlight. No one will love you now."*


"Allison!"

She jumped at Thomas's voice, heart pounding. With a small smile at her foolishness, she turned to see him standing at the back door.

"Yes, Thomas?"

"It's time for Ishi to go back to the museum. Aren't you finished pruning those roses yet?"

Only then did Allison realize that the sun had sunk lower in the sky, and the shadows in her garden were as long as those in the story.

Ishi stood and walked toward Thomas, but Allison didn't move. She couldn't. The spell of the story was still woven too tightly around her.

When Ishi reached the door, he turned and spoke so

softly that Allison wasn't sure she heard him right. "Who is the eagle, Lissie? *Achi djeyauna?*"

With that he left the garden, but his question lingered, haunting her.

"*Achi djeyauna?*"

"*Do you know his name?*"

# ELEVEN

The countertop glittered like freshly washed coins. Thomas sat on a high blue stool and rapped his knuckles on the silver surface. Small electric lights reflected off the countertop in white circles. Behind, the mirrored wall reflected a shop lined with blue booths and wallpapered in pink-and-white stripes. Thomas spun in his seat, then glanced up at Ishi. "Come on, my friend, pull up a stool." He patted the seat next to him.

Ishi lowered himself onto the second stool. It swiveled. He leapt to his feet and his eyebrows shot up. He put his palm on the seat and turned it left, right, and left again. He pressed his palm into the cushion. "*Su!*" He glanced at Thomas.

Thomas waited.

Ishi sat again, very carefully, without moving. The stool stayed still. One long breath. Then two. The tension eased from Ishi's shoulders. He folded his hands in his lap and smiled at Thomas.

The shadows beneath Ishi's eyes seemed deeper today, the lines in his forehead more pronounced. Even his smile could not erase the pallor that washed his cheeks. Thomas felt just as weary.

The ding of the cash register at the far end of the counter caught Thomas's attention. He looked over to see Sam, the counter attendant, handing some coins to the teenager on the other side of the register. Thomas turned his gaze out the windows that lined the front of the shop. People hurried up and down the street. One man walked a dog. Another rode a bicycle. He could hear the hum of motorcars and the murmur of a dozen voices. And for the twenty-fifth time that day, Thomas wondered if it was wise to bring Ishi into the heart of the city. But he had put it off long enough, just as he had put off telling Ishi what he intended to tell him today.

Still, perhaps it would have been better to wait until tomorrow. It had been a long day. Ishi had sung for over an hour into the tin funnel of the phonograph, recording several songs onto Edison wax cylinders. Thomas took over three hundred notes on Yahi customs, then transcribed them with meticulous care onto white sheets in his notebook.

Allison had finished the arrowhead display at last and asked for Thomas's input. He'd had meetings with Dr. Kroeber, Mrs. Whitson, and even the janitor. And now . . . now he was tired. Now it was time to make fingerprints on the pristine counter and eat a little of his favorite ice cream with a friend who'd never had the pleasure. The rest could wait, at least for the moment.

Thomas plucked a bright red lollipop from the glass on the counter. He tapped the stick across his hand. No, no lollipops today. He glanced at the tall, flute-shaped glasses that sparkled behind the counter. He looked at the silver ice-cream scoop hanging beside them. Thomas replaced the lollipop and rubbed his hands together. *Two scoops? Or one?* One, he decided. For each of them. Today, Ishi would have a real treat. And then maybe, just maybe, Thomas would find the strength to do what he'd come here to do.

A bell jingled as the front door opened and a woman entered with her small son. Thomas turned to Ishi and pointed at the list of ice-cream flavors written on a piece of cardboard.

Sam sauntered toward him in his red-and-white hat and stained apron. "How ya doin', Professor?" He wiped his hands on the rag.

"Good, good. Any special flavors today?"

Sam tucked the corner of his rag into his pocket so that the majority of it hung over his pant leg. "Nothing more special than your usual chocolate cherry. As if you'd ever order anything else."

Thomas smacked his hands against the smooth counter-top. "You know me too well." He grinned.

Sam chuckled. "And for your friend? What can I get for . . . *oh.*" The word escaped him like a breath of smoke. "Is that . . . ?" His eyes grew round as walnuts.

"Yes. This is Ishi. The last Yahi."

Sam kept his eyes fixed on Ishi, but he moved no closer. "Likes ice cream, does he?" His voice cracked.

"Don't know." Thomas rested his elbows on the immaculate counter. "Guess we'll find out today. I think we'll try vanilla for him. What do you think?"

Sam didn't answer. Instead, he pulled his rag from his pocket and again began to methodically wipe his hands.

Ishi didn't say a word. He just sat on his stool, his bare feet dangling inches from the floor.

Thomas reached over and touched Sam's arm. "Vanilla, and chocolate cherry. Cones."

"Hmm?" Sam's gaze drifted to Thomas. He blinked. "Oh, yes, ice-cream cones. Right away. Of course. Chocolate, you said?"

Thomas hid his smile. "Vanilla for Ishi, please. Chocolate cherry for me. Same as always."

"Sure, Professor. Coming right up." Moments later, Sam returned with two bowls of ice cream. He set them both down in front of Thomas, along with two spoons. "Here you go, Professor. Does he—" he tipped his head in the direction of Ishi—"know how to use a spoon?"

Thomas's mouth twitched. "Yes, he does it quite well, in fact." Thomas looked down at the bowls and decided not to remind Sam he'd asked for cones.

Sam scurried to the far end of the counter. He glanced back twice, then bent to polish a spot that already glistened.

Thomas pushed a bowl in front of Ishi and handed him a spoon. "Ice cream." He said the words slowly.

Ishi repeated the words.

Then Thomas took a bite of his own ice cream.

Ishi looked at the pale vanilla ball in his bowl. He glanced up at the mirrored wall. Then he poked the ice cream with his finger. "Cold!" His eyebrows darted to his hairline, and Thomas grinned. Was he thinking of the streams of ice in winter?

Tentatively, Ishi picked up his spoon and dipped it into the bowl. He lifted a spoonful of ice cream and placed it into his mouth. His lips puckered. His eyes widened. He swallowed. "It is good."

132

Thomas laughed.

Ishi dug his spoon into the bowl again and raised it to his mouth. Not a stray drip dropped from his spoon. Not a smudge stained his lips.

Thomas watched, his chocolate cherry forgotten. There was a civility that went beyond training, he decided. Something that sprung from the soul and no amount of etiquette training—or lack thereof—could change it. Ishi was proof of that. Uneducated? Yes. But uncivilized?

Not at all.

Ishi paused in his eating. He looked at Thomas, then down at Thomas's bowl. He motioned for Thomas to eat.

Thomas nodded and took a bite. It *was* good. Cool, creamy, and soothing, and probably completely unlike anything Ishi could have tasted before.

"Look, Mom." Thomas heard the voice of a young boy from the booth behind them. He glanced at the mirror.

The boy pointed at Ishi.

His mother leaned toward him and frowned. "Shhh, Charlie, it's not nice to point."

Ishi turned in the chair and smiled at the boy. Then he faced forward.

"Did you see that, Mom?" The boy's loud whisper echoed through the room. "Huh, did ya? He looked at me. Can I go see him? Can I, Mom?"

"No, dear." The mother's words were as decisive as a book snapping shut.

Thomas heard the scraping of fabric against the seats of the booth. He looked up again to see the mother dragging her son from the booth. His one arm was caught in his mother's grip, while his other hand held a huge ice-cream cone. The boy's cream-covered face broke into a grin as he looked at Ishi.

"Hope you like your ice cream!"

The boy's mother pulled him from the shop. Through the glass, Thomas saw them hurry away.

Ishi's attention stayed fixed on his bowl. Soon he finished his ice cream and pushed back the dish.

Thomas toyed with the last spoonful of his ice cream.

"Aiku tsub, Majapa?"

Thomas felt a weight pressing into his shoulders, and he knew that Ishi was no longer talking about the ice cream. "Yes . . . No." He didn't want to say more.

"Lissie?"

"Yes, Allison, and everything else."

"Aiku tsub? No?"

Thomas coughed. "Yes. Yes, I'm well. Everything's fine. Did you like the ice cream?"

Ishi didn't answer.

Thomas fell silent. He picked up his spoon and let the last bits of melted ice cream drip off its tip. He could feel Ishi's gaze on him. The ice cream was gone. The excuses had faded. The time had come. But Thomas wasn't ready. What had ever possessed him to think that this was a good time to share the story of Jesus with a man who could barely understand a single word he said? He pushed his bowl to the back of the counter. He'd brought Ishi here to tell him the greatest story of all. And even if it seemed ridiculous to try, he had to say the words. At least then he could look Pop in the eye again.

Thomas turned to Ishi. "There was a man—" No, that wasn't quite right. He started over. "Jesus was God's Son. He came to earth and died for people's sins, so that they could be forgiven by God."

Ishi just stared at him.

"The Great Spirit—" He bit back the words. This wasn't going well at all. He cleared his throat and tried again. "It wasn't the Great Spirit; it was God."

"Achi djeyauna?"

"His name?" Thomas rocked back on the stool. "His name is Jesus."

Ishi nodded and turned away. He looked at the shiny glass bowls behind the counter, then down at the clean white floor.

Thomas leaned forward and dropped his head in his hands. He wasn't making any more sense than Pop had. Allison should have been talking to Ishi during all that time they spent in the garden, but she hadn't. And lately, there was something strange going on with her. She had headaches on Sundays. She grew flushed when he spoke of Jesus. Last night, she'd even walked out of the room.

Thomas sighed. Perhaps it wasn't Ishi who needed to hear the truth about Jesus . . . Yet Thomas doubted his wife would understand his words any better than Ishi.

The jingling of the bell announced another customer. Thomas turned in his seat, glad for once to be interrupted.

A thin man with glasses perched on the end of his nose hurried up to him. "You Dr. Morgan?" He pushed his glasses farther up his nose.

"Yes." Odd anxiety surged through him.

"Dr. Kroeber said you were here." The man spoke the words to Thomas, but his eyes were fixed on Ishi.

Ishi ignored him.

Thomas leaned forward. "And may I inquire—"

"Grant Wallace." The man dragged his eyes away from Ishi. "From the *San Francisco Sunday Call.*"

Thomas felt his fingers relax and only then realized that he'd been clenching them. "And?"

"And I want to do a story on Ishi."

Thomas sat back. "Now is not a good time for an interview."

"Oh, I don't want an interview." He dropped onto a stool on the other side of Thomas.

"Then what do you want?"

"I want to take Ishi to tomorrow night's vaudeville show." He splayed his hand and swept it in the air as if reading from a headline. "Can't you just see it? *Wild man finds enchantment in a vaudeville show.* What do you think?"

"I think you're mad."

"Maybe—" he laughed—"but will you do it? Dr. Kroeber gave his okay already."

Thomas felt as if someone's hand was pressing into his back. "I suppose so. If Dr. Kroeber—"

"Great!" Wallace leapt from the stool as if he'd been poked with a needle. "See you tomorrow. I'll send tickets over to the museum in the morning."

"Is it a box seat?" Thomas called as the man reached the door.

"Of course." Wallace rushed out before Thomas could say more. The door thumped shut behind him.

"You think that's a good idea, Professor?" Sam stood on the other side of the counter drying a fountain glass.

Thomas sighed. "Probably not."

"Then why do it?"

"Because I'm a fool, Sam. I'm a fool." Thomas spoke the words slowly, and they sank into his heart like rocks in a river.

# TWELVE

They were brown—brown as the eyes of a grizzly. And to Wanasi, just as frightening. He picked up one of the leather things between his thumb and forefinger and held it out away from him. "Shoes." The word tasted foreign on his tongue. He licked his lips and tried again. "Shoes." But the naming didn't help. They were still brown. They were still awful. They were still hanging midair, waiting to be forced onto feet that had never felt the likes of them before. Why did the saldu wear such unnatural things?

Wanasi picked up the second one by the strings and held it out beside the other. It circled right, then left, before it stopped. Hanging there, the shoes became like two eyes staring at him, daring him to step fully into the white man's world. Wanasi sighed and set the shoes in front of him. Somehow, they looked less intimidating on the brightly colored rug.

He rubbed his hand over his chest. He was rather fond of the crisp white shirt he wore. He didn't mind the black pants, or even the soft thing called a *cravat* that he'd tied around his neck after Majapa showed him how. But the shoes? They were a different matter. Could he really put them on his feet and then walk? It seemed impossible. But he must try. For Majapa. And for Lissie.

Wanasi stood and checked his reflection in the shiny circle on the wall. His cravat was tied neatly in place, his hair was combed, his face washed. "You can do this thing," he told his image. The reflection did not answer. He stood for a moment before the shiny circle and stared into eyes he knew were his own. Then he returned to the bed, picked up one shoe, and held it in his palm.

From outside his open window he could hear the usual noises of the saldu world—the growl of the metal horses in which they rode, the creak of the wooden wheels from a handcart, and the distant murmur of sounds he could not distinguish. And then into the hum of sound came voices, like boulders rolling down a hillside. Heavy voices, wavering voices, a sharp one, and one so low that it sounded like rumbling water. Voices speaking words Wanasi felt he should understand but didn't. Because he didn't care to. It was an ugly language, this thing called *English*. Even so, Wanasi paused and listened. He heard the name *Ishi* spoken once by the low, rumbling voice—the voice of the saldu called *Pop*. The other voices he didn't recognize. The sharp one spoke, and again Wanasi heard the name Majapa had given him. Wanasi swallowed. He didn't like that voice. It reminded him of things best forgotten.

The voices drew closer. Then they grew more distant, as if the group had been walking toward him, then veered away. Wanasi was glad.

A burst of laughter echoed from the direction of the

road. Someone called out. Another answered. He listened for the sharp voice, but it had disappeared. Now the voices were friendly, jovial. They made Wanasi smile.

The growl of a metal horse grew louder, then sputtered to a halt. There came a muted thud, and then Majapa's voice joined that of the others. Wanasi's gaze flew back to the shoe in his hand. He must hurry. They would come for him soon.

He drew a deep breath, then leaned over and slid his bare toes into the shoe. He let out his breath. Maybe it wouldn't be so bad. He slipped the rest of his foot into the brown trap.

"*Su!*"

The exclamation choked from his lips. It was worse than he'd expected. Much worse. It was as if the bear itself had swallowed his foot in one bite. He pulled off the shoe as fast as he could and dropped it onto the floor. He rubbed his toes. Footsteps sounded from the other room. Wanasi clenched his teeth and tried again. First the toes, next the foot, finally the heel. Then the other one.

He looked down at his feet, now encased in two leather shoes. He eased up, placed his right foot in front of his left, shifted his weight, then took one more step. It was awful. Horrible. He couldn't do it. Not for Majapa. Not even for Lissie.

Wanasi sat back on the bed and pulled the miserable things from his feet. Then he got on his hands and knees and shoved them as far under his bed as possible.

"Ishi?"

Majapa spoke from the doorway, and Wanasi leapt up. His face grew hot. "No shoes."

Majapa glanced down at his feet and nodded.

Lissie peered over Majapa's shoulder. She smiled. "Hello, Ishi." She stepped around Majapa and into the room.

Wanasi's eyebrows rose. Lissie was dressed like a butterfly, in shimmery orange that rose from her shoes all the way up to her neck. It puffed out over her shoulders and flared near her feet. Even her headdress had a black feather, like a butterfly's feeler. "Lissie, *jupka.*" He grinned at her.

Majapa's gaze darted to his wife. *"Jupka?"*

Wanasi searched his mind for the saldu word. Finally, he found it. "But-er-fly." He pointed at Lissie. Then he covered his mouth with his hand.

Majapa chuckled as he strode to Wanasi's side and patted him on the shoulder. "Come." He motioned to the door.

Wanasi grabbed his flute, stuck it in his coat pocket, and headed out of his room. In the main museum, pale sunlight slanted through the windows and glinted off the clear boxes like white ribbons. Wanasi rubbed his eyes.

Behind him, Lissie closed the door to his room. As she did, Wanasi heard a sound like rain after a hot summer. For the first time, he heard Lissie laugh.

Agnes paced. Back and forth, back and forth, until she feared there would be a path worn on the rug in front of the fire in the parlor. For a moment, she paused and pinched the bridge of her nose. Then she started again. Back and forth. Back and forth. In just nine days, the museum would open. Nine days! And they had yet to catch the scoundrel who had ruined the displays. Not that the exhibits mattered so much anymore. But still, the menace was out there.

The others, Thomas, Dr. Kroeber, even Allison had become complacent. They didn't understand how easy it was for things to slip through your fingers if you failed to grasp tightly enough. But Agnes knew. She knew all too well. Teddy had made sure of that.

So she watched, waited, ready to protect what was hers. *Just as the others ought to be doing.*

But instead, Thomas was taking Ishi to that loathsome entertainment called *vaudeville*. Agnes's shoulders quivered. Of course, the reporter who'd invited them insisted Ishi attend. He wanted a story. And the good Lord knew they could use the publicity for the museum. But vaudeville? Just the name made her feel in need of a bath. Vulgar, heathen thing. Women prancing about half dressed on the stage, their faces painted with shocking colors. Men in tights tossing perfectly good dishes in the air. And the music! Well, it was enough to make a poodle yowl.

Agnes stopped and placed both hands on her hips. "Mary!" She walked over and clanged the bell. Where *was* that dratted woman?

Mary stepped through the doorway. A tendril of hair had escaped her cap and now lay curled over her ear. The sight annoyed Agnes.

Mary reached up and tucked the stray hair behind her ear. "You called, mum?"

Agnes twisted the strand of pearls at her neck. "Fetch my shawl. It's cold in here."

"Yes, mum." Mary bobbed and turned away.

"Wait!" Agnes dropped the pearls. "Bring me my mink stole instead. Yes, that's it."

Mary nodded.

"And be quick about it."

Mary's back stiffened, but she turned and clomped down the hallway.

"Banks!" Agnes's voice echoed out of the room.

A moment later, the butler appeared in the doorway. "Yes, ma'am?"

"Get the carriage ready. I'm going out."

"This late, ma'am?" He stepped forward.

Agnes rose to her full height and stared down her nose at the man. "Do I pay you to question my orders?"

Banks seemed to shrink before her. "No, ma'am. I'll get the carriage now, ma'am."

"Yes, you will." Agnes straightened her spine and walked past the butler without looking at him. Then she mounted the stairs to her room. "I will return shortly. Send Mary up. I must change into my evening wear."

"Yes, ma'am."

Agnes paused on the stairs until his footsteps faded away. Then her hand gripped the polished wooden rail. She looked up at the chandelier hanging from the ceiling.

"Lord, help me. I'm going to vaudeville."

The great rock structure loomed in front of Wanasi like a mountain out of a nightmare. He stared up at its bold carvings and doors large enough for a herd of horses to pass all at once. But it was not horses that passed through the openings now. It was saldu. A whole flock of them, chattering like mockingbirds. It was enough to make Wanasi's stomach feel as if a dozen snakes wiggled within. "Hansi saldu."

Majapa laid his hand on Wanasi's shoulder. "Yes, there

142

are many, but it's all right. Aiku tsub." He tightened his fingers. A horse whinnied on the road behind him.

Lissie stepped to his side. "Haxa, aiku tsub." She spoke the assurance for his ears alone, then looked into his eyes and smiled.

Wanasi stepped forward.

Together, they joined the mass of saldu flowing through the doorway. Strange scents assaulted Wanasi's senses: cigars mixed with wildflowers gone sour and overlaid with sweat. He put his finger to his nose. Then they turned to the left, toward twisting steps whose end could not be seen. Wanasi hesitated for only a moment before the red line of stairs. Then he mounted them. One, two, ten, twenty— soon he lost count.

Finally, the steps ended in a curved hallway with many doors. Majapa led him to one of the doors, opened it, and motioned for Wanasi to step inside.

Wanasi did. He caught his breath at the sight before him. He stood in a huge red box, like a square cave in the side of a cliff. A man sat to one side of the cave. He looked up at Wanasi, but Wanasi paid him no heed. Instead, he walked to the edge of the cave and looked out over a wide river of saldu beneath him. Above, glittering lights shone on a dozen other box-caves surrounding his in a broad circle. Women and men sat in them, looking down at the mass of bodies below. "Hansi, hansi saldu." He breathed the words.

Noise rose from the crowd like the roar of many waterfalls. Headdresses swayed and turned. White faces flashed. Wanasi stared at the colors, like the reflection of trees, flowers, and sky on the surface of troubled water. He stepped back. Crimson material hung around the cave's opening. He dug his toes into the soft red material on the floor. It was like the finest grass, though it was not grass at all.

Wanasi sidled over to a chair with the same red material as the wall hangings. He sat and gripped the leather arms. The man in the far chair bent over and began making black marks on the thin white sheets that he held in his lap.

Majapa and Lissie sat on either side of Wanasi, and he relaxed. They would not let the saldu overwhelm him. They were twin trees, holding him in place so that the river would not sweep him away.

Wanasi tipped forward and again looked over the cliff's edge. To the left, a huge sheet of red material hung from the high ceiling to a raised floor. All the saldu looked in the direction of the material. But Wanasi could see nothing there that would hold their attention.

The room grew darker. But not so dark that Wanasi couldn't see the saldu below. Suddenly, the wide material opened to show a fat wooden platform. The noise quieted. A man, dressed in black, stepped out. He spoke words Wanasi recognized as some kind of greeting. Then he walked back behind the red cloth.

A moment later, men ran onto the platform. Their clothes, in more colors than the flowers in springtime, clung to them like the skin of a lizard. Shimmering things flashed from their waists and arms. Wanasi leaned forward and grabbed the edge of the cave's opening. Below him, the men on the platform whirled their bodies over their heads and flipped like stones skipping over water. Red lights snapped on.

Wanasi blinked.

The strange dancers continued to twirl and vault in the red glow. Wanasi frowned. This looked like no dance he knew. He leaned over to Lissie. "Are they sick?"

Lissie giggled. "No. Dawana saldu."

Wanasi nodded. Crazy white men, indeed. Then the men tumbled toward the pulled-back cloth. The crowd slapped their hands together. The men ran away. They did not come back.

Wanasi touched his fingers to his chin. His gaze returned to the crowd of saldu on the floor. They had great power, these saldu, he decided. They could drive away the dancing demons with just the slapping of their hands. Were they all *Mechi-Kuwi*, demon doctors?

Dread slithered down Wanasi's spine. What would happen if those slapping hands were turned upon him?

# THIRTEEN

Agnes gaped at the ridiculous Brazilian dancers cavorting all over the Orpheum stage. Her cheeks warmed as full-grown men flounced and flipped their bodies like ill-trained children. She averted her gaze as the main dancer stood on his head and spread his legs wide. Goosebumps rose on her arms. She shuddered and turned her opera glasses toward the box just across from her. There Ishi perched, his hands clutching the rail. His cravat hung perfectly straight. His coat framed his thin shoulders without wrinkle. But despite all that, miniscule beads of sweat shone on the side of his face. Agnes pressed her fingertips into the cool brass of her glasses. She squinted. Was that fear in Ishi's eyes? Or simply confusion?

The crowd clapped. Ishi pulled back into the shadows of his box. His head tilted, and Agnes knew that he was no longer ogling the stage but the people below, two thousand of them, packed shoulder to shoulder into symmetrical rows. Agnes pursed her lips as she peered over the crowd, noting the outlandish colors, the women in makeup, the men smoking cigars. It was positively unseemly. She shuddered again, then returned her gaze to the stage.

Australian woodchoppers pranced out with axes slung over their shoulders and their short pants held up by bright blue suspenders. Uncouth fiddle music filled the hall. The men lined up. A tree was rolled out in a large box. Then in time with the music, the men whipped their heavy axes across the stage. One ax after another whistled through the air. The blades sank deep into the massive trunk. Dead branches stretched out like eerie arms from either side of the tree. Axes continued to spin through the air. A branch fell with a sharp crack.

Agnes lowered her glasses. Theirs could be considered a formidable task, she supposed, though it was utterly outrageous. Brawny men like that should be home chopping wood for their wives. But men didn't always do as they should. Even the sophisticated ones.

The ax throwers were soon replaced by a troupe of comedians who skipped out onto the stage wearing pink ruffled shirts. Agnes ignored them. Instead, she blew on the ends of her opera glasses, wiped them with the handkerchief from her handbag, and looked into the opposite box. Ishi seemed to have given up all pretense of watching the show and was now staring at the crowd.

Agnes scrutinized each occupant of the box in turn. Thomas, looking his usual well-dressed, relaxed self, had a hand on Ishi's shoulder. Agnes smiled. Thomas was a good man. Allison was lucky to have him. *He* wouldn't take up with some no-account—

Agnes cleared her throat. Yes, Thomas was a good match. A trifle weak, perhaps, but so far she had not needed to intervene.

148

She shifted her gaze to Dr. Kroeber, who sat behind Thomas. The good doctor was not watching the show either. Instead, he studied Ishi. His cravat was crooked, and his jacket looked like he kept it in the bottom of a trunk. But Agnes was not deceived. Unlike other men, Dr. Kroeber could not be judged by his attire.

She moved her glasses to the left. A man she didn't recognize perched on the edge of his seat. *That fool reporter, I suppose.* He was scribbling madly on his pad of paper.

Agnes paused. Did she want to look further? Did she dare? She moved the glasses back toward Ishi, and there was Allison. The glasses shook. Agnes lowered them to her lap as the image of Allison leaning over and whispering in the Indian's ear caused a slow ache to swirl in the pit of her stomach.

Even without her glasses she could see Ishi tugging at his collar as he turned toward Allison.

Agnes shoved the opera glasses into her handbag and stood. Her hands gripped the edge of the theater box until her knuckles turned white. *How* dare *she!* Heat filled her cheeks. *And right out in the open, where the whole world could see!*

Allison looked away from Ishi at just the right moment to catch Agnes's glare. Even across the distance, Agnes could see Allison's cheeks pale. For a full five seconds, Agnes shot silent messages to Allison. Then Allison stood and retreated from her box.

Agnes lowered herself back to her seat, then pulled out a handkerchief and dabbed her nose. How many times had she lectured that girl about appearances? Sometimes, a reputation was all one had. Allison should remember that.

A flash of white from the stage caught her attention. She turned her head. A man dressed in a white shirt with a bright purple sash around his waist swaggered onstage. With a flourish, he raised his hand to the ceiling, fluttered it, and bowed. "Mr. Harry Breen," a voice announced.

Agnes glanced back to Ishi's box. Allison had returned. But now, at least, she held herself at a respectable distance from the Indian.

Mr. Breen began to sing. But not a real song. Instead, he chirped out horrible little ditties containing impromptu jokes on individuals he recognized from the audience.

> *I spy Mr. Dithers,*
> *Who sat on some withers*
> *And oh did he fly.*
> *The horse bucked him off*
> *Right into a trough,*
> *And then Mr. Dithers did cry.*

The crowd laughed. Agnes frowned. Mr. Breen pointed to a top box.

> *And there's Mrs. Beamer*
> *With her dress from the cleaners,*
> *But still I see a spot . . .*

Agnes shrank back in her chair. What if he saw her? What nasty little rhyme would he make up then? She could scarcely think of anything worse, except . . .

Mr. Breen thrust his hand toward the box opposite Agnes. Then he began a new song. Agnes blanched.

> *The Indian cavman next I see*
> *With the professors from the university.*

150

*He smokes a bad cigar and he hasn't any socks.*
*And he's laughing, although he's sure in a box.*

It wasn't a very good rhyme, but still four thousand eyes turned toward Ishi. Two thousand mouths laughed. A thousand fingers pointed.

Agnes again raised her opera glasses. What she saw made her stomach churn. Ishi's hands grasped the arms of his chair. His face was white. His eyes wide. Allison had her hand on the Indian's shoulder, in plain view of the crowd. Oh, why, *why* had they allowed him to attend this repulsive show in the first place? But it was too late. The damage was done.

Agnes rose to her feet. She should go over there and get him out now. She should *do* something. But before she could move, Mr. Breen ended his act, and a vision in red floated out onto the stage. Lily Lena of the London music halls. Spangles dangled. Glitter winked from skin white and firm. Eyes, stained coal black, swept over the crowd. Agnes felt her gaze held by the woman on the stage. Mary had looked like that when she was younger. With hair as sleek as a black panther and skin like the ivory keys on a piano.

Lily Lena gazed up into Ishi's box. Her eyes grew large, like those of a forlorn lover. Her arm reached toward him as her voice rose in song. "Have you ever loved another little girl . . . ?"

Agnes felt her chest constrict. Her vision blurred. Suddenly, twenty-five years dropped away, and it was no longer Ishi in the box but her husband, Teddy. And a woman was singing a love song. The notes trilled like the pure sound from a nightingale. But it was not Agnes who sang. It was another. It was always another.

The handbag dropped from Agnes's arm. She leaned down and grabbed it. She had to get out. Fast. Why had she even come? She didn't remember anymore. She stumbled from the box, the words of the woman's hateful song chasing her like angry hornets. Voices babbled. Her head spun.

Like an ocean's wave, the memories surged forward. She forced them back.

But some things could never be forgotten.

Vaudeville was a disaster. A complete, utter, miserable debacle. At least Allison thought so. She was glad it was over, glad to be rid of all those awful, staring people, glad to be free of the glittering lights and flashing spangles, glad she didn't have to feel Mrs. Whitson's condemning eyes on her for one more minute.

Now, only the stars glittered, only the leaves shimmered like spangles in the moonlight as she, Thomas, and Ishi walked back to the museum. Peace breathed into the night; darkness enfolded them. Enough darkness to hide them from prying eyes eager to find fault.

Streetlights dropped flickering circles of light onto the sidewalk. Distant voices became a gentle rumble as the quiet clop of horses' hooves faded into the night. Somewhere, a horn beeped. A man shouted for a cab. A dog whined.

Thomas slid his hands in his pockets and whistled a merry tune. He glanced at Allison and smiled with his eyes. She smiled back as Ishi walked between them.

Allison tilted her head and gazed at the stars. They winked and twinkled like a thousand friendly faces. Faces that didn't condemn, didn't judge. If only she and Thomas and Ishi could walk this way forever. If only tomorrow would never come . . . and yesterday had never been.

Thomas ceased whistling. A barge tooted far off in the bay. He reached his hands over his head and stretched his back. Then he turned toward Allison. "Do you think Jesus would go to a vaudeville show?" His voice was quiet, though in her heart it sounded like a shout.

"I don't know." Her tone was sharper than she intended. Why did he have to bring up religion now? Why did he have to say that name?

Thomas shrunk back. He still walked beside Ishi, still kept pace, but she sensed the distance expanding between them.

Ishi pulled his flute from his pocket. She hadn't known he'd carried it. He lifted the instrument and began to play. Thomas hummed with the music, his question, thankfully, dropped.

A light breeze tickled Allison's ears. A stray leaf fluttered down the sidewalk, as if dancing to Ishi's song. She tucked her arms around herself and tipped back her head to again gaze at the stars. But the mood was gone. Peace had vanished. The once gentle wind seemed cold.

Thomas's question whispered through her mind, and with it a memory that had lay long buried.

A faceless woman stood over a small girl, but the woman had eyes—eyes like stone. They studied the girl. They saw a smudge on the girl's cheek, a spot on her dress. A handkerchief appeared. It rose to the place where the woman's mouth should have been. Then it wiped the girl's cheek. The girl's skin turned red. The handkerchief wiped and wiped and wiped.

Allison shivered and lifted a hand to touch her own

cheek. She could almost feel the bite of the rough material. It hurt.

In the memory, a voice came. "Jesus, but you're a dirty child."

The child looked up. "Who's Jesus again, Mama? I don't remember."

"Nobody. At least nobody who helps the likes of us."

A chill coursed from Allison's head to her heels. It was a strange memory. One she hadn't recalled before. One she wished she hadn't remembered now.

The flute music faded. The stars seemed to dim. Allison dug her fingers into the shawl covering her shoulders.

"What's that?" Thomas's voice dropped like a mallet into her thoughts.

"What?" She turned toward him.

"Look!" He pointed to the museum, now visible through a line of trees. "Someone's there."

Allison could just make out a motorcar parked in front. Light glowed in the windows. "Dr. Kroeber? Or the reporter? What was his name?"

"Wallace." Thomas shook his head. "But it can't be either of them. Alfred was going straight home. And Wallace was headed to his office."

Allison quickened her pace. "Maybe it's our vandal."

Thomas ripped off his jacket and tossed it to her. "Well, I'm sure going to find out." He squeezed Ishi's shoulder, then took off at a run.

Allison attempted to follow, but Ishi put his hand on her arm. "Walk with me."

She looked up at the museum and then at Ishi's face. "But my exhibits . . ."

"Walk with me."

154

She drew an uneven breath. Thomas was halfway to the museum already. The lights still shone from the windows. A vision of ruined displays and broken glass swept through her mind. "But . . ."

Ishi tightened his grip on her arm. "Majapa goes. You stay."

Allison nodded.

Ishi released his grip, lifted his flute, and played a single long note. Then he slipped the flute into his pocket and began to speak in slow, clear sentences so that she could understand.

*The sky rumbled, long and deep. Clouds grew black as a raccoon's eyes.*

Ishi circled his eye with his fingers. "Like raccoon eyes."

Allison studied him for a moment, then nodded. "Raccoon. I understand."

Ishi dropped his hand.

*Rain splashed into Yuna's camp. It poured from the sky. It poured into puddles. And Yuna was happy. The rain will make me clean, she thought. But the rain did not clean her. Instead, the dirt soaked deeper into her dress. Mud oozed between her toes and splashed up her feet and ankles. And still it rained.*

*Yuna huddled beneath a tree and cried until she slept.*

Allison frowned. "I don't like this story." She glanced again toward the museum. "Don't tell me any more."

Ishi ignored her. "It is a good story. Listen."

*In the morning, the rain had gone. Yuna's camp was wet, but the ground around her was dry. How could this be? She looked up. There, the Great Eagle sat on a branch overhead. His wings outstretched.*

Ishi demonstrated with his arms.

*His feathers were spotless and perfect. They glistened in the morning sun.*

Allison looked at him. "Who is this Great Eagle? You asked me his name the last time we talked, but I don't know."
"Listen." Ishi placed a finger over his lips. "No questions now. Only listen."

*Yuna drew her knees up to her chest and wrapped her arms around her legs. Perhaps the eagle would not notice that she was not clean as he. "Have you been there all night, Great Eagle?"*
*"I have," he replied.*
*Yuna cringed. He had seen her filth, then. He had seen it all through the long night. He knew she was not clean. She crept into the shadows, away from him. "Good-bye, Eagle," she whispered.*
*The eagle did not answer. He leapt from the branch and flew into the sky. A single leaf fluttered from the tree. It caught in the breeze and landed on her grinding stone.*

*Yuna watched the leaf; then she looked up at the eagle. He was only a speck now against the white clouds in the sky. And Yuna was alone again. Dirty, and alone.*

Ishi's voice faded as they drew closer to the museum. Moments later, they reached the steps. Thomas stood there with another man. They were speaking but stopped as Allison and Ishi approached.

Allison hurried up the steps toward them.

The man looked at her through eyes set too close to his roman nose, and Allison was reminded of a hawk. The eyes blinked. "Hello, Mrs. Morgan."

Allison stepped closer to Thomas. "Hello, Mr. . . ." Her voice sounded faint in her ears.

He smiled. "I'm Mr. Reynolds from the Bureau of Indian Affairs."

Fear sluiced through her. "Good evening, Mr. Reynolds. What brings you here?"

Thomas answered, his voice as cold as winter fog over the bay. "He's come to take Ishi home."

# FOURTEEN

Pain seared Allison's chest and left her breathless. "No! No, you can't." Her arm stretched toward the stranger. Her voice cracked. "You can't take him away."

She could hear Thomas's harsh breathing beside her. She shoved his jacket back into his arms. Ishi again held his flute, but he did not play. He only held it close, turning it in his hand, the wood silent, waiting.

Allison swayed between them. She too waited. Waited to hear that Thomas was mistaken, that Ishi would not be stolen from her, that there was a God who would intervene.

Mr. Reynolds's voice broke the silence. "I can. And I plan to, Mrs. Morgan."

*At least nobody who helps the likes of us . . .*

Perhaps Mama was right. Allison struggled to still the trembling in her knees. "Why? Why are you doing this? What have we done?"

The breeze ruffled Mr. Reynolds's dark hair. "It's only right, miss." The words darted at her like tiny needles.

Ishi touched his fingers to her arm. She flinched. He held his flute out to her in a flat palm. She shook her head. He didn't understand. He could not know that at this very moment their lives were being torn asunder.

Thomas sidled close to Ishi, but he didn't speak. He didn't even utter a single word in their defense. *Thomas, please. Say something! Do something. Thomas . . . I need you!*

Her husband remained silent. The night dimmed, until all Allison could see were the bureau man's narrow eyes— and a long, dark tunnel that was her future without Ishi.

Ishi hid his flute back in his jacket.

"You can't take him. I won't let you." Allison pressed nearer to Ishi until her arm brushed his. "He's mine."

Mr. Reynolds chuckled. *"Yours,* is he? Like those gloves that you've changed twice since we've been standing here?" He raised an eyebrow.

Allison's gaze shot down to her hands. They were clenched together like a knot of ecru silk. She yanked them apart and stared at the beige fabric. She had been wearing white. "No, that . . . that's not what I meant. He's ours. No, not ours. *His.* I mean—" Allison swallowed and found her fingers again reaching for the small reticule hanging from her wrist. She stopped them before they touched another pair of gloves. "What I mean is that he belongs here. With us." Thomas could say this so much better. He could make the bureau man understand. *Thomas!*

Mr. Reynolds crossed his arms over his chest.

In the shadows behind her, the wind rattled the leaves of the trees. A branch fell.

"He belongs with his own kind." Mr. Reynolds's voice snapped through the darkness. Sharper than the crack of the branch.

*I am his own kind.* Allison could not say the words aloud.

When Thomas spoke at last, his voice was the merest whisper in a storm. "There are no more of his kind. He is the last. The last Yahi."

Mr. Reynolds's gaze skittered off into the darkness. "You know what I mean."

Thomas lifted his head until his eyes were level with Mr. Reynolds's. "No, I don't."

*Tell him to go away. Make him leave us alone.*

Thomas crossed his arms.

Words spurted from Allison's lips. "This is ridiculous!" She stepped in front of Ishi and dug her fists into her hips. "You don't care about him at all. If you did, you wouldn't be here."

The man shifted his gaze to Allison. Time slowed like a salmon swimming upstream. He took a single step toward her, then stopped. A carriage passed on the road behind them. Ishi coughed.

"Mrs. Morgan, I don't think you understand." Mr. Reynolds's voice turned soft. "No one speaks this Indian's language or even anything similar. He can't communicate with you, or you with him. He knows nothing of the white man's ways. He knows no one. He's living in a museum. A museum!" He cast his hand backward toward the open door. "Don't you think he'd be better off with other Indians? People who at least might understand him?"

A lump lodged in Allison's stomach. *I can; I do!* She longed to say the words out loud, but they stuck in her throat like a fishbone. Her gaze darted to Thomas. He would never understand why she hadn't told him. He would scorn her. And Mrs. Whitson would find out she'd been spending time alone with Ishi. She'd be shamed. Disgraced.

She had to speak, but she couldn't. Her head fell forward. Her vision blurred. She reached into her reticule and gripped a pair of gloves.

Mr. Reynolds sighed. "I was intending to explain it all to Dr. Kroeber and Dr. Morgan here in the morning. I didn't expect to see you tonight."

"Then why are you here?" Thomas's question seemed to come from a mile away.

"Just examining the Indian's accommodations before I retire to the hotel. They are as I expected."

Allison trembled. "What do you mean?"

Mr. Reynolds drew a piece of paper from his jacket pocket. "We received this letter nigh onto a week ago now." He handed it to Thomas. Allison edged closer so that she could read the words over his arm.

*Dear Burro of Indian Fares,*

*I am riting to tell you of a terible thing that is hapening here in San Francisco. A indian that they are calling Ishi got captured by some purty greedy folks and they are making him stay at the new moozeeum of the universitee. They won't let him walk in the trees or do anything by himself. They got him working all the time kleening the moozeeum. All they care about is themselves. He is very sad and lonly and wants to go back and live with peeple like himself. But they won't let him. Pleese come and help. Pleese take Ishi back to other Indians. He don't belong here with them mean folks. You got to do something quick. If you don't, the Indian will be dead by winter.*

*Signed, a concern citisen*

Allison grabbed the paper from Thomas, then shook it under Mr. Reynolds's nose. "Surely you don't believe a word of this, of this—"

162

Mr. Reynolds snatched the letter from her. "I don't know what I believe yet, Mrs. Morgan. That's what I've come to investigate. So far, though, it looks like the writer might be correct about a good many things."

Allison sucked in her breath. "No—"

"Clearly the Indian *is* living here." Mr. Reynolds stabbed his finger at the wall. "Clearly you two aren't Indians and can't speak Yahi. And—" he drew himself up to his full height—"I wouldn't be surprised to find out that the Indian is doing the janitor's work."

"He's not *the Indian*," Allison sputtered. "He's got a name."

"Does *Is-hi*—," he spoke the word as two long syllables— "clean the museum?"

Allison lowered her eyes.

Thomas sighed. "Yes, yes he does."

Mr. Reynolds clapped his hands. "There, you see."

"But only because he wants to."

"Mrs. Morgan, we can stand here all night discussing this, or I can go to my hotel and you can go home. The facts are that Ishi is alone here. Don't you see?"

Allison sniffed. "No, I don't see." She clutched Ishi's arm. His skin felt damp beneath her hand.

"Mrs. Morgan—"

"Thomas, tell him. Tell him that Ishi's perfectly happy here. Tell him to go away."

But Thomas said nothing. He only looked at the ground and brushed his foot over the top stair. Allison could see defeat in his bowed shoulders, in the way his eyes refused to meet hers.

She stumbled backward. They couldn't take Ishi away from her. They couldn't! She wouldn't lose someone again. *Not again. Not like this.*

The wind stole her words. Her legs crumbled beneath her. But tears would not come.

⁓

Something bad was happening. Wanasi knew it. He saw the pain in Lissie's eyes and the look like death in Majapa's. Who was this hawk-saldu standing before them?

Wanasi studied the saldu's dark eyes, his long nose, his lips arching into words that somehow had the power to frighten Lissie. Wanasi was frightened too. He'd heard that voice before. The sharp voice that spoke from outside his window. The voice that Pop had led away. But not far enough away.

The man pointed at Wanasi, then motioned back toward the museum. Wanasi thought of his room, of the bright colors in the thing called a *rug* on his floor, of the softness of his bed, of the way the sun slanted through the opening in the wall and shone off the clear substance that blocked out the wind. He wanted to go there now, to escape the pointing finger, the harsh words, the evil that hung in the air like blue-flint dust. He took a step toward the door.

"Ish-eee."

Wanasi froze at his name on the man's lips. More words tumbled around him, words spoken too quickly for Wanasi to catch their meaning.

"No." Lissie groaned, and by the paleness of her face, he knew the evil remained. Her words had not defeated it.

Wanasi reached into his coat and caressed the smooth wood of his flute. He had offered the flute to Lissie to drive the evil away, but she would not take it. Perhaps the music was too weak for this kind of spirit. Maybe the hawk-saldu would only laugh at the melody. Maybe he would have forced the flute to swallow its song.

The saldu slapped his hands together. The sound echoed in the night. Cold fear splattered over Wanasi's nerves. The flute was useless. Words were useless. This man was the Mechi-Kuwi, the demon doctor. Even now he was muttering the incantation to send Wanasi away. Just like the saldu had sent the dancers off the platform. As he'd feared, the hands were turned on him. Would they make him disappear like the men who danced in bright skins?

Wanasi felt a drum beating in his head. He couldn't go. Not yet. He must resist the Mechi-Kuwi's power. The story was not finished. There was much left to tell. And Lissie had to hear. He would tell no one else.

The Mechi-Kuwi spoke again, his voice like that of a coyote choking on a bone. And Wanasi knew that he was that bone. Would he be swallowed or spit out? Would he be driven into the darkness or spewed out into the light of the *museum-watgurwa*, his museum-home?

Lissie stepped beside him. Her hand clutched his arm as she attempted to hold him back from the abyss, but she was not strong enough. Wanasi felt the blackness of the night sweeping in on him. He needed Majapa. Majapa was strong. Majapa would help.

But Majapa moved away. Wanasi saw his chin drop. It was not a good sign. Lissie looked at Majapa. Her mouth did not speak, yet words shot from her eyes like poisoned arrows. Words of accusation. Words of shame. Then Wanasi knew that Majapa would not save him.

And still Majapa stood there, like a man who stares into the mouth of the bear when he has no tomahawk in his hand. Wanasi turned. His eyes caught Lissie's. She twisted away from him, and then crumpled on the step. Hope fled from Wanasi's heart.

"Hexai-sa!" He threw the word at the Mechi-Kuwi, but the man did not go away. He stayed. He stared. He spoke again. And his voice was like the hiss of a snake in Wanasi's ears.

～

For the briefest breath, the vision of a bedroom door flashed before Thomas's vision. He could see the tiny crack that ran from left to right, the bit of blue paint that had peeled to show white beneath, the touch of rust on the hinges. *Stay behind the door. In a moment, it will be over. The bureau man will be gone. I will be walking in the moonlight with my wife, and she will be smiling at me. And Ishi will be with us.*

Thomas closed his eyes, then opened them. But the Bureau man was still there. Allison was still piercing him with a look of cold fury, and a cloud had blotted out the light from the moon. He rubbed his hand over his forehead. Long shadows spilled from the door, dripped down the steps, and splashed onto the gravel pathway below. Shadows as black as those that had once flickered beneath his bedroom door.

But what could he do? Mr. Reynolds had come, his accusations were valid, and every excuse Thomas could think of sounded hollow. *Was* Ishi happy here? He didn't know. He'd thought Allison was happy, but he'd been mistaken there too. Would Ishi be better off with other Indians who might understand more than a scant handful of the words he spoke? He didn't know that, either. He pressed his fingers into his temples. What did he know? Nothing—except that something inside him ached at the thought of losing Ishi. And not just because the museum would suffer.

Thomas lowered himself to the step beside Allison. She turned away. He looked at the back of her prim orange hat, with its tiny silk flowers and pert black feather. A tendril of her hair had escaped the pin and now hung in a single, soft curl at the nape of her neck. He longed to reach out and stroke the silken strand. But he didn't dare.

"I think I'll be going now." Mr. Reynolds's voice floated down to him.

"Ishi belongs here." It was all he could say in response. "This is his home now."

"Dr. Morgan—" the man sighed—"I can't argue with you all night. This Indian here—"

"Ishi."

"Yes, Ishi." Mr. Reynolds cleared his throat. "Let's just ask him, why don't we?"

Thomas's head shot up. "He won't understand."

"My point exactly."

"Try it." Allison's murmured words were spoken so low that Thomas barely heard her.

Mr. Reynolds stepped close to Ishi. He bent and stared into his face, then spoke, his words slow and overly loud. "Ish-eee, do yoooooou—"

"He's not deaf. Or stupid." Allison glared at the man.

Ishi squared his shoulders and lifted his chin. His finger jabbed toward the museum. *"Wowi."* The word rang clearly in the night.

"What did he say?" Mr. Reynolds turned toward Thomas.

Thomas rose to his feet. "I don't know."

*"Wowi."*

Thomas thought of rushing to his office to find the list

of Yahi words he started to make weeks ago. But before he could, Allison's voice drifted from the steps, as faint as mist at midmorning. "He said *home*."

Thomas squatted beside her. "How do you know that?"

Allison didn't answer. She wouldn't even look at him. Instead, she stared out into the night. "I think you'd better go now, Mr. Reynolds."

"I've been trying to." Mr. Reynolds pushed the words from between gritted teeth. His gaze shifted from Allison to Thomas. "Something odd is going on here, Dr. Morgan. That letter writer knew it. And I'm starting to see it too." He trotted down three steps, then turned. "Make no mistake, I'm going to make sure that Indian gets what he deserves."

Allison rose from the stairs like a cougar ready to pounce. "Get! Go!"

Mr. Reynolds backed down the remaining steps. "I'll return tomorrow." He disappeared into the darkness. His footsteps echoed back to them, fainter, fainter, the gravel crunching beneath his shoes.

Thomas sat back on the step and dropped his head into his hands. Mr. Reynolds had one thing on his side: Someone had sent that letter to the Bureau of Indian Affairs. Someone watching the museum, who knew enough to cause them trouble.

Someone who said Ishi would be dead by winter.

# FIFTEEN

Tension dripped through the cab of the Model T like rain from autumn leaves. Allison shivered in the dampness. Light from a streetlamp slanted through the window and illuminated the drawstring reticule clutched in her lap. She stared at it. Had her fingers ever looked so white, or shaken so noticeably? She pulled her gaze from her lap as the light dipped and retreated. Then the shadows fell.

The Model T turned a corner and rumbled toward home. Allison's head throbbed. Her shoulders felt so tight she was sure she could string a bow between them. Outside, another streetlamp threw a rosy glow onto the cobblestone. A mutt darted in front of the car, then disappeared down a dark alley.

Allison listened for the sounds of the night but heard only the quiet chug of the Ford's engine. There was no chirping of crickets, no distant singing, no jingle of harnesses or shrill catfights . . . and no husband telling her that everything would be all right.

She peeked at Thomas, his hands stiff on the steering wheel. His gaze focused ahead. He pushed back the hair from his forehead, but he didn't look her way, didn't speak. Nor had he since they'd taken Ishi to his room in the museum. Perhaps for the very last time.

Allison closed her eyes and remembered Ishi's face—his eyes wide, his mouth drawn down—as they'd left his room. He'd gripped his flute in one hand, much as Allison gripped her reticule now. As if it could save him.

"Lissie?"

She couldn't answer him. Couldn't look him in the eye.

"Majapa?" Thomas paused at the door. She remembered the way the candlelight flickered over his features. The light hadn't reached his eyes. "Aiku tsub," Thomas whispered. "Aiku tsub, Ishi. Go to sleep."

It was the last thing Thomas had said. All is well, when all was *not* well. Not even close. But how could they explain that to Ishi? They couldn't. They hadn't. So here they were, bumping along in silent agony, with the weight of unspoken words pressing down like a great fist in the darkness.

Allison studied the way Thomas's hair curled around his ear. She watched the glint of the streetlamp flash over his jaw, then recede into the shadows. She saw his eyes narrow. What was he thinking behind those silent eyes? Was he finding fault with her? With what she had said to Mr. Reynolds? Allison dropped her grip on her reticule and folded her arms.

*Thomas, why didn't you make everything right? Why won't you say something now? Reach toward me. Tell me it's going to be all right. Please, I'm afraid . . .*

Finally, as if the wind had summoned the words from across an ocean, Thomas spoke. "How long, Allison?"

The words were too quiet for accusation, too stinging

for comfort. "How long for what? How long before they take Ishi away?" Was that her voice? So harsh? So unyielding? Her fingers dug into the flesh of her arms. "How should I know?"

The car slowed. Thomas leaned forward. Still, he did not look toward her. "No. How long have you been lying to me?"

Foreboding tingled over her skin. "W-what do you mean?"

Thomas turned the Ford down the last narrow street. Then he answered, spacing each word as if they were pebbles dropping into a still pond. "How long have you been lying to me about Ishi?"

Allison shifted in her seat. Her back stiffened. Fear pattered through her. "It's not *my* fault that Mr. Reynolds wants to take him away. I didn't do anything wrong. I don't know what that man was talking about."

The car slowed to a crawl. Thomas turned in his seat. His eyes pierced her. "What are you talking about, Allison? This isn't about Reynolds. It's about *you*. And me." He paused as if waiting for her response. Then he leaned forward until his elbows touched the steering wheel. "Why didn't you tell me the truth about what you were doing all those days in the garden? Why didn't you tell me you were learning Yahi?"

Allison pressed back into the door, as if by doing so she could lengthen the distance between herself and his questions. She opened her mouth, but no answers came.

Thomas straightened and shook his head. His foot jammed into the C pedal, and the car leapt forward.

Words clogged in her throat. She wanted to explain. To admit she was afraid Thomas would take Ishi away from her. That Thomas wouldn't bring him to her garden anymore.

But it wouldn't matter. He would still accuse her. He would never understand. So she remained quiet

But she hadn't lied, had she? She'd only done what she needed to.

Silence stretched between them, as though waiting for her to make peace. She drummed her fingers against the silk of her reticule bag. "Maybe Mr. Reynolds won't take Ishi now, since someone can communicate in Yahi."

Thomas didn't answer.

"It'll save us, don't you see?"

For five long breaths, Thomas said nothing. Then he sighed. "Do you truly believe that we improve our case by telling Mr. Reynolds that a married white woman is the only one who can speak with Ishi?"

"Why not?" But the answer to her question hit her almost as soon as she asked it. She bit her lip. "If I tell him, they'll find out I've been spending time alone with Ishi."

"That's right."

"Mrs. Whitson will find out. She'll say—"

Thomas's face became like granite. "I don't *care* about Mrs. Whitson." He pulled the Ford into the narrow alley alongside their house. The glow of a gaslight lantern flickered from the side window. The car sputtered to a stop. Thomas turned toward her. "It's you I'm worried about. Are you going to tell me why you lied?"

Allison looked out the window. Wisps of cloud drifted over the moon, like smoke from an ancient fire.

"I'll tell you why, then." His voice was so soft that it reminded her of a prayer. "It's because you don't trust me. You never have."

Thomas opened his door and vanished into the night.

For the first time, Majapa had lied to him. Wanasi knew it. Knew it as surely as he knew the sound of the wind across the waters of the Daha. "Aiku tsub," Majapa had said, but it wasn't true. He'd heard those words spoken in that tone before. As he stepped from a bloody river, then again the day his mother died. Words of defeat, not victory. Words that told him that he was alone.

Wanasi knew the truth. The bad saldu wanted to send him away.

He strode to the window and stared into the night. He watched the branches sway like black dancers in the darkness. His chin tipped up. "I will not go back. They cannot make me." He listened to the words and heard in them the echo of Lissie's fear, of Majapa's despair. He pulled his flute from his jacket pocket and smoothed his hand over the carved wood. "This time, it will be different."

Wanasi slid to the floor and rested his head against the wall. The flute lay silent in his grip. Tonight was too bitter for music. He closed his eyes. Forty years ago, the saldu drove him from his home, but they would not do it again. He would stay here in this place he had made his own. He would tell his story to Lissie. He would finish the task.

Or die trying.

Dread trickled down Agnes's backbone and pooled like sour milk in her stomach. A paper trembled in her grip. *Reynolds, Bureau of Indian Affairs, a letter, the Yahi* . . .

The words blurred before her vision. She didn't want to read more. She didn't need to. She knew what they wanted.

Ishi. They wanted to take Ishi.

"Mrs. Whitson?"

Agnes glanced up at the messenger boy who waited in the doorway. His eyes blinked like an owl's.

"Did you hear me, ma'am?"

Agnes's hand tightened on the note. "Yes, I heard you. Of course I heard you." But she hadn't. She hadn't heard a single thing since the boy had handed her the note and she'd read the first line. *Agnes, we have trouble . . .*

"Well, ma'am?"

"What?" She fixed her gaze on the bucktoothed youth in front of her. "Oh yes. Well, I suppose you are waiting for a tip?" She reached for her handbag on the side table.

The boy blinked twice.

Agnes withdrew a nickel and gave it to him. "Now, get. Go on now."

He turned and trotted down the stone steps toward the street.

Agnes closed the door and tossed her handbag back onto the table, not caring that it landed askew. She crumpled the paper in her fist, listening to the sheet crackle, then strode into the parlor. A fire blazed in the grate. She threw the wad of paper into the flames and watched the edges curl and smoke. A moment later, the ball burst into orange light.

Agnes turned away. If only this Mr. Reynolds could be as easily dealt with. But men were not as simple to manage. They did as they wished. They betrayed you.

Agnes sat on the wing chair with her spine tilted so as not to brush the seat's back. She massaged her forehead with her fingertips. She must think. Someone had done this evil thing. Someone had sent that letter to the bureau.

Well, that someone could not, *would* not, win. She had lost too much to lose Ishi as well. This time, she would not be the one who suffered.

Light from the morning sun made an elongated rectangle on the wooden floor. Agnes studied the pattern of light. Dust motes glowed in the sun's ray. Agnes frowned. There shouldn't have been dust in the air. Just as there shouldn't have been a Mr. Reynolds, nor that ridiculous letter to the Bureau of Indian Affairs.

She stood and stared up into the painted face of her dead husband. "How did you do this to me, Teddy? Why must everything always go wrong?"

But Teddy only stared back at her with dead eyes, eyes that did not see, did not know, had never cared. She would find no answers there. She never had.

Agnes walked to the window and gazed outside. The hill sloped away from the house and ended at the road below. A horse-drawn carriage hurried past, followed by a motorcar. In the distance, the bay shone like a ribbon of silver. Out there, everything seemed to go on as usual. But here, closer to home, nothing seemed right. Below the window, the nasturtiums looked wilted. The grass was too long. A weed scarred the stone walkway.

Agnes drummed her fingers on the sill. In the old days, the lawns were perfect, drooping flowers were plucked and discarded before they had a chance to fade. But somehow, she'd lost the beauty of the garden. It had slipped through her grasp, just like so many other dreams, so many other hopes. But this time she would not lose what was hers. No one would take him from her hand.

Agnes reached up and locked the window. The click of the lock resonated through the room. In three strides, she crossed the parlor, then grabbed the bell and rang it. "Mary!"

No one came.

She rang the bell harder. As the sound faded into silence, footsteps hurried down the hall. A moment later, Banks appeared in the doorway.

"You called, ma'am?"

Agnes twisted the bell in her palm. "Where's Mary?"

Banks took a step backward. "She's out. Left quite early this morning, ma'am. She didn't say where."

Agnes's eyes narrowed. Mary. It was all Mary's fault. "Have cook bring me a cup of tea and some laudanum."

Banks nodded and turned.

"And Banks?" Her voice arrested him.

"Yes, ma'am?"

"The newspaper clipping on my bureau, the one regarding the museum's anticipated success, take it and put it in Mary's room."

"Ma'am?"

"Just do it, Banks." She turned back to the fire and watched the flames twist and curl. No, she hadn't lost control yet. Things may have slipped, but she would not allow them to fall. She was still the mistress of this house. The mistress of her life. And she would find a way to make sure the Indian stayed. She would show that bureau upstart. She would show the letter writer. She would show them all.

She would throw a dinner party. Tonight.

# SIXTEEN

Thomas adjusted his tie and studied his image in the mirror. Defeat. That's what he saw there. Failure, dressed in a new Kuppenheimer jacket with a shiny silk cravat. Maybe Pop was right. Maybe something *was* missing in his life. Ishi had come to him as an answered prayer, but now . . .

He should've said something, *done* something to stop it, to make it right. But he couldn't find the strength. He never could. He supposed he was weak—that's what Allison wanted to call him, that's the indictment he'd seen in his father's eyes all his life.

Weakness. Defeat. Failure.

A chill slithered into the crevices of Thomas's stomach as his mind turned to the upcoming dinner party. He didn't know which was worse—Mr. Reynolds's intent to take Ishi away, or being forced to attend another of Mrs. Whitson's horrible parties. Last night, Mr. Reynolds's threat would have won without argument. But tonight . . . well, tonight it seemed like a dead heat.

Still, they would go. As always, they'd bow and say "yes, ma'am" when Queen Whitson called. Thomas hated it. He hated every last thing about those parties, from the flickering gaslights, to the false laughter, to the hors d'oeuvres he couldn't pronounce. Most of all, he hated what these parties did to Allison.

It was always the same. Allison would take two hours to dress, changing her clothes five times in the process. He could hear her in their room now, a drawer closing, the wardrobe doors banging shut. She would come out too pale, her small reticule bag bulging with extra gloves. Before the evening ended, he would see that look of shame, of humiliation, on her face. The same look he saw in the mirror now. And he knew there was nothing he could do for either of them.

Thomas dabbed at a small shaving cut on his chin and leaned closer to the mirror. He stared into deep blue eyes. *When are you gonna grow up, boy? When are you gonna stand up and be the man God's called you to be?* But those weren't his words; they were Pop's. Always Pop's.

Suddenly, Allison's bulging reticule bag didn't seem so silly.

As if conjured by his thoughts, an image appeared in the glass behind him. Unshaven chin, black mole, eyes that pierced his like a matching blue sword.

Thomas smoothed his tie. "Hello, Pop. I didn't hear you come in."

"Side door. Wasn't locked." Pop grunted. "Heard you were going to *her* house." Odd . . . that *her* sounded as if it hurt him.

"We're going. How could we not? Mrs. Whitson thinks a dinner party will help convince the bureau that Ishi should stay."

"Or show them just how out of place that Indian is."

Thomas heard the echo of his own fear in Pop's words—and heard the words left unsaid: *You should have converted that Injun when you had the chance. Should have taught him to talk English. Should have taught him to pray. Should have, shoulda, should.* Accusations beat like a hammer on Thomas's temples.

"We're expected to go."

Pop shook his head. "She ain't God, boy."

*She may as well be.* Thomas turned from the mirror and picked up his jacket from the wingback chair.

"And you can tell her that for me."

Thomas shrugged into his jacket. "Why don't you tell her? You're invited too. Just like always."

"Me? Trussed up like a spitted pig and served in the Whitson dining room?" Pop coughed. "No, boy, there'll be ice on the devil's horns before I put one whisker in Mrs. Agnes Whitson's house. You can take that to the bank."

Thomas smiled. He hadn't seen Pop in a tie for anything but church in a long time. But there was more to his refusal than a simple dislike for fancy getups. There was something sharp, something unfinished between his father and Mrs. Whitson. Something Thomas suspected went back to their childhood, when Grandpa Morgan worked as a gardener at the Spencer estate.

A vision of Miss Agnes Spencer in pinafores and ribbons, and his father in short pants with a smudge on his cheek, fluttered through Thomas's mind. But the image vanished, leaving behind the same icy feeling in his middle.

Pop stomped a bit of dirt off his boots. "Bible says bad company corrupts a good man."

"It also says that Jesus ate with tax collectors and sinners."

"Humph." A small smile lifted the corners of his mouth.

"Don't let Agnes Whitson hear you calling her a sinner. She won't cotton to that."

Thomas didn't answer.

Pop chuckled and settled onto the couch. "Nope, Mrs. Agnes Whitson never much cared for the truth. Found it mighty bitter, she did. And I suspect she still does." He paused and rubbed his chin. His voice lowered. His smile faded. "Can't say as I blame her, though." Pop sniffed and shook his head.

Thomas tugged at his collar, straightening a place where the fabric had curled. "Why not?"

Pop stared at a spot on the ceiling until his eyes seemed to lose focus. "Well, boy, sometimes God don't rescue us from our choices." His voice turned soft, distant. "No matter how many times we preach His name. Sometimes there ain't no going back."

Thomas's hands stilled as he contemplated his father. "Is this one of those times?"

Pop's gaze dropped back to Thomas. He blinked as if trying to regain focus. Finally, he nodded. "Maybe. Just maybe. Though I don't suspect she'll believe it." He crossed his arms. "She thinks this tomfoolery will work, doesn't she?"

"I suppose so." Thomas brushed a final bit of lint from his lapel. He was tired of this conversation. Tired of hoping everything would be fine when he knew it wouldn't. Tired of Pop's cryptic comments and Mrs. Whitson's domineering ways.

Pop pulled a small pillow from behind his back and tossed it to the far side of the couch. "Always thought she could get what she wanted. Thought she could have the world. Never learned. Shoulda." He clucked his tongue. "You tell her your Pop sends his greetings. You tell her that for me. Tell her I remember."

"Sure, Pop." Thomas took a step toward the hall.

"Tomfools." The couch creaked as Pop rose. "Suppose I'd better get to praying."

Thomas turned. "What for? I thought you wanted Ishi gone?"

Pop rubbed his chin. "Maybe I do, maybe I don't. Don't matter what I want. Never has. You go to your party, boy, but don't expect no miracle. I can't see one coming tonight."

Thomas didn't see one coming, ever. Not if he prayed a hundred prayers. Not if he prayed a thousand. Maybe that was what caused the glacier in his gut.

It was foggy again. Not the nice kind of fog that kisses rooftops and wraps the sidewalks in fluffy moistness. No, this was a drizzling mist, like the spitting of an alley cat over the neighbor's fence. Allison wiped the dampness from her cheek, then examined the dark spot it made on her white gloves. She would have to change them, but not now. Not while Thomas was looking.

And not while the Whitson mansion glared down at her as if she were a mere rodent.

She shuddered and clutched Thomas's forearm. Before them, the great white mansion crouched like a pale lion— grand, pretentious, devouring—its mouth two gaping oak doors, its eyes flickering with yellow gaslight.

Allison's gaze followed the cobbled path. Fog-drenched nasturtiums stood on either side, ending at the edge of a fountain where a fat cherub spilled water from its ivory cistern. Beyond the fountain, roses with bent heads bowed along the twisted path until it stopped at the porch of the Victorian mansion. The Whitson manor. Each time Allison came here, the very bricks seemed to sneer down at her, questioning how one such as she dared approach.

Thomas put his hand over hers. She felt the warmth of his skin through the fine silk. He leaned close, his breath tickling her ear. "You're certain about this? Ishi and I could go alone."

She glanced back at Ishi. He stood just a few feet behind her, waiting, watching, wondering, she supposed, why they paused. Allison smoothed her dress. "No. I'm ready."

Ishi stepped beside her. Light reflected in his eyes. He smiled, and she saw there, in the upturn of his lips, in the brightness of his eyes, interest and trust and willingness to go wherever they led.

Even into the lion's jaws.

Thomas dropped his hand and led her to the stairs. A motorcar rumbled behind them as the great door swung open. Allison swallowed. Light swarmed out around the silhouette of a tall man in a dark suit, who bowed and beckoned them forward. "Good evening, Dr. Morgan. Mrs. Morgan." His voice faltered. "Ishi." He sniffed. "Do come in. Mrs. Whitson has been awaiting your arrival."

Allison glanced inside. Dr. Kroeber and his wife were already there, as was that awful Mr. Reynolds. She could see them circled in the parlor with long-stemmed glasses held delicately between their fingertips. Waterford stemware, she assumed. Nothing but the best.

The butler stepped aside. Allison put a trembling hand on the pleats of her dress. "Is it wrinkled, Thomas?"

His palm touched the small of her back. "No, it's fine. You're beautiful, love."

"Perhaps I should have worn the brown one. Brown is more appropriate in the fall."

"It'll be all right, Allison."

"Is my hat straight?"

Thomas sighed. "You look . . . you look perfect." He said the word as if it were more accusation than compliment.

Her eyes flew to his, but she saw only weary resolution. Her eyes widened. He dreaded this party. But why? Was he embarrassed by her? Did he wish for a wife who could walk with confidence into a place like the Whitson manor?

Thomas glanced down at her and sighed again. "Come."

A flutter of blue taffeta and silk caught Allison's eye as Mrs. Whitson glided toward them. Her fingers stretched out to Thomas. "Welcome, Thomas. Thank you for bringing Ishi." She smiled at the Indian, then turned her gaze to rake Allison. "I thought you were going to be late again, my dear. A lady must always be punctual."

Allison looked down at the damp toes of her shoes.

Thomas cleared his throat. "My father sends his greetings, Mrs. Whitson. He apologizes for not being able to come himself."

Mrs. Whitson's fingers fluttered to her chest. "Silas still won't come." Her voice turned wistful.

"No."

She turned away, her gaze traveling out the door to somewhere beyond where any of them could see. "Someday, perhaps. One day he will come." Her features softened, then her eyes fixed again on the butler. Mrs. Whitson shook her head. Her voice sharpened. "Do shut the door, Banks. You're letting the wind in." She whirled and retreated to the parlor, her words trailing like a ribbon behind her. "Ishi's here, Mr. Reynolds. Come, you must have a proper introduction to our Indian friend."

And just like that, Allison and Thomas were forgotten.

Thomas stood in the doorway of the parlor and watched Mrs. Whitson directing her guests as if they were actors in a play. She positioned Ishi in front of Mr. Reynolds, with Dr. Kroeber at his side. She drew Dr. Pope toward the window, where a photographer stood. She hurried Mrs. Kroeber toward the seats near the fire. Only then did she seem to remember Allison. She swept back toward them. "My dear, *do* entertain Theodora for a while."

"But . . . Mr. Reynolds." The feather in Allison's hat quivered.

Mrs. Whitson's lips thinned. "It is unseemly for a woman to push her way into men's conversations. The chair by the fire is quite comfortable, I assure you."

She drew Allison toward Mrs. Kroeber; then her gaze fixed again on Thomas. He turned away, pretending not to notice her. In the shadows, a serving woman stood with a tray of small tarts in her hand. Her eyes watched Allison, or was it Mrs. Kroeber? Thomas couldn't tell. Was the woman dreaming of what it would be like to mingle with such guests, to be served instead of serving? What if he gave her the chance? Wild thoughts dashed through his mind, put there, he knew, by his desire to forget why they'd come tonight.

He imagined what would happen if he walked over to the woman, lifted the tray from her hands, and invited her to nibble hors d'oeuvres and sip from crystal glasses. The thought made his lips twitch. But of course he'd never do it. He'd never dare.

Would he?

He took a step toward the woman, but Mrs. Whitson

reached him first. "Now, now, Thomas, we'll be needing you soon. There will be time for hors d'oeuvres later."

The jingle of a bell shimmered through the room. A frown scurried across Mrs. Whitson's face. "The dinner call is early. Where has Mary got to?"

"Something amiss?" Thomas almost smiled.

Mrs. Whitson's raised an eyebrow. "Amiss? Of course not. I do hope you like lamb."

Before Thomas could answer, the bell rang again. The serving woman, now trayless, stood in the doorway leading to the dining room. Mrs. Whitson beckoned them forward, then dropped back to take Mr. Reynolds's arm.

Allison and Ishi walked into the dining room together, with Thomas just behind them. Crisp white linen covered a long cherrywood table. Light danced off the Tiffany silver flatware. Thomas knew it was Tiffany, as Mrs. Whitson had been sure to tell him so on his first formal visit. Apparently *Tiffany* meant something, though Thomas had never bothered to discover what—not even when he found Allison sighing over their own plain silverware some weeks later.

He pulled out a chair for his wife, then settled beside her. Ishi sat across from them. A light green soup that Thomas didn't recognize was placed before them. He watched as, moments later, Ishi picked up his spoon and politely dipped it into the bowl and lifted a taste to his lips. From the corner of his eye, he saw Mr. Reynolds's eyebrows rise.

Thomas hid his grin.

"You'd think he'd been having dinners here all his life, wouldn't you, Mr. Reynolds?" Mrs. Whitson was all but purring.

Mr. Reynolds's spoon clattered in his bowl. "Yes." He

pushed the bowl away from him. "But that isn't the point. As I explained—"

"Yes, we all know what you explained. Don't we, Thomas?"

Thomas felt the soup clog in his throat. "Ah, um, well . . ."

Mrs. Whitson laid her spoon beside her bowl. "We had hoped, of course, to speak of this after dinner. But perhaps we could talk a bit now, while the next course is being set." She turned in her chair. "Mary, clear the soup, please. It appears Mr. Reynolds doesn't care for it."

The servant woman bustled out from the doorway and began removing bowls. As she did, Mrs. Whitson turned piercing eyes onto Mr. Reynolds. "Now, my dear bureau man, perhaps we could reach some kind of compromise, don't you think? Cut straight to the main course, so to speak?"

"If you wish."

Mrs. Whitson flicked her fingers toward the serving woman. "The lamb, please, Mary." Then she turned back to Mr. Reynolds. "Now, as I was saying, poor Ishi has barely arrived here. How would it be for him to be uprooted so soon? He's already lost one home."

"A museum is no home."

"Now, now, let's not quibble over terms. How much harm would it do if he stayed, say, another month? Maybe two? The museum will open soon. What are a few more months?"

"You are quite persuasive, Mrs. Whitson."

"Ishi is a miracle for modern anthropology. At a reservation, he's just another Indian. He's special here."

"Too special." Mr. Reynolds shifted in his chair. "He

needs to be with people like himself. Other Yana Indians who at least might understand him."

"In good time, Mr. Reynolds. In good time. Oh yes, Mary, put it here, please." Mrs. Whitson motioned toward an empty place on the table.

Mary placed the platter of lamb in the center of the table and began to cut thin slices with a large knife. Her brows knit together as the conversation continued.

"What can it hurt to allow the good people of San Francisco to see him, to learn about the lost Yahi culture? Ishi is our only link to a people long dead."

"Perhaps, perhaps."

The knife slipped and made a loud clunk on the serving platter.

Mr. Reynolds frowned and sat forward. "I can, perhaps, agree to allow Ishi to stay until after the museum opens. But then he must return to his own kind."

"What if he doesn't want to go?" Thomas was almost as surprised as the others by his question.

Mr. Reynolds's eyes slid to Thomas. "My dear sir, we cannot be sure *what* the Indian wants. Unless, of course, you've learned to speak Yahi since last night?"

"Dr. Sapir will come."

"Dr. Kroeber tells me Sapir has refused."

Thomas swallowed. "We'll ask him again." The words sounded unconvincing, even to his own ears.

Mr. Reynolds let out a long sigh. "Ishi must go to a reservation. Say what you will; the fact remains that the Indian is all *alone* here." He jabbed a finger down at the table.

The fork shook in Allison's hand.

Thomas touched his fingers to her arm. "Shhh." He hissed the warning under his breath.

"Think of how you would feel," Mr. Reynolds continued. "Being all alone."

*Alone.* The word seemed to echo around the table. Allison leapt to her feet. Her glass tipped.

Thomas caught it before it fell.

"He's *not* alone! He's not!"

*Not now, Allison. Not yet. Wait.* Thomas willed her to read his thoughts, but she wasn't even looking at him, didn't notice the hand he'd placed on her arm.

He might as well not even exist.

"Sit down, Allison. Don't make a scene." Mrs. Whitson's voice sliced across the table as cleanly as the blade had carved the lamb moments before.

Trembling, Allison sank into her seat.

Mrs. Whitson reached for her glass, and her gaze shot toward Thomas. *Control your wife,* those eyes seemed to say.

Thomas wished that he could, if only to protect her.

Mr. Reynolds wiped his mouth with a napkin. "As I was saying, he is alone here, and—"

Allison leaned forward. "I won't lose him. Not like this. Not again." Her voice rose. "No, sir, Ishi is not alone."

"Mrs. Morgan?" Mr. Reynolds returned his napkin to his lap. "Do you have something to say?"

*No, Allison.*

"I understand him. I can talk to him."

*Wait.*

"I speak Yahi."

*No!*

Mrs. Whitson's water glass stopped halfway to her lips, and Thomas felt the silence descend like a bucket of cold water running down his back.

# SEVENTEEN

A chill drove deep into Allison's bones. The room swayed. She could hear someone breathing. In and out. Raw. Harsh. Was it her own breath in her ears? Thomas's? Or some monster's that had risen from fear long suppressed?

She pushed her fingertips into the linen tablecloth and sat back in her chair. Words echoed in her mind: *I speak Yahi.* The truth forced itself from her. Beat in her chest until she felt she would burst if she didn't release it. But now . . .

She'd give anything to pull it back, swallow it, make the words as if they'd never been.

*"You?"* The question shot from Mrs. Whitson's lips like a poisoned arrow. "How?"

Allison trembled. Eyes bored into her from every side. Staring. Accusing. Mocking. She glanced at Thomas for help, but he was not looking at her. Instead, his eyes were closed, his forehead in his hand. Was he condemning her too? Couldn't he stand by her, believe in her, just this once? Wasn't she worth even that much to him?

*Thomas, please . . .*

"Well?" Mrs. Whitson's fingers rapped on the table.

Allison's gaze swept over the linen tablecloth, the perfect Wedgewood Queen's ware, the sparkling silver of the knives and forks. In that moment she knew she could not erase the enormity of her error. Her fingers curled against the white linen. "I-I learned. He taught me."

Mr. Reynolds lifted his napkin and rested his elbows on the table. His arms formed a triangle in front of him. "Do I understand correctly—" his voice oozed over the gathering —"that the Indian came to live with the top professors of anthropology at the University of California, Berkeley. He is surrounded by men of learning. He is, as Mrs. Whitson has so eloquently stated, a miracle for modern anthropology?"

He paused, and Thomas shifted in his seat beside Allison.

Mr. Reynolds continued. "And yet this *woman* is the one you assigned to learn his language? An uneducated, unlearned wife of a junior professor?"

With each word, Allison felt more and more like a tiny, shabby mouse caught beneath the lion's paw.

Dr. Kroeber cleared his throat. "We did not assign her." His voice sounded strained. "We did not even know." His eyes turned to Thomas. "Did we?"

Slowly, Thomas raised his head. His face looked pale in the gaslight. "Alfred . . ." He motioned with his hand.

"Oh, no." The serving woman's whisper hissed behind Allison.

At the same moment, Thomas's sleeve caught the edge of his water glass. Time slowed as the sparkling Waterford goblet wobbled. Then tipped. Then fell to the floor and shattered into a dozen glittering shards.

The serving woman hurried forward. She dabbed at the tablecloth with a towel, then began sweeping the broken pieces of glass into a dustpan. For a moment she paused. Her gaze rose to pierce Allison's.

Allison caught her breath. Something in those eyes . . . Shame bubbled up inside her like snakes writhing on the surface of water. She ripped her gaze from the woman's and stumbled to her feet. Her legs shook beneath her. Even the servants blamed her. Even they accused her.

Was learning Yahi really so wrong?

The woman brushed the last bits of glass into the dustpan, then turned and left the room.

Mr. Reynolds waited until the door thumped shut before he leaned back in his chair and allowed his glance to wander from Dr. Kroeber to Thomas. "You didn't know, you say? How interesting. How very amusing." He tossed the words out as if he were but a newspaper critic, sitting in the plush seats of the opera house as he fashioned phrases for a drama-turned-comedy. "Tell me, gentlemen, is that admission meant to inspire my confidence in your care of the Indian?"

No one answered. Allison heard the creak of a chair, the rustle of fabric, the soft ping of a fork touching china. She glanced around the table. Mr. Reynolds smiled. Mrs. Kroeber smoothed the napkin in her lap. Dr. Kroeber studied his fingertips. Thomas sat with his head bowed. And Ishi . . .

Warmth stole through her. Ishi cut a piece of lamb, raised it to his mouth, and ate as if nothing unusual were happening around him. He did not condemn. Did not accuse. Did not scorn.

She frowned. Was that only because he didn't understand? Allison raised her chin. "Why does it matter who can understand him? Someone can. He's not alone."

At the head of the table, Mrs. Whitson straightened. Her voice bit through the tension in the air. "Allison, I think you'd better leave the room now."

The command cut Allison like a knife, slicing between her heart and breastbone. The bits of confidence she'd gathered from Ishi vanished. A final plea tore from her. "Why can't you see? Why can't any of you see?" She took a step back, away from the averted faces, then she turned and hurried away.

But not fast enough. Before she reached the door, she heard Mrs. Whitson's sigh. "She's always been a wayward girl. It's in the blood, I say."

*It's in the blood . . .*

The words chased Allison from the house, nipping like a mutt at her heels, as surely as Mr. Mayweather's words did all those years ago. Only this time, there was no carriage. No mother. No hope that somehow, someone would make everything all right.

Wanasi chewed the meat slowly, as if he could draw from its flavor the wisdom he sought. The saldu had changed since that day when the river flowed red. They no longer warred, it seemed, with sticks that shot fire. Now they sat around a long table, smiled, and shot words just as deadly. Or perhaps *they* had not changed so much. Only their weapons had. Only the method by which the enemy was shattered.

And shattered she was. Wanasi could see it in the droop of Lissie's shoulders, in the sound of her steps as she fled from the room. But no one cared. Soon the sound of footsteps was buried beneath a babble of saldu voices as they all spoke at once. Arguing, pointing, jabbering like a flock of crows over a dead rabbit—or a well-cooked lamb.

Suddenly, Wanasi was no longer hungry. He pushed back his plate and placed the thing called *fork* next to it. Something bad had happened tonight. Something that no one else seemed to notice, except perhaps for the woman who brought food. She looked ill, as if she had swallowed a poisoned berry.

This was a strange place. This cave-house that held images of strange people on the walls; where knives glittered like stars but were cold as the Daha in winter; where cups captured the light then spat it out again in handfuls of sharp, tiny daggers. This was not a good place. Not a happy place. He wanted to go home.

But Lissie needed him. Majapa too. He couldn't help them now—not with that saldu sitting there with ice in his eyes and fire in his voice . . . not with Majapa too weary to look up. Not with Lissie fleeing like a deer before the hunter's arrow.

Only his story could help them. Only it could say the words they needed to hear. Maybe, just maybe, it could heal them. It was all that mattered now.

Thomas felt Allison's last words like a weight pressing into his chest, drowning him beneath a flood of "should haves." He never should have taken Ishi to the garden. He should have found another way. He should have foreseen this moment. He should have realized someone would find out.

And most of all, he should have been the one planting flowers with Allison in the garden.

But he sent Ishi instead. And in doing so, he'd failed her. He knew that now. Knew it as clearly as the sound of his glass shattering on the wooden floor, as distinctly as her footsteps dashing away from them. Away from him. Did she count him, too, as the enemy?

Thomas pressed his palms into his forehead. Perhaps she was right about him. After all, wouldn't a better man have defended his wife tonight? Wouldn't a better man have protected her from herself, from Ishi, from the piranhas of the past that took the form of Mrs. Agnes Whitson? But he had failed. Again. Why couldn't he be the man Allison needed him to be?

And yet . . . if he'd intervened, wouldn't that only make things worse? It was best to stay back, to be quiet, to wait for the storm to pass. He knew that. *Oh, God, God, God . . .* The prayer whispered through his mind, so soft that he wasn't sure if it was new or an echo from days long past. *God, it's Thomas. I'm here behind the door . . .*

As if waking from a muddled dream, he realized the conversation continued without him. Reynolds, Mrs. Whitson, Dr. Kroeber, each speaking words that no longer mattered. Arguing. Reasoning. With "howevers" and "what ifs" and "therefores." But it had become no more than children playing a game of kick the stick. Except here, the stick was made of words. Back and forth, around the table. Words without meaning. Words without hope. Thomas didn't want to hear them anymore. He couldn't.

He pushed his chair back from the table.

"Where are you going, Thomas?" Mrs. Whitson's question halted his flight.

*Out. Away. As far away as possible from you vultures. Just like Allison.* He placed his napkin on the table and rose.

"Sit down, Thomas. You have some questions to answer."

He shuddered. "Such as?"

Mrs. Whitson twisted the napkin in her hands. "How could you allow your wife to spend all that time alone with a man, a *savage?* Have you no decency?"

Thomas swayed on his feet. He almost smiled. Yes, he should have known he could not escape so easily.

Mr. Reynolds clucked his tongue. "Had I known you were allowing the Indian to become attached to a *married* woman . . ."

"Do sit down, Thomas," Mrs. Whitson repeated. "How can we have a conversation with you standing there like a reprimanded child?"

Thomas glanced at his chair. Would he? Should he?

"Gracious, are you ill?"

Thomas suppressed a surge of bitter laughter. He looked over at Reynolds, then at Mrs. Whitson. "Yes. No. What do you want me to say?"

The serving woman leaned over and removed the barely eaten lamb from the table.

Mrs. Whitson's voice lowered to a hiss. "I want you to tell us why you allowed this atrocity to occur. I *trusted* you. We all did. Don't you know that Allison needs someone who—" She stopped and drew a quick breath. "Someone who will keep her from making mistakes."

*Atrocity? Mistakes?* The words stuck in Thomas's heart. *The atrocity is what we've done to Allison. The mistake is what we will do to Ishi.* Thomas lowered his head. He had no better answer for them. In a way, they were right, of course. And they were wrong too. But he didn't have the strength to fight them. He didn't even know how.

Mr. Reynolds dropped his hands to the table. "I will remove Ishi immediately, of course. If our letter writer had had any idea of this—"

The serving woman dropped the platter of meat. Juice flew over the white linen and spattered across the polished floor.

Mr. Reynolds leapt to his feet.

Mrs. Whitson gasped. "Heavens, Mary! Have we not endured enough disasters tonight?"

Mary knelt to retrieve the platter. "Sorry, mum. I'll clean it up right quick."

Mrs. Whitson wiped her napkin over a spot on her sleeve.

"Mum? Perhaps the nice gentlemen would like to retire to the parlor? Or to the porch for a pipe, while you change into some fresh things?"

Mrs. Whitson frowned. "Yes, yes, of course. Gentlemen?" She gestured toward the outer door.

Thomas pushed himself away from the table like a man granted a reprieve. Moments later, he stepped out onto the porch and watched his breath rise in misty puffs before his eyes. He savored the cool night air, the dampness of the mist, the quietness of crickets playing tunes in the dark.

"Majapa?" Ishi placed a hand on Thomas's shoulder. With the other, he pointed toward the black shapes of trees in the garden. "Lissie?"

Thomas shrugged. "No, she's back in the house, I think."

"Lissie." Ishi's tone softened.

Thomas sighed. Where *had* Allison gone? To the powder room, as he'd assumed? How long would she stay in there until she came and sought him? And when she did, would he know what to do to help her, to help them all?

Mr. Reynolds stepped behind him. "Do you smoke, Dr. Kroeber?"

Dr. Kroeber sat in a chair near the edge of the porch. "No. Not tonight, thank you."

Mr. Reynolds pulled up the seat beside him. "Will you sit now, Dr. Morgan?"

Thomas took a chair on the other side of Dr. Kroeber, with Ishi beside him. For a moment, they sat in silence, looking out into the darkness. The glow of a match illuminated Reynolds's face as he lit his pipe. The sweet smell of tobacco filled the air. Beside him, Ishi closed his eyes for a brief moment and inhaled the aroma. Did it remind him of home? Or of people long dead? Thomas looked away. Thoughts, unbidden, unwanted rose in his mind.

Were they doing Ishi a disservice by keeping him here? Would he be happier among his own kind, smoking pipes, remembering . . . ?

"Listen, Reynolds." Dr. Kroeber's voice interrupted Thomas's musings. "I don't see why everything is happening in such a rush. Ishi lived alone three years in the wilds before he came to us."

"Hmmm." A puff of smoke rose from Reynolds's pipe.

"Give us time to appeal to Dr. Sapir again, tell him of our urgent need." Dr. Kroeber nodded. "In the meantime, the museum will open. Surely you'll allow Ishi to demonstrate his skills for the people of San Francisco? Arrowhead making, bow shooting, Yahi skills that will soon be lost to us forever. And we still have more recordings to make of Ishi's songs and stories."

"Hmmm," Reynolds said again.

"He is well fed here." Dr. Kroeber pointed to Ishi. "He is happy. Come, Reynolds. What are a few months?"

"The bureau only wants what's best for the Indian."

Thomas leaned forward. Their conversation, their debate didn't seem to matter. What was happening to him?

Reynolds took two more puffs on his pipe, then drew a piece of paper from his pocket and tapped it against his knee. "The word of some anonymous letter writer against the arguments of a renowned professor? Hmmm, yes. Well, I will agree, Dr. Kroeber, to allow you a few more months with Ishi."

Dr. Kroeber clapped his hands together. "Very good."

Reynolds raised a finger. *"But."*

"But?"

Thomas turned toward him. Reynolds's gaze was fixed on Thomas. A slight smile played on his lips.

"But only, doctors, if you can assure me that Mrs. Morgan will have no further dealings with the Indian."

Dr. Kroeber reached out and gripped Thomas's forearm. "That will not be a problem, Mr. Reynolds. That was an oversight. Nothing more."

Reynolds blew a smoke ring into the air.

As it dissolved, Ishi rose from his chair and stood at the porch railing. Thomas watched him, a black shadow against the dark sky. For a moment, they all fell silent, waiting. Then Ishi began to speak. But not to them. To someone none of them could see. He chanted, his voice low, then flowing, like a song sung on a lonely day. He did not turn around. He did not look back. He only spoke into the night, as if expecting the shadows to answer him.

"What is he saying?" Reynolds whispered.

"Is he praying?" Dr. Kroeber glanced at Thomas.

*Praying?* The question brought an image of Pop to mind. Pop was praying, too, but no miracle had come tonight.

"He's calling for someone."

Mr. Reynolds looked at Dr. Kroeber. "Who?"

Thomas closed his eyes and allowed Ishi's song to wash through him like a cleansing breeze. "He's calling for Yuna." And for one moment, Thomas wanted to believe that the unknown Yuna would answer the call.

# EIGHTEEN

A single candle burned low on the hutch behind the dining room table. A single yellow flame. Alone. Flickering. Growing dimmer. Soon it would die, drowning in the last bits of wax that had once fed its life. For a moment, Agnes watched it grow bright, then sputter in a puff of black smoke. The sight chilled her. She could hear the murmur of the men's voices on the porch and Mrs. Kroeber's footsteps on the way to the parlor.

Agnes massaged her temples. The scene from moments before replayed in her mind. How had she not seen it? How had she not known? Thomas should have intervened. Should have kept it from happening at all. But he was too weak. She would have to do something about that. If the evening's misfortunes were to be managed at all, she'd have to take control.

She flicked away a speck of lamb that had landed on her bodice. Drat that girl! She had warned her about mingling with that Indian. But sometimes blood would tell. *Allison,*

*Allison, how could you do this to me? After all I taught you. After all I sacrificed.*

The girl was just like her mother.

"You ought not have said those things, mum."

Agnes turned. Mary stood in the doorway with a lamb-spattered rag in her hand.

Heat traveled up Agnes's neck. "You spoke?"

Mary twined the towel around her palm. "You got no right."

Agnes dug her fingers into her hips. "Don't I?" She stepped forward. "After all I've done?"

Mary backed away until her features were half hidden in the shadows of the doorway. Her voice drifted back to Agnes. "Especially after what you done."

Agnes froze. "Don't say another word, Mary. Don't you dare."

Mary quivered in the doorway. The rag dropped to the floor. Briefly, Agnes thought Mary might defy her. Might say the words that would sever their bond forever. But Mary didn't have the strength. She'd never had it. The moment passed, and darkness swallowed up the place where Mary stood, leaving Agnes alone again.

She rubbed a finger over a dark stain on her sleeve. She would have to change her dress, of course. And then return and somehow repair the damage Allison had done.

*You should have trusted me, Allison. You should have listened. Don't you know it's for your own good . . .*

Agnes glanced at the blackened wick of the candle one last time before she hurried out of the dining room, up the stairs, and into her dressing room. There, she paused before the mirror. A woman with thin, tight lips looked back at her.

A woman with too much gray in her hair, too many wrinkles lining her face.

"No. Do not believe it. You are not old yet, Agnes Spencer. There is still time." Time to remember. Time to forget. Time to remedy the mistakes made. All the hurt endured. The disappointments suffered.

Agnes's hand reached for the top drawer of her bureau. Her fingers trembled as she clutched the knob. Then she pulled open the drawer, reached far in the back, and withdrew a tiny photo. A young man looked back at her. She touched a fingertip to the mole on his cheek. "You should have been here tonight. You should have come. I needed you."

But he couldn't. He wouldn't. Agnes had made sure of that forty years ago. And too little had changed since then.

The bench was cold, the air heavy, the night quiet but for the chirping of a few crickets beyond the garden wall. Allison pressed herself into the cool marble of the bench and willed the darkness to enfold her like a shroud. To hide her, for now, forever, from the accusations spinning in her mind.

*Don't listen to them. Don't remember. Forget.*

But she could still hear Mrs. Whitson's voice. Could see the way the light glinted off Thomas's hair as he turned his face from her, refusing to meet her gaze.

*They're all gone now. They don't matter. No one will find you here.*

If only she could believe the words. But they, too, were a lie. Everything was an awful mess. She was in disgrace. Ishi would be taken away. And somehow, it was all her fault. She didn't know how, she didn't know why, but she knew she was to blame.

Just like always.

A breeze ruffled the leaves of the hydrangea bush beside her, the sound like a hundred whispering voices telling secrets, telling lies. She wrapped her arms around her waist and rocked back and forth until the voices grew silent. A fat slug trailed along the path in front of her. Behind it, a ribbon of dull silver caught the glow of starlight. Allison looked up to see a rift in the clouds overhead.

Mist moved and shifted, revealing a handful of scattered stars, twinkling above her like beacons to another world. A better world, but one she'd never reach.

"So, would you tell me that even in the darkness, there is light?" she asked the stars.

*Not today. And not for you.*

Allison leaned back against the slender trunk of a birch tree behind her. The rift in the clouds drifted east, and still she watched it and wondered. Was there a God up there somewhere, looking down through the slit in the clouds? A God who saw, who knew, who cared? Sister Catherine had thought so. But Allison hadn't believed it. Not when she was seven. And not now.

"Jesus is always with you, Ally. He sees you. He loves you."

How often had Sister Catherine spoken those words? Allison had wanted to believe it as she looked up at the blind-eyed statue of a man with arms extended, red marks on his palms. But fear took her then. Took her and bound her, whispering in her ear.

*If He really saw, if He really knew, how could He love?*

She knew right at that moment that Mama was right.

There was no Jesus. There couldn't be.

Her heart grew colder that day, but she buried the fear, the doubt, under a thousand murmured "Our Fathers," under ten thousand hours of sitting in the church, wishing, praying, hoping that those eyes really didn't see, that Jesus really didn't know the depths of darkness in her heart. She learned how to play the good Christian girl. She knew how to go to church, say her prayers, and mutter the right words at the right time. She'd performed her part, done as she was expected to.

Until Ishi came.

Somehow he'd cracked the guise just a little. Enough for them to see and condemn. Enough for the fear to seep from that sealed place deep within her. But this time, she would find a way to show them, to prove to them all that she was not afraid. That she was worth their love.

She dropped her gaze and saw the starlight reflected in the snail's dim path.

As if summoned by her thoughts, voices drifted from the direction of the house. Men's voices, low and deep. Were they looking for her? Had Thomas come, after all? For a moment, she held her breath, waiting.

"Listen, Reynolds . . ."

That was all she heard. The rest was lost in the sounds of shuffling feet and chairs being repositioned on wood planking.

Allison shrank farther into the shadows, then turned and peered from behind the birch. Through the branches, she discerned the glow of a pipe and the dark outlines of three, maybe four, men on the porch. They were close, just thirty or forty feet away. But the night was thick between her and them. Thick enough to hide her. She shifted to the left, allowing the hydrangea flowers to blot out the pipe's glow, but not the sound of those voices.

Were they deciding her future? And Ishi's? Were they discussing what should be done about Thomas's wayward wife? She shuddered. Wasn't it enough that they would take away the only one who understood her? The only one who didn't judge and find her wanting?

One of the dark shapes separated from the others. It drew closer until it stood by the porch railing and looked out into the night. It lifted its chin, and Allison recognized the gesture. Ishi. It had to be Ishi. Did he know she was hidden out here?

Then he began to speak Yahi words that flowed out from the shadows like a song. The story of Yuna. The tale he kept only for her. Allison closed her eyes and let the story wrap its arms around her.

And this time, she had no trouble understanding the flow of Yahi words.


*Summer dropped from the mountains like a stone thrown from the sky. Summer, hot and dry and lonely.*

*One day, Yuna found some blackberries along the path in the forest. Big, juicy berries. She was very hungry and ate one after another after another, until they were gone. When she finished, she looked at herself and saw that the berries had made dark purple stains on her fingers and the front of her dress. Terrible stains. Stains that could not be hidden.*

*She looked into the forest, into the sky, down the long, winding path. But no one was there. No one had seen her stains. She hurried to the stream to wash her clothes. The waters were deep, clean, and cool. She scrubbed her clothes against the rocks. She* scrubbed them with sticks. She scrubbed them until her knuckles were red. But the stains would not come out. They only spread.

"Yuna, Yuna." She heard a call far above her. A call from the clouds. "Yuna, Yuna."

As she listened, Allison knew Ishi was speaking to her, calling her out from the darkness just as the eagle called Yuna. But she wouldn't come. Not yet. She opened her eyes. How could she while the men sat on the porch, eager to tell her what else she had done wrong?

For a long moment, Ishi paused. She could see him at the railing, his posture as still as a deer who'd caught a scent on the wind. Allison didn't move. Didn't respond. Didn't dare to break the silence.

Finally, Ishi leaned forward. She could see his chin drop. Then the story continued.

Yuna did not answer. She did not even look up to the sky. The eagle should not see her now, she thought. If he did, he would see her stains. He would know the truth. She would clean them first. She would wash away the dark marks. Then she would look up and answer his call. Then she would not be ashamed.

Yuna stepped deeper into the stream. The waters swirled around her. Colder. Much colder. But Yuna did not care. She rubbed at the stains. And rubbed. And still they would not come out.

The sun dipped low in the sky. Shadows crept from beneath the trees. Closer they came. Dark shadows. Black fingers that pushed Yuna from the water. Cold. Dripping. Still not clean.

Then a voice fell from a rock above her. "You are dirtier than ever, Yuna," Coyote called. He looked down his long nose and laughed. "No one will love you now."

Allison felt the night grow as cold as the stream in Yuna's story. Goosebumps rose on her arms. "Hexai-sa!" She breathed the words. "Go away, Coyote. Stop whispering in my ear."

She shook her head. What was she saying? The coyote was not talking to her. He was just a character in some old fable. It was Yuna's story, not hers. It didn't have anything to do with a modern woman, sitting in the dark, in a garden, in San Francisco, in 1911. How could it? Unless . . .

Suddenly, Allison wondered if Coyote had gray, perfectly coiffed hair and wore Gibson Girl dresses from a decade past.

"Listen, listen," came Ishi's voice again from the porch. "Listen to the branches crack. Listen to the leaves crumble. Listen to the sounds of footsteps among the trees."

Allison leaned forward, but she could hear none of those things. Only the crickets. Only her own breathing. Only Ishi's story spoken again from the shadows.

Yuna ran into the forest. Branches cracked. Leaves crumbled. She ran and ran. The forest grew darker. Twigs caught and ripped her clothes until the bottom of her dress was torn and tattered. Moon rose in the sky and peeked through the tops of the trees. Light glimmered on her dress. And Yuna saw again the stains. So she ran no more. She sat on the trunk of a fallen tree and looked at the long tears in her dress. She could not mend them now. But in *time, maybe in time, the holes would close and the stains would fade. Maybe she wouldn't notice them anymore.*

*Moon stared down at her. And she knew he saw her stains, her tatters. She huddled close to a tree, out of the sight of Moon face. There, she waited. Her stomach rumbled. She was hungry. But she had not gathered food. Only the berries. And they were gone.*

Allison's stomach grumbled too. She pressed her hand into her abdomen. Silly story. Why should she listen at all?

*Now it was too late. Moon hid behind a cloud. Yuna watched the darkness grow deeper; then she slipped from her hiding place beside the tree. Moon could not see her. No one could. She hurried back to her camp. Branches cracked. Leaves crumbled. Her stomach gnawed at her backbone like Beaver felling a log.*

*When she reached her grinding stone, she saw two splashes of silver shining from the rock's surface. She drew closer. Two fresh plump trout lay on the stone beside an ear of yellow corn. Where did they come from? Who could have left them? The leaves rustled above her. She looked up. It was only the wind.*

Allison looked up, almost expecting fish to fall from the sky. None did, of course. But Ishi's tale was winding itself around her heart so that she wouldn't have been surprised if they had.

She smiled. Was Ishi inventing the story for her? Or was it truly a fable told by his grandfather, and his grandfather's grandfather before him?

*The next day, Yuna tried to soak her clothes in a turtle shell. The sun beat hot upon her. "If only I had some shade," she moaned. She scrubbed at her dress again and again, but the stains remained and the tears only worsened. Then she saw the sun was no longer upon her, though it was now midday. She put a hand to her eyes. She looked above her. The eagle was there again, his silhouette dark against the bright sky.*

*"Hello, Yuna," the eagle said.*

*Yuna lowered her head. She did not answer.*

*All day, the eagle remained above her, but she was too ashamed to speak with him. If only her clothes were clean, then perhaps she would dare to ask the eagle's name. Perhaps then she would call out to him and he would fly down and talk with her and tell her the secrets of the clouds, the mysteries of the sky, the wonders he saw as he flew above the earth.*

*But Yuna did not call out. And the eagle did not speak again.*


Nor did Ishi.

Silence fell across the night. For several minutes, Ishi remained at the rail, looking into the darkness. Then he turned and joined the other men. Allison heard the murmur of voices. Her name spoken once. And Thomas's muttered reply.

The men rose. The light of the pipe grew dim, then extinguished. A door creaked open. A swath of light spilled into the night. Footsteps pattered on the floorboards of the porch. The door swung closed. The light was gone.

And Allison was left alone.

She settled back against the tree trunk and allowed her gaze to drift to the clouds overhead. The rift had grown wider, revealing the glow from a still-hidden moon. A bird flew across the opening, soaring higher, then dipping into the mist.

*A seagull, probably.*

Still, the graceful flight reminded her of Ishi's Great Eagle. Was there a Great Eagle out there somewhere, flying among the clouds? And if so, what was his name? Ishi had asked her that once. But she didn't know. Did he know himself? Or was he searching too? Could she call to the eagle if he flew now overhead? Would he come and lift her above the clouds, above the mist, above the cruel and accusing eyes? He would, perhaps, if she knew his name.

Allison sighed and rose from the bench. "Take me away, Great Eagle. Rescue me from these coyotes. Tell me your name."

She heard footsteps on the porch again and turned. Had Thomas come to find her at last? No. It wasn't Thomas, but the silhouette of the serving woman, the frills of her cap outlined in the light of the half-closed door. She moved to the top of the steps.

"I know you're there, Mrs. Morgan."

Allison froze.

"You can come out now."

Allison held her breath.

"I see you there on the bench, beside the hydrangea."

"Leave me alone."

"They'll come looking for you soon. You gotta come in now." She raised her hand to her brow as if peering into the darkness. A rag fluttered in her grip. "Come, girl, don't make them go looking for you as if you was some naughty child."

Allison raised her eyebrows. The woman was certainly outspoken for a maid, and yet her words carried no sting.

Allison brushed off her dress. "I'm coming, then. If I must." She stepped from behind the birch and slipped up the short path toward the porch.

The woman waited as Allison reached the stairs.

"Go on in now." The woman motioned with a sweep of her hand.

"I will. And thank you." Allison crossed the porch and reached for the door.

A low voice whispered behind her. "Remember, girl, you're as good as any of them. It's in your blood."

"How do you know what's in—" Allison turned to face the woman, but there was no one there. Nothing remained but the shadows.

# NINETEEN

The museum opened, right on schedule, on a warm, sunny day in mid-November. The storm clouds ran away the night before, leaving only white fluffy wisps that pranced across the sky like sheep frolicking in a turquoise meadow. Outside the museum, reds, greens, purples, and yellows were splashed across the yard in the form of dozens of bright balloons. Children ate hot dogs off sticks while mothers pushed strollers up the gravel path. A juggler tossed bowling pins in a high circle. A boy in short pants blew a merry tune on his pennywhistle. A clown handed out bits of peppermint. Fathers lifted little children onto their shoulders and pointed up to the wide doors of the museum.

It was perfect. Beautiful. Everything Allison had dreamed of.

And she was miserable.

She tucked a piece of peppermint into her handbag and stepped inside the museum. Crowds meandered from room to room, their voices, like the babble of water over rocks, drifted around her and drew her forward. She followed one group into the Indian exhibit room. Her room. The room that once held so many hopes.

Now she crept into a corner and watched as old, white-haired gentlemen with glasses leaned over her displays, while a woman with a baby on her hip paused to consider the leather papoose hanging from a hook above the Apache exhibit, and a group of teenagers hurried past to get a glimpse of Ishi in the far room. It was just as Allison had imagined.

Except it was meaningless. Completely, utterly empty.

It wasn't fair! Why hadn't someone told her that accomplishment wouldn't cure the ache within?

Applause erupted from the room beyond, and Allison shrank into the corner. Ishi was there, where the people clapped and cheered and laughed. Had he finished another arrowhead? Had he shot his arrow through the target on the far end of the room? Or sung a song from his people? Allison didn't know. She would never know. Strangers could crowd in to watch him share a piece of his history, a piece of his heart, but she was banned.

How could they be so heartless as to forbid her to see him? She supposed she deserved it. But still . . .

For a moment, she contemplated defying them all. What would it feel like to march into that room and call out a greeting in Yahi? How would the crowd's astonishment feel, and Ishi's smile? She sighed. She knew how she'd feel. She'd feel like a fool. Which was why she would never do it.

Mrs. Whitson had made sure of that.

Allison turned to walk out and found Pop standing behind her. The mole on his cheek twitched. "Going somewhere, girl?"

"Oh! You startled me." Allison pressed her fingers to the base of her throat. "Thomas said you weren't coming."

Pop stared at her for a long moment, then glanced away to look over the Indian exhibit room. "Humph, well, yes. Almost didn't come. Didn't really want to."

"Why did you then?" She said the words before she could consider how the question might sound.

Pop only smiled, then sucked his teeth. "Couldn't miss the grand opening of the Mrs. Agnes Whitson show, now could I?" He stuffed his hands into the pockets of the grubbiest gardening overalls Allison had yet seen on him. "Dressed up special for it, I did."

The words pricked Allison's skin like a tailor's needle. "We *all* worked hard for this, you know. Not just Mrs. Whitson."

"Did you?" He raised his eyebrows and made a show of looking around the room. "Looks a lot like Agnes Whitson to me. Too much like her."

Allison jabbed a finger toward an arrangement of Ute baskets. "You *know* I set up this room."

"Hmmm. Yep, that's what the rumor was." He turned to pierce her with his eyes. "Indian kind of stole the show though, didn't he?"

Allison felt a lump lodge somewhere in her windpipe. For a second, she couldn't breathe. Then the air came again. "The . . . the Indian?"

"You know, I heard about you and that Indian. Heard plenty, I did."

Allison crossed her arms. She'd been expecting this. The condemnation, the scorn. She opened her mouth to make a defense, but there was none.

Pop rubbed his hand over the stubble on his chin. "That Thomas is a doggone fool."

She stared at him. "W-what?"

"You heard me." Pop crossed his arms. "There's no helping it. Lord knows I've tried." He clucked his tongue. "You'll just have to forgive him, you will. It's the Christian thing to do. I ain't saying he deserves it."

Allison had no response. Of all the things Pop could have said, this was something she'd never imagined.

Pop let out a long breath, then continued as if Allison wasn't there at all, as if he was no longer talking to her but to someone who lived only in his memory. "Though sometimes, when someone you love hurts you bad enough . . ." Pop shook his head and cleared his throat. "Hmmm, well, yes." He turned and studied Allison, as if really seeing her for the first time. "It ain't easy though, is it?"

"What?"

"Losing."

Allison pulled in her breath.

Pop put a hand on her shoulder, stopping her words. "Don't say it. I know. I lost too once. Lost bad."

Allison's voice softened. "Thomas's mother?"

Pop's gaze flew to hers. His eyes widened. "Elizabeth? Naw, I wasn't talking about her." He tugged on his ear, as though reluctant to continue. Then he dropped his hand and spoke again. "There was a girl once, when I was young. Before Elizabeth. That girl was something to behold."

"I didn't know."

"Don't like to talk about it much. Don't see the point."

"What was she like?"

A smile crinkled the corners of his eyes. "Like a fine

flower most of the time." His grin widened. "But sometimes like a hornet too."

"A hornet?"

"Aye. Fiery and confident, full of life." He dug his hands into his pockets. "Hair like wheat. Voice like an angel. Never dreamed she would love me, but she did. At least, I thought she did." He sighed and shook his head. "The dreams we had . . . We were gonna grow up and defy the world." He paused. His eyes fixed on Allison. "Instead, we just grew up."

"What happened to her?"

"Did what her papa wanted. Married some rich fella. Moved into a big house. Became Mrs. Fancy Pants. Ain't such an unusual story."

Allison laid her hand on Pop's sleeve, hoping he could feel the sympathy in her touch. "And what did you do?"

"Came to my senses, I suppose. Married Elizabeth. Turned my life to important things, to telling folks about Jesus. Figured that's what God wanted. Figured that's why He let things happen like they did. You think about that, girl."

Allison pulled back her hand and stepped away. "You don't believe—"

"Ain't for me to say. Ain't for me to answer. It's up to you. Are you going to sulk here in the corner all day, or are you going to figure out what Jesus wants and do it?"

Allison felt the hairs on her arm stand on end. She pressed her handbag into her abdomen. "What are you saying?"

His forehead beetled. "You know what I'm saying."

Allison's fingers fumbled with the opening to her handbag. Her voice cracked. "How am I supposed to know what He wants?"

"Good heavens, you're as dense as that son of mine! Not a lick of wits in this whole family." His eyes rose to the ceiling. "Lord, help them." He returned his gaze to Allison. "Well, girl, you're supposed to *ask* Him, that's what. You do know how to pray, don't you? Know how to ask Jesus to help you? To tell you what to do now, huh? You ain't some kind of heathen, are you?"

Allison backed farther away. "Th-that's ridiculous."

Pop grunted.

She reached toward the side door that led out of the exhibit room. "Let's not talk about that . . . that . . ." She couldn't say the name. "Let's not talk about Him now, Pop. Okay? I can't. Not now." Her hand gripped the door's handle.

"Not ever?"

She stepped through the door. She couldn't turn back. Couldn't answer, though his eyes bored a hundred holes in the fabric of her fine silk jacket. But that didn't matter. It was the holes in her heart that hurt. Why couldn't Pop just leave bad enough alone?

Hansi saldu. All breathing. Whispering. Pointing. Watching with wide eyes and blinking stares. Like salmon pulled too soon from the river. Hansi, hansi saldu. How could there be enough breath for them all in this one long room?

Wanasi shifted on his stool. Beside him, a small basket held bits of material that Majapa had called *bottle glass.* Wanasi's bow and a quiver full of arrows sat against the wall behind him. In the corner, a long harpoon leaned against a wooden bench. He put his hand over his heart and felt the flute he'd tucked there. He would not pull it out. He would not play the sacred music for them. Such things were not for the crowds. But it pleased him, having the flute there, like an old friend who knew, who understood the spirit of the Yahi could not be captured by simple arrowheads or bows or toggle-heads tied to harpoons.

More saldu pressed into the room, but Lissie was not among them. Would she come? He waited all through the morning, but she hadn't appeared. Not when he made the arrowheads, nor when he shot the bow, nor when he demonstrated how his people had harpooned the big fish. Why? He needed her. There was so much he could tell these strange saldu, so much he could share with them about his people. Things they should know, things that might make his people live again, if only in the shadows of memory. But no one would understand if he spoke to them. He didn't have the saldu words. Only Lissie would know what to say.

Wanasi picked up a piece of bottle glass and began to chip away at its edges. The glass felt cool against his skin. A bit broke off and spun onto the floor, scattering bits of green light across the shoes of the nearest saldu.

A cry rent the air.

Wanasi looked up.

There, at the front of the crowd, a woman stood with a bundle in her arms. The bundle shrieked again.

Wanasi caught his breath. *Daana?* He stood.

An angry face peeked from the blankets. So tiny, so pink. A miniscule foot poked out beneath the folds.

Wanasi glanced up at the baby's mother. Would she be afraid of him? Would she shrink back if he approached? He reached out one hand. The woman did not draw back. One finger. She didn't move. He touched, ever so gently, the soft skin of the baby's toes. He smiled.

The woman smiled back.

His people had had babies once, but that was long, long ago. So long that he barely remembered it. Too long for the memory to sting.

Wanasi withdrew his hand and returned to his stool. *Chip, chip* . . . The sound of hard rock on bottle glass. His hands moving in the familiar motion. The glass sharpening to a point. And the steady rhythm soothing, drowning the noise of the saldu breath, the rustle of their feet on the floor. He could still feel their eyes pressing him, but they were kind eyes, for the most part. Women and men and children. And some who were not yet men.

Those eyes were not so kind.

Three boys hung their arms over the red-covered rope separating him from the saldu. They spoke words Wanasi did not bother to understand. Words that sounded harsh in his ears. Their fingers pointed. One laughed.

"You stop that!"

Wanasi looked up at the familiar voice speaking through the crowd. A yellow-haired boy appeared beneath the elbow of the woman with the baby, and Wanasi smiled. "Wee-lee!"

Willy scowled at the older boys. "Go on now, or I'll get Dr. Morgan right quick."

The boys pushed their hands into their pockets and slunk into the crowd like coyotes denied their evening feast.

Willy leaned over the rope much like the other boys had done. "Hey, Ishi." Willy grinned. "Came to see you. Almost couldn't squeeze through the crowds, though."

Wanasi flipped the arrowhead in his hand. "Wee-lee, come to see."

"Yeah, I came. How are you doing? Are you happy with all this?" He motioned to the crowd.

The baby started to cry again. Someone coughed. Wanasi shrugged his shoulders. "Aiku tsub."

The door opened at the back of the room, and Wanasi paused. A man with white hair under his nose stepped through. Wanasi sighed and turned toward Willy. "Lissie? Lissie come?"

Willy shuffled his feet. His eyes darted away from Wanasi's. "She's not coming."

"Lissie not come?" Wanasi continued chipping at the arrowhead.

"Look, Ishi, they, they . . ." Willy paused and rubbed his hand over his nose until the skin turned red. "They won't let her, you know." He swung back and forth with the rope beneath his armpits. "They told her she can't see you anymore."

Something cold and awful settled in Wanasi's stomach. "No Lissie?"

Willy sighed. "No, no Lissie. Not anymore."

The cold thing grew and gnawed. "Not ever?"

Willy's cheeks turned the same color as his nose. He shook his head.

"Wee-lee?"

Willy dropped his gaze.

Wanasi's hands fell still. How could this be? And why hadn't Majapa told him? Or had he? A memory flickered to the surface of Wanasi's mind. Majapa mumbling something. Majapa looking ill as he spoke. Wanasi had thought Lissie might be sick too; that's why he hadn't been brought to her garden. That's why they were keeping her from him. But this, this he had not expected. "This not good." The arrowhead tumbled to the floor. He didn't bother to retrieve it.

Willy's eyes leaked. "I'm sorry, Ishi. I'm so sorry." He

backed away, into the crowd. "This is all my fault." With that, Willy turned and disappeared behind the elbows, arms, and backs of the mass of saldu.

Wanasi's voice rose over the noises of the crowd. "Wee-lee!"

But Willy did not come back.

Wanasi looked down at his arrowhead, glinting in the false light. A green arrowhead. Strange, unnatural green. The bottle glass made sharp arrowheads. Good arrowheads. But something about them just wasn't right. Something that would never be right. Not even if he lived with the saldu for a thousand winters.

Thomas leaned against the wall in the Egyptian room. The air clung to him like a damp tissue. It was too warm for November, too warm for the close woven shirt that stuck to his back and underarms. It would be cooler in the big room where Ishi was. But Thomas didn't move. Somehow he felt more at home among the dusty relics of thousands of years ago than with the bustling crowds pressing to get a look at the last living Yahi. At least the mummies couldn't speak, or see, or tell him all the things he should have done, could have done, to make things right. No, the mummies didn't care. The mummies were silent. And so Thomas stayed, watching the few straggling groups that meandered through the Egyptian exhibits.

Of course, he should be on the other side of the wall, in the room where Ishi was. He ought to move out of the shadows, ought to be sure that Ishi was well. But he couldn't. Not yet. He knew what Ishi was doing—making arrowheads, shooting his bow, and watching for Allison. Thomas couldn't face that. Couldn't face the disappointment he knew would be there, knew was his fault.

How had he ever gotten himself into this mess?

A dust bunny tumbled from under a cabinet as a woman walked past. Thomas heard the rumble of voices, the patter of footsteps, and the quick explosion of someone sneezing from another part of the museum. Someone spoke Ishi's name. A child cried. Thomas pushed his shoulder off the wall. He had to move. He had to do his duty. Why was it so difficult?

"There you are, Thom."

Thomas glanced back toward the open doorway. "Dr. Kroeber?"

"Didn't expect to find you skulking in the shadows today." Dr. Kroeber pulled a piece of paper from his jacket pocket.

Thomas shrugged.

"Well, can't say as I blame you, especially after you see this." Dr. Kroeber held out the paper, and Thomas recognized the familiar type of a telegram. "From Sapir."

Thomas's fingers trembled as he took the telegram. "Don't tell me . . ." He glanced over the paper. It felt like he was reading his own obituary. "Can't come . . . middle of a project," he mumbled the words, "impossible." Thomas folded the telegram in half and handed it back to Dr. Kroeber. "Can we get someone else?"

Dr. Kroeber shook his head. "That's not an option. It has to be Sapir. Reynolds made that quite clear in our last meeting."

Thomas stared down at the telegram now dangling from Dr. Kroeber's hand. "What are we going to do, Alfred?"

Dr. Kroeber patted Thomas on the shoulder. "Pray for a miracle, Thom—pray for a miracle."

Thomas swallowed the words like bitter herbs. Pray? For a miracle? That was Pop's job. Not his. He'd stopped believing in miracles.

Dr. Kroeber stuffed the telegram back into his pocket, turned, and left the room. In time, Thomas followed. For a moment, he paused outside the crowded room that held Ishi. He glanced through the door. Through the mass of people, he could just make out Ishi talking to a blond boy at the front. Pope's son? Thomas stood on his toes. He could see Ishi frown. The boy was speaking to Ishi.

Thomas dropped back to his heels. He couldn't do this. He needed some time alone.

A woman with a baby pushed by him, and Thomas watched her, then turned and retreated through a small door and down a corridor that led to his office. Halfway there, he paused. A low, muttering voice sounded from a storage room on his left. The public wasn't supposed to come down this corridor, and the janitor was off for the day. So who could be in the storage room? Their saboteur? He edged toward the door. It was slightly ajar. He leaned closer. The voice came again. Thomas straightened. Pop?

He peeked through the door to see Pop's flannel-covered back leaning near the floor. Whom was he talking to?

"They've made a right mess of things, Lord . . ."

Ah, Pop was praying. Of course. Thomas started to draw back, then hesitated. Pop's prayers should be private, but still he stood there. What could Pop be saying that couldn't wait until he got home?

"An awful mess. That son of mine . . ."

Pop's next words were lost in a mumble that Thomas couldn't understand. He leaned closer.

"Don't know what to do now." Silence drifted through the room for a long moment, and then Pop spoke again. "You know, Lord, this Indian thing is completely out of control."

Thomas pushed the door a bit wider.

Pop was kneeling beside an empty bucket and broken cabinet, head bowed over folded hands. "We need You, Lord Jesus. We need You bad." A hefty sigh echoed through the tiny room. "All right, then, I'll trust You. Don't got no choice anymore." He coughed, straightened his shoulders, and rose from the floor.

Thomas opened the door wider and stepped inside.

Pop turned, a handkerchief clutched in his hand. "Oh, Thomas, my boy. Didn't know you were there." He blew his nose.

Thomas cleared his throat. "Heard a voice. Thought I should investigate."

Pop stuffed his handkerchief into his pants pocket. "I ain't no robber, if that's what you're afraid of."

Thomas's forehead wrinkled.

"Are you the one . . . ?" Thomas couldn't finish the accusation.

A wintry smile passed over Pop's face. "Do you think so, Thomas? Do you really think it's me been doing those things?"

Thomas looked away. They'd been here before, in this place of suspicion and doubt. And then as now, Thomas couldn't make himself believe that Pop would go so far as to sabotage his career. Still . . .

"I don't know what to think anymore. I just don't know."

To Thomas's surprise, Pop chuckled. "Well, thems the

225

most honest words I've heard out of you in some time. Maybe there's a bit of hope for you yet, boy." He motioned toward the place on the floor where he knelt to pray just moments before. "The floor is free, if you want to ask Him."

Thomas looked at the old bucket, at a dark stain on the floorboards beside it, at the smudged rag that had been flung over a hook on the wall above. "Maybe I will, Pop. Maybe I will."

Pop looked into Thomas's eyes. "Something bad happen today?"

Thomas sighed. "Sapir's not coming."

"He's that fancy language fella?"

Thomas nodded. "They're going to take Ishi away. They're going to come and take him, and there's nothing I can do to stop it."

"Ain't there?" He pointed again to the spot on the floor.

Before Thomas could take his advice, footsteps pattered down the corridor. A moment later, a small blond head poked through the doorway. "Dr. Morgan?"

"Hello, Willy."

"I heard what you was saying about Ishi just now." He sidled into the room. "Is it really true?"

"Don't you worry about that Indian, young man." Pop ambled toward the open door. "Enough folks worried about him already. God knows what He's doing."

The look Willy gave Pop wasn't full of assurance but fear. "G-God? *God* knows?"

Pop stopped and looked back over his shoulder. "That's right, boy. Jesus is looking out after us here. Ain't nothing going to take Him by surprise."

Willy turned white. His eyes darted down to his feet.

Thomas reached out and squeezed Willy's shoulder,

much like Dr. Kroeber had done to him earlier. "We'll find some way for Ishi to stay. We have to."

Willy shuffled one foot over the floor. "I-I just wanted you to know, Dr. Morgan, there ain't gonna be no more letters."

Thomas's hand froze on Willy's shoulder. "No more letters? How do you know that?"

Willy looked up, his wide eyes like twin pools about to overflow. "Cause I won't write no more, that's why. Not again." His voice rose. "Not even if I'm offered a whole quarter." He spun and raced out the door. The sound of his footsteps echoed back, followed by Pop's slower ones.

Thomas stared at the half-open door, Willy's last words replaying in his mind. So he'd found the letter writer. But he was no closer to discovering who was bent on sending Ishi away.

With a deep sigh, Thomas turned and knelt in the spot where Pop had prayed.

# TWENTY

Winter grew into a monster. Gray. Cold. With teeth of freezing wind that devoured light and hope, consumed the last bits of happiness that Allison had hoarded from her friendship with Ishi. Winter swallowed it all. All but the aching loneliness she kept hidden from Thomas, from Mrs. Whitson, and on good days, even from herself. But most days, storm clouds blotted the sky, and rain whipped the branches of the maple next door. Then Allison would turn away, close the draperies, and remind herself to forget. To do her duty and dream no more.

Which was what she did. She performed her household duties. She maintained the exhibits at the museum. She cleaned; she cooked; she kept the windows closed against the wind. But nothing helped. There were too many things to remind her of her shame. Too many times when she wished she, too, could be among Ishi's friends. One day he sang a Yahi wedding song onto the Edison wax cylinders. Another day, he told a group of the department's anthropologists a story of a wood duck. Thomas said it took six hours, but Allison wasn't invited to hear even one word. She was exiled. Treated like some disease-carrying vermin, as if she would infect Ishi if she were even in the same room.

So she continued her work alone, took care of her duties alone, did everything a good wife and assistant curator was supposed to do. Alone. But it didn't matter. No one cared. Not even Thomas.

Then one day, something happened. Something Allison didn't expect. The breeze was light that day. It skipped over the waters of the bay and dropped tiny bits of moisture over the streets of San Francisco. Allison wrapped her scarf over her head as she walked home from the museum. The steps to her front door were slick with moisture. And there she found it. A shiny golden jewel on her doorstep. A single acorn glistening on the wet brick. And she knew she was not alone after all. She stood there, the acorn in her palm, feeling its smoothness, basking in its beauty. And she wondered, for the first time in months, about the tale Ishi was never allowed to finish. Did Yuna ever learn the Great Eagle's name? Did she ever call out to him? Had she ever found a way to be clean?

Another acorn came a week later, and another some days after that. And another, and another, until the tiny porcelain bowl on Allison's dressing table was filled with a dozen proofs that she was not forgotten.

Allison held one of the acorns now. It felt so smooth, so warm against her skin. One tiny acorn, reminding her how much she missed Ishi's friendship, missed the story he told only for her. She opened her hand and looked down at the golden surface. Yuna's story should not be lost. She slid the acorn into her apron pocket, then strode over to a small table tucked into the living room corner. She pulled open the top drawer and removed five sheets of paper, a quill, and an inkwell. Then she sat down and began to write.

*It happened in a time long ago, when the moon still shone orange and fat in the night sky . . .*

Pen scratched over paper. Pages filled as Allison relived the story. Page after page she wrote, blowing the ink dry, tucking the finished pages into a bottom drawer of the desk. Hiding them where Thomas would never bother to look. It was *her* story. It would always be hers.

She dipped the quill again, but a knock sounded at the door. She paused, the quill halfway to the page. The knock came again. Louder, more insistent. Only one person would knock like that.

Allison returned the quill to the inkwell and put away the last sheet. She rose and hurried toward the door. The wood shuddered as the caller rapped again. Allison reached for the doorknob, only then noticing the black smudge of ink on the right index finger of her glove. She pulled off the gloves and stuffed them into her pocket. Then she drew a deep breath and opened the door.

Mrs. Whitson stood like a pillar in the doorway. "Good day, Allison."

Allison hid her bare hands in the folds of her apron. "Mrs. Whitson, how nice of you to stop by."

"This is not a social call, my dear." She folded her umbrella and tucked it beneath her arm. "I've come on important business." She swept into the house.

"Business? Thomas isn't here."

Mrs. Whitson unwrapped her scarf and hung it on the hat rack near the door. She placed her umbrella beside it. "I am not here to see Thomas."

"Please, have a seat. Would you like some tea?" Allison reached out and stopped the hat rack from tipping.

"No tea, thank you." Mrs. Whitson perched on the couch. "No gloves, today, my dear?"

Allison stuffed her hands back into her pockets. "Um, I . . . is there something I can help you with?"

Mrs. Whitson smiled. "No indeed. I am here to help you."

"Help me?" Allison lowered herself to the edge of a stuffed chair. "Why?"

"The time has come, my dear, for us to be wise. For us to forget those things behind and make the future what it ought to be." She leaned forward. "I believe both you and I want the same thing."

Allison felt her hands clutch her pockets. "What is that?"

Mrs. Whitson touched the pearls at her neck. "We want Ishi to stay."

Allison nodded.

"The winter is drawing to a close. Spring is coming, and when it does, Mr. Reynolds will come with it. You know what that means."

"Yes, I know."

"And?"

Allison felt a flush of heat beneath her collar. She rose from her chair and for the first time looked directly into Mrs. Whitson's eyes. "What does it matter? Mr. Reynolds has taken him from me already."

Mrs. Whitson twisted her pearls into a figure eight. "Hmmm, yes, I've given that much thought over these last months." She dropped the necklace and pressed a finger to her chin. "Perhaps I judged with too great a haste that night at the dinner party. But still, you acted imprudently."

Allison turned away. "Appearances."

"Exactly. Sit down, Allison."

"Why?" The question choked from her in a whisper.

Mrs. Whitson's voice flowed over her like the smooth water of a winter stream. "Do you remember the first time you saw me at the orphanage?"

Allison did not turn, did not sit. "Yes."

"You were seven years old, I believe. A skinny little thing. Knobby knees, scraggly hair, red nose."

"They told me I had a visitor. They brought me to the blue room, saying someone was there to see me." She had thought that someone would be her mother. But it wasn't.

"Yes, I asked for you. I picked you out of the dozens of little girls. Do you know why?"

Allison turned around. "No, I've never known."

Mrs. Whitson lifted her chin until her gaze caught and held Allison's. "I chose you because I thought you could be more than a knobby-kneed, scraggly haired girl. You were a poor, abandoned child, born of bad blood. Yet I thought that perhaps, with a little help, you could be somebody."

Allison pulled her hands from her pockets. "I am somebody."

Mrs. Whitson's eyebrows rose. "Are you?" The question dangled between them. "You could be. You could be still. I will help you. Again."

Allison dropped her gaze, then sat back down on the chair.

"Do you remember what I told you that day when I met you for the first time?"

Allison's voice caught in her throat. "You told me to brush my hair."

"Yes."

"And to sit up straight."

"What else?"

Allison felt the words freeze in her gut before she could speak them.

"You remember."

She sniffed. "Yes, I remember. I've never forgotten."

Mrs. Whitson reached out and gripped Allison's chin. She raised it until their eyes were level. "I told you to stop crying for a mother who was never coming back. I told you it was time to grow up. Time to forget the past." Her grip softened. "Harsh words, I know. Especially for a little girl. But you needed to hear them. Then. And now."

Allison clutched her hands in her lap until the blood fled from her fingers. "It's hard to forget."

"Yes, I know." She dropped her grip on Allison's chin. "But we must be strong. We must go on. We are women, Allison. If we do not make our dreams come true, no one will."

"But Thomas—"

"No." She raised her hand. "Don't rely on men. Even Thomas. They always fall short of the need. It's time to grow up, my dear. It's time to stop moping and act."

"It's too late for that."

Mrs. Whitson stood and towered over Allison like a great rock cliff overshadowing a rabbit. "Not yet it isn't. Not until I say so."

"What am I supposed to do?"

"You'll know, when the time is right." She leaned closer. "Only you mustn't fail me this time."

Willy lied. Thomas knew that now. The winter had come and stayed and fled. And Ishi was still alive. Dead by winter? It was nothing more than an empty threat written by a boy who had read too many tales.

So why did the thought still haunt Thomas?

Earlier that morning Dr. Pope had come by his office to offer yet more assurances. "You can be sure Willy's not written any more letters, Thom."

"And what does he say about the person who paid him to write the last one?"

Pope grunted. "Nothing more. Seems to feel his silence is a matter of honor. I'm not going to keep asking him about it. I just can't."

And that was that. A dead end, again. So why think any more about it? No one had died. No one.

Thomas tapped his pencil on his desk and glanced down at the order for another box of green bottle glass. "No one has died," he told the order form.

*No one? Nothing?*

Thomas sighed. "Nothing, except perhaps Allison's spirit." He hadn't wanted to admit it. For months, he'd willed himself to believe everything was all right. After all, Allison still prepared his favorite meals, starched his shirts, darned his socks. She kept up with her work at the museum. Her exhibits were flawless. She never complained. The perfect wife, the perfect worker. Yet, sorrow hung around her like fog over the bay. Just as dense, just as impenetrable.

Sometimes he saw her running her fingers through a porcelain bowl of acorns on her dressing table, or staring into the mirror as she brushed and braided her hair before bed. What did she see in the mirror? She certainly wasn't seeing him. Nor hearing him as he laid his hand on her shoulder and asked if everything was all right . . . when he leaned over and kissed her cheek or told her that he cared.

It was as if he were kissing a shadow overlaid with mist. The shadow of a person he once knew and loved.

He grabbed up the order form and stuffed it into his desk. It was time to go home, yet he found his feet reluctant to move toward the door. If he went home, he would have to face her. And the fact that he couldn't make her happy.

Thomas pushed himself back from his desk, rose, and grabbed his coat. He would go home again today, just as he always did. They would sit at the table like strangers, and he would pretend nothing was amiss. Just like yesterday. Just like the day before.

And just like every day, he drove his Model T from the museum, up the hill, and into the alley beside his house. Raindrops the size of grapes splattered on the windshield. A narrow beam of sunlight dripped through the clouds. Thomas watched the ray fade behind a dark cloud, then got out of his Model T, opened the side door of the house, and stepped inside.

He paused. Something was different. There was no smell of roast drifting from the kitchen. No sizzle of pork chops crackling on the stove.

Thomas pulled off his coat and tossed it onto the back of a chair, and then he wound his way to the kitchen.

Allison stood there in front of the back window, as still as a stone in the dark. Her back was to him, her arms wrapped around her waist like a little girl too sad to cry.

He walked toward her. "Allison?" His voice echoed through the kitchen.

She didn't move.

He stepped beside her. Rain pattered on the window, obscuring his view. Outside, branches, touched with green, danced in the breeze. A few pink roses budded on the trellis.

"What's out there? What do you see?"

"The tulips are coming up." She spoke without turning.

He followed her gaze, noticing the tiny sprigs of green where she and Ishi had planted the bulbs last fall.

"Ishi will want to see them."

Thomas turned his back to the window. "Allison, you know I can't—"

For the first time, she looked at him. "Of course you can't, Thomas. You never can." She turned and walked from the room. Down the hallway, a door opened, then closed.

Thomas dropped into a chair. He didn't go after her.

Wanasi couldn't rid himself of the coldness of winter. It seeped into his bones, dripped down his spine, froze along the fine hairs on his neck. He fought it with blankets, with songs, with fires built in his mind. But the coldness remained. He could not defeat it. There were too many ghosts, too many memories in the chill of the wind. It had been winter when the saldu came and stole their blankets. It had been winter when the sickness came. It had been winter when the last of his people died.

Winter was an evil time.

Even here, in his new home among the saldu, it had found him. It hunted him, captured him, and forced him to remember dreams best forgotten. For a time, he believed he could fight it. He continued to show his Yahi skills to the saldu. He shot his bow, made his arrowheads, and sang Yahi songs to a people who would never understand. Some people came regularly; others he'd see only once. They came; they watched; they smiled and wondered about the strange creature before them. He was like a green tree in a forest of white. So they paused, looked, and marveled. To them, he was someone to be gawked at, an exhibit like those dead things in the room beyond. But for a few, he was more. To Majapa; Wee-lee and his father, Popey; the Big Chief they called Kroeber; and of course Lissie. To them he was more than just the last Yahi.

He was a friend.

It should have been enough. But it wasn't. At least not in the cold of winter.

The memory of his people demanded more. They demanded that he finish the tale he began, that he tell Yuna's story. That he finish what he started when he walked out of the woods and into the saldu world. He was failing them. He was failing Lissie.

Wanasi sat on his chair and placed his plate of food in front of him. Beef, potatoes, and an odd green vegetable that they called *broc-lee*. Saldu food. But he didn't mind. It was better than anything he'd found in those three long years he wandered the hills alone. It was good food. It should have been enough.

He looked down at his pants, his shirt, the thick coat they gave him when he complained of the cold. Good clothes. They should have been enough.

Wanasi stood. It was time to answer the call of his people. It was time to finish the story.

He lifted his plate and strode toward the window. With one hand, he opened it. A breeze drifted through the opening. A cold, winter breeze. He clutched his plate in both hands. Soon, they would let him tell his story. Tell it to Lissie. He would make them.

Wanasi reached out his arms and dropped his food out the open window.

# TWENTY-ONE

Thomas heard the roll and flap of the window shade before he reached Ishi's room. The *thump, thump, thump* of the shade being pulled down. Then the whoosh and slap as it again flew up. He smiled and adjusted the tray of food in his hand. Ishi seemed to never tire of the wonder of a window shade. Automobiles, aeroplanes, men on tall bicycles—none of that impressed him. But the simplicity of a retracting window shade, or the beauty of piped water, still captivated him. Those remained the unsearchable wonders of the white man's world.

The shade again flew into place as Thomas pushed open Ishi's door. As usual, Ishi's never worn shoes sat neatly beneath the bed. His blanket was folded, his extra set of clothes tucked in their place on the shelves. And on the opposite wall, the unsmudged mirror reflected Ishi standing by the window, pulling down the shade and running his hand over the smooth surface of the cloth. He tugged the bottom, and the shade again retracted. Ishi grinned. He touched the tiny roll at the top and muttered words Thomas did not need to hear to understand. His expression spoke them clearly enough. *Where did it go?* He pulled down the shade again.

Thomas stepped into the room. "Good afternoon, Ishi. Chicken soup today."

Ishi gave the shade a final tug. It flew to its hiding place. Then he turned. "Majapa come." He glanced toward the doorway behind Thomas. "No Lissie?"

Thomas sighed. Ishi asked for Lissie every time he saw him. "No, Ishi. Not today."

Ishi frowned and walked toward Thomas. He paused and stared down at the steaming bowl of soup on the tray. "No Lissie." He reached out and touched the chunk of buttered bread next to the bowl. Then he pushed the tray into Thomas's chest. "No Lissie. No eat."

Thomas felt his grip tighten on the tray. "No eat? What do you mean? Don't you care for soup today?"

"I no eat. I see Lissie."

Thomas extended the tray toward Ishi again. "Of course you'll eat. You like chicken soup."

Ishi stepped away and folded his hands behind his back. "I see Lissie. I no eat."

"Don't say that!" He looked into Ishi's calm eyes. His gaze swept over the immovable features, the firm jawline, the tilted chin. Fear oozed into Thomas's gut. He butted the tray against Ishi's ribs. "Please."

"No, Majapa."

Thomas's hands shook. The soup sloshed from the sides of the bowl.

Ishi withdrew his hands from his back and took the tray.

Thomas backed away.

With slow steps, Ishi walked to the window, opened it, and took the bowl in his hand. He looked back at Thomas. "I see Lissie. Majapa listen now."

"Ishi, no!"

The soup slid from the upended bowl and landed with a splash on the ground below. The bread followed. Then Ishi brought back the empty bowl and tray and handed it to Thomas.

Thomas took it in hands suddenly numb. "I-I understand." His voice scraped like a carriage wheel over gravel. "I need to talk to Dr. Kroeber." *He'll know what to do.*

Thomas turned and stumbled out the door. Behind him came the roll and slap of a window shade being pulled and released, pulled and released.

He wove his way through the displays in the adjacent room. He had to find Dr. Kroeber. He had to speak to him as soon as possible. But what would he say? How would he explain? He dropped the empty tray onto a table, then leaned over and gripped the table's edge. He lowered his head and closed his eyes. How had things come to this? He'd prayed. He'd hoped. He'd waited. What more did God want of him?

A door creaked open in the far room. Thomas straightened. He would have plenty of time to decide what he'd say to Dr. Kroeber. He'd figure something out on the long way through the city, across the bay, and to the university in Berkeley. He'd have time to craft an explanation, *any* explanation that would make sense.

Thomas strode to a side door and flung it open. "Alfred!" He nearly ran over the man. "What are you doing here?"

"Thom!"

They both spoke at once. "I was coming to see you."

241

Thomas stepped back and opened the door wider. "Has something happened?"

Dr. Kroeber appeared more tussled than usual, with his tie askew and his hair looking as if he had gotten caught in a windstorm. "News, Thom. Surprising news."

Thomas grimaced. "Mine too."

"Your office?"

Dr. Kroeber stepped past Thomas and made his way toward the door that led to the offices. He started speaking again as they reached the long hallway. "Delivered this morning. Most unexpected."

Thomas quickened his pace. "What was?"

Dr. Kroeber chuckled. "Why, a telegram from Dr. Sapir."

"Sapir? But I thought—"

"We all did." Dr. Kroeber opened the door to Thomas's office and motioned him inside. "It seems, Thom, that our Willy wrote one more letter."

"Oh no." Thomas dropped into a chair in front of his desk.

"Oh, yes. But I don't think he was paid for this one."

"Why not?"

Dr. Kroeber clapped his hand on Thomas's shoulder. "Well, from what I gather, Dr. Sapir received a very persuasive letter from one contrite little boy who begged him to come work with Ishi. 'Please don't let them take my friend away' were the exact words, I believe." He pulled up a second chair and leaned back into it. "It seems Sapir's heart was quite moved by the plea."

Thomas sat forward. "Moved? Are you saying—?"

Dr. Kroeber laughed. "Sapir arrives on today's train."

Thomas hit his fist against his thigh and let out a whoop. It was a miracle! *His* miracle. It had come after all.

Dr. Kroeber rested his hands on the arms of the chair. "Now, what did you have to tell me?"

Thomas looked into Dr. Kroeber's face and knew he didn't have the heart to spoil that smile. Besides, maybe it didn't matter anymore. Sapir was coming. Surely now everything would be all right. Ishi would forget about Lissie. And Thomas could get back to life as it ought to be.

Three hours later, Thomas had convinced himself that the trouble with Ishi would simply disappear. Dr. Sapir had come. And he was everything Thomas had imagined. A willow thin man, with a firm grip, sharp eyes, and a voice as melodious as a Greek orator.

Thomas shook hands with his miracle and escorted him through the room filled with Allison's exhibits.

"We've not had time to explain your arrival to Ishi," Dr. Kroeber was telling Dr. Sapir, "but I'm sure he'll be quite pleased."

"*We* certainly are." Thomas paused beside the display of Yahi artifacts. "These are some items from Ishi's tribe. Of course you may use whatever pieces you might find helpful."

Dr. Sapir glanced at the exhibit. "I will need the subject to speak, gentlemen. I assume I will not have to shoot him with an arrow or jab him with a spear in order to get him to do so."

The term *subject* grated on Thomas's nerves. He ignored it, reminding himself again that what mattered was that Sapir had come. "This way." Thomas indicated the door that led to Ishi's room. "I think you will find Ishi most amiable. We hope you enjoy working with him. He is quite a unique person in many ways. A friend, really."

A wry smile curved Dr. Sapir's lips. "Here I thought my purpose was to map the Yahi language. And now I find you

243

have brought me halfway across the country so that the Indian might make a friend. I do believe I will have to adjust my fee structure for this new task."

Thomas swallowed anything further he had hoped to say. Perhaps Dr. Sapir was not what he'd expected after all. But still, he was here. That was all that mattered. For the second time that day, Thomas pushed open Ishi's door.

Ishi was polishing his shoes.

Thomas stepped into the room. "Hello, Ishi. I've brought someone to meet you."

Ishi placed his shoes back under the bed and stood. "Lissie?"

Thomas sighed. "No, not Lissie. Dr. Sapir. He has come to learn Yahi." He stepped aside so Dr. Kroeber and Dr. Sapir could enter the room. "This—" he gestured toward the thin man—"is Dr. Sapir."

Ishi walked up to Dr. Sapir and held out his hand.

Sapir took it. "Nice to meet you, Ishi." He spoke slowly.

Ishi nodded and turned away. He looked out the still open window. An icy wind swirled into the room. He glanced back at Sapir and raised his head. "Nice meet you." He inclined his chin; then he stepped toward Thomas. "No, Majapa. I no speak Yahi. I see Lissie."

Ishi turned and walked out of the room. The door closed behind him.

"Thom, what's going on?" Dr. Kroeber's question echoed through the room like a thunderclap.

"Perhaps I will need that bow and arrow after all," Dr. Sapir muttered.

Thomas stared at the closed door. He could feel Dr. Kroeber's perplexed gaze, could sense Dr. Sapir's sardonic surprise. But he couldn't turn. Couldn't face them.

He couldn't tell them that somehow he had gotten his miracle, but it had come too late.

~~~~~~~~

Wanasi stood in the damp mist and gazed out over the tops of the saldu roofs. In the distance, he could see the glint of stormy water. Nearer, tall trees glistened with moisture. Wanasi held his breath and listened to the slow drip of mist from the leaves. He often walked up this short hill to see the water beyond. Majapa could see him here from the museum, and sometimes Wanasi could see the sun.

But not today.

Above, some great bird swept through the clouds and soared toward the twinkling water. Wanasi could almost see the air move beneath its wings, could hear the mist swirl through the leaves of the trees, could taste the dampness on his lips, and could feel, deep in his bones, the same awful coldness that no ray of sunshine could penetrate. But this time, with the coldness came doubt, and that was colder still. Was he doing the right thing? Would they yield to his will? Was the story truly worth the risk?

Wanasi tipped back his head and allowed the breeze to caress his face. He felt the rub of the saldu clothing on his skin. He listened to the faint sound of saldu voices on the wind. He lowered his gaze and looked at their homes, their horses, their streets. Their world. Nothing was his. Nothing but the story. It was all he had left. All his people had left to give. He would tell it for them. He would tell it for Lissie. For everyone who wept without tears, who wondered, who hurt. Then he would know that he chose well that day when he decided to leave the land of the Yahi forever.

Wanasi heard the rustle of footsteps on wet leaves behind him. He recognized the sound. "Aiku tsub, Wee-lee?"

"Hiya, Ishi." The boy came up to stand beside him. "Thought I'd find you here. Nice view." Willy shook his shoulders like a dog shedding water. "Kinda wet up here, isn't it?"

"Birds fly." Wanasi pointed up at a black silhouette against the gray sky.

"Dr. Morgan says you won't see that language fella. Says you walked out."

Wanasi continued looking into the sky.

"Is it true?"

"Yes."

Willy sniffed. From the corner of his vision, Wanasi could see Willy wiping his arm across his nose. "But I thought . . ."

Wanasi glanced down at the boy's red cheeks.

"I thought Dr. Sapir was going to make everything all right. So why won't you talk to him?"

Wanasi brushed his fingers over the boy's cheek. "Wee-lee, fren." He looked deep into Willy's eyes.

Willy dropped his gaze. "Yes, I know. So why won't you—"

"Lissie fren too."

"Please, Ishi."

Wanasi stiffened his jaw. "I see Wee-lee. I see Lissie." He willed the boy to understand.

Willy reached out and grabbed Wanasi's arm. "But that bad Reynolds man will take you away. Please, won't you talk to Dr. Sapir? For me?"

Wanasi studied the boy's face—the round, pleading eyes, the ghost-colored skin, the pale hair curling around his ears. Willy was his friend. A real friend. Wanasi laid his hand on the boy's shoulder. "Yes. I talk to thin saldu."

Willy smiled.

Wanasi squeezed his fingers tighter. "I talk to saldu. If Lissie help."

"If Mrs. Morgan helps?" Willy nodded his head. "I'll try, Ishi. I promise I will." He threw his arms around Wanasi's waist and squeezed; then he dashed back down the hill.

Wanasi watched him until the boy's golden hair disappeared inside the museum. Then he turned back toward the water.

One day, he knew, the last Yahi would be no more. But perhaps, if he was faithful, Yuna would live on. For Lissie, and for Willy too.

The boy had done his job, just as Agnes had known he would. Now the stage was set, the musicians ready, the actors in their places. She needed only to raise the curtain, and the play would begin. So raise it she did.

Agnes lowered herself onto the leather chair behind the desk in Theodore's study. She folded her hands and leaned forward. "Good afternoon, gentlemen. Shall we begin?"

Three grim faces looked back at her. She nodded to each in turn—Dr. Kroeber, Dr. Morgan, Dr. Sapir, all sitting across from her in chairs lower than her own. Just the right amount of gaslight flickered over the dark walls. Heavy leather-bound books lined the shelves on either side of the desk. A fire crackled in the wood-burning stove. And, as Agnes had insisted, the one window in the room was closed, with the draperies shut tight.

In this room, the shadows were her ally, and the one who sat behind the desk ruled. It had always been so. Today, she needed every ally. For her own sake, and for Allison's too. Today, she must not fail.

Agnes rapped her fingers on the smooth cherrywood. "So, gentlemen, how shall we solve our dilemma?"

The men shifted in their seats.

"According to Thomas here—" she inclined her head toward him—"Ishi refuses to speak with Dr. Sapir unless we allow him to see Allison. But Mr. Reynolds was quite clear in his stipulation that we keep Allison and Ishi separate."

Thomas cleared his throat. "We can give in to Ishi's demand, or we can refuse. Either way, we lose Ishi."

Dr. Sapir rubbed a long finger over the arm of his chair. "Unless I can speak to the Indian, I will be on the train home tomorrow."

Thomas tipped forward. "You can't leave now!"

*Hush, boy. Let me handle this.* Agnes shot a quick look at Thomas, then quelled her irritation. "We know, of course, good Doctor, how valuable your time is. However, we beg you not to be hasty. Surely these intelligent men here will come upon a solution." She swept her hand toward Dr. Kroeber.

Dr. Kroeber rocked back and forth. "Mrs. Whitson is right. We must not lose Ishi." He dug his fist into the chair's arm. "There's got to be a way."

"But what?" Thomas breathed.

"What if—?"

"No, that won't work—"

"Could we—"

"No—"

And so the conversation continued, just as Agnes

planned. It turned, twisted, doubled back on itself. And all the while, Agnes sat, her fingers laced beneath her chin, and waited for the moment to ripen. If all went well, if all went perfectly, she would save Allison, save Ishi, save them all.

Finally, Dr. Kroeber burst from his seat. "Come now, Thom! It is simply not enough to place Allison under Sapir's supervision."

Thomas ran his fingers through his hair. "What else can we do?"

"It's not proper, and Reynolds will know it. We can't get around this thing like that."

"I know, but—"

Agnes felt the tension melt from her shoulders. Soon, very soon, the moment would come.

Dr. Sapir's gaze traveled from Agnes to Dr. Kroeber. "I could use the help, especially if she can understand the language as you say she can." He nodded at Thomas.

Thomas leaned back and groaned. "She can."

"Of course, I will be focusing on writing the language systematically, not just learning to recognize and speak a few words. Is she up to the task?"

Agnes leaned forward, careful to keep her voice calm. "She is. But that does not solve our problem, gentlemen."

Thomas glanced at the fire. His voice lowered like a man who had run too long without seeing the finish line. "We can't have her working alone with a man, whether that's you or Ishi. And Dr. Kroeber and I cannot take the time to be there every moment."

Dr. Kroeber retook his seat. "If only she were a man."

A tremor ran up Agnes's back. The moment had come. All eyes turned toward her. She placed her palms on the desk and caught Dr. Kroeber's gaze with her own. "Since we cannot make her into a man, perhaps what we need is another woman."

Dr. Kroeber's eyes widened.

Yes! He understood. Agnes inclined her head toward him. "Myself, perhaps?"

Dr. Kroeber nodded. "Of course, if you would be willing?"

Agnes repressed the urge to cheer. Instead, she lowered her gaze and nodded. "For the sake of the museum."

"It is preferable to shooting the poor man with an arrow." Dr. Sapir's eyebrow quirked upward.

Dr. Kroeber rubbed his hands together then wagged a finger in her direction. "Yes, that's it! You will supervise Allison's work with Dr. Sapir and Ishi. She will answer to you, and we avoid any appearance of impropriety."

She heard Thomas's quick intake of breath.

Agnes tilted forward, solidifying the decision before Thomas could speak. "Quite a workable plan, I believe, Dr. Kroeber. I will, of course, require complete control of Allison's schedule in this matter."

"Of course."

It was done.

Agnes could see Thomas's scowl from the corner of her eye. She turned and looked directly at him. "Do you have any objections, Dr. Morgan?"

*Don't you dare, Thomas. You had your chance, and you failed. You allowed Allison to risk her reputation. And for what? For nothing! Now it's my turn. I won't make the same mistakes.*

Thomas read her gaze and drew a long breath before answering. "No, no, I suppose not."

Dr. Sapir clapped his hands together. "Good. That's settled then. I shall begin work as soon as this new assistant is ready. Your wife *will* agree to this, Dr. Morgan?"

He nodded slowly, like a man in a dream. "She will. She would do just about anything, I think, to work with Ishi again."

Dr. Sapir raised his eyebrows. "Was this Mr. Reynolds correct then? Are we doing right in bringing them back together?"

"We'll see," Thomas murmured. "We'll see."

Agnes rose to her feet. "We are agreed, then." Her voice sounded a shade louder than she'd anticipated. Quickly, she lowered it. "All of us. Together."

Dr. Kroeber stood. "Yes, we are agreed." His gaze flickered toward Thomas. "We shall allow Allison to work with Dr. Sapir and Ishi, under your exclusive supervision." He smiled at her. "Ishi will agree to work with Dr. Sapir, and Mr. Reynolds will be satisfied. I see no other way. Do you, gentlemen?" He motioned to Thomas and Sapir.

"It is a solid plan," Sapir agreed.

Thomas said nothing. Instead, he rose from his chair and walked toward the door. "I guess I'd better talk to Allison." He hesitated as his hand reached for the doorknob; then he pulled the door open and turned. His gaze fastened on Agnes's, but before he could say a word, Dr. Kroeber and Sapir strode out the open door.

For a moment, Dr. Kroeber paused. "Thank you, Thom. This will work. It has to." Then he hurried down the hallway.

Agnes glided out from behind the desk, her eyes still locked with Thomas's. He knew. Knew what she had done. Knew that she had crafted this meeting as carefully as any playwright. But it didn't matter. She'd done what she had to do, for Allison and for the museum. Thomas had had his chance. And look what came of that. This time, she would see things were done right. There would be no more embarrassing revelations. No more whispers of impropriety.

Agnes strode forward, her heels clicking on the floor as she drew abreast of Thomas. There, she halted. Light tumbled in from the open door, casting a golden glow over the side of his face.

A cynical smile brushed over his lips. "You got what you wanted, didn't you?"

She stabbed him with her gaze. "You left me no choice."

Thomas narrowed his eyes. "So I'll either get my wife back or lose her forever?"

Agnes leaned toward him and lowered her voice to a mere whisper. "You lost her a long time ago."

Fear flashed through Thomas's eyes, and Agnes knew the truth.

That there was no turning back. For either of them.

# TWENTY-TWO

Thomas found Allison in the kitchen, busy at the stove. He watched her scuttle to a cabinet and back again. Steam rose from the pots on the burners. She dropped some spices into a kettle, then plopped a handful of freshly washed green beans into a pot of boiling water. He hated beans, but he'd never told her so.

Water splashed from the pot and hissed like a rattler on the stovetop. Thomas stepped into the kitchen and placed his coat over the back of a chair. "Allison?" He grimaced at the waver in his voice.

She glanced over her shoulder. "We're having lamb chops tonight. Fresh from Roscoe's."

"Hmmm, sounds good." His gaze swept over her yellow dress, clean and crisp, her hair pulled back in a simple but elegant knot, her eyes like two coals, devoid of fire. How he wished he could make them spark again.

She turned back to the stove.

He moved to the kitchen table and laid his hands on the

back of a chair. She was beautiful, standing there with a wisp of hair fallen from the knot to curl over her slim neck. Beautiful, yet inaccessible. Like a fine golden chest, locked tight for fear of thieves and flood. Would today's news be the key to unlock her? If so, was it worth it? He didn't want to lose her. Not to the waters of despair that flowed between them now. Nor to Mrs. Whitson. Yet what choice did he have? Either way, she would slip farther away from him. He gripped the chair until the wood bit into his fingers. *Lord, please . . . I don't want to make another mistake.*

Allison checked under the lid of a second pot on the stove. She picked up a wooden spoon and began to stir. "I heard that Dr. Sapir has come."

"Yes."

"Mr. Reynolds will let Ishi stay then?"

"Well . . ." Allison didn't seem to notice Thomas's hesitation. She nodded. "That will be good for the museum. You must be pleased."

Thomas rocked the chair back and forth. The legs knocked rhythmically on the wooden floor. "Yes, um, about that."

"Hmmm?" She continued stirring. The smell of carrots and cream wafted through the room.

He pulled back the chair. It scraped along the floor in a loud screech. "They've, well, we've decided that Dr. Sapir needs an assistant."

"An assistant?"

"Yes." He spoke the word slowly, wishing she could read his mind.

"That's nice." Her voice held no emotion. "Will you be taking an ad in the paper?"

"No, we, uh, decided Sapir should work with someone Ishi already knows."

"Someone in the department will be eager for the job, I imagine." *Tap, tap*, went her spoon against the metal pot.

"We . . . well—" his words finally escaped in a rush—"we wanted that assistant to be you." There, it was done.

The spoon stopped. Only the sound of boiling beans broke the silence. Allison turned, the spoon dripping. "Me?" She barely breathed the word. "You want me to work with Ishi?"

He winced at the wonder in her eyes. "There's only one thing—"

Her shoulders drooped. "Naturally, there's a catch." She turned back to the stove. The spoon descended back into the pot, stirring, clanking against the side.

*Walk away. Don't tell her the rest.* Thomas swayed on his feet. *Don't open that chest. You'll lose her.* But he couldn't stop now. Allison would have to make her choice. "It's just that you'd have to work under Mrs. Whitson's supervision. She'd arrange your schedule, set your tasks, and oversee your work. With the help of Dr. Sapir, of course."

Allison dropped the spoon. "Mrs. Whitson will supervise me? Is that all?"

Desperation flared through Thomas, then died into embers of defeat. "She'll run your life. You know how she is."

Allison spun around. "Don't be silly. Is that the only problem?"

Thomas gripped the top of the chair tighter. "Yes. That's all." He ground the chair's legs into the floor. "You . . . you want to do it, then?" For a moment, he grasped at the wild hope that she'd refuse. That she'd see the danger and back away.

Allison squeezed her hands together and grinned. "Of *course* I do! Working under Mrs. Whitson won't be any problem at all. You'll see." She stepped toward him. "I'm going to be the *perfect* assistant, Thomas. I promise. You won't need to be ashamed of me." She threw her arms around him and squeezed.

Thomas dropped his grip on the chair and held her close. He inhaled the scent of her hair, felt her soft cheek against his. And for that single breath, he wished it were real. He wished that everything were right between them.

"Thank you." Her words whispered against his ear. She pulled back and smiled up into his eyes. "I'll be the best linguistic assistant Dr. Sapir has ever had."

A loud sizzling sound erupted behind them. Allison turned. "Oh, the beans!" She hurried back to the stove, her skirt swaying.

Thomas again leaned on the chair back.

"You won't be sorry," she called over her shoulder as she removed the pot of beans from the burner. "I won't make a mistake. I'll do everything just like Mrs. Whitson says."

The chair beneath Thomas's hands tipped and clattered to the floor. "That's what I'm afraid of."

But she didn't hear him. No one did, though the words echoed in the sudden hollowness of his heart.

Allison wore her best pair of ecru gloves. They were spotless, perfect. Today, she would leave her shame behind. Today, she would begin to prove she was more than Thomas, Dr. Kroeber, or even Mrs. Whitson ever believed. Today, she would see Ishi again.

The Model T lumbered over a bump in the road as the museum came into view. The building sparkled like a gray jewel in the aftermath of rain. And there, on its steps, stood a figure as straight and inflexible as a hat pin.

"I see Mrs. Whitson is waiting." Allison inclined her head toward the museum.

Thomas glanced her way. She could see the deep grooves in his forehead, the unhappy lines around his mouth. "Are you sure about this?"

She straightened her shoulders. "I'm sure. I can do this. Don't you trust me?"

He sighed. "Of course I do. It's just—"

Allison pressed her gloved fingers to her ears. "Stop it, Thomas. Don't say another word. I don't want to hear it."

His jaw tensed, but he did not speak again. Not as he parked the Ford in front of the museum. Nor when he got out and slammed the door behind him. Not even when he opened her door and helped her from the automobile.

Allison checked her gloves one last time, twitched the folds of her skirt, then mounted the steps toward Mrs. Whitson. A breeze tickled the hair at the back of her neck and played at the ribbons in her hat. And yet, Mrs. Whitson's dress remained motionless, her hair still, her hat ribbons unmoved. It was as if even the wind didn't dare ruffle her.

Allison reached the top of the steps.

Mrs. Whitson's gaze swept over her. "Are you ready?"

"I am."

Mrs. Whitson nodded. "There will be no playing, no wasting of precious time, no idle chitchat." She pressed a handkerchief to her nose.

Thomas opened the museum door and beckoned them inside.

Mrs. Whitson turned and strode forward. "You are to work efficiently and effectively. And report directly to me at the end of each day. Do you understand?"

Allison stumbled over the threshold.

257

"Pick up your feet, child."

"Yes, ma'am."

"You will meet with Dr. Sapir and Ishi each day. You will complete your allotted amount of work and you will go home. This time, there will be no cause for disgrace."

"Yes, ma'am." Allison longed to press her hand to her heart, to calm the rapid beat pounding at her chest. But she kept her hands at her side. She was going to see Ishi soon. That's what mattered most.

Thomas gave her a final, inscrutable look, then hurried away. She wanted to call after him, beckon him back to share her first moments with Ishi. But she quelled the urge. She didn't need Thomas. She didn't need anyone. Just Ishi. And this one last chance to prove herself.

Mrs. Whitson removed a sheet of paper from her handbag. "Here is a list of your responsibilities." She handed the paper to Allison. "As you will see, Dr. Sapir will be working on the mechanics of the Yahi language, and you will be cataloging vocabulary."

*Cataloging?* Allison frowned. She could do so much more! "Just vocabulary? But I thought—"

"What you think is irrelevant. You are not in a position to think but rather to do as you are told."

Allison clenched her fist, then forced her fingers to relax. *It doesn't matter. Think only about Ishi. Think only about the job you need to do.*

"I will expect neatly categorized lists of words with complete definitions, phonetics, and sample sentences for each term. You will focus on words, Dr. Sapir on the language structure. You will have four scheduled hours a day to work with the Indian, in which time you will complete a minimum of two hundred words, with the accompanying information. Any less will be unacceptable."

Allison's breath left in a sudden rush. "Two hundred?"

Mrs. Whitson stopped and turned. One eyebrow lifted. "Is the task too difficult?"

Allison swallowed. "No, I can do two hundred words. I promise." If Mrs. Whitson wanted two hundred words, Allison would do *three* hundred. Somehow she'd manage it. She had to.

Mrs. Whitson continued toward the Indian exhibit room. "Very well, then. As long as you understand the expectations, I will take you to Ishi. And—" she looked over her shoulder—"you must remember to conduct yourself as a proper lady at all times. You must!"

Allison's chin dropped. "Yes, ma'am. I will."

Suddenly, Mrs. Whitson stopped, turned, and gripped Allison's hands in her own. Her voice faltered. "Be wise this time, Allison. Show them you can do this thing properly. Make me proud." For a moment, Mrs. Whitson's gaze grew soft, even caring. She blinked and glanced away.

"I'll remember." Something tightened in Allison's chest. "You won't be ashamed." She felt the warmth of Mrs. Whitson's hands on hers, the grip that was firm yet gentle.

Mrs. Whitson sniffed and released Allison's hands, and her rigidity returned. She stepped forward and opened the door to the exhibit room.

Sweet, lilting flute music, like the song of a bird calling Allison by name, flowed through the doorway. It made her want to run, laugh, throw her arms around Ishi and beg him to tell her more about Yuna. Just before she rushed through the door, her gaze caught Mrs. Whitson's.

"Make me proud."

Allison slowed to a subdued walk and nodded. This was no time for running or laughing or stories told to amuse. It was no time for music. She clutched her handbag to her chest and willed herself to ignore the call of Ishi's song.

A man with spectacles and a long nose stood outside Ishi's door. Mrs. Whitson introduced him as Dr. Sapir.

Allison nodded in polite acknowledgment, and then the moment came.

Mrs. Whitson opened Ishi's door. The flute music stopped.

Allison stepped inside the room.

As if in slow motion, Ishi turned from where he stood at the window. The flute shook in his hand. His eyes crinkled as he breathed her name. "Lissie?"

The sound was like a warm breeze encircling her. She savored it. Savored the welcome in his eyes, the joy of his smile, the knowledge that he, at least, had not blamed or condemned her. "Hello, Ishi." She reached out with one arm. Then she moved forward, intending to cross the room and take his hand in hers. But before she could, Mrs. Whitson's fingers descended on her arm. Allison stopped.

Mrs. Whitson's eyes flashed a warning.

Dr. Sapir moved in front of Allison, blocking her view of Ishi.

Mrs. Whitson loosened her grip and turned toward the window. "Ishi, you remember Dr. Sapir. You will be working with him now."

Allison moved sideways until she could see Ishi glancing from her to Dr. Sapir, and back again. At Ishi's slow nod, Allison released a breath she hadn't even known she was holding.

Dr. Sapir rubbed his hands together and stepped back

toward the door. "Good, then. Shall we get to work? Dr. Kroeber has assigned us a room."

Mrs. Whitson steered Allison down the hall to the room, Ishi and Dr. Sapir following. In the middle of the room sat a table with a stenographer's phonograph, a stack of Edison wax cylinders, paper, an inkwell, and three fountain pens. Two electric lights chased dismal shadows over the gray walls. Behind the table, a long bench lay covered with a number of familiar items—an arrow, a blanket, a basket, a bow, apples, a few heads of wheat, a drum, and a ceramic bear.

Dr. Sapir snapped on a small lamp near the door. "Come in, Ishi, Mrs. Morgan. Please take a seat." He motioned toward the ladder-back chairs surrounding the table.

Mrs. Whitson moved forward. "Allison, you will sit here." She touched the chair closest to the door. "Ishi will sit there." She pointed to a chair on the opposite side.

Allison and Ishi took their seats.

Dr. Sapir grimaced and pulled out a chair between them. "Now that we all know precisely where to sit," sarcasm laced his tone, "let's begin by hearing Ishi talk. I'd like to get a feel for the cadence and basic structure of his language. Mrs. Morgan, if you please?"

Allison smiled at Ishi. He appeared thinner, paler than she remembered, and for a moment, she was reminded of how he looked the first time she'd seen him there on the edge of the ferry—skinny and cold, with that blanket wrapped around his shoulders. But that was a lifetime ago.

"Allison?" Mrs. Whitson spoke sharply from the doorway. "Ask Ishi to speak."

Allison looked across the table into the brown eyes searching hers. "Talk to me, Ishi," she said in Yahi. "The man wants to hear you."

Ishi began, as somehow she knew he would, with Yuna. There was no greeting, no mention of the long months apart. Only Yuna. Just as if those months had never been.

*Summer turned to autumn, and Yuna grew lonely. Many days the eagle soared above her, but she did not call out. Did he see her there, far below in the forest? She hoped he did. She hoped he did not. Foraging among the trees had made her clothes ragged. Her face was splotched with dirt. Scratches covered her arms—*

"What is he speaking about?"

Allison jumped at Sapir's sharp question. For a moment, she had forgotten the man was there. "He is telling a story."

Dr. Sapir tapped his pen on the page in front of him. "I believe it would be better to start with more simple sentences. Please have the Indian describe the objects on the bench behind us." He pointed over his shoulder.

Allison leaned forward and fixed her gaze on Ishi. "No more Yuna now. Dr. Sapir wants you to talk about those things on the bench." She gestured toward the arrow and basket.

Ishi glanced at the bench and frowned. "I do not want to speak of those things. I want to tell you about Yuna."

Allison adjusted her hat. "I know, but you can't now. We have to do what they tell us."

"You should be writing words now, Allison." Allison's shoulders tensed at Mrs. Whitson's cold voice from behind her. "Unless there is a problem."

"No—" Allison shook her head—"it's fine. Everything's fine."

"You can be writing as Ishi tells the good doctor about the items on the bench. There is no time to waste, you know. We must show Mr. Reynolds we are making progress now that Dr. Sapir is here."

It was as though someone squeezed a band around her throat. Allison forced words out despite her discomfort. "Yes, ma'am. Of course."

Dr. Sapir laid down his pen and laced his fingers together. "Thank you, Mrs. Whitson. Your help, as you know, is invaluable." He smiled. "However, we must not take up more of your time."

Allison turned to see Mrs. Whitson arch her eyebrows. "Are you throwing me out, sir?"

Dr. Sapir chuckled. "Not at all, ma'am. Though I do recall that Dr. Kroeber asked to see you."

Mrs. Whitson regarded him for a long moment. "Very well, then." She stepped through the doorway. "I will leave you to it." Her footsteps clicked down the hall.

Dr. Sapir turned again to Allison. "Proceed, please." He picked up the pen. "And do feel free to change seats if you wish. I don't believe I saw your name on that one."

Allison remained in her chair and tried to make her voice sound firm. "Tell me about the things on the bench, Ishi. Describe them to me."

Ishi crossed his arms over his chest. "No. I must tell you about Yuna."

"Not now, Ishi, please. The story doesn't matter now."

Ishi raised his chin. His jaw became like stone. "The story is all that matters, Lissie. Don't you see?"

Allison sighed. This wasn't going at all as she'd planned. She could feel Dr. Sapir's eyes on her, judging her, scorning her for her incompetence. She could hear Mrs. Whitson's doubts ringing in her ears. She could see Thomas's face, dis-illusioned, accusing.

No! She would not disappoint them. She would not fail. Ishi *would* cooperate. He would do as she asked. "All I see is what's on that bench back there. Tell me about those things, Ishi!"

Ishi didn't even look at the bench. He folded his hands on the table, closed his eyes, and began to speak. "Listen, then perhaps you will see."

*Winter came to the forest. The beaver no longer swam in the stream, and the moon shone like ice in the sky. Yuna grew so cold that she shivered even in the day. Even when the sun looked through the clouds and dropped its light upon her. Wind whistled through the holes in her clothes and bit at her skin. But Yuna did not have a fur to wrap around her. She had nothing but her one dirty dress. Torn, old.*

*Then one day when the wind blew most bitterly and the snow fell like great stones from the dark sky, she heard a sound near the grinding rock. She was not alone. There stood the Great Eagle, his feathers gleaming against the snow.*

"He is talking about the objects now?"

Allison bit her lip. "Not yet."

"Mrs. Morgan—"

"I know." She put her palms on the table and leaned toward Ishi. "Listen to me. You must stop the story."

"Yuna hid her face."

"Please, Ishi." Allison reached across the table. "Not now."

Ishi straightened, then tipped forward until his face was

level with hers. His voice dropped to a whisper. "Do you hear the eagle's call, Lissie? Do you know his name?"

"No, I don't." Allison pushed back in her chair and rubbed her hands over her suddenly chilled arms. "How can I know?"

Ishi turned his face away from her and continued speaking.


*Come to me, little one." The eagle's voice was like the wind, only warmer.*

*Yuna looked up. "But I will soil your feathers, Great Eagle."*

*The eagle spread his wings wide. "You cannot soil me. Come."*

*The eagle's feathers looked soft and warm. And Yuna was very cold. She crept toward the eagle until she sat within the circle of his wings. The eagle wrapped his feathers around her. "Are you warm now?" he whispered.*

*"I am," she answered. "Why haven't you come to me before? I've been so cold."*

*"I have been here always, but you did not call for me."*

*"How can I call you? I do not know your name."*


Sapir shot a glance at Allison, and panic rose in her throat like bile. She leapt from her seat. "No, Ishi! Stop!" She could taste the fear in her voice.

Ishi halted. His eyes grew round as though he, too, could taste her fear.

"We have to do as the man asks. You must tell me about the things on the bench. If not . . ." She couldn't finish the sentence.

Ishi looked down at his hands.

For the first time, Allison noticed the ticking of Dr.

Sapir's pocket watch. *Tick, tock, tick* . . . The sound seemed to grow louder until it filled the whole room. Allison waited.

Then as if the words were bitter, Ishi began to speak. "The arrow is made of yew. The arrowhead is white. It is made from bone. The basket is woven poorly. It would not hold many fish."

Relief washed through Allison. "He's doing it now. Starting with the yew arrow."

Dr. Sapir nodded, then began scratching notes on his pad of paper.

"Keep going, Ishi."

"The apples are wrinkled. They will not be sweet."

Allison reached for a pen and paper and began to write the Yahi words with their definitions.

"The bear is made by a saldu. The saldu maker does not know the bear. A bear does not stand like that. The bear is brown."

Hours passed, and weariness settled over Allison. Darkness crept beneath the door. The words blurred on the page before her, but Ishi continued speaking, his voice dull, lifeless. He spoke of the color of the floorboards, the shadows on the wall. He spoke of anything, everything—and of nothing at all.

Finally, Sapir replaced his pen in the holder. "Good, good. That's enough for today." He waved his hand at Allison. "Mrs. Whitson will be waiting for your report. You may go."

Allison stood and stretched her back.

Dr. Sapir rose. "May I see your list before you go, Mrs. Morgan?"

She gave it to him.

Dr. Sapir's eyes narrowed as he scanned the pages. "Well

done." He tapped the edges of the papers until they formed a straight line. "Mrs. Whitson should be pleased." He handed the list back to her. "Perhaps tomorrow she will even allow you to choose your own chair."

Allison took the pages as if they had suddenly turned to gold. She'd done it! Tomorrow would be the same. And the tomorrow after that. Soon, very soon, they would all have to say "well done."

She started for the door, but before she reached it, Ishi began to speak again. His voice was no longer lifeless.

*For a long time, the eagle was silent. Yuna feared she had offended him by asking for his name. But finally, the eagle spoke. "You will know my name when the time is right, Yuna. I will show it to you soon. Then you will know who I am."*

Allison whirled around. "Ishi?"

He rose from his chair, his gaze as soft as his whispered words. "Soon, Lissie. Very soon the Great Eagle will come."

# TWENTY-THREE

Allison felt it first as a tickling in the back of her throat. Then her nose stuffed, her ears plugged, and a cough came. A cough so bad that it made purple spots appear before her eyes every time it shook her. She clutched a handkerchief and fought to hide the symptoms. There was no time to be ill. No time to pause for a throat that ached, for a head that spun.

Thomas opened the door of the museum and peered at her through squinted eyes. "Are you sure you're feeling well? Your cheeks are flushed."

Allison dabbed her nose with the bit of lacy cloth in her hand. "It's just the brisk morning air."

"And the cough?"

Allison frowned. "A little dry throat from the winter weather. And some sniffles. Nothing to be concerned about." She made her voice confident as she walked into the museum, but she wasn't so sure. It had been over a week now, and the cough was only getting worse. She hid it most of the time, but if it didn't improve . . . She twisted the handkerchief between her fingers and glanced back at Thomas. "Don't worry about me. I feel fine. And I have work to do." She strode toward the room where she and Dr. Sapir met with Ishi.

"Just don't be foolish, Allison," Thomas called after her. "Mrs. Whitson's approval isn't worth it."

"Oh yes, it is," she murmured, too low for him to hear. She listened to Thomas's footsteps echo across the room toward the long hallway that led to his office; then she continued to the workroom.

Dr. Sapir and Ishi were already there. "Ah, you've arrived." Dr. Sapir rose from his seat. "And not a moment late."

Allison smiled. "Thank you." She glanced around the room. "Where's Mrs. Whitson?"

"Somewhere between Market and Polk, I'd say."

"Pardon me?"

Dr. Sapir grinned. "She had to take a trip into the city today, but fear not!" He waved his hand in the air. "The dear lady promised to return to examine your daily work so that you may sleep in peace tonight. So all is well."

Allison pulled out a chair.

"Oh, you mustn't sit there."

Allison dropped her grip on the chair and turned, wondering if this was yet another of Sapir's jokes. "Why not? Is one of the legs loose?"

"Um, no." Sapir's neck reddened. "But that's not your chair."

She glared at him.

He laughed, and then his voice turned serious. "No, really, Mrs. Morgan. Could you and the Indian work in the outer room today? I know it's not allowed, but . . ."

Allison's eyes widened. "Just the two of us? Alone?"

"Don't make it sound so outrageous. It's just that I really must have some quiet to concentrate on these recordings." He pointed toward the wax cylinders onto which Ishi had sung a number of songs the day before. "Would you mind? I won't tell Mrs. Whitson if you won't."

Allison rubbed her nose with the handkerchief. He trusted her! Sapir trusted her to work alone with Ishi! She almost clapped her hands, but instead she tucked her handkerchief into her pocket and smiled with what she hoped was quiet dignity. "No, of course not. Besides, hearing Ishi's disembodied voice on those recordings is too eerie for me. I don't want to be here if you'll be playing those."

"Boo!" he teased. "Go on, get out of here. I'll even let you take your chair if you wish."

"Come on, Ishi." She motioned for him to follow her into the other room. She would be able to accomplish so much today! Two weeks had passed since the first day she'd worked with Ishi, and in that time she'd kept him from wasting time on Yuna's story. She'd kept him on task, and her work had flowed. Mrs. Whitson seemed pleased enough, but today she could do even more. Today, Mrs. Whitson would be especially proud.

Allison sneezed, then coughed into her handkerchief. She rubbed her chest. If only it weren't for this annoying cold! She sniffed, then led Ishi into the larger room where she found two chairs and a small table to use as a writing desk.

Ishi pulled his chair close to the window. "Aiku tsub, Lissie?" They were the first words he had spoken to her that day.

"Yes, yes, I'm fine." Her cough belied her words. She pressed her handkerchief to her mouth, then dipped her pen into the inkwell. The pen hovered for a moment over the stack of papers she'd placed on the desk. "Let's begin with the names of animals and plants."

"I will tell you about the eagle. And the coyote." Ishi folded his hands and leaned forward in his chair. "Especially about the eagle."

Allison sneezed. "Maybe later. For now, just the words."

Ishi sighed. "Will there be a later, Lissie? Are you certain?"

For a long time, Allison didn't answer. Then she tapped her pen on the edge of the paper. "The words, Ishi. We must focus on the words."

After a moment, Ishi nodded.

For hours, Ishi spoke, then waited for Allison's pen to flow in long sentences over the paper. The pages filled. The shadows grew long. Finally, Ishi stood and pulled his chair closer to Allison. "I am tired of words now. Let me tell you about Yuna. There is not much time left."

Allison blew her nose, then pulled out a clean piece of paper. "Just fifty more words. Then we'll stop."

"No more words. Not today."

Allison shuffled through the sheets piled to one side of the desk. They had done well. Three hundred terms. But not well enough. She could do more. She knew she could.

Ishi's voice broke through her thoughts.

*All through the dark winter, the eagle came and kept Yuna warm. She would wave to him as he flew overhead, and he would swoop down and tuck her into his wings.*

Allison opened her mouth to stop him, but instead she coughed. She pressed the fourth handkerchief she'd used that day to her forehead. Perhaps a few minutes of Yuna's story wouldn't hurt.

*Through the long nights, he amused her with stories of life beyond the clouds. He told her of the lands he had seen and how he would take her there someday.*

*But Yuna only laughed. "I cannot go to the clouds," she said. "I am too dirty."*

*"Yes," the eagle replied. "You cannot go to the clouds like that."*

*Yuna was very sad. It was the first time the eagle had mentioned her clothes.*

Allison felt a chill travel from her spine down to her heels. She should stop him now. She should stop this story before it was too late. But Ishi kept on.

*When the spring sun shone down on the earth, Yuna was no longer cold. Soon, she did not wave to the eagle when he flew above her. Sometimes, she would see him on a branch in the forest, and he would look at her.*

*She would remember her clothes and the words he had spoken about the clouds. Then Yuna would hurry away into the trees where he could not see her.*

*One day as she was gathering nuts near the pond, Coyote came out of the brush. He looked at her with eyes like arrows. "How dirty you are, Yuna," he whined. "I'm surprised the eagle is not ashamed to speak with you."*

*"But what can I do?" Yuna cried. "I've tried washing, soaking, scrubbing, but it only makes it worse."*

273

*"You must cover yourself, Yuna," Coyote said. "Perhaps the eagle will not notice then."*

Allison closed her eyes and leaned her head back until her chin pointed at the ceiling. Her temples pounded. Her throat burned. She swallowed, focusing on the story instead of the pain.

*Yuna plucked leaves from the bushes around her and poked the stems through the holes in her clothes. Soon, leaves covered her.*

*"That is much better," Coyote said. "You are beautiful now. As beautiful as the eagle."*

*Yuna stood straighter. She was beautiful. The eagle would be glad to be her friend now. "Thank you, Coyote. I will look at myself in the water." She stepped over to the pond and looked, but what she saw was not beautiful. Bits of dirty clothes peeked through leaves that lay askew over her chest. The wind picked a leaf from her skirt and settled it on the grinding stone.*

*Then Yuna remembered the eagle.*

Ishi fell silent.

Allison opened her eyes. "Is that all?"

Ishi studied her for a long moment. "It is getting late, Lissie. You are pale."

She massaged the back of her neck. "Am I?"

"Except for your cheeks." He leaned toward her. "They are very red. You must go home."

Allison jolted upright, only then noticing how low the sun had slipped in the sky, how gray the light looked as it spilled through the window. "No, I can't." She grabbed her pen and poised it over a fresh sheet of paper. "Mrs. Whitson hasn't come yet. I must show her my work. We haven't done enough."

Ishi's voice softened. "It is enough for today."

Allison scribbled the word *coyote* on the paper. "We have to do the words. I shouldn't have let you tell the story for so long."

Ishi reached out and pulled the paper from beneath her pen. "I will tell you more of the story tomorrow." He placed the paper on top of the completed ones. "I will help you with the Yahi words tomorrow. Now go home, Lissie. It is time for rest."

Her hand trembled. "I can't."

Ishi removed the pen from her fingers. "I am tired too."

"There's not enough time."

He placed the pen back in its holder. "There is time, Lissie. There is always time to choose well."

She waved away his words.

He stood and looked down at her with eyes as deep and troubled as the ocean on a windy night. "How many, Lissie?" The question washed over her.

"How many what?"

"How many words will it take for you to be free?"

Thomas stretched out full length in bed and hooked one arm behind his head. The sheets rustled as he laid his other hand on his stomach and watched the dawning sun gild the windowsill. The swath of sunlight lengthened until it splashed across the middle of the bed and sent currents of warmth up his chest. Thomas smiled. It was going to be a beautiful day. A day when hearts would sing, couples would stroll on the beach laughing, and he and Allison could remember what it meant to be in love. A good day. A day to do things right.

He rolled over and put his hand on Allison's back. His fingers ran down the length of her braid, which trailed over the covers toward him. He felt the softness of her hair against his fingers, then lifted the end of her braid to his lips and breathed in the fragrance of soap and lavender.

Allison turned onto her back, pulling the braid from his fingers. "Hmmm," she mumbled, her eyes still closed in sleep.

Thomas leaned closer. "Morning, love."

Her eyes flew open. "Morning? Have I overslept?" She sat up.

"No, it's early still." Thomas's hand pressed into her shoulder until she sank back to the bed. Then he tipped onto one elbow and gazed into her still-sleepy face. A line from a wrinkle in the pillow creased one of her temples. He traced the line with his finger, then brushed his knuckles across her cheek. "I have to go across the bay to the university this morning. Do you want to come with me?"

Her eyebrows puckered. "What for?"

Thomas shrugged one shoulder. "Just so we can spend some time together. Are you feeling well enough?"

She sniffed. "The cold's almost gone. That chamomile tea is quite the cure."

Thomas tucked a stray hair behind her ear. "I thought maybe we'd take a short drive up the coast afterward. There's that little restaurant overlooking the ocean."

Allison sat up. "That will take all day. What about my work?"

Thomas pushed himself to a sitting position as well. "Your work will still be there tomorrow."

Allison's frown deepened. "You know I can't do that. I have to work with Ishi today. That little cold put me behind. I can't miss a whole day now."

"You've been working with Ishi every day, every hour, it seems. No matter how you've felt." Thomas sighed. "You deserve one day off. I've hardly even seen you these past weeks."

"But Mrs. Whitson—"

Thomas flopped back down onto the pillow, causing Allison to bounce up beside him. He looked out the window, away from her. "What about Mrs. Whitson?"

He heard Allison fluff her pillow. "Well, she hasn't said anything about having a day off. I don't think she'd approve."

Thomas sat up again and flung his legs over the side of the bed. "Why don't you run and ask her permission, then?" His words crackled between them. "Maybe if you bend down and kiss her toes—"

"Oh, Thomas. Stop." The bed creaked behind him as Allison rose. "I just don't want to give her the impression that I'm shirking my work."

Thomas grunted as he leaned over to pick up a slipper.

"She might think—"

He hurled the slipper across the room. It slammed into the wall, then fell into a potted ficus. "She might think! She might think what?"

"Well . . ."

Thomas glared at his wife over his shoulder. She stood there, like a prim, white post, dressed in a starched nightgown with a high neck and long sleeves. Unapproachable.

Unassailable. Utterly unaware of how her choices were tearing them apart.

He turned back around. "I'll tell you what she might think, then. She might think that you have your own life. That you can make your own decisions. That she isn't the master of us both." He threw his hands in the air. "Heaven forbid she think that!" Thomas lurched from the bed, stomped across the room, and retrieved the slipper from the ficus pot.

"This job with Ishi is important to me, Thomas."

He heard her rustling behind him as she spoke, but he didn't turn around.

"Obviously." Bitterness stained his voice.

"I don't ask you to dodge your duties at the department."

Thomas shoved his foot into the slipper, not caring that he nearly split the seam. "Of course you don't. You don't ask for anything." He grabbed his robe from the hook behind the door and threw it over his shoulders. "Forget it. Go to the museum. Do your job. Show Mrs. Whitson what a good little worker you are. And someday, maybe, she'll be impressed." He stormed out the door.

"Thomas . . ."

He didn't stop. He didn't even pause. What was the point? It wouldn't change anything. He had lost her. He knew it, even before he asked her to come with him to Berkeley, before he mentioned a drive up the coast. He knew it as soon as Mrs. Whitson looked him in the eye.

Thomas opened the door to the washroom and pulled a towel from the hook near the basin. He opened a tiny, high window and breathed deeply of the salty air. From outside, the sounds of a city just waking blew through the window and danced around him. The rumble of carts, the beep of a horn, and way off in the distance, the sound of church bells ringing in the new day. He sank onto a wooden chair and leaned his head against the wall.

*Lord, help us. Give us, give me* . . . The words scattered from Thomas's mind, and he knew he no longer had the heart to pray for a miracle. Now he just asked for hope. Hope that the truth would come to free them before it was too late.

# TWENTY-FOUR

The room fluttered around Wanasi's head like a hundred squawking crows. He blinked once. Then twice. And the room came into focus. The same room they took him to every day, the same table, the same stale air, the same long bench covered with items gathered from the dead. He was tired of it. Tired of the long hours of speaking about nothing. Weary of talking into the strange tube that captured his voice and caged it on fat circles. Worn out with watching that stiff woman come and hover and strut as if she were the chief of their small tribe. He missed the trees, the flowers, the wind that danced through the leaves and made them glitter in the afternoon sun. He missed planting those secret flower-stones, called *two-lips*, in Lissie's garden.

But most of all, he missed telling Yuna's story to someone who cared.

Lissie cared once. Now nothing mattered to her but pleasing that hard, gray-haired woman. Lissie didn't see anymore. She didn't understand.

Wanasi looked at her across the table. Her hat perched on the top of her head, her hands hidden in spotless gloves, her brow furrowed in concentration. He tipped toward her, but she did not look up. Instead, she kept pushing her writing stick over the white sheets until black marks covered one sheet, then another, then another. It would never end.

He allowed his gaze to wander to the man hunched over his own sheets in the corner. There, too, the writing stick scratched and flowed and made marks Wanasi didn't understand. Marks that somehow were more important than life or laughter or songs in the wind.

Lissie's writing stick paused. She glanced up. "Just a few more minutes. Then we'll start again."

Wanasi turned away. He didn't want to think about Lissie or the man in the corner. They did not know him. They did not see that he was more than words, more than a string of sounds that would die with him, or a voice that spoke a language shared only by the dead. Lissie knew that once, but she had forgotten. In these last weeks, she had forgotten many things.

A cough tore through Wanasi's chest. A strange taste filled his mouth. The taste of meat cooked over too little fire. He shuddered again, but now he knew it wasn't just the winter. Something had gone wrong somewhere in his middle. The coldness was growing in him like ice spreading over a lake. But this ice was mixed with a strange fire in his chest that made his breath burn within him while his limbs shivered.

Wanasi rubbed his hands over his arms and felt their thinness. He had come to these strange saldu because he could no longer endure the loneliness. He had come to tell a story one last time. But he was still alone. The story was only half told. Perhaps he should not have left the graves of his people. Perhaps he would return to them soon.

Lissie's writing stick slowed.

Wanasi placed his palms on the table. "Rest now?"

Lissie shook her head. "Not yet. We've more work to do."

He dropped his gaze to his hands, folded now on the smooth wood before him. They looked thin and pale. Like the hands of his mother before she took the long journey south.

Another cough shook through him, lighting fire in his breast.

Lissie looked up and frowned. "Let's move to words about the water now."

Wanasi sighed. For hours and hours he had spoken already. His throat hurt. His mouth felt dry. He had started early in the morning with that "Sap-ear" man. And now Lissie was pushing, pushing, always wanting more. Could he go on? Were there more words within him?

"Water words, please, Ishi. Then we'll be finished."

Wanasi nodded. If he gave her what she wanted, perhaps she would listen as he told her more of Yuna's tale. Even if it was only a little more. That was enough to keep him pressing forward, to give him hope. He wet his lips. "Water runs quickly in the spring. Streams dry in summer. Rains come. Noisy chatter of water over rocks. Water speaks to stone. Stone speaks to land. Land speaks to sky." He paused.

Lissie's writing stick flew over the thin white sheets. "Go on."

Wanasi drew a pained breath. "Water falls as snow in winter. Snow crunches under hunter's feet. Hunter sees tracks in snow. Tracks of deer. Tracks of big cat. Tracks of small rabbits." He stopped. His vision blurred. He could see the tracks now in his mind. Tracks of animals, birds, and sometimes of saldu. But never, never the small tracks of a Yahi child. No tracks of tiny feet running to the larger feet of a mother, or circling in a game, or dancing to the sound of flute music. Only deer and rabbits and booted heels of pale saldu hunters. If only there had been children. If only the winter had not come at all.

Another cough ripped through Wanasi's throat. He struggled to catch his breath.

For once, Lissie stopped writing. "Aiku tsub?"

Wanasi could not answer. All was not well; it was not good. But he couldn't tell her that. If he did, he would never be allowed to share even small snatches of Yuna's story. He pushed his chair back from the table. "Enough words. Yuna, now."

"Not again, Ishi." Lissie set aside a sheet covered with marks and placed a clean sheet in front of her. "Mrs. Whitson will be here in a moment to see how well I've done."

Wanasi thumped his hand on the table. "Listen to Yuna's story now, Lissie. Listen, until stiff woman comes."

A smile almost reached Lissie's lips, but it fled before Wanasi could be sure he saw it.

Lissie placed her pen on the table. "Okay, but just a little."

"Yes. Just a little." He didn't think he had the strength for more.

Lissie rearranged the sheets on the table while Wanasi pressed his back into the slats of the chair. He would tell his story, would tell it though his throat felt as if it were made of jagged stones in a river. He would squeeze the words through. He would find a way to tell her what she needed to hear. He would. He must.

Lissie again picked up her writing stick.

Wanasi pulled in a pained breath and began.

*Coyote screamed. A terrible scream. Of hate. Of pain. Of anger. A scream that shook the leaves free of the trees above them. It made Yuna shiver to hear it. She turned, but Coyote was gone. He had fled into the trees. Silence followed him.*

*"What are you wearing, Yuna?" It was the eagle's deep voice from behind her.*

*Yuna dared not move. She looked at the leaves poking from her clothes. She looked at the dirt on her arms. And she was ashamed.*

*"Turn around, Yuna."*

*But Yuna ran. She hid behind a bush.*

*The eagle waited.*

*Yuna hid her face in her hands. "Go away! I don't want you to see me now. I won't come out." She peeked through her fingers. The eagle was gone. "I cannot bear for him to see me. I will stay here until I find a way to be clean."*

*Day after day, Yuna hid in the shadows and scrubbed at her clothes. And each night Coyote came to her and said, "You are very dirty, Yuna. No one will love you now."*

Wanasi locked his gaze on Lissie's face, willing her to hear, to understand.

But she did not look back at him. Instead, she rapped the end of her writing stick on the white sheet in front of her, while her eyes moved with restless scrutiny over the marks she'd written there.

Wanasi reached out and touched her hand with his own. *"Listen*, now. Write later."

She dropped the writing stick. Her eyes darted to the man in the corner.

He touched her hand again. He needed her to listen. He needed her to hear.

Finally, she looked at him. So, Wanasi continued.

*Summer came, hot and sticky and dry. Mud turned to dust and blew through the trees. The sun beat on Yuna until her skin turned dark with earth and heat. The river slowed. Clouds vanished. The sky pressed down like a bearskin wrapped too tightly.*

*Then Yuna recalled other days when the sun beat down and the eagle came to spread his wings and shade her. She remembered how he comforted her in winter and told her stories of life beyond the trees. "I will stop hiding now," she said. "I will face the Great Eagle."*

*As she spoke, the eagle landed beside her. "Hello, Yuna. Why did you run from me?"*

*"My clothes are torn and dirty. My hands are stained with earth, and my face is full of mud. No one will love me now."*

*"I love you," said the eagle.*

*Yuna looked down at her tattered, soiled garments. She saw the stains on her hands, the streaks of dirt on her arms. "Then it doesn't matter that I am dirty?"*

*"It matters," replied the eagle. "It matters very much."*

Lissie gripped the writing stick again, but she didn't write. Instead, she clutched it tight, as if to ward off words she did not want to hear.

Wanasi studied her pale fingers for a long moment. Then he nodded. Maybe she did understand after all.

*What will I do?" Yuna asked. "I cannot clean them. I cannot clean me. I have gone to the river. I have scrubbed in the turtle's shell. But the stains will not come out. There is nothing I can do to be clean."*

*Then the eagle did something that Yuna had not heard him do before. The eagle laughed. A great, ringing laugh that was like a song, a story, and a promise all in one. It was a laugh of great happiness.*

*Yuna did not understand. "Why do you laugh, Great Eagle?"*

*He looked at her with deep, dark eyes. "Because you cannot clean yourself."*

*Yuna touched a finger to her skirt, to the tears in the cloth that once covered her arms, to the smear of mud on her cheek. "Then what shall I do? Can I never be clean? Must I always be like this?"*

*"I will clean you," said the eagle.*

*Yuna shivered. "You can clean me?" Would he take her to the high cliffs where the water was fresher? Would he fly her through the clouds for the sky to wipe her clean?*

*She looked at the eagle's sharp talons and curved beak. "Will it hurt very much?" she whispered.*

*"It will," he answered.*

*Wind shook the trees above her. And suddenly Yuna was afraid. She looked at the Great Eagle. He looked at her.*

*"Be ready tomorrow, Yuna," the eagle said. "Then I will show you what I will do."*

"Have you still not finished your work?"

Ishi frowned at the sharp voice shooting from the doorway. He did not like that voice.

Lissie leapt from her seat. "Yes, yes, we're just finishing now."

And Yuna was lost.

The stiff woman strode to the table.

Lissie handed her a stack of white sheets. The woman peered down her nose, her eyes darting back and forth over the marks written there. Then she dropped the sheets. "Very well. Ishi, come along."

Wanasi pushed himself to his feet. Then he felt it. A cough rising from deep in his chest. It erupted out of him, like shards of ice breaking, scraping in his throat. He shuddered and sat back down.

"Heavens, Allison!" The woman fluttered her fingers at the base of her neck. "Do get this poor man a handkerchief."

Lissie pulled a cloth from her bag and handed it to Wanasi.

He clutched it in his fist, then pressed it over his mouth as another cough tore from him. He lowered the white cloth.

And there, on the snowy cleanness, shone a dozen specks of bright red blood.

# TWENTY-FIVE

Allison's eyes riveted on the spatter of red. Fear tiptoed up her arm, whispered in her ear. *It's over. It's too late. It's your fault.* She stumbled backward until she bumped into the wall.

Mrs. Whitson reached out and took the handkerchief from Ishi's hand. It hung there, like a flag of surrender, as she turned it toward Allison. "How long has this been going on?"

Allison stared at the handkerchief and shook her head. "I . . . I don't know."

"Dr. Sapir?"

The man rose from his desk on the far side of the room. He removed his reading glasses and tucked them into his vest pocket. "He's been coughing for some time, on and off at first. More frequently of late. I didn't think much of it since Mrs. Morgan here . . ."

Mrs. Whitson stabbed Allison with her gaze. "Allison?"

Allison balled her fists into tight knots.

"What have you *done?*"

She released her grip and felt the blood rush to her fingertips. "Nothing. I've done nothing."

Mrs. Whitson lifted a corner of the handkerchief, then shook out the cloth until it jerked and twisted like a marionette performing some macabre dance.

Allison looked away. "I had a cold, that's all. Just the sniffles."

Dr. Sapir made a sound in the back of his throat.

Allison glanced up at him.

He watched her for a long moment, then began to gather his papers into a neat pile.

Mrs. Whitson folded the handkerchief into a square, with the specks of blood facing upward. "This, my dear—" she tapped the edge of the cloth with her fingertip—"is no common cold." The cloth bunched in her hand. Then she sighed. "Maybe you're right, Allison. Maybe you did nothing. Nothing more than I should have expected of you."

Allison felt fingers of ice creep over her.

Mrs. Whitson's voice lowered. "No, I suppose I should have known something would go wrong. I should have suspected she would beat me in the end." Mrs. Whitson stepped forward and pressed the handkerchief into Allison's hand. "But she hasn't won yet."

Allison held the handkerchief far from her body. "Who?"

Mrs. Whitson whirled toward Ishi. "Come. We shall see Dr. Pope. Perhaps something can be done." She extended her hand and motioned toward the door. "Popey, Ishi. Let's go see Popey." Her gaze flashed to Allison. "That is what he calls the doctor, is it not?"

Allison nodded. "Popey." Yes, Popey would tell them that everything was all right.

"Dr. Kroeber can meet us at the hospital."

Allison dropped the bloodied cloth onto the table. "He's in New York."

"And Thomas?"

"At the university. It'll be hours before—"

"We'll send a messenger. And do what must be done here." Mrs. Whitson smoothed the bodice of her dress. "Come, girl, see to the messenger. There's no time to waste."

Allison almost laughed. *No time to waste.* How often over these past weeks had she used those very words? But they had deceived her. If she had known, if she'd only taken the time to see that Ishi was ill.

"Come, Ishi, quickly." Mrs. Whitson took Ishi's arm and guided him out the door.

Silence followed in their wake, and Allison reached out to turn the handkerchief over so that only white cloth was visible in the fading light. Shadows crept from the corners of the room. Closer, closer, like a pack of wolves stalking prey.

"May I see it?"

Allison jumped. Dr. Sapir stood next to her, his hand extended.

"The handkerchief?"

Allison flipped over the cloth to again show the spattering of blood, already turning brown.

Dr. Sapir studied it, then returned to his desk and gathered up his notes. "Tell Dr. Kroeber that I will send him my findings after I return home. Maybe he'll still find them useful." He rapped the edges of the paper on the desktop.

Allison listened to the sound of paper hitting wood. *Thump, thump, thump,* like the beating of a stick on a funeral drum. "What do you mean? You aren't leaving now, are you?"

He fanned the papers in his hand. "I'm sorry, Mrs. Morgan. But the university won't be needing my services any longer. Not now, anyway."

Allison's legs trembled. He didn't mean . . . he couldn't be saying—"No! We have work to do. We'll go slower; take our time. He'll get better."

"Mrs. Morgan, please—"

"No. You can't give up."

Dr. Sapir looked at her with such pity that it made her chest ache. "You know what that blood means, don't you, Allison?"

Fear pierced her, slicing, cutting, and she pressed her hand into the pain and willed it away. "It-it doesn't mean anything. Just a bad cough. He'll recover. I know he will."

Dr. Sapir tucked the pile of notes under his arm. "The truth can be a cruel master, can it not?" He patted the glasses in his pocket, then spoke again, quietly, almost to himself. "I only wish I had known. I never would have pushed him so hard."

"Don't say that!"

His smile was bitter as he turned toward her. "The truth. Ah, the truth . . ." The smile faded.

The knife twisted in Allison's chest. "You don't think—"

"We'll never know for sure, will we?" He grabbed his satchel and strode from the room. He never looked back.

Allison stood there, alone, silent, as the darkness deepened and the shadows closed in around her. She could feel them, the wolves, the coyotes, drooling and snapping at her heels. She let them come. It seemed wrong somehow to chase away the shadows now. Now, when her life seemed to be slipping back into the darkness she had always known was there. Into the same darkness where all she could see was the image of stone angels, with mist making tears in their eyes. All she could hear was the voice of a little girl crying.

*Don't leave me alone . . .*

⌒

Wanasi shivered in the white, white room, with his feet bare on the white floor, his chest exposed to the bright white lights. He could hear shoes clicking in the hallway outside his room. Hard, white-soled shoes, belonging to saldu women with white hats. They scampered back and forth, like colorless squirrels harvesting a summer's worth of nuts. A white bed stretched by the window, with white sheets turned down and a white pillow smoothed flat. Wanasi hugged his arms around himself and blinked into the light. His chest hurt. There, a battle raged and grew. He could feel it. Fire fighting ice, with blood marking the clash.

It was the blood, he knew, that had frightened them. The blood that seemed so red against the whiteness. The same blood that stained the river so many years ago.

A man in a white coat hurried into the room. Wanasi looked up and recognized Popey, Wee-lee's father. He could trust Popey. Popey was a friend. Popey would help him feel right again.

Popey twirled the board in his hand, then tugged at the strange silver thing that hung around his neck. Earlier, he had pressed that thing into Wanasi's chest while the stiff woman watched and held her breath. Then Popey left, and he and the stiff woman waited. Waited in the whiteness. In time Majapa came, and Lissie. Then they waited some more. Waited in the awful silence.

Now, Popey had come back, still dressed in white. White, like the faces of those around him. Majapa, the stiff woman, Popey, and Lissie. His gaze lingered on Lissie. Lissie, who refused to cry.

Popey took the silver thing from around his neck and tossed it onto the bed.

"Well?" Majapa's question shattered the silence.

Lissie rocked back and forth on her heels, while the stiff woman stood like a tree braced against the wind.

Wanasi sat on a hard wooden chair and folded his hands on his lap. His throat stung, but he would not cough again. Not yet. Not while they all waited for what Popey would say.

Popey dropped the board onto a table by the door. The white sheets that were attached to the top fluttered, then grew still. He took a deep breath. "I'm sorry, Dr. Morgan."

Majapa closed his eyes. The muscles in his neck flexed, and Wanasi knew he was struggling with words that did not want to come. "How bad?" Majapa forced out the question.

Popey did not meet Majapa's eye. "Quite bad, I'm afraid."

"No! I won't believe it!" Lissie swayed on her feet, then slumped onto the bed. "It's not . . . It can't be . . ."

"It is, Allison." The stiff woman spoke without moving. "You knew it the moment you saw the blood. We both did."

Popey's gaze rested on Wanasi, but his words were for Lissie. "It could have been there for months. Then another sickness triggered it. A simple cold, perhaps."

"A cold?" Lissie choked on the word.

"That's all it would take, with the stress of long hours . . ." He shrugged. "There's nothing we can do now. He has—"

All eyes turned to Wanasi. The whiteness closed in around him like a blizzard in a mountain pass. Then Popey spoke a

294

name, a name that painted fear on all their faces. A name that burned in his chest and made bloodred spots on the snowy, clean cloth. *Tu-ber-cu-lo-sis,* Popey called it. A strange saldu word. Wanasi had never heard it before. But from their faces, he knew what it meant.

Death had found him at last.

# TWENTY-SIX

Allison sat in the cold hospital room on a hard metal chair and held Ishi's hand. His eyes were closed, his breathing like sandpaper over stone. For weeks he had lain there, growing weaker, coughing more and more blood. Every day, for the hour they'd let her come, she sat at his side, held his hand, and wrestled the daggers of guilt that stabbed through her mind.

*You were sick. You should have stayed home. You shouldn't have worked him so hard. You should have allowed him to tell his story of Yuna. You should have laughed with him more, taken him on walks, planted more tulips in the garden. What kind of woman are you?*

Then she'd answer the accusations. *I was given a job. I did my best. Besides, they wouldn't allow it.* They barely allowed this, this one short hour each day in which she could sit here and argue with the unseen foes in her mind.

*A real friend would have—*

*I don't hear you.*

*A good woman would—*

*It's their fault.*

*If he dies . . .*

Then Allison would push her fingertips into her temples and drive the thoughts from her head. Ishi was *not* going to die. He couldn't. She wouldn't let him.

Ishi stirred on the bed. She held his fingers tighter. Maybe he would wake now. Maybe he would smile and tell her about Yuna. She leaned forward.

His eyes did not open. She waited, but he only moaned in his sleep.

Gently, Allison laid his hand on the blanket, sat back, and massaged her forehead. Her hour was almost up. And he still hadn't told her any more about Yuna. That first week, he had shared with her a little of the story every day. Just a few sentences were all he could manage. She remembered the first words he'd spoken to her from the hospital bed.

*All night long Yuna thought about the eagle's promise. To be clean, unashamed. It was all she'd ever wanted. All she'd ever tried to attain. And now, the eagle promised to do it for her. But how? And how much would it hurt?*

"What would you do, Lissie?" Ishi had asked. "What would you say if you were Yuna? What would you risk to be clean?"

She rubbed his hand between her own and shook her head. "I don't know, Ishi."

He smiled then. "Don't you? Do you still not know the eagle's name?"

Those words stirred something in her soul, a longing, an

298

ache that frightened her. Yet she wanted to hear more, to know the secrets that Ishi's people had handed down from their grandfathers, the secrets of Yuna's story. Somehow, that first week Ishi was in the hospital, she believed she just might find her answers there too. But still, the answers had not come.

The second week, Ishi had told her more of the story. He told her what happened before sunrise.

*The sky glowed with the hint of coming dawn. The dawn of promise. But before the sun colored the clouds, Yuna heard a whisper outside her hut. She knew she should not listen. She knew Coyote did not love her. He did not care. But she left her ears open. She heard Coyote hiss. "You must not let him hurt you. He will cause you much pain. Come out to me. He does not love you. Only I do."*

*Yuna stepped from her wowi. "You do not love me."*

*Coyote grinned with teeth sharp and yellow. "Haven't I been with you always? The eagle has not even told you his name."*

*The dawn was cold and gray, but Coyote's words were colder still.*

*Yuna gripped her torn, dirty dress. "He said he will make me clean."*

*"You cannot be clean, Yuna. It's too late to hope for that."*

*"But he said—"*

*Coyote stood on his haunches and opened his arms. "You will be safe with me, Yuna. I will protect you. I am your only friend."*

*"You cannot save me."*

*Coyote turned. And Yuna saw a bow and a quiver full of arrows strapped to his side—*

"Is everything okay in here, Mrs. Morgan?" Allison looked up to see a nurse in a square cap. The nurse smiled. And Allison was wrenched into the present. "Yes, yes, everything's fine."

The nurse nodded. "He's still sleeping, then? Well, that's good."

*That's good.* The words echoed in Allison's mind as the woman returned to her station. *That's good.* But it wasn't. Her time with him was so short, too short to be wasted with sleep. Yet she didn't wake him. She just sat there and looked at the thinness of his hands on the sheets, the darkness of his lashes on his gaunt cheeks, the labored breath that caused his chest to rise and fall in so uneven a pattern.

His right hand stayed on the sheets where she laid it, while his left held his flute in a light grip, with his fingers just encircling the running bear. He would probably never play the flute again.

Allison ran her finger over the carved surface of the instrument. That was one thing she did right. She gave Ishi his flute. Next time, she would have to remember to tell *that* to the accusing voices in her mind. She shifted in her chair and allowed her gaze to wander over the room.

As usual, on the table across from the bed, Pop's thick-black Bible sat open. Sometimes, Pop came and read to Ishi, glowering at him with those big, dark eyebrows and talking about heaven and hell. At least, that's what Allison had found him doing one day last week. Thomas came too. More frequently, and often late at night. He didn't glower, and he didn't read. He just sat and stared and sometimes whispered under his breath.

Willy visited, too, though his father only allowed him to stand by the door and wave his greeting. And sometimes, others came, the nurses said. The janitor from the museum, a woman no one recognized, and once, Mrs. Whitson herself.

Occasionally, a stranger wandered in to glance through the door and wonder what they had done to the world's last Yahi. But the visitors were fewer since the museum was now only opened on Saturdays. And then there were small crowds that, without Ishi there to make arrowheads and stir their dreams, seemed solemn and silent. So briefly he'd shown them the ways of his people, opening a doorway to a past only imagined. So briefly he'd come into all their lives. So briefly . . . yet long enough for tuberculosis to catch and consume him.

It wasn't fair.

Allison sighed and continued her perusal of the now familiar room. Ishi's favorite blanket from the museum lay folded at the foot of the bed. In the corner sat a stenographer's phonograph, with a large tin funnel. A number of Edison wax cylinders lay beside it for those rare times when Ishi had the strength to sing or speak. That first week, when he was stronger, he told the story of U-Tut-Na and U-Tut-Ni, the two sisters of the wood duck. But lately he had told no stories. Had sung no songs.

She brushed her fingers along his arm. "I'm sorry, Ishi." Her whisper filled the room. "I'm sorry you never got to see the tulips."

His eyes fluttered open. "Lissie?"

She tipped forward, into his line of sight. "I'm here."

But he didn't seem to see her. "Is it night already?"

"No, not yet." The afternoon sun slanted through the window and made a wide wedge of light across his bed. He didn't see that either.

"It feels so dark."

"It's light yet. Can't you see the sun?"

301

He blinked and seemed to focus. "The sun. Yes, I see it now. He peeks through the smooth glass. But the wind can't get in."

"No, there's no wind. Not in here."

He stretched out his hand into the wedge of light. "I miss the wind."

"Tell me about Yuna."

He fell silent, his hand still lit by the sun. "Yuna?"

Allison laid her hand on his and squeezed. "Yes, tell me the story." It made him happy, she knew, to tell her about Yuna, and it kept her sane, in the dark of night, to sneak down the hall at home and write down what he told her. When fear stole out of the shadows to taunt her, she would remind herself that soon the eagle would tell Yuna how to be clean. Did Ishi know that? Did he know that she dreamed of Yuna in the night? Sometimes, she thought he did.

"The coyote was with Yuna. You remember, Lissie?"

She smiled. "Yes, I remember. He had a bow. What was the bow for, Ishi?"

Ishi gazed at the ceiling. "Coyote is very bad. You should never listen to the coyote when he howls."

"I know. I won't listen to him."

"Promise? Do you promise me, Lissie?"

She patted his hand. "I promise. Now, tell me what happened next."

He closed his eyes again. The words came slowly. So very, very slowly.

*J*ust as the sun shone over the mountains, the eagle swooped from the sky. He was beautiful. Perfect. Glorious. "Are you ready, Yuna? Are you ready to be clean?"

*"Yes!" she answered.*

*Coyote grabbed his bow and fitted an arrow to the string. "Leave her alone," Coyote howled. "She's mine."*

*"Never!" With a powerful sweep of his wings, the eagle rose from the ground and hovered over Yuna.*

*Coyote laughed. The sound was like ice shattering on rock. "She's not worth it!"*

*Yuna felt the wind of the eagle's wings on her face. She felt the warmth of his body above her. And she heard his words like a song in her heart. "She's worth it to me."*

*"Then die," Coyote cried.*

*The arrow flew through the air.*

Ishi coughed. Blood spattered over his lips.

Allison leaned forward and dabbed his mouth with a cloth, but he batted the cloth away. "Tell more. Not much time left." He coughed again.

She lifted the rag.

Ishi intercepted her hand. His eyes held hers. "Just a little more. Just a little more, and it will be done."

Allison lowered the cloth.

Ishi lifted his head from the pillow. His eyes focused on the window. Then the story came again, between labored breaths.

*Yuna screamed, but it was too late.*

*The arrow pierced the Great Eagle through his heart. His cry filled the morning. His blood poured over Yuna. Red, hot blood.*

*She crumbled to her knees.*

*Then the Great Eagle fell dead before her.*

Allison dropped the cloth. *"No!* No, Ishi. The eagle *can't* die. That can't be how the story goes."

Ishi's head fell back to the pillow. "He dies, Lissie. He has to die."

She pressed her fingers into her forehead. "Don't talk about death."

"The Great Eagle must die." His voice weakened. "Grandfather said he must."

"Not today."

Another cough erupted from Ishi's throat. "Yes, today. Tonight. I must finish it now, before it's too late."

Allison twisted her gloved fingers in her lap. "What more is there? What more could there be? The eagle is dead."

"More, Lissie. Just a little more." Flecks of blood appeared on his lips as he spoke.

Allison picked up the cloth and pushed it into his hand. "No more today, Ishi."

He wiped the blood away. His eyes lost focus. "But the eagle—"

Allison stood. Her hour was up. She knew it. Thomas would be coming soon, and he must not find her tiring Ishi. He mustn't think she was pushing him again.

Ishi's hand reached out and grabbed her. "Wait. Just a little more. You have to know—"

"Tomorrow."

"No." Another cough halted him.

She touched her fingertips to his lips. "Tomorrow, my friend. We'll finish the story tomorrow."

# TWENTY-SEVEN

*Wanasi . . .*

The wind called his name, like a sigh through the branches of the giant oak.

*Wanasi.*

He stood at the edge of the Daha River. Sunlight rippled on the water, nearly blinding him in its brightness. The river flowed south, always south.

*Wanasi.*

The water added its voice to the wind. Calling, beckoning him forward.

"Not yet," he told the river. "Not yet," he said to the wind. "I have not finished Yuna's story. I cannot go. Not yet."

*Wanasi.*

*Wanasi.*

Trees swayed in the breeze. Damp earth compressed beneath his feet. And still, the wind and waters called.

Overhead, an eagle circled ever lower in the cloud-free

sky. Light shone through its wings. It called out to him in one piercing cry. Yet, the cry was like a song, a series of notes that lilted through the air and caressed him with their music.

*Wanasi.*

"I'm coming." He stepped forward into the flowing river. It swirled around his bare feet, soothing them. The water felt warm, soft. Sand crept between his toes. And he knew he was almost home.

*Wanasi.*

Then he remembered Yuna. He remembered the eagle dead at her feet. "Just a little more time," he called to the bird above him. "Just one more day," he told the river.

But the river didn't hear. The water pulled at him, pushed like a hundred hands, firm yet gentle, guiding him deeper. He took one step, then another. The river swirled around his calves, his thighs, his belly, his chest. It felt so good, so right. But not yet.

"I cannot come now," he whispered to the wind. "The Great Eagle is dead."

*Wanasi.*

He heard his mother's voice, carried on the wind.

*Wanasi.*

The water turned cold.

*Wanasi, it is time.*

He opened his eyes and found the white room around him. Cold light shone down on his face. The flute was still in his hand, and the strange wax tubes remained in the corner.

But there, in the quietness of his mind, he could still hear the Daha calling his name. And he knew that the river's voice was too strong to resist.

Thomas raced down the hospital corridor as if rabid dogs were biting at his heels. Pale faces passed in a blur as he rounded a corner and sprinted toward Ishi's room. His shoes seemed to make a terrible racket on the hard floor, but he didn't care. Voices called out as he passed, but he paid them no heed.

A red light flashed somewhere ahead. Thomas sped toward it. A nurse in a square white hat stepped from behind a counter to block his way. He swerved and darted past her.

"Dr. Morgan! Please!"

He didn't stop. He didn't even slow. He wouldn't. Not until he reached Ishi's room. Not until he knew if he was already too late.

Time had seemed to speed up from the moment the messenger appeared in his office doorway. Thomas was reading papers from his *Anthropology and the World* class when the red-haired boy with freckles on his nose burst through the door.

"Dr. Pope says to come quick! He said the Indian doesn't have much time." The boy seemed too young, too innocent to bring a message of imminent death.

For that one instant, Thomas hesitated. Then the pen dropped from his hand and splattered ink over the students' papers. He leapt from his chair. He remembered it bumping against the wall behind him, but he didn't reach back to stop it. He didn't even pause for his coat or to put on the scarf that Allison had knit for him. He just bolted out the door with not even a hat on his head. He dashed over the museum grounds, across the street, and up the stairs of the hospital. Some rude person in an automobile beeped his horn at him, but Thomas didn't stop. All that mattered was to get to Ishi. Quick.

And then he remembered Allison. Allison would want to be there too. She'd want to say good-bye, to sit beside Ishi one last time before it was too late. He should have sent the messenger to her. He should have thought of her sooner.

Thomas skidded to a halt before Ishi's door. His breath sounded harsh and fast in his ears, blocking the sounds of the hospital staff in the corridor behind him.

Dr. Pope stood near the bed, his fingers pressed to the thinnest part of Ishi's wrist.

Ishi lay motionless on the white bed. His face was ashen, his eyes closed, his hand open on the sheets.

A full second passed before Thomas found his voice, somewhere beneath the thudding of his heart. "Am I . . ."

Dr. Pope laid Ishi's arm gently on the bed and shook his head. "No, you're not too late." He pulled his stethoscope from around his neck and stepped toward the door. "But the time is short now. Very, very short."

Thomas moved to Ishi's bedside. He looked down at the pale figure on the bed and felt his breath leave him in a pained rush. "Oh, Ishi, if only—"

Ishi opened his eyes. "Majapa?" His voice was so faint, so weak, that it barely rose to Thomas's ears.

Thomas leaned over to catch every precious word.

A muted cough rumbled from Ishi's throat. "The river is calling me, Majapa. I have to follow it now."

Thomas took Ishi's hand in his own. "No, Ishi, fight. Stay with us."

Ishi's eyes glazed. "The river, Majapa. The river will take me south."

Thomas lowered himself onto the chair next to the bed, his hand still holding Ishi's.

Dr. Pope cleared his throat. "Call me—" his voice caught—"call me when you need me, Thomas. I've done all I can for him, until . . ." He didn't need to say the rest.

Thomas nodded, then glanced up. "Allison." Her name trembled from his lips, and he started again. "Can you send someone to tell Allison?"

Dr. Pope twisted the stethoscope in his hands. "Of course. I'll dispatch another runner right away." He strode out the door, then turned back. "Though, honestly, I don't think she'll get here in time."

Thomas listened to Dr. Pope's footsteps echo down the corridor. Tears formed in his eyes. Outside the room, nurses bustled back and forth, voices called down the hallway, wheelchairs squeaked. But inside, silence hung like a damp cloak. And Thomas could find no words to free himself from it. He bent over Ishi's hand and allowed his eyes to fall closed.

"Majapa."

Thomas sniffed back his tears. "I'm so sorry, Ishi. I'm sorry we couldn't save you."

For a brief moment, Ishi's grip tightened. "Lissie?"

Thomas opened his eyes. "She's coming. Soon. Just hold on a little while longer."

Ishi's arm flopped out toward the corner of the room. "Lissie's story." He drew a labored breath. "Yuna."

Thomas leaned closer. "Who is Yuna?"

"Tell her."

Thomas pressed Ishi's hand between both his palms. "Tell her what, Ishi? What do you want me to say?"

"Tell her the end of the story. Tell her the eagle flies."

"I will. I'll tell her." Thomas rubbed his thumb over Ishi's knuckles to solidify his vow, even though he had no idea what Ishi was talking about. He'd never heard of Yuna, had never known Allison to care if an eagle flew. But, if somehow, someway, he could keep this last promise, he would.

Ishi smiled, a feeble gesture that scarcely lifted the corners of his mouth. But it was enough. "It is done now. I want to go home."

"What will we do without you?"

"You will live." Ishi's smile dissolved into a spasm of pain. He coughed deep in his chest. A flow of blood, no mere spattering now, escaped his lips and poured down his chin. He didn't wipe it away. Nor did Thomas.

It didn't matter now.

For a moment, Ishi's eyes cleared. He lifted his trembling hand and touched Thomas's cheek. "I go. You stay." His eyes clouded. His hand dropped.

Sorrow such as Thomas had never known broke over his soul. He reached for Pop's Bible, still lying on the table beside the bed. The leather felt cool to the touch. He picked it up and clutched it to his chest. "Oh, God . . . Father . . . no."

One last cough ripped through Ishi's frame. Another flow of blood washed down his chin.

And there, on white sheets stained red with blood, the last Yahi died.

# TWENTY-EIGHT

Fear. Terror. They coursed through Allison's veins like broken glass, jagged edges tearing, shredding. It couldn't be. It must not be. There had to be some mistake. Ishi could not be dying today. The messenger was wrong. Ishi would not leave her now, the story unfinished, his pledge of tomorrow's telling unfulfilled.

Allison pelted from the carriage, hurried up the stone steps, and flung open the door of the hospital.

A woman in white smiled at her. "May I help you, ma'am?"

Allison pushed by without answering. She rushed along the main hall, up a staircase, and down a thin corridor. There, the door of Ishi's room stood open. She paused. And listened. And heard nothing but the murmur of nurses and the sound of their soft shoes on the tile floor. Was she already too late?

She stepped forward on shaking limbs. Thomas appeared in the doorway, his eyes red and swollen, his hair tousled. A smear of blood marked his sleeve. But what was worse, much worse, was that he clasped a big black Bible to his chest.

Allison knew that her world had shattered.

Thomas looked up at her. His hand reached for the doorjamb as if to steady himself against a stiff wind.

"Thomas?"

His eyes pleaded with her. "Allison, I'm sorry. I couldn't. I didn't . . ." His gaze swept away from her, then back again.

Her mind screamed words that refused to be spoken. *No, no! It cannot be!* But Thomas's face confirmed her fear. His eyes told her more than she wanted to hear, more than she could bear.

"He was my friend. And I killed him. I let us kill him." His arm dropped. He stared at her for a second longer, then staggered away down the hallway.

Allison watched him go, her feet frozen in place by the words he had spoken. In a moment, he was gone. The noises of the hospital—a scratching pen, a squeaking cart, voices and footsteps and closing doors—rushed in around her. Then she found she could move again. She crept forward, slowly, so slowly that it seemed she would never reach Ishi's door. But she did. All too soon, she did.

She looked in and saw him there, lying straight and silent on the bed. A thin wraith covered in white. Blood stained his chest. His eyes were closed. His hands lay crossed over his stomach, with the flute resting between his fingers. If not for the stillness of his chest and the silence where once there had been labored breath, she could almost believe he was asleep. It was the silence that convinced her, the awful, awful silence of death.

Ishi, her only friend, was dead.

There would be no story now. No planting of tulips. No lilting tunes piped on the little flute to help her to remember. It was all gone now. He was gone. And she never even knew his name.

Allison took a few unsteady steps forward. One, then the next, until she stood near the bed. Her hand reached out, trembling, to touch the smooth wood of the flute. She pulled it from his grasp.

Ishi's fingers dropped away.

Allison lifted the flute and pressed it to her ribs. She started to shake. Her gaze riveted on Ishi's pale face, on the blood covering his chin, on the lifelessness of his closed, unseeing eyes.

"I did this. I killed you." She squeezed her eyes tight shut, but the image of Ishi's dead body could not be erased from her mind. "I did this. And everyone knows it."

Then Allison turned and fled, the flute still clutched in her fist. She didn't know where she was going. She didn't care. All she knew was that she was never, ever coming back.

He noticed the darkness first. No flicker of gaslight shining through the front curtains. No glow of electric lights coming from the kitchen. No candles. No lanterns. Just the darkness. Thomas stepped out of his Model T and walked with halting steps up the stairs to his house. He opened the door. Silence. Only darkness and silence. "Allison?"

Silence.

He pulled the door shut behind him. "Are you here?"

No one answered.

Thomas stepped over to the side table, picked up a

match, and lit the lantern. Light and shadow flared over the walls. "Anyone home?"

The match burned his fingers. He flicked it out, then dropped the charred stick onto a glass plate on the table. "Allison!" His voice echoed through the house.

Thomas dropped his coat on a chair and hurried down the hallway. At the bedroom door, he stopped to turn on the electric light in their room. The glow illuminated their perfectly made bed, a clean basin on the bureau, and the open window on the right wall. Thomas strode over and flung open the wardrobe door. Allison's dresses hung in tidy alignment, not one missing except the dress she was wearing. He ran his fingers through his hair. She hadn't been home, at least not since he'd seen her. So where could she have gone? Not the museum. He had just come from there. Not the hospital. Dr. Pope said she'd left hours ago. Mrs. Whitson's? He couldn't believe that. So where? Maybe she'd just gone out walking. Maybe in her sorrow she'd lost track of the time.

A cold wind blew in from the window. Thomas walked over and slammed the pane shut. Then he sat in the straight-back chair beside the drapes and waited.

Minutes crept into hours, and still Thomas waited. He paced before the window. He strode down the hall and back again. He got a glass of water from the kitchen, drank it, and washed the glass. He turned up the lantern in the living room. He hung up his coat. He wiped the dirt from his shoes. He watched the stars grow brighter and brighter in the nighttime sky.

And still, Allison did not return.

Fear settled in his chest. He strode back to the bedroom and lay down, fully clothed, on the bed. *Lord, she's gone. Bring her back to me. May the front door open. May I hear her coming down the hallway with those light, brisk steps that could only be hers. Today has been filled with too much sorrow to endure this too. Please, God, make her come home.*

He closed his eyes, held his breath, and listened. But there was no sound of the front door opening, no footsteps in the hall, nothing but an old tomcat yowling from the neighbor's fence. His breath escaped in a pained whoosh. He pulled out his pocket watch. Ten minutes to midnight. He punched the pillow. He'd failed and she'd run away. In the midst of her grief, he left her standing alone in the hospital hallway. He was the first to run. So could he blame her for not coming home now?

Thomas waited a moment longer, then vaulted from the bed. He'd lost Ishi. He couldn't lose Allison too. He pulled open the drawers of her dresser and rifled through the stacks of gloves, the handkerchiefs, the stockings held there. He opened the wardrobe, searched its floor, poked his fingers into the pockets of Allison's coats. Nothing. Not a single clue as to where she might have gone.

He rushed back to the front room. Her reticule bag was missing. His gaze fell to her writing desk in the corner. He pulled out one drawer, then another, then a third. Finally, he found something. A neat stack of white pages, covered with writing in Allison's firm, fine hand. He pulled the pages from the drawer, crossed the room, and turned up the lantern.

*Yuna's Story,* read the title on the first page. *Yuna!* He'd heard that name before. *Could it be?* He began to read. All about Yuna. About the Great Eagle. About the coyote, who shot the eagle through the heart. Page after page of heartbreaking story that could only be the secret tale that Ishi had begged him to finish. But how could he? He didn't know the ending. He didn't know anything except that Ishi was gone, and Allison had fled. What did it matter, then, if the eagle flew?

Thomas moved to the couch and settled on the tapestry surface. Yuna, Coyote, the Great Eagle. The story haunted him. Perhaps because Allison had never mentioned it. Or perhaps because of Ishi's last wish. He lay back on the couch and placed the pages over his chest.

Above him, shadows played on the white ceiling. It was just a story, after all. Just a simple tale from a pagan culture. Maybe it didn't matter if the ending went unheard.

He touched the papers on his chest. They seemed heavy, weighted, as if they held all the sorrow, all the pain of Ishi's death, and all the fear of Allison's disappearance.

Weariness stole through him. His eyelids drooped. "I can't do it, Ishi." His words trickled into the darkness. "I can't finish a story I don't understand."

The shadows flickered on the ceiling. He paused and waited, but the door did not open. Footsteps did not sound on the gravel outside. "Oh, Allison, come home to me. Please, come home."

There, with the pages still spread like a white cloth over his chest and silence pressing down like a fist over his eyes, Thomas let sleep overtake him. And for a moment, he forgot that somehow, in a single day, he had lost the two people he held most dear.

# TWENTY-NINE

Thomas woke with the morning sun shining across his face and the smell of burning oil tickling his senses. He bolted upright. White papers fluttered to the floor at his feet. He glanced down at them and shuddered as the memories came rushing back. Ishi's death, Allison's disappearance, and the strange tale of Yuna and her Great Eagle. He gathered the pages with one hand and set them beside him.

On the table, the lantern still burned, the oil nearly gone now in the clear bowl beneath the flame. Thomas rose and blew it out. The quietness of the house sent chills over his skin.

"Allison!"

But even as he called, he knew she wasn't there. The house's emptiness grated against every nerve in his body.

Thomas sat on the edge of the wingback chair and pushed the hair from his forehead. He wished he could just lie back down and return to the blissful nothingness of sleep. Maybe, if he closed his eyes tight enough, he could forget all his troubles and awake to find that everything was as it should be. If only life could work like that, if only prayer could make it happen. But it never had. Perhaps it never would.

He pushed himself up and glanced toward the window. *Let her be right outside. Let me look out and see her.* He strode to the window and pulled back the drapes. A horse trudged by, pulling a grocer's cart. A black motorcar turned a corner. A robin hopped along the branch of a myrtle tree across the street. But no Allison.

Thomas sighed and let the drapery fall back into place. He'd really hoped that today he might have a miracle. A real one. Not like Sapir's coming but one that lasted.

He turned from the window and stared at the papers on the couch. Allison's story. He wished he could finish it for her, finish it with a miracle. He wished he could do at least that one thing right. But he didn't know how. And so he would fail her again. Just as he failed her at the hospital.

A good husband would know where she had gone. A good husband would find her and bring her home. He would sense what he ought to do. But Thomas didn't have any idea at all.

He knew only one thing: The responsibilities of the day would not wait any longer. He had to face them, do what he must, and then, just perhaps, he would figure out what to do about Allison.

The sun had crept to its zenith and started its descent before Thomas found another moment to think. He'd sent telegrams to Dr. Kroeber in New York and to the Bureau of

Indian Affairs. He'd gone to the hospital to oversee the removal of Ishi's things from the room. He crafted and sent a statement to the newspapers, then declined three interviews and avoided a gaggle of pesky reporters lingering outside the hospital. He'd done all that was required of him, said the right words, given the proper instructions. And now, here he was, swaying like a raft adrift in the silence of Ishi's room at the museum.

Thomas wandered through the small room Ishi had called home for so short a time. He ran his fingers over the clean, folded clothes that lay in neat piles on the shelves. He touched the blankets on the bed, then walked to the window and pulled down the shade. He let it go again and listened to the roll and thump of the material as it retracted. Roll and thump, roll and thump.

Would he ever be able to pull a shade again without thinking of Ishi?

He turned from the window and glanced toward the bed. Someone had brought Ishi's shoes back and placed them beneath the headboard. Dr. Pope, he assumed. And the blanket too. But the flute was missing. Thomas frowned. What happened to the flute?

He bent down and pulled a clean shirt and pants from the shelf along the wall. The fabric felt soft against his fingers. White man's clothes. Yet Ishi would wear no others. A sad smile lifted Thomas's lips. He waved his hand in the air, as if by doing so he could disperse the ghosts, the memories of Ishi that whispered of the way things could have been, the way things should have been.

"Dr. Morgan?"

Thomas straightened and turned to see a boy hovering at the door. "Hello, Willy."

Willy scratched his red nose, then ran the back of his hand over one blotchy cheek. "I miss Ishi." He dragged himself across the room and plopped onto the bed.

"So do I." Thomas laid Ishi's clothes back on the shelf.

Willy's booted feet swung back and forth over the edge of the bed. For a long moment, he didn't say a word. Then his gaze shot to Thomas. "How come my father couldn't save him? Why did Ishi have to die?"

Thomas looked into Willy's innocent bloodshot eyes and felt his own soul echoing the question. "I don't know, son. Only God knows."

"I wish God wouldn't have taken him away."

"I do too, Willy. I do too."

"Dad says answers never look like you expect them to."

"Answers to what?" Thomas sat on the bed beside Willy and looked out at the trees shaking in the wind.

"Answers to prayer. That's how you know it's really God answering you. Do you think that's true, Dr. Morgan?"

Thomas laid his arm over Willy's shoulders and considered the wisdom in the boy's words. "It just may be, son. Just may be." He sighed. "Though sometimes, I wish it weren't so."

"I wish I coulda talked to him before he died. But Dad wouldn't let me go into the room."

Thomas glanced down at Willy's bowed head. He squeezed the boy's shoulder. "You could see him from the doorway though. He knew you were there. He knew you were his friend."

Willy scuffed the toe of his boot over the floorboard. "I could only wave. Then Ishi'd wave back. Woulda rather sat by him like you did, and like Mrs. Morgan."

"He couldn't say much at the end anyway. He was too sick to talk."

Willy's gaze darted to Thomas. "Was saying plenty yesterday. Didn't even see me in the doorway. Didn't even wave."

Thomas sat up straighter. "What do you mean?"

"I mean he was sitting up, talking real slow like into that funny funnel machine."

Thomas dropped his arm from around Willy's shoulders. "The wax cylinders. Of course! I didn't even think . . ." He gripped Willy's arms and turned the boy to face him. "Are you sure? Are you positive he was talking into the stenographer's phonograph?"

Willy shrugged. "Don't know what it's called, but I do know he was talking into that funnel. Seemed important, so I didn't call out or anything. Didn't want to bother him." He paused. His lower lip quivered. "But if I'da known it was the last time . . ." His voice squeaked to a stop.

Thomas leapt to his feet. His hands clenched into fists. That cylinder. He had to find that cylinder! With a final word to Willy, he turned and sprinted from the room.

# THIRTY

A thin line of sweat had gathered on Thomas's forehead by the time he pushed open the door of the back storeroom at the museum. To his surprise, the light was already on. He glanced up at the single electric bulb, then pulled the door closed and placed his pen and papers on the first ledge near the door. His gaze traveled over the rows of dusty shelves that filled the room. There were a dozen rows in all, most covered with frayed baskets, clay pots, boxes with broken arrowheads, and worn leather moccasins. A shelf creaked. Then Thomas heard a soft thud.

"Hello? Anyone here?" He wiped his hand over his brow. Silence answered him.

He slipped down the first row of shelves, his eyes skimming the collection of old Civil War swords and pans filled with coins from the Mexican American war era. He touched the edge of a threadbare Mexican flag. The phonograph was supposed to be right here. Thomas ran his finger over an empty spot on the middle shelf and frowned. They had to be here somewhere. Dr. Pope told him someone was asked to bring the cylinders and phonograph to the museum's storeroom just an hour before. Apparently someone had not done his job.

Thomas rounded the corner to search the next row of shelves. A sniff came from the row beside him, followed by a gruff cough. He bent and tried to peer through the shelves to the row beyond. A large wicker basket blocked his view. "Who's there?"

Someone in the next row sniffed again. "It's just me, boy."

"Pop?" Thomas strode around the corner and found Pop sitting on a crate in the middle of the aisle. The stenographer's phonograph rested on his lap. "What are you doing here?"

Pop rubbed his handkerchief over his pink nose. "Didn't mean no harm. Just doing as I was asked." He stuffed the cloth back into the pocket of his dirt-stained overalls, then stood and pushed the phonograph onto an empty space on the shelf.

"Did you bring the cylinders too?"

Pop waved his hand toward the opposite shelf. "They're all there."

Thomas hurried toward the black cylinders, half hidden behind a small wooden box.

Pop sat on the crate and pulled the handkerchief from his pocket. He blew his nose.

Thomas paused. "Pop?"

Pop looked up at him with eyes as bloodshot as Willy's.

"Are you ill?"

Pop turned away and grunted. "Ain't nothing wrong with me. Just a little dust in my eyes, that's all." He rose from the crate. "Better be going. Ain't got no cause to sit around here all day. Got some roses that need planting at the parsonage. Some tree trimming too."

Thomas put a hand on Pop's arm, stopping him. "You didn't know that Ishi died, did you?" His voice was soft.

Pop wiped the handkerchief under his nose again. "Don't matter. Shoulda figured it."

"Sorry, Pop. I should have let you know."

"Came to talk to him about Jesus. They said he was dead." Pop's fingers twitched. He blinked rapidly, his eyes not meeting Thomas's. "Had to hear it from strangers."

"I didn't think you'd care." The words slipped out before Thomas could censor them.

Pop snorted, then twisted the handkerchief into a ball. "Why do you say that?"

Thomas looked at Pop, standing there, his shoulders slumped, his eyes averted. He squeezed Pop's arm. "He was just a pagan, after all."

Pop grimaced. "Aye, so it would seem."

Silence crept between them.

Finally, Pop sighed. "But he was a good pagan, wasn't he?"

An ache started in Thomas's chest. "He was a good friend."

Pop nodded, his eyes catching Thomas's for the first time. "You came down here for him, didn't you? Something with those sound tubes." He flicked his fingers toward the Edison wax cylinders. "I know you didn't come down here to find your old pop and tell him what happened."

"I said I was sorry."

"I know. Guess I'll be going, then." He took a step toward the door.

Thomas called after him. "Stay, Pop. Stay and hear Ishi one last time."

Pop cocked his head. "Hear Ishi? How?"

Thomas moved toward the phonograph and replaced the recording mouthpiece with the reproducer attached to the side. Then he removed the instrument and positioned it on the crate. "Ishi was telling Allison a story about an eagle. A story that he wanted me to finish for her. It seemed important to him."

"So important that you think he talked it onto one of them Edison tubes before he died?"

"I'm counting on it."

"Humph." Pop pointed to the front roll. "I'd try that one, then. It was sitting separate from the others."

Thomas picked up the cylinder, mounted it on the phonograph's threaded axle, then held up the stylus.

"Ain't you going to need to write it down?"

"I brought paper and a pen. Over there on the shelf near the door."

Pop nodded and retrieved the writing materials.

Thomas still held the stylus.

Pop set the paper and pen on the crate and stared at Thomas. "What's wrong, boy?"

Thomas shook his head. "What if it's not what I think? What if it isn't the story at all?"

Pop laid a finger on his arm, then reached over to turn on the phonograph's battery-powered motor. "Put down the stylus. That's the only way you'll find out."

Thomas didn't move. Now that he was here, with the last cylinder spinning in place, he was no longer sure that he wanted to hear the rest of Yuna's story. Did he really want to hear more about the death of the eagle? Hadn't there been enough sorrow? Enough tragedy? He cleared his throat.

"It's a heathen story, Pop. I don't even know why I wanted to find the end."

Pop flicked the pen so that it twirled on the crate. "Too late now, ain't it?"

"Is it?" His voice lowered to a whisper. "What am I doing here?"

Pop smiled. "Honoring a friend." He took the stylus from Thomas's hand and placed it carefully on the wax cylinder.

The cylinder spun beneath the stylus. And then words, low, harsh, and barely discernible, floated from the funnel like disembodied spirits. "For Lissie," Ishi's voice said.

The sound pierced Thomas's heart. He had guessed right. He picked up the paper and pen. His hands trembled.

The sound of Ishi coughing rose from the phonograph. Pain seared Thomas's chest. His throat clogged. From the corner of his vision, he saw Pop dab at his eyes, then turn away.

Ishi's voice came again in halting, rasping sentences, speaking words Thomas did not understand. Yahi words. Thomas wrote down the sounds. Allison would know what they meant. She would understand.

Slowly, Ishi spoke. Thomas wrote. And Pop waited. Eventually, the words came to halt. A final racking cough issued from the phonograph. Then two words, spoken in English, "No more," followed by a scratching nothingness, and the steady sound of the cylinder spinning around and around.

Thomas stopped the machine and looked down at the precious paper in his hand.

"So, that's it, then," Pop murmured. "You know what it means?"

Thomas shook his head. "Allison will."

"Well, let's go then." He rubbed his hands together. "Take it to her. I want to hear this story too. Reverend's roses can wait."

"Pop." Thomas hesitated. He took a quick breath, then let the words spill from him like water over a dam. "Allison's gone. Disappeared. I haven't seen her since Ishi died."

Pop's eyes grew round. "Gone, and you haven't found her?"

"I don't know where to look."

Pop scowled. "What are you doing here when your wife's missing?" The words came like rapidly fired gunshots.

Thomas turned away and put the phonograph back on the shelf. He could feel Pop's accusing gaze on his back. Finally, he turned back around. "I don't know where she is! I've prayed and prayed. What more do you expect of me?" He flung his hand in the air.

Pop scratched his mole. "I see. You've *prayed*, have you? It's up to God now, is it?"

"I guess it is."

"So you trust God enough to hear you when you're praying, but not enough to be with you when you're doing. It's time to stop the talk, boy, and walk!"

Anger rose from deep inside Thomas, choking him. "You're a fine one to talk about that. When you and mother—"

"That was a long time ago. You ain't a little boy anymore." He clucked his tongue. "You never have been one to want to do the hard thing. Always want the easy way. But life ain't easy. No, it ain't."

"I don't want to talk about this. Allison will come home. Then I'll show her the story, and everything will be all right."

"What if it ain't? What if she don't?"

"I've prayed for God to bring her back. Isn't that what I'm supposed to do? Isn't that what you've always preached?"

Pop glared at him. "Aye, you're supposed to pray. But prayer ain't a substitute for doing what's needed. You've got to trust God in the *doing* too."

"I can't!" The words tore from Thomas's lips, and he knew they were true. He couldn't step from behind the door. He didn't know how. Or he was too afraid to try . . .

"You've got to!" Pop's voice sliced through him. "You don't just let the lady you love—" Pop stopped as abruptly as if someone had slapped him. He lowered himself to the crate, then gazed up at the ceiling. A strange, sad smile played around his mouth. His tone softened. "You don't just let the lady you love leave you." He paused. "You go after her. You do everything you can in the strength God gives you. You lay down your life. That's what you do when you love. That's what He did."

"What do you know about love, Pop?" Thomas sighed, his voice no longer harsh but gentle, pleading.

Pop's chin lowered until his eyes were level with Thomas's. "Take the plank out of my own eye; is that what you're saying, boy?"

He shook his head. "I didn't mean that."

"Didn't you?" He ran his hand through his grizzled hair. "You should have."

Thomas looked into his father's familiar eyes, and for the first time in his life, he saw a man with hurts, secrets, regrets that he'd kept hidden beneath the gruffness. He saw a man trying to fight back emotions, a man wounded and trying to be strong. But most of all, he saw a man. Not a father, not a judge, but just a man. A man Thomas loved, despite it all. He put his hands on Pop's shoulders. "You're right. I should have."

Pop laid his hands on Thomas's and squeezed. His eyes watered.

"I should have said a lot of things, a long time ago," Thomas continued. "And not just to you." He dropped his hands and stepped back. "I love you, Pop, and I'm sorry."

Pop's head bobbed up and down. "Me too, boy. Me too." He rubbed his palms on his thighs. "About time we did what was needed. Both of us. Long time in coming, it is."

Thomas glanced toward the door. "I need to find Allison."

Pop waved his hand, as if urging Thomas forward. "That you do. Been down here long enough yammering with an old man."

Thomas started toward the door, the paper in his hand. He heard the creak of the old crate as Pop rose.

"And I need to go see Agnes." Pop chuckled. "Looks like the ol' devil will be wearing long johns tonight."

Thomas halted and turned. "Long johns?"

A smile quirked the corners of Pop's mouth. "Hell's a'freezing over, boy. Suppose I ought to go put on a tie."

Gray clouds painted the sky the color of dishwater. The sun refused to shine, but Allison didn't care. Not when the sky darkened. Not even as the wind howled down the alley like a wolf hungry for prey. She felt the cold biting her nose, her chin, the tips of her ears. But she didn't bother to tighten the collar around her throat or to retrieve the hat that had fallen into the gutter the day before. Instead, she turned to face the wind, accepting the slap of cold on her cheeks, the sting that brought moisture to her eyes.

She lowered herself to the broken surface of an old milk box and pressed her back against the damp stone wall of the orphanage. On the other side of the alley, a brick and wood wall rose to cut off the dismal light of the sky. Cracks from the earthquake of six years ago zigzagged across the rough surface. She noted places where the wall had crumbled, then been repaired with haphazard rock and wood. She allowed her gaze to travel up the wall until it met the gray sky above. Somehow, it had seemed much taller when she was five.

The odor of rotting fish and molding squash rose from the trash bin beside her. The stench brought back memories. It was here, just here, that she had been left all those years ago. It was here that her life had become what it was. Life had begun. Life had ended. She could almost hear the sound of her mother's footsteps retreating, could almost sense the moment when the footsteps stopped and the creak of carriage wheels began.

An orange cat leapt onto the bin beside her and started to rummage through the newspapers stained with fish. Allison shivered. The cat raised its head and looked at her with unblinking green eyes. A fishbone dangled from its mouth.

Allison grimaced. The garbage, the cat, and the cold, cold wind . . . nothing had changed in all these years. She remembered it now. Remembered the terrible chill of the wind, the fear, the deep, sinking knowledge that she had been thrown away like a bit of rotting squash. And now, all these years later, she'd returned here.

*Why?* Why had she come to this most hated of places?

She knew the answer. She'd returned because she had finally, utterly failed to prove she was somebody. So this place had called her back to face the barrenness of that truth. And face it, she must.

The cat stuffed its head back into the garbage, its tail lashing upward, from side to side, like the flag of an advancing army. The other cat had been gray and striped . . . That awful, bony cat that stared at her five-year-old self with bold and accusing eyes. She'd hated that cat.

Allison leaned her head back against the wall, watching the cat. "I belong here. Just like you do. It all started here. And here it will end."

The cat didn't look up.

Allison picked up a small stone from beside the milk crate and tossed it into the garbage bin.

The cat jumped and ran.

Allison watched it go. "This is my alley now. At least for a little while longer."

The wind picked up speed.

Allison dropped her gaze to the long tear in her dress, the dark stain that marred the hem, the wrinkles that covered the once pristine fabric. She touched a finger to a blot of dirt on her bodice. "This is where I belong. Right here by the trash bin. It's where I've always belonged. Mama was right."

She gripped the hem of her dress and pulled until the tear lengthened. *I won't pretend anymore. I can't.* She tore a swath of cloth from the bottom of her skirt and twisted the material in her fists. *I've spent my whole life trying to convince the world that I don't belong here in this alley, that I am good and worthy and beautiful. But it was all a lie.* Her gaze fell to her gloves, marred with dirt that would never come out. *Even gloves can't cover the truth.*

"They never could." Her words echoed against the stone and brick. "I just didn't know it." But Ishi had. He'd known all along.

Allison removed the flute from the pocket of her bolero jacket and blew a single mournful note. The wind snatched the sound and carried it away. She slid the flute back into its hiding place. She couldn't make it sing like Ishi had. She couldn't force it to weave melodies of peace. Even the flute knew the truth. It knew who she was.

*I am dirty, selfish, unclean. I cared so much about proving my worth that I killed my best friend. I pushed and pushed. I didn't care that he was weary. I only cared about making them all believe I was somebody.* A bitter laugh escaped her throat. *But who am I now? What am I?*

A cat meowed.

Allison looked up to see the creature peering around the corner. She stared into its eyes. "Hello, Coyote. Yes, I know the truth."

The cat crept forward.

Allison clutched her tattered skirt in both hands. "I am Yuna. No one will love me now." She closed her eyes. The wind chilled her face, stripping away the masks she had made for herself. Stripping away the lies that said she was okay, she was clean. Blowing away the falseness, the feeble attempts to hide the filth within, and leaving only the knowledge that she was dirty, helpless, without hope.

But the wind couldn't make her clean. And she couldn't clean herself. She had tried, oh, how she had tried. Ishi had known that. He'd attempted to tell her. But now it was too late.

The Great Eagle was dead.

Allison opened her eyes. A glint of green beneath the

trash bin caught her attention. She leaned forward to see a shard of green bottle glass, like the kind Ishi used to make arrowheads. She reached down and retrieved it. The glass shone dully in her hand. A single splinter, shaped like a blade. Sharp. And deadly. Its edge glinted in the gray light. Allison touched the tip with her finger, and a drop of blood appeared on her glove.

She set the shard of glass on her knee. Slowly, ever so slowly, she peeled off one glove. Then the other. She dropped them onto the cobbled ground. They lay there, like a pile of filth, mute testimony to the truth of what she had become, what she always had been. She kicked them away. Her fingers, cold and pale, shook in the dim light. She would never wear gloves again. Never.

Allison picked up the glass in her bare fingers. It felt like ice in her grip. She looked down at her image, distorted in the glass. Then she touched her sleeve.

# THIRTY-ONE

Ridiculous! Absurd! Agnes tore the note in two and let the pieces flutter to the parlor floor. The words seared her mind: *"Ishi is dead."* They taunted her. *"Dead . . ."*

"No!" She flung the word away from her. It seemed to echo, then fade into the crackling of flames in the grate behind her. Agnes stared out the closed window. Storm clouds gathered in the gray sky. Trees dipped and quivered in the wind. Down below on the street a carriage stopped.

Agnes turned from the window. Tears threatened. She blinked them back. *It cannot be true.* She'd worked too hard. Planned too well. But tuberculosis was not something one could plan against. She knew that. What she didn't know was how to accept the defeat. She sighed and pressed her fingers into her chest. Ishi was dead. They'd warned her. Dr. Pope had told her the time was short. But she never dreamed it would be this short.

She rubbed at the chill creeping over her skin and sat on the overstuffed chair by the fire, for once allowing her back to curve into the cushions. She looked up at the white plastered ceiling. "How could this atrocity occur? I planned for everything. *Everything!*"

*Everything but death,* the air seemed to whisper back.

Agnes lowered her eyes. It was funny, really, how much life was like water. The harder you grasped it, the more easily it slipped through your fingers. Agnes knew that now. She had grasped hard. Very hard indeed. She'd controlled the issue with the Bureau of Indian Affairs, convinced Dr. Sapir to come, and repaired the damage to Allison's reputation. For a moment, she'd ruled her world. Life was what it ought to be. But it all slipped away . . . like everything else she'd ever really wanted in her life—a faithful husband, a child of her own, Silas . . .

Her thoughts staggered to a halt when a man stepped through the parlor door.

Agnes blinked. Stared. "Silas?" It wasn't him. It couldn't be. It was just a vision conjured by her thoughts. She passed a hand in front of her eyes.

"Hello, Aggie-girl." He stood there, his shoulders rounded with age, his hat in his hand, turning the brim.

Agnes rose from the chair. It was just a dream. It had to be, after all these years. Her glance swept over him—from the tie askew around his neck to his unevenly pressed trousers and scuffed and worn shoes. It *was* him. Her Silas. But how? Why? She looked into his face with its deep-lined wrinkles and fringes of once dark hair now gray. Tears welled in her eyes. "You've come? You've come to me at last?"

His gaze caught hers, as keen as ever and just as piercing. "Mary let me in."

*Mary . . .*

The name caused a burning deep in Agnes's chest. Mary

had gotten what she wanted, just as she always had. Agnes pushed away the thought.

"What are you doing here?"

"It's time we talked, Aggie. Time we put the past where it belongs."

"I've watched for you. I've wished . . ." Her throat tightened. Here was another thing she'd never been able to control, never been able to make right. She took a step forward, toward him. "I needed you, Silas. But you didn't come."

His chin lowered. He twisted his hat into a tighter ball. "I know. But we promised each other, remember?"

"I remember." A vision of their younger selves washed through her mind. They were sitting on their special bench beneath the old oak, the same bench where he kissed her for the first time. But that day there were no kisses. That day she told him she was going to marry Teddy—wealthy, refined Teddy. Forty years had passed since then, the last time they spoke, but the memory was still fresh, still painful.

"It was a long time ago."

Agnes nodded. "Too long. But not long enough to forget." She shot him a quick glance.

He looked away, and Agnes knew she was right. Silas had not forgotten what she'd done to him. He hadn't forgotten, but perhaps, just perhaps, he'd forgiven her at last.

"Come, sit down, Sy." She motioned toward the chairs by the fire.

Silas dropped his hat on the small table, crossed the room, and sat on the edge of the chair. He never had been comfortable among fine things. *"I'm like a long-tailed cat in a roomful of rockin' chairs,"* he always used to say. He certainly looked like that long-tailed cat now.

Agnes perched on the chair beside him, her heart

jumping when Silas reached over and took her hand in his. "Roomful of rocking chairs." He smiled.

Just like that, the years standing between them dissolved. Agnes curled her fingers around his. His skin felt rough and thin, against her thumb, so unlike the hand she had held in her youth. But the warmth was the same. And his eyes, deep blue and searching—those were her Silas's eyes. Could he see in her, too, the girl she once was? "I'm glad you've come."

Silas's hand tightened on hers. "I should have come sooner. I should have come after Elizabeth died."

"She was a good wife to you."

"She was. And Whitson—"

Agnes touched her fingers to his lips. "Don't say it. We both know it isn't true."

He grunted, then rubbed the back of his neck. "Shoulda come. Coulda. Didn't." He shook his head. "I was a fool, Aggie. A stubborn old fool." His voice lowered. "But mostly I was afraid. You know that, don't you?"

She dropped her gaze to their hands, spotted with age, frail, but linked together for the first time in forty years. "Afraid that I would hurt you again?"

He reached out with his other hand and touched her hair. "Being hurt ain't the worst thing that can happen to a man. I know that now."

Agnes trembled at his caress. "What is the worst, Sy?"

"Not knowing how to live."

Silence swept between them.

Finally, Silas coughed. "But I know how to live now. Least I think I do. Gonna try anyway." He cleared his throat. "Been doing all my living through Thomas. Been meddling in his life instead of running my own. Been preaching instead of living. But preaching can't make up for mistakes."

Agnes dropped her gaze. "They were my mistakes."

"They were ours."

The truth floated like a feather between them.

Silas rubbed his thumb over her skin. "I'm gonna start over, Aggie." He shifted in his seat. "Want to know if you'll start over with me. Start over, like we should have done years ago."

Agnes pulled her hand from his. "I-I don't know how, Silas."

He nodded. "We'll remember. We'll remember together."

Agnes shook her head. Her throat tightened. "It's too late. Everything has fallen apart. Again. I can't keep it together."

Silas's fingers caressed her cheek, then wiped away the tear that had fallen there. "You try too hard. You always have."

"I've had to. You know that." Her voice sounded strained. She turned her face away from him. "How else . . ."

"Aggie?"

She sniffed. Was this why he came? To remind her of her failures? To tell her how she had lost what she wanted yet again? It wasn't fair. It wasn't right. Why did God always have to be against her? "How else could I hope to get what I want?" She paused and dabbed her eyes with her fingertips. "But it hasn't worked, has it? It never does. Why won't God ever allow me to have what I've labored so hard to gain? Why must He turn everything sour?" She glanced back at him.

Silas's lips pressed into a tight line. "You know why."

"He let Ishi die. There was nothing I could do to stop it."

"You aren't God, Aggie. You've got to stop pretending you are." He gripped her fingers.

She stared at him for a long moment, noting the shadow of whiskers on his cheeks, the black mole she once adored. "Are you saying—" she could hear the hardness in her tone, the scarcely concealed anger—"that God let Ishi die because of me?" She pulled her hand from his.

Silas sighed and settled back on the seat beside her. "You know what I'm saying. I've been saying it since we were seven years old." His fist clenched, then opened. "Let go, Aggie. There ain't nothing left to hang on to. I know. I've been hanging on too." He turned his hands palms up. "Let go."

Breath shuddered from her lips. "It won't bring Ishi back. It won't turn back time."

"This ain't about the Indian anymore."

"Then who?" Scorn laced her voice. "Us?" She almost laughed. She'd been a fool to think they could go back, become the two young lovers they once had been. The Indian's death had made her vulnerable. For a moment, she'd forgotten how many years had passed. But she remembered now. She remembered the woman she had become. She was someone to be reckoned with. She didn't need to let go.

Silas leaned forward, his elbows on his knees. "Us, yes, maybe us. But mostly Allison now."

Agnes's back stiffened. Her eyes narrowed. "Allison? What does any of this have to do with her?"

"She's gone, Aggie."

Fear pattered over her nerves. "Gone?"

"She didn't come home the night the Indian died. Nor last night either." Silas pressed his hands into his thighs and tilted toward her. "It's time for the truth. You know it. I know it. We've kept quiet too long."

"You're wrong, Silas."

He touched her hand. "Jesus says the truth will set us free. And maybe it will, Aggie-girl. This time, maybe it will."

Pure terror surged through Agnes's frame. Goose pimples raised on her arm. How dare he! She stood and backed away from him. How dare he ask that of her now? After all this time. "You have no right! I can't. You *know* I can't." Agnes took another step back. She felt the wall behind her.

Silas rose from his seat, and his finger jabbed toward her. "She's not your daughter, Agnes." His voice sharpened. "She never was."

Fury sliced through her like a burning knife. "She should have been. You know she should have been!" Pain laced up through Agnes's chest. Words jammed in her throat, choking her. She pushed her palm into her breast, quelling the tightness. "She should have been *ours!*"

The words echoed between them, shattering her anger, leaving only the pain. The age-old pain. The pain that had driven her for so many long years. Tears blurred her vision. She leaned against the wall behind her. "She should have been ours." Her voice dropped to a mere whisper. "Oh, Silas . . ."

Silas reached her in two strides. He took her in his arms —once strong arms, now thin, frail, but still strong enough for her. Still gentle. "Shhh, Aggie-girl. Shhh. You've got to let it go. It's time to move on." His hand stroked her hair.

"I will never forget what they did to me. When all I wanted was a daughter of my own . . ."

"Let go, Aggie." She could hear his heart beating, steady, strong. He massaged her shoulder. Gently, so very, very gently. "Thomas needs to know the truth. He needs to know if he's going to find Allison. You must, for Allison, and for Thomas. It's time."

She felt the rough fabric of his shirt scratching her cheek, muffling her words. "How will the truth help now?"

"He thinks her parents died."

"One did." She paused, her voice barely audible. "They both should have." Agnes looked up through her tears.

Mary stood in the doorway, her face as cold and sharp as a knife of ice.

Agnes pushed Silas away. She brushed her fingers over her cheeks to dash away dampness. "What do you want?"

Mary dropped her serving tray onto the table that held Silas's hat. Tea spilled as a cup clattered to its side, the sound echoing in the room.

Agnes smoothed her dress, her eyes never leaving Mary. She tried to make her voice stern. "You should tell Thomas to look for Allison at the orphanage, Mr. Morgan. Perhaps she has gone there."

Mary's gaze flickered to Silas. "He won't find her there."

Silas turned toward the serving woman. "Where should he look, Mary?"

Mary regarded him for a long moment. A log fell in the fireplace. Shadows shimmered over the walls. Mary's gaze dropped. Her face colored with shame. "The alley. Tell him to try the alley."

Agnes held her breath. It was coming. She could feel it.

Mary squared her shoulders. Her eyes narrowed into slits.

"No. Don't." Agnes reached toward Mary.

Mary shook her head. "It's time to face the truth. For good." Before Agnes could move, Mary marched over and flung open the parlor window.

An icy breeze blew in from the bay. The curtains billowed. The fire sputtered out, spitting ash onto the wood floor.

Agnes trembled as the wind lifted the hem of her dress.

# THIRTY-TWO

He appeared like an apparition out of the grayness, like a ghost from a dream, standing there at the end of the alley, the breeze ruffling his hair. "Allison?" His voice reached out to her. "Is that you?"

She shrank back into the shadows. *Thomas?* The shard of bottle glass slipped from her hand and broke on the cobblestone. Pieces skittered away, refracting light.

Thomas moved toward her, his features becoming clearer in the dimness. She noticed the way his hair drooped over his forehead and how his shirt lay open at the neck. But the difference in his appearance was more than dishevelment. *He* had changed. His chin was hard. The set of his shoulders, determined. Something had finally stirred Thomas to action. She rose from the milk crate.

"Allison!" He broke into a run. "Allison!"

Allison swayed. She raised a hand to her matted hair, brushed her fingers over the filth on her sleeve. He came. He cared enough to find her. But—her fingers trembled— he shouldn't see her like this.

"I found you." His arms extended toward her.

She put out a hand, stopping him. "Go away, Thomas. Go home."

"Allison?"

"I want you to go home!"

For a moment, he paused.

"Leave me *alone!*" Her shout rang through the alley.

"No." Thomas took two strides forward and caught her in his arms, engulfing her, drawing her close. One hand stroked her tangled hair, the other pressed into her back. "I found you. I won't lose you again."

She pushed against him and felt his muscles tighten. "Leave me alone," she whimpered.

He didn't loosen his grip.

She pounded a feeble fist on his chest. Didn't he know what she was? What she'd always been? Did he know that this alley was where she belonged?

"It's time to come home, Allison."

"I can't." Her hands grew still. She rested her forehead on his shoulder. "Let go of me, Thomas. I belong here."

Thomas released her, then leaned over and tenderly wiped his finger across her cheek, as if removing a smudge of dirt that clung there. "You belong with me. I thought I'd lost you too."

She stepped away from him and again sat on the crate. "Why? You know what I did to Ishi."

Thomas studied her for a moment, then sighed and sat down beside her. "I know what we both did. I, because I was too weak; you, because you were too strong." He reached out and touched her leg as if he feared she might somehow get away. "We make mistakes. We fail. I don't blame you."

*You should.* Allison felt the warmth of his hand through the stained fabric of her dress. "Look at me, Thomas."

He glanced toward her.

"No, I mean really look at me."

His eyes, so blue, so clear, caught and held hers.

"This is what I am." She waved her hand over her filthy clothes, then pointed to her matted hair. "I'm not the woman you thought you married. I'm—" she swallowed— "I'm this woman. This mess. That's who I really am."

Thomas's gaze shifted from her dress to her hair, then rested on her hands. "You've taken off your gloves." His eyes grew round. He reached out and took her bare hand in his. "I always thought you had lovely hands."

She pulled her fingers from his grip. "I'm finished wearing gloves. They can't help. They never really did."

He looked at her and nodded. "I see."

She laughed. "Do you? Do you finally see what I really am?"

Confusion spilled over his face.

"I'm dirty, I'm filthy, I'm just a piece of trash that my mother decided to throw away one day."

"I thought—"

"I know what you thought. I'm not an orphan. I was *left*. No one wanted me." She paused and clenched the dirty cloth of her dress in her fist. "Can you blame them? I've pretended for so long, so very long, that I was somebody. But I know the truth now."

"No, Allison."

She scooted away from him, trembling. "I can't live the lie anymore. I won't." She stood and turned her back to him. "The Great Eagle is dead."

Thomas rose behind her. He placed a hand on her arm, pulling her back toward him. "Maybe. Maybe not."

She paused, then glanced over her shoulder. Did he know . . . ? "What do you know of the eagle?"

His fingers tightened on her arm. "I found the story. The tale you wrote down, the one Ishi was telling you."

She nodded. "So you understand, then. You know what I am. You know there's no hope for me."

She heard his sharp intake of breath. "But there was more, Allison. More of the story. Ishi told me so."

She swayed on her feet. "He's dead now. Yuna's tale is dead with him." *And so am I.*

"He finished it."

Allison heard the crackling sound of paper unfolding.

"He finished it for you."

She turned around.

Thomas held a page, extending it toward her. "Only I don't know what it says." His voice was soft, entreating.

She glanced down at the paper, fluttering in his hand. Yuna's tale? But how?

"Take it, Allison. Read it to me."

She reached out and took the sheet. Words, Yahi words, written phonetically, scampered across her vision. Yuna, Coyote, the Great Eagle. Could it be? And what did it matter now?

"Sit down, Allison." Thomas's voice came from beside her. "Read it to me. Tell me how the story ends."

Allison lowered herself to the milk box. Her eyes skimmed the page. Ishi's last words to her. The story he would share with no one else. "Do you think I should?"

Thomas knelt before her and placed his hand on her knee. "I know I don't deserve anything from you. I haven't been the husband you've needed me to be. I was too afraid to face the hard things in our life. I learned early the cost of fighting, of angry words. And I thought hiding behind the door would keep me safe, even now, even in our marriage. So I looked away. I stepped aside. I blamed Mrs. Whitson. But hiding won't save me. I know that now. Only God can do that. We just have to trust Him."

Allison made a sound of denial in her throat.

Thomas put up a hand. "No, don't say it. You know I'm right. Things are going to change. I promise. I'm going to trust God to see me through the uncomfortable parts of life as well as the triumphs. I'm stepping out from behind the door, Allison. I owe it to you. I owe it to Ishi."

"But, Thomas, I—"

He touched her lips. "I know you don't owe me anything. But I'm asking you anyway. Ishi wanted you to see the story. Read it for him. For me."

Allison wondered if she could read, now with her vision strangely blurred and her chest feeling so tight that her breath came in labored spurts. "All right, but it's just an old Indian fable, after all."

"Perhaps." Thomas rose and settled onto the crate beside her.

Allison flattened the paper on her knees and began to read, translating into English.


*Yuna knelt over the dead eagle. Blood stained his chest, flowed over his wings. Her fingers shook as she touched his still form.*

*"I've won! I've won!" chanted the coyote behind her.*

*She turned toward him.*

*"You are mine, Yuna!" Coyote howled. "No one will love you now."*

*Yuna bowed her head. The sky turned black above her.*

Tears all but choked Allison, and she looked up into the gray sky. "I don't want to read. It hurts to hear it."

Thomas brushed his hand along her arm. "Keep going."

She touched the edge of the paper, took a deep breath, and continued.

*Suddenly, a piercing light shone through the clouds. Coyote screamed. His eyes grew wide as stones in the river.*

*"No! It cannot be!" With a shriek, he fled into the forest.*

*Yuna watched him go. Then she stretched out her hands toward the eagle. Clean hands. She looked down. The blood was gone. The dirt vanished. She touched her clothes, white and clean; her feet, spotless; her arms, perfect; her face . . .*

*She jumped up, ran to the turtle shell, and peered into the water. Her nose, her cheeks, her mouth. Not a spot, not a blemish.*

*Yuna pressed her palms to her shiny cheeks. "His blood . . . his blood did this." Then she knew that the eagle had given his life for her, so that she could be clean. He had done as he promised, but now he was dead. "Oh, Great Eagle," she muttered, her heart breaking.*

*The light in the sky grew brighter, stronger.*

*"Hello, Yuna." The words washed over her like a mighty wind.*

*She turned. "Eagle?"*

*"It is I."*

*"You're alive!" The blood was gone, though now there was a scar over his heart.*

*The Great Eagle spread his wings. His feathers touched her cheek. "Do you know my name now, Yuna?" he asked.*

*"Yes," she answered. "Your name is—"*

Thomas finished the story with a single word: "Jesus."

# THIRTY-THREE

The name shimmered between them like a sapphire in the sun.

*Jesus.*

Thomas held his breath. Would she accept it? Would she understand? He waited for an eternity while Allison sat silently with her head bent and the paper wavering on her knee. "Allison?"

She looked up.

Thomas felt his heart thump in his chest.

There, on her cheek, shimmered a tear. The only one he had ever seen her shed. A single, pure, cleansing tear. "Mama was wrong." The words flowed from her like a soft breeze.

Thomas touched a finger to the wetness on her cheek. *Oh, Father, does this mean . . . can it possibly mean that . . . ?*

Allison smiled. "Ishi told me I would know the Great Eagle's name when the time was right. *Achi djeyauna?* he would say. What is his name? I never dreamed—"

"It was Jesus all along?" *How did Ishi know? Did Ishi know?* The questions darted through the back of Thomas's mind. Was Yuna's tale a story told by some long-ago missionary? They would never know. Maybe they didn't need to.

Allison leaned her head against Thomas's shoulder. "I've been a fool, haven't I? I've spent my whole life trying to make myself worthy of love."

"You've always been worthy to me."

She shook her head. Her hair tickled his chin. "No, I haven't been. But God has loved me all the same."

Thomas gathered her in his arms and hugged her to his chest. "It seems too easy, doesn't it?"

Allison didn't answer for a long moment. Then she pulled back and looked up into his eyes. "But it wasn't easy, was it? Someone had to die for me to hear. For me to understand."

A tremor shook her, and he held her closer. It would take time, he knew, for the truth to take root, for hurts of the past to be healed and the habits of a lifetime to be changed. But this was a start, a glorious new start that Ishi had given them. It was his final gift, a legacy more lasting than a hundred bottle glass arrowheads, than a thousand words written in long, dull lists.

The rumble of a Model T's engine woke Allison from dreams of dancing maple leaves and flute music. She yawned and stretched her arms above her head. The wooden swing creaked beneath her. The sound of the engine sputtered to a halt. Thomas was home!

Allison rubbed her eyes. In a moment, he would fling open the front door, look out the back window, and see her sitting here on the swing he'd made for her. Then he'd hurry to change his clothes before he came out to sit with her. They'd swing together and talk about Ishi, about the museum, about all the ways their lives would be different from now on. Allison hugged her arms around herself and waited. He'd come soon, just as he'd done for the past three days.

Three days. It seemed so short a time, just a blink, really, on the backdrop of eternity. Three days from a cold, gray alley to a garden lit with the warmth of the sun. Three days from despair to hope. Three days—the same amount of time Jesus was in the tomb.

Three days was enough time to change one's life forever.

Allison tipped back her head and allowed the sun to caress her face. Sunshine and promise and hope. She'd found them all since that day in the alley, found them like newly blooming flowers in the corners of her heart. Like the first blossoms after a long winter. Fresh and fragile, with dew still on their petals.

A smile curved over Allison's lips. She was becoming positively poetic these days. She glanced out over the garden—the pink roses climbing the trellis, the swaying branches of the crepe myrtle, the brightly colored tulips, and the old stone fountain gurgling water from its algae-stained bottom. A scene like that would bring out the poetry in anyone. Even Thomas would agree. She settled back into the swing and tucked one foot under her leg. She pushed against the ground until the swing rocked in a gentle arc.

Today, she'd talk to Thomas about the flowers. She'd tell him that flowers didn't strive; they didn't pretend. God had made them what they were. He tended them. He gave them their beauty. Just like He'd done for her.

Allison brushed her bare fingers through her hair. Yes,

much had changed. It didn't even matter anymore if she remembered her mother's face. She didn't need to remember to know who she was. She knew. She was Yuna. She was dirty, just as she'd always known, but the Great Eagle . . . *Jesus*—she savored the name—made her clean. Finally she was somebody.

She was a child of God.

She wouldn't forget that. Not even when the sun disappeared, when doubts came, or—she bit her lip—when Mrs. Whitson had her next dinner party. For Ishi's sake, she would remember what Jesus had done for her.

She leaned back and closed her eyes, relishing the scent of roses on the breeze. She drew in a long breath and let it out slowly. *Thank You, Jesus, for making me clean. Thank You that I don't have to be good enough. Don't let me forget, especially when—*

A shadow passed over Allison's eyelids. She opened her eyes and blinked into the sunlight. "Thomas?" She shielded her eyes with one hand as the outline of a flowered hat materialized before her vision. A chill swept over her. "Oh, Mrs. Whitson, I wasn't expecting—"

"Clearly." Mrs. Whitson stepped out of the sun's path enough so that Allison could see the scowl on her face. She touched the brim of her hat.

Allison glanced down at her own hat sitting on the seat beside her. She reached for it, then drew back her hand. She hadn't expected to be tested so soon. "Would you care to sit down?" She pushed the hat aside to allow Mrs. Whitson to sit.

Mrs. Whitson balanced on the edge of the bench swing. Her gaze swooped over Allison.

Suddenly Allison realized her spine was resting against the back of the swing and one foot was still tucked beneath her. She sat up and straightened her leg. "The sun is pleasant today." Her voice cracked. "Would you care for some tea?"

Mrs. Whitson smoothed a wrinkle in her dress. "No, I didn't come here to sip tea and exchange pleasantries. I came because there are some important matters I must discuss with you."

Allison glanced at Mrs. Whitson's profile—the rigid jaw, the chin slightly lifted, the eyes focused on something beyond the garden fence. "Important matters?" A trembling began in the pit her stomach. Had Mrs. Whitson come to list all the ways Allison had failed? Had she come for an apology for making them all worry? Thomas told her he'd taken care of that, but knowing Mrs. Whitson . . .

Allison folded her hands in her lap and began the speech she'd rehearsed, just in case. "I sincerely regret the worry I caused you. I know I shouldn't have run away after Ishi's death, but—"

Mrs. Whitson raised her hand, stopping Allison's words. "No, child. Say no more. I'm not here for that either."

Allison's brows drew together. "Then why?"

Mrs. Whitson caught her lower lip between her teeth. She glanced back toward the house.

Allison followed her gaze. There, like a shadowy reflection through the window, she could just make out the shape of a woman watching. The image caused a pang in her chest. For a moment, she couldn't breathe. Then the woman stepped back. "Who is that?"

Mrs. Whitson's eyes fixed on Allison for a long moment. "It is only Mary, my maid." She paused. "Does her presence trouble you?"

Allison shivered. "Oh, no." She tried to smile and failed.

"I just wasn't expecting to see anyone there, that's all." She touched her hand to her hair.

Mrs. Whitson reached out and captured her fingers in a tight grasp. Slowly, she turned Allison's hand until the palm faced upward. A gloved finger traced a line from her thumb to wrist. "Where are your gloves, my dear?" She released her grip.

Allison's hand curled into a fist.

"A lady always wears gloves."

Allison massaged her thumb over the knuckles on her clenched hand. "Yes, I know." She spread her fingers and studied the way the light made her skin seem to glow. "But for me, they are no longer right." She laid her hands on her lap and tried not to twine her fingers too tightly together.

Mrs. Whitson's eyebrows darted upward. "Is that so?"

Allison nodded, not trusting her voice to speak. *Please don't ask me any more. Don't say another word about the gloves. Lord Jesus . . .*

Mrs. Whitson turned away. "No matter."

Allison sighed. The breeze picked up. A cloud passed in front of the sun. The sky darkened. From next door, she heard the clatter of wood falling from the woodpile. A cat yowled.

Mrs. Whitson drew a deep breath. "Now, about why I am here. It seems it is time to make you aware of some—" she cleared her throat and began again— "to apprise you of a few facts regarding your past."

Allison leaned forward. The swing quivered beneath her. "My past?"

Mrs. Whitson threaded the drawstring of her reticule bag around her finger. "When you were a child . . ." Her hands clenched. Her knuckles turned white. "I cannot do this. They cannot make me."

"Mrs. Whitson?"

She turned away, her shoulders tense. "No, this is insanity. I cannot do this alone. I never should have tried." She stood and moved away from the swing.

The door creaked open behind them. "Aggie?"

Allison looked up, surprised to hear Pop's voice.

Mrs. Whitson twisted her reticule into a figure eight. "I can't do it, Silas."

"Oh, Aggie." He sighed and came toward them.

*Aggie?* Allison knew they'd been friends as children, but this was new. Had God been breaking through more barriers than just her own in these last few days?

Mrs. Whitson turned as Pop reached her. "I—"

"Shhh." He put his hand on her arm. Allison noted the tenderness in his touch. Her gaze flew to Pop, but he just smiled at her.

"Pop?"

His head inclined toward Mrs. Whitson. "My hornet. My flower." His smile spread into grin.

"Ohhh." Warmth washed through Allison.

Pop searched her face for a long moment as his hand caressed Mrs. Whitson's arm. "You know, there's something different about you, girl."

Allison saw a softness in his expression, a gentleness she had missed before. Yes, God had certainly been at work in him as well. "And you, Pop."

He chuckled. "Aye, though God's still working on me, He is. Got a lot of years worth of pigheadedness to make up for." He tapped his temple with one finger.

Allison giggled. "Me too."

"We got some ways to go, we do. All of us." His gaze shifted to Mrs. Whitson. Yes, something *had* happened

357

between them. Something private, something good. "Time to tell her what you come to say, Aggie. No use hiding anymore."

The door slapped shut.

Allison turned. There, on the steps leading from the back door, Thomas guided the maid out to the garden. His eyes caught Allison's in a single penetrating look before they turned to Pop. "Has she—?"

Pop shook his head. "Not yet. Time now to do it. Now . . . with all of us here." He motioned toward a bench near the swing. "You just sit right there, Mary. Thomas . . ."

Thomas led Mary to the bench, then strode over to Allison and put his hand on her shoulder. A tremor raced through her. "What's going on, Thomas?" Her gaze sought his.

*I'm here,* his eyes told her as his fingers squeezed gently into her skin.

Peace flowed through her, replacing her fear. Thomas was with her, beside her. She was not alone.

The maid fixed her gaze on Mrs. Whitson and remained silent.

"It's okay, love," Thomas murmured. "I guess we're not the only ones who need to start over." He smiled down at her, then settled on the swing beside her.

Mrs. Whitson's fingers fluttered to her hat. As they did, Allison noticed something in her face that she'd never seen before—a tightening at the corners of her mouth, a tremble in her chin. Was it fear? It didn't seem possible, and yet . . .

Mrs. Whitson's gaze slid away from them. She smoothed her hand over her bodice and straightened her shoulders. Then her eyes rose to meet Allison's. "It's time for the truth."

"Truth?"

"You should have known long ago, I suppose. But, well, I've had my reasons." She paused and twined her fingers through the reticule's string again. "I would like to tell you that what I did was for your own good. I told myself that it was."

The maid made a noise in the back of her throat.

Mrs. Whitson threw her a sharp glance, and the woman quieted.

"But it wasn't for your good. It was for mine. It was because they hurt me, and I wanted them to pay." Mrs. Whitson's fist clenched. Her jaw tightened until it looked like chiseled stone. "You have to know that, Allison. I never meant to hurt you. Just them."

"Who?"

"Your parents, my dear. I'm talking about your parents."

Allison quaked at the hardness in Mrs. Whitson's voice. "You . . . knew my parents?"

Mrs. Whitson's eyes narrowed into angry slits. "I knew them very well. You see, your father was my husband."

*My father* . . . It took several moments for the words to penetrate her senses. Her father, Mr. Whitson . . . She'd never thought about her father before. The irony struck her, and she fought to stifle a laugh. Why, her father was a gentleman, an aristocrat! She frowned. No, her father was God. That's what mattered. A few days ago, knowing that she was Mr. Whitson's daughter would have really mattered, but now she knew the truth. Her blood, Mr. Whitson's blood, none of that was important. It was *Jesus'* blood that made her somebody. She couldn't forget that.

Allison glanced at the faces of those around her. Did they care that Mr. Whitson was her father? Thomas wouldn't. He was watching her face carefully, his arm still around her shoulders. The maid didn't. She was staring out at the rose trellis as if none of this concerned her. Pop didn't. He had moved to Mrs. Whitson's side, his hand on her arm. Only Mrs. Whitson cared. Only her gaze was tortured.

"I didn't know about you, though, didn't know until he died." Her voice grew ragged.

Allison spoke softly. "A deathbed confession?"

Mrs. Whitson grimaced. "No, child, nothing so dramatic as that. I knew for years, of course, about Teddy's little affair with my personal maid." Allison could hear the chill in her voice, the pain that had not dissipated over the years. "But I chose to ignore it." She raised her chin. "Cultured women do that, you know. They overlook; they rise above such sordidness." Her back straightened. "And that's what I did. I was Mrs. Theodore Whitson. I had a reputation to protect." Her mouth twisted into a sad smile. "That's what I told myself. And for a while—a very little while—it was enough.

"In time, I dismissed your mother. Then later I found that Teddy had been paying rent for a cheap little house outside the city. I didn't care. The woman was gone. Teddy was mine. Then Teddy died of the fever. And I found out about you. A little girl . . . a beautiful, perfect little girl."

The drawstring ripped from her reticule. "A *girl*, when God refused to give me any children at all." The bitterness of a lifetime overflowed that one phrase.

Allison shuddered.

"So I did what I did. Your mother couldn't get work after it was known what she'd done. Who would want her in their home?" Mrs. Whitson's lips grew tighter, until Allison wondered if she'd be able to squeeze the words through such a narrow opening. "But I offered her a choice. A single chance to save herself, and you."

Allison caught her breath, sudden understanding striking her heart. "You didn't!"

Mrs. Whitson's mouth thinned. "I did. I made her give you up. If I couldn't have a child, why should she?"

Allison's mind reeled. "You. It was you all along. That's why you—"

Mrs. Whitson jammed her fists into her hips. "Yes, that's why I took a special interest in you. That's why I've done everything for you."

Allison gripped the edges of the swing. "But you took my *mother*."

Mrs. Whitson turned her face away. "She didn't deserve you. You should have been mine."

Allison bolted up. The swing tipped back, then jarred the back of her knees. "You had no right!"

Mrs. Whitson's chin jutted up. "I had every right."

Mary leapt to her feet and glared at Mrs. Whitson. "You finish the story. You tell her!"

Mrs. Whitson blanched, and her shoulders hunched.

"Mrs. Whitson?" Allison spoke slowly. She couldn't bring herself to look at Mary. "Is my mother still alive?"

Silence pervaded the garden until all Allison could hear was the quiet gurgle of water in the fountain and the sound of Mrs. Whitson twisting, twisting, twisting the broken string of her reticule bag.

Pop coughed.

Mary crossed her arms over her chest. A blackbird squawked from the maple.

"Yes, she's alive."

Allison sat back on the swing. "And?"

"Mary . . ." Mrs. Whitson motioned to her maid. The words stopped, as if stuck behind a lifetime's worth of bitterness. Then she took a deep breath.

"It's okay, Aggie," Pop murmured. "It's time."

"I know." Mrs. Whitson's voice grew hard. "Allison, Mary is your mother."

# THIRTY-FOUR

Allison gazed into the face that had haunted her dreams. The dark hair, the watery blue eyes, the narrow nose.

She looked nothing like the stone angels.

"Mother?"

Mary took a step forward. "It's me, Allison." The woman's voice sparked no memory, no joy of discovery, nothing.

Mary stopped, as if sensing the rejection that Allison fought to suppress. She touched her fingers to her throat. "I never wanted to give you up. She gave me no choice. She made me. You understand?" Her hand extended toward Allison.

Allison pressed back into the swing. Her emotions swirled in an eddy of confusion. "You left me. Next to a trash bin."

"It weren't my fault. I'd nowhere to go." She put her hands out, palms up, pleading.

Allison stood and approached her mother. From somewhere above, a robin answered the blackbird's call. The swing squeaked. The sun dipped behind a cloud. And Allison looked into the face that had evaded her for as long as she could remember. She noted the quivering lips, the weak chin, the eyes that darted sideways as if judging the reaction of her rival. Allison glanced at Mrs. Whitson, standing like a statue, jaw set, eyes narrowed.

And she understood.

These two women were locked in a world all their own. She stepped back. Two women with masks thick enough to hide the truth from others, to hide the truth from themselves. That's why she never recognized her mother. That's why she never knew the secrets buried in Mrs. Whitson's heart. Masks. Masks of civility concealing anger, disguising hate. Masks that hid the faces beneath until nothing was recognizable but the bitterness.

Allison lifted her hand and touched her mother's cheek with one finger. Dry, weathered, like old papier-mâché that had just begun to crack. She'd always thought that this face would heal her, that even the memory of it would connect the missing pieces of her life. But memory did not heal. Only Jesus could do that.

Her finger traced the wrinkled surface of Mary's chin. She looked deeper into the woman's eyes and saw the weariness, the guilt she hid there.

*This could have been me. I could have lived my whole life trying to fool the world, trying to fool myself. I could have spent my life living behind the mask.* She dropped her hand. Peace flowed through her. *Thank You, Jesus, for showing me my mother's face. For showing me what I could have been.*

"I'm sorry, Allison," Mary choked. "Maybe I shoulda been stronger. Maybe I shoulda stood up to her. But that's behind us now, now that you know the truth."

"All the truth, Mary?" Mrs. Whitson's voice cut through the air like a gardener's spade.

Mary started. "What else is there? You made me give away my daughter. You kept me from her." She turned to Allison. "But I've always watched over you. I've always been there, even when you didn't know it."

Mrs. Whitson strode forward and gripped Mary's arm. "Yes, you always have been, haven't you?" She thrust the question from between gritted teeth. "But it hasn't always been her that you've been watching."

Mary's face turned red. "What are you saying?"

Mrs. Whitson tightened her fingers until Mary's skin became pale beneath them. "I'm not the only one with secrets."

Mary shook free. "I love my daughter. It ain't my fault I didn't know about the displays or—" her voice turned as brittle as shattering glass—"or about that Indian."

"Ishi?" The hair rose at the back of Allison's neck.

Mrs. Whitson nodded. "I thought it was you. I always suspected."

"I did it to get back at you." Mary stabbed a finger toward Mrs. Whitson. "Like you hurt me. That museum was *your* baby."

"Yes, but the displays were Allison's." Mrs. Whitson's voice was soft as churned butter.

A pained expression flitted over Mary's face. "I know." Tears formed in her eyes. She turned them to Allison. "I'm real sorry about your exhibits. I'm sorry I told Willy to write that letter to the Indian bureau. I didn't know. I swear I didn't."

"We wanted to hurt each other." Mrs. Whitson sighed. "Instead, we hurt Allison. She's always been the one to pay for our hate."

Mary reached her arms toward Allison one more time. "Can't we forget all that?"

Allison massaged her fingers into her temples. "I can't forget. How could I possibly forget?" She felt a tremor in her stomach. She'd wanted so desperately to please these two women—the phantom mother of memory and the woman who had filled her mother's place. Yet in all that time she'd only been a symbol to them, a pawn to manipulate in their games of hate and revenge. And now they wanted her to forget, to forgive?

Thomas stepped behind her. She felt the warmth of his hand on her back, supporting her. "While we were yet sinners," he whispered in her ear, "He died for us."

Allison gazed at the two women before her, women twined together by hate, linked in bitterness. Yes, she had reaped the poison of their schemes, but Jesus rescued her. Rescued her and set her free. She hadn't deserved it. She hadn't earned it. But Jesus loved her all the same.

"I cannot forget," she repeated. "But perhaps I *can* forgive." She moved toward them. The image of a golden eagle soared through her mind. "I don't understand all you've done. Maybe I never will. But this one thing I know: Jesus died for you too."

Allison reached out and took each of their hands in her own. "Even you can be clean."

They stood there, three women bound by pain, linked by love. And Allison knew at that moment—Ishi had fulfilled his dream.

# EPILOGUE

The tulips were in bloom again. Vivid colors spattered over the garden like the threads of a brightly woven Indian blanket, reminding her of Ishi. Allison walked along the garden path with one hand in Thomas's. With the other, she rubbed her rounded belly. "The tulips are especially lovely this year. I wish Ishi could have seen them."

Thomas squeezed her hand and pulled her closer to his side. "It's hard to believe he's been gone a year now."

"Gone, but not forgotten. Never forgotten."

"I wonder what he would have thought about Pop and Mrs. Whitson?"

Allison chuckled. "Missionaries to the Indians, who would have believed it?" She still could hardly believe those two had married and gone off to Arizona like two twenty-year-olds. "I never dreamed Mrs. Whitson could change so much."

"I don't know. Pop said she wouldn't let him take his gardening overalls. Said she threw them in the garbage and insisted he wear clothes *befitting a man of his station.*"

"Ah, but I heard he rescued the overalls in the end."

Thomas laughed. "I pity the poor Indians who will have to put up with those two."

Allison leaned into Thomas. "But Ishi wouldn't. You know, I think he would have smiled and said, 'Aiku tsub.'"

Thomas rubbed his hand along her side. "Aiku tsub. Yes, I believe he would have. And he'd be right."

Warmth spread through Allison's body. It had been quite a year, a good year. Forgiveness had come, slowly and hard fought. Allison had gotten to know her mother, and in doing so found a woman completely different from the one she imagined. Mary didn't care about proper hats and fine dresses, but she couldn't abide an overcooked roast. She was distant sometimes. And occasionally, Allison would find her staring out toward the edge of the city with tears in her eyes. But at least Mary and Agnes had finally let go of their hold on each other's lives.

Yes, forgiveness had come, and with it freedom for all of them. All because of Jesus, the Great Eagle. All because Ishi had died to tell the story that healed their hearts.

"I miss him."

Thomas smiled at Allison. "So do I."

She paused and touched the velvety petal of a red tulip. "You know, sometimes I think I still hear flute music." She straightened. "But then it's only the wind."

"Only the wind." Thomas pulled her closer. "And the memory."

Allison rested her hand on her expanded belly. She smiled up at Thomas. "If it's a girl, I'd like to name her—"

"Yuna?" He grinned at her.

She let her joy out with a smile. "Yes, Yuna. A name is a powerful thing, you know."

Inside her womb, Allison felt the baby kick.

# HISTORICAL NOTE

*Only the Wind Remembers* was inspired by the true story of Ishi, the last Yahi, who walked out of the woods in Oroville, California, on August 29, 1911. Dubbed the last Stone Age Indian in North America and named *Ishi* (the Yahi word for *man*), he took up residence at the Museum of Anthropology in San Francisco. There he learned about the *saldu* (white man) and shared his culture with the anthropologists who became his close friends.

In *Only the Wind Remembers*, I've attempted to paint a picture consistent with the historical record. For example, as in my story, the real Ishi shared the Yahi culture through songs and stories etched onto Edison wax cylinders. He made arrowheads out of bottle glass, demonstrated Yahi hunting techniques, and even did some janitorial work at the museum. He went to a vaudeville show in October of 1911 where Harry Breen sang the ditty about Ishi that we read in the story. The real Ishi was fascinated by retracting window shades and piped water. He cared little for shoes and remained unimpressed by either aeroplanes or San Francisco's tall buildings. No one ever knew his true Yahi name, but those who did know him counted him a friend.

However, while I've tried to be true to Ishi's life and spirit, *Only the Wind Remembers* is a fictional story. As such, I've introduced characters and events that are not part of recorded history.

In my story, I've shortened the time line of Ishi's life at the museum and created a conflict with the Bureau of Indian Affairs. Dr. Alfred Kroeber, whom Ishi called the *big Chief*, and Dr. Saxton Pope (*Popey*) were actual friends of Ishi's, as was famous linguist Dr. Edward Sapir, who worked with Ishi prior to his hospitalization for tuberculosis. However, Thomas and Allison Morgan are fictional creations. The young professor of anthropology, who brought Ishi to San Francisco and became his first friend, was Thomas Waterman. Mrs. Agnes Whitson is also a fictional character. The patron whose support established the Museum of Anthropology in San Francisco was Mrs. Phoebe A. Hearst, after whom the museum was named in 1991.

Today, you can visit the Phoebe A. Hearst Museum of Anthropology in Kroeber Hall at the University of California, Berkeley. (The museum moved from its San Francisco location in 1931.) There you can see the largest and most comprehensive gallery of California Indian artifacts in the world, as well as a section devoted specifically to Ishi.

While the real Ishi told many stories, including those of the wood duck and U-Tut-Na and U-Tut-Ni, the wood duck's sisters, there is no record of a tale of the Great Eagle. Nor do we know if Ishi had any knowledge of Jesus. It is often assumed that he shared a religion similar to that of other Yana tribes of the Eastern Sacramento Valley, but the data is inconclusive.

On March 25, 1916, the real Ishi died of tuberculosis—a white man's disease to which he had no resistance. Yet, the world did not forget him. Even today, his name is in the news. Lately, the story has centered on the return of his brain from the Smithsonian. Tomorrow, who knows? But one thing is certain: Ishi is remembered. His story lives on.

# GLOSSARY

| | |
|---|---|
| *Aiku tsub:* | all is well |
| *Banya:* | deer |
| *Daana:* | baby |
| *Daha:* | the Sacramento River |
| *Dawana:* | crazy |
| *Ishi:* | man |
| *Hansi:* | many |
| *Haxa:* | Yes |
| *Hexai-sa:* | Go away. |
| *Jupka:* | butterfly |
| *Majapa:* | headman |
| *Mechi-Kuwi:* | demon doctor |
| *museum-watgurwa:* | museum-house |
| *Nize ah Yahi:* | I am Yahi |
| *Saldu:* | white man |
| *Siwini:* | white pine |
| *Su!:* | So! Ah! |
| *Waganupa:* | Mount Lassen |
| *Wanasi:* | hunter |
| *Watgurwa:* | house, particularly a man's house |
| *Wowi:* | home, family home |
| *Yahi:* | the People |
| *Yuna:* | acorn |

Dear Reader,

When I first started writing *Only the Wind Remembers*, my daughter, Bethany, was two years old. As I finish, she has just passed her third birthday. Much has changed in the course of a year. She's learned how to count to ten, to recognize her ABCs, to make poo-poos in the potty, and to sing "tinkle tinkle little tar" in a voice loud enough to shake dust from the rafters. But, more important, she has discovered the wonder of Jesus.

Every night now, as she crawls in bed and pulls the blanket up under her chin, she says, "You want to tell me about Jesus? Tell me about Jesus on the cross."

And so I tell her the story again. I talk about how they nailed Jesus to the cross, how the sky turned black, how He died and the curtain in the temple was torn in two.

"That's sad, Mommy," she says as she clutches the sea otter toy we bought her for her birthday.

Next, I tell her how they took Jesus down from the cross and put Him in the tomb for one day . . . two days . . . three days (she loves to count the days on her fingers). Then my voice grows quiet. "The ground shook. The stone rolled away, and—" I stop.

Bethany finishes the story. "Him not die anymore! Him risen!"

We laugh together, and then I say, "And that is the most wonderful, incredible, amazing, important thing that has ever happened in the whole wide world from the beginning of time until now."

Her eyes grow wide. She snuggles deeper into her blankets, and whispers, "Wow."

"Wow," I say in return.

And that, I think, is what Ishi's story is all about. The

*wow* of what Jesus did for us—how that changes everything, how that gives us hope.

Through the parable of the Great Eagle, I pray that you, too, can regain some of the wonder, some of the "wow," of what Jesus did for you. May He wrap you in His wings of love, and may you fly with Him into the winds of truth and beauty.

If you enjoyed your journey with Ishi, Allison, and Thomas, please drop me a note at the address below, or visit my website at www.marloschalesky.com. I'd love to hear from you!

Write to Marlo at:

> Marlo Schalesky
> c/o Moody Publishers
> 820 North LaSalle Boulevard
> Chicago, IL 60610-3284

SINCE 1894, Moody Publishers has been dedicated to equip and motivate people to advance the cause of Christ by publishing evangelical Christian literature and other media for all ages, around the world. Because we are a ministry of the Moody Bible Institute of Chicago, a portion of the proceeds from the sale of this book go to train the next generation of Christian leaders.

If we may serve you in any way in your spiritual journey toward understanding Christ and the Christian life, please contact us at www.moodypublishers.com.

*"All Scripture is God-breathed and is useful for teaching, rebuking, correcting and training in righteousness, so that the man of God may be thoroughly equipped for every good work."*
—2 TIMOTHY 3:16, 17

MOODY
PUBLISHERS

THE NAME YOU CAN TRUST®

# Dust and Ashes

ISBN: 0-8024-1554-7

Nazis flee under cover of darkness as American troops near the town of St. Georgen. A terrible surprise awaits the unsuspecting GIs. And three people —the wife of an SS guard, an American soldier, and a concentration camp survivor—will never be the same.

Inspired by actual events surrounding the liberation of a Nazi concentration camp, *From Dust and Ashes* shows the healing power of forgiveness.

*What a story! It sweeps us back to a time when the world swore "Never again" and gives us raw hope to walk away with.*
Anne De Graaf, International best-selling author & Christy Award winner.

# The Brother's Keeper

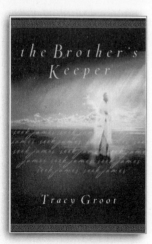

ISBN: 0-8024-3105-4

Thirty years after he followed a star to Bethlehem, one of the Magi is back on another mission. This time, he is sent not to an infant "king of the Jews," but to the king's brother James.

The sons of Joseph run a successful carpentry business in Nazareth. At least, it was successful until the oldest brother, Jesus, left home to tell the world He will forgive their sins and save their souls. Now everyone is hearing outlandish reports of healings and exorcisms. Business is suffering; not many people want a stool made by the family of the local crazy man.

## Valkyries Book 1
### some through the fire

Streetwise freshman Tracey Jacamuzzi knows that if anyone discovers the whole truth about her, they'll give up on her entirely. She isn't so sure they'd be wrong.

This is where Tracey's story begins—but certainly not where it ends. Because God has set His sights on this young woman. And His plan is to use all of her experiences to draw her to Himself. Along the way, He enlists the help of some unlikely friends.

ISBN 0-8024-1513-X

## Valkyries Book 2
### all through the blood

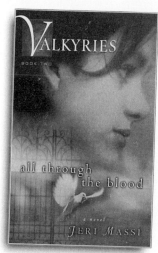

Most days, life seems more like a prison than an adventure to Tracey Jacumuzzi. She feels more like a failure than a Valkyrie. And it's no wonder. Her junior year is marred by her parent's divorce, the death of a classmate, and the continued violence of a fellow basketball player.

Tracey's faith in Christ is growing, and she is achieving excellence as an athlete. But she can't seem to control her own actions or rise above her violent past. Even at her lowest point, she begins to understand the potent mercy of the God who refuses to give up on her.

ISBN 0-8024-1514-8

MOODY
PUBLISHERS

THE NAME YOU CAN TRUST.

1-800-678-6928  www.MoodyPublishers.com

# ONLY THE WIND REMEMBERS TEAM

*ACQUIRING EDITOR:*
Michele Straubel

*COPY EDITOR:*
Karen Ball

*BACK COVER COPY:*
Julie-Allyson Ieron, Joy Media

*COVER DESIGN:*
Barb Fisher, LeVan Fisher Design

*INTERIOR DESIGN:*
Ragont Design

*PRINTING AND BINDING:*
Dickinson Press Inc.

*The typeface for the text of this book is*
***Weiss***